"I said it once, and I'll say it again: CASSIDY JONES ROCKS!...Ms. Stokes writes on-the-edge-of-your-seat adventures that are appropriate for kids and adults. I am a huge fan..."
—Erik, This Kid Reviews Books

"Elise Stokes has outdone herself...The Luminous delivers a great read, with enough action to satisfy the adrenalin junkie, but without losing the depth of the characters or their relationships."
—Vered Ehansi, Author of the Myth & Dragon and Ghost & Shadows Series

"Cassidy Jones does it again. She keeps the world safe while dealing with the ordinary stresses of teenage life..."
—Diane Rapp, Author of High Seas Mystery, Heirs to the Throne, and The Alphas Series

'Cassidy Jones is a spunky heroine who hooks you with her charm and vulnerability right before hitting the fast forward button on a rocket ride of an adventure. You won't be able to put this down until the very last zinger! Enjoy the ride."
—Tara Fairfield, Ed.D., Licensed Psychologist and Author of *Makai Queen* and *Makai King*

CASSIDY JONES AND THE SECRET FORMULA

"Brimful of danger, secrets, a bit of romance and fun, this debut author's entertaining plot and well-drawn characters not only is all it promises to be, but will leave readers looking for more…Highly recommended!"
— Gail Welborn, Examiner

"I was hooked from the beginning…The plot was generally original, the climax was pretty epic, and the story had some complex concepts that were explained incredibly well. Not only that, but Stokes painted vivid pictures in my mind with her fantastic use of imagery…"
— Gabbi, Book Breather

"Everything about this book sucked me in completely…nail-biting action scenes kept the story flowing at a perfect pace, pulling me along on the roller-coaster ride that was Cassidy's life. She was a complete kick-butt heroine who pulled out an arsenal of moves and weapons…"
— Kristin, Better Read Than Dead

CASSIDY JONES AND VULCAN'S GIFT

"Imaginative!—Modern!—Unpredictable! Riddled with delightful characters, magical adventure and a captivating plot, Stokes again captures young reader's attention with another dangerous, action-packed adventure..."
— Gail Welborn, Examiner

"As in her first book, Elise Stokes proves herself to be a master of suspense for tweens and teens with her ability to unfold a mystery with shocking twists and unexpected turns, all the while entertaining the reader with story lines of high school drama, relationships and pending romance..."
— Stephanie Laymon, Five Alarm Book Reviews

"Elise Stokes has done it again...This is by far turning out to be one of the most amazing and well-written, middle grade to young adult series I have ever read...This book has it all, wild adventure, non-stop action, hilarious banter, family value and love, teenage angst, and excitement at every turn...simply stunning and beyond superb!"
— Kitty Bullard, Great Minds Think Aloud

 AND
THE
SEVENTH
ATTENDANT

ELISE STOKES

CASSIDY JONES AND THE LUMINOUS

BOOK FOUR

JACE
Publishing LLC.

CASSIDY JONES AND THE LUMINOUS Copyright © 2014 by Elise Stokes

JACE Publishing LLC,
15600 NE 8th St., Suite B1, 287,
Bellevue, Washington 98008

Edited by William Greenleaf, <u>Greenleaf Literary Services</u>

Cover illustration by Kelly Carter

Cover design and layout by David C. Cassidy, <u>davidccassidy.com</u>

Interior book formatting by Amy Eye, <u>The Eyes for Editing</u>

ISBN: 978-0-9881851-2-8

Publishing LLC.

Printed In The United States Of America

For the love of my life, David

Contents

Prologue

"There it is again," Patrick Grimm said to himself.

He pressed his ragged coat sleeve against the warm blood that was trickling through his whiskers, keeping his gaze on the glimmer. Something had punctured his cheek when he'd rolled down the embankment—a rock or a stick, maybe.

A moment beforehand, he had dismissed the twinkle in the dark water as a reflection from the star-studded sky that canopied the lake. On the far end, moonlight exposed shadowy oil rigs, ominously lined up like the statues on Easter Island. *Moai*, he believed was the name of those giant human figures that the Polynesians had carved from stone to warn off invaders.

Patrick hadn't any idea about the name of the lake. It just happened to be the spot where those rednecks he'd hitched a ride with had shoved him out of their vehicle—a beat-up truck sporting monster tires and a Confederate flag painted on its dented hood. The only thing he knew was that he'd landed somewhere in Montana. *Or was it North Dakota?*

Truth be told, Patrick didn't really care where on God's green Earth he was.

"Idiot yokels," he grumbled, busying himself with lighting a cigarette.

Those hicks had dumped him in the middle of nowhere. And they'd all been getting along just fine until his wee-little blunder.

"Who's the heifer?" he'd sniggered, after he'd glimpsed a snapshot of what had to be the ugliest woman he'd ever seen clipped to the sun visor. He'd assumed it was

1

a joke, seconds before noticing the resemblance between the big boys he'd been sandwiched in between and the woman in the photo.

"That'd be *Mama*."

Patrick shook his head and took a drag off the cigarette. He was always sticking his foot in his mouth, saying and doing the wrong things. If mistakes were dollars, he'd be mighty rich.

Patrick had had every opportunity to make something of himself—an education and a family tree full of shining examples of success. He'd had doors of opportunity opened for him, welcoming him in. But had he taken his shot? No, not him! Instead, he had traveled down the road of screw-ups, with bad choice after bad choice eventually causing him to hit the actual road.

Exhaling a stream of smoke, he narrowed his eyes on the glimmer, making out a distinct speck of light. It was moving.

"Firefly?" He sopped up some more blood with his sleeve.

Suddenly, two more specks of light appeared, a dozen or so yards away from the other sparkle, each coming from opposite directions.

Patrick dispelled the firefly theory. The sparkles didn't appear to be flying. By their slow movement and the way the flashes faded in and out, he guessed that they were underwater.

"Only one way to find out."

Clamping the cigarette between sun-cracked lips, Patrick scooped up his military backpack and hoisted all his worldly belongings onto his back. As he made his way down to the water, he marveled at the fact that the big rednecks had thrown his backpack out of the truck after him. It had been pretty generous, considering he'd called their mother a cow.

The song "Bad to the Bone" skittered through Patrick's mind. He hummed the tune around his cigarette, noting that five more sparkles had joined the ranks. By the time he stumbled onto the rocky beach, he'd counted thirteen specks of light, no more than ten feet from shore, swirling through the water as if searching for something. The first sparkle had been in the middle of the lake.

He scrutinized the strange phenomenon for another moment, then decided the sparkles were just some type of water insect that probably posed no danger. At worst, he might get a little bite or sting if he came into contact with one.

The sparkles danced closer toward the shore. "What the—?" Patrick flicked his cigarette onto the rocks. "You attracted to my rugged good looks?"

Squatting down, he stuck his hand into the cool water and wiggled his fingers. "Well, come on. Let's have a look at you."

Like bees catching the sweet scent of a fragrant rose on the breeze, the sparkles ceased their whirling and moved straightaway toward Patrick's hand, bumping up against it.

Enchanted, Patrick laughed. A warmth filled him. He couldn't remember the last time he'd felt happy.

"You're beautiful." He gently swished his hand and watched the sparkles dance around his fingertips, like miniscule forest fairies. The white shimmer they cast reflected in his delighted eyes.

He scooped up a single sparkle with some water in his cupped palm. The twinkling glow immediately began to fade. Alarmed, Patrick submerged his hand in the lake. The sparkle instantly regained its luster.

3

"Guess you need your brothers and sisters to shine," he deduced. After another moment of observation, he recognized a curious pattern in their twinkling, almost like Morse code. "Do you communicate with those bright flashes?"

All at once, the sparkles swam away, as if summoned home by a dinner bell.

"Where are you going?" Patrick felt a strange panic.

He slipped off his backpack, dropped it on the rocks, and stepped into the lake. Water seeped into his boots.

"Come back!" He trudged after the sparkles that lured him onward, deeper and deeper.

"Stop!" Waist-deep, Patrick took another step and the rocky floor beneath him disappeared. He plunged with a splash.

Opening his eyes in the dark, murky water, he stretched his arms as he prepared to swim to the surface. Then he noticed that the sparkles had stopped moving.

In fact, they were drawing closer.

Patrick again felt unusually happy.

He watched with amazement as they hovered about two feet from his face, as if observing him, appearing even more luminous underwater. The bright flashes came more quickly, like a speeding heartbeat.

The dark underneath him illuminated.

Patrick dropped his gaze and saw a mass of sparkles rising from the depths like an incandescent cloud. The glare from the light they radiated was so intense that he could barely look at them. Panic began to rise in his chest, prompting him to try to escape—while he still could.

But another part of him overruled the instinct. The part that craved the immense joy amplified in his being as the shimmering wonder came ever closer. It was the joy he had ached for his entire, miserable life, a feeling he had instantly become addicted to the moment the sparkles had touched his calloused hand.

Patrick's lungs burned. His head grew dizzy. Grudgingly, he surfaced, took a gulp of air, and submerged again, right into the cluster of sparkles.

Blinded by their collective brightness, he jerked in surprise. Before he had time to understand what was happening, the sparkles attacked, rushing into his ears, up his nose, and into the open wound on his cheek, flowing into him like relentless rivers of light.

Terror-stricken, Patrick clawed his way through the water. The invaders continued to swarm into his body. His toe kicked a rock, and he sprang to his feet, screaming. He lifted frantic hands to claw at his ears, but suddenly his fingers dissolved into water.

It's impossible to describe what Patrick felt as he watched his hands turn into water—then his forearms, and upper arms, which poured from the empty coat and shirt sleeves now dangling at his sides. Fear, obviously, disbelief, and denial. Yet blanketing the expected emotions was one not normally experienced when life is coming to an end:

Euphoria.

It was as though an internal choir of angels celebrated in song when Patrick felt his physical core give way like a ruptured dam. A sweet cherubic voice caressed his mind with a promise:

You will be a new man.

Patrick exploded into water.

Chapter 1

Thick as Thieves

"**A**ren't we the brave crooks?" I asked out loud. I was sitting crossed-legged on the steel catwalk of a billboard a hundred feet above the street, watching four burglars cut a hole into the adjacent building's rooftop. "Especially with all the extra police everywhere."

Right on cue, a squad car crawled down Spring Street below. There were definitely more police on patrol that evening.

Probably because of Jeff Ferrell.

The twenty-one-year-old University Of Washington student had been reported missing that afternoon. The case had come right on the heels of two other local disappearances: Anita Hart, a mother of three, and Sebastian Romero, owner of Champion Health Clubs.

Three people in two weeks— has to be a serial killer.

I could see no other explanation. However, according to my dad, Drake Jones, host of *In the Spotlight* for Channel Five News, missing person reports were filed with the Seattle Police Department almost every day. Only about one percent turned out to involve actual crimes, he said.

These particular cases had made headlines mainly due to Romero. I'd recognized him immediately when his face had flashed across the television screen eight days earlier. I'd had many opportunities to ogle the twelve-foot-high picture of him that graced a billboard off I-5 advertising his health clubs. His chiseled jaw and ripped biceps had been seared into my brain.

The guy is all muscle. He had to have been taken by gunpoint, or drugged.

I shook off the grim thoughts and redirected my attention toward the crime-in-progress. The thieves' attire, similar to mine—black clothing and a ski mask—had been a dead giveaway that these four were up to no good when I'd happened upon them about thirty minutes earlier. The high-tech power tools they'd produced from two large duffel bags snuffed out any lingering doubts.

Chunks of cement blasted into the air as they drilled. The group wasn't exactly being quiet, but wasn't loud enough to draw attention from that high up, either. Good thing I'd decided to leap rooftops that night, or there wouldn't have been any eyewitnesses.

While three of the thieves cut the hole in the roof, the fourth anchored four ropes to air conditioning units and put on a rappelling harness and backpack. The calm and proficient way the men worked suggested that breaking and entering was old hat for them. I could guarantee, however, their playbook didn't include a fifteen-year-old mutant foiling their heist.

The harnessed thief lowered himself through the hole as the others shrugged on their own equipment. One man slid on a backpack, too, and rappelled into the dark office, followed by the next man. I expected the remaining thief to go down, as well, but he didn't.

Plan B? I surmised, searching for reasons why he'd geared up but had stayed behind. *Rappelling over the side of*

7

the building, if—I glanced at an access door to the roof—*things go badly and they can't escape the way they had come up.*

Time for things to go badly, I thought, and pulled on a pair of soft, black angora gloves, embellished with a purple heart, dead center.

I gathered the handles of the colorful polka-dot gift bag nestled in my lap, and stood up. Then I gently tucked the bag against my side, drew several steps back on the catwalk, and took a running leap.

I soared over the alley separating the two buildings, dropping a full story, and landed, solidly and silently, in a crouch. My eyes darted to the pretty gift bag. I frowned. All this jumping was wrinkling the tissue.

No biggie, I reassured myself, setting down the bag.

The thief directed a flashlight into the hole. He had no clue that he was no longer alone on the rooftop. I slunk up behind him and tapped his shoulder. He started, but didn't scream or drop the flashlight. The guy was a real pro.

He whipped around. I introduced my fist to his jaw.

The blow snapped his head backward, and his body followed the motion. My hand shot out and secured the harness. The man dropped the flashlight, which tumbled into the hole, but his abrupt stop caused him to whiplash in the harness. A series of pops rippled along his spine.

I winced. I hated the sound of cracking joints.

I heard the flashlight strike the floor and bounce across it.

"Paves," one of the men hissed.

Gripping the harness, I lowered Paves into a sitting position so his legs dangled over the ledge, as though he were just chilling.

"Paves!" A flashlight beam caught the unconscious man's face slumped to his chest.

I stifled a giggle.

"What are you doing?"

Paves's cell phone vibrated inside his jacket.

I unzipped his jacket with my free hand, ran my hand down his chest, and located the pocket his cell was in. The flashlight beam caught me.

"I see you," the man hissed as I pocketed Paves's cell. "Let him go."

By all means.

I shoved Paves's backside off the edge with my foot. The rope raced through my palms, which would have been torn to shreds if my skin hadn't turned rock-hard—a little defense mechanism of mine. My cute gloves wouldn't have been enough protection.

The men below shrieked as their cohort plunged toward them, then they scrambled out of the way. I tightened my grip moments before Paves reached the floor, stopping his descent. He swung back and forth in the harness like a wrecking ball, his chin bobbing flaccidly against his chest.

I adjusted my eyes and absorbed the available light, until the dark recesses of the room below were visible. Safe-deposit boxes lined the walls, and there were bars behind a closed steel door. The robbers hadn't broken into an office. They had broken into a vault.

"Who are you?" the hisser demanded as the men cautiously approached Paves. "The Seattle Shadow?"

A giggle escaped as I let go of the rope.

Paves crashed to the floor, taking out the other men.

Moaning, they crawled from beneath their cohort. I ripped an air-conditioning unit off the roof and carried it to the hole. A bullet struck the metal.

"Not cool," I grumbled, placing the air conditioner over the hole. The thieves had the gall to protest after shooting at me.

I brushed off my gloves and retrieved Paves's cell, then dialed 911. When the dispatcher answered, I cleared my throat and forced my voice down a few octaves.

"There are four *armed* men trapped in a vault on the top floor of a building on Spring Street, right next to the billboard—" I glanced right at the billboard. I hadn't paid attention to the advertisement. "—for Group Health."

"It is illegal to call 911 if there is no emergency," the dispatcher droned.

"I told you they have guns!" My voice pitched. Coughing, I forced it low again as the dispatcher threatened to trace the call.

"Good," I replied deeply. "You do that. Don't forget about the guns. Approach with caution. Oh, and tell the cops that the Seattle Shadow said so," I added as a last-minute flourish before disconnecting. Maybe that would give this phone call some credibility.

A reporter for *The Seattle Times* had dubbed me the Seattle Shadow after a cashier called me a "phantom" when I'd intervened in a convenience store holdup. I'd thrown the two robbers into shelves, which toppled over, one after another, like enormous dominoes. It had been pretty cool.

Since the MO matched a few other crimes I'd hampered—a slight person dressed in black and wearing a ski mask, appearing from nowhere, going to town on the baddies, and then vanishing in an instant—naturally the conclusion had been drawn that our city had gained a new crime fighter—one who could disappear into thin air, like a phantom.

I hadn't looked for those crimes per se, but I did seem to have the uncanny ability of being in the right place at the right time, or within a one-mile radius. What can I say? Not much gets past super-enhanced hearing, sight, and sense of smell.

"Speaking of which, you smell like salami, Paves," I said to the air-conditioning unit plugging the hole. "Hope you have a breath mint on you."

I dropped his cell phone on the rooftop for the police, then collected my gift bag, taking a moment to straighten the tissue.

"It looks awful," I grumbled, giving up.

I tucked the bag under my arm and headed to Joe Jackson's new digs.

~~~

I climbed down the fire escape over Joe's new home, pausing to watch another police car drive by the alley. Once it passed, I hopped down to the asphalt.

With a heavy heart, I observed the refrigerator box tucked inside the alcove of the back entrance of a vacant store. This was no way for my friend to live, even though this lonely and miserable existence was Joe's choice. Living on the streets was his self-inflicted punishment for delivering a single blow that had killed his childhood friend, Theo. They had gotten into a fistfight over a girl when they were eighteen, almost fifty years ago. Joe had served his time in prison, but as far as he was concerned, he was condemned for life.

"Knock, knock," I called, pasting on a grin. Joe didn't like me worrying about him.

His salt-and-pepper dreadlocks poked out of the box, followed by a big smile that lit his dark face and revealed a couple of missing teeth. The smile didn't reach his sad brown eyes, however. His smiles never did.

"Hey, Green Eyes!" He wiggled out of the box, pulling his thin frame upright. "Mighty glad to see you."

Since the evening was fairly warm, especially for April, Joe wasn't wearing the Seahawks jacket that he was typically bundled in. Instead, he wore a gray hoodie like kids my age wear, stained jeans, and tennis shoes, all of which needed to be run through the wash.

What I wouldn't have given to do that for him, and to get him in a decent home.

As it was, Joe didn't even know my name, nor had he ever seen my face, other than what was visible through the openings in my ski mask. A couple of times, locks of my dark-red hair had escaped from the mask, but Joe had just stared at them without comment.

"For you!" I produced the gift bag from behind my back.

Joe's grin widened.

"Me?" He tugged at his coiled beard, looking pleased. I noted how his facial hair had become whiter since I'd met him four months earlier, after he'd caught me scaling the Space Needle. "You're too good to me."

"Ditto." I handed him the bag. He handled it as though it were a precious jewel.

"Thank you." Joe's thick tone and gratitude made me blush. My gift was really no big deal.

"Well, come on. Open it."

He carefully removed the rumpled tissue. "Let's see what we have here," he said as he pulled out the box of Turkish Delight.

"Oh, wait!" I grabbed the candy from him before he'd had a chance to get a proper look at it. "This won't make sense if you don't see my other gift first."

"My, oh, my. Two gifts?" His eyes twinkled. He plunged his hand into the bag and pulled out a copy of *The Lion, the Witch and the Wardrobe*.

"This is the story your mama read to you and your twin," he remembered.

"Yep. And she'd give us a piece of Turkish Delight as she read. The White Witch tempts Edmund with it in the story. That's one of my best childhood memories."

A distant look came onto Joe's weary face. He glanced away and tugged at his whiskers. I assumed the void into which he stared held images of days gone by—much better days.

Perhaps of a bedtime story being read to him.

"Thank you kindly." His grin returned. "What do you say we break into this Turkish Delight?"

"Oh, no, no, no! That'll ruin it. Save it for the story."

"Well, I certainly don't want to spoil the story." He winked and then gestured to the cement steps. "Take a load off. I'll just put these away."

I sat down on the second step, scooting to the corner so Joe had room to climb into the box. A siren wailed past the alley. Another joined it blocks away. I smiled with satisfaction. They were headed in the direction of the thieves.

Good thing you heeded the Seattle Shadow's warning.

My gaze moved to a neatly folded newspaper that Joe had been reading. I picked it up and frowned at the headlines.

UW Student Reported Missing

Police Baffled by Champion's Owner's Disappearance

Search Parties Organized to Look for Missing Seattle Woman

Seattle's Loch Ness: Is Something Lurking in Lake Washington?

"Has the world gone crazy?" I asked.

"Crazier than a road-runnin' lizard," Joe said as he backed out of the box.

I laughed. Joe had the funniest sayings.

He held up two bottled waters and parked himself beside me. He offered me one.

"No, thank you." Joe needed the water more than I did. It wasn't like the box had plumbing.

"You sure? This is real good vitamin water," he tempted. "A bunch was donated to the soup kitchen, so they're passing them out like hot cakes. I got five more bottles in there." He jerked his thumb toward his current residence.

"Thanks. But I'm not thirsty." I smiled and looked down at the newspaper. I wasn't taking his water.

"Suit yourself." Joe set one bottle next to me and twisted the top off the other. "It's mighty refreshing," he

14

enticed, then took a luxurious drink. After a couple of loud gulps, he smacked his lips and let out a satisfied *ahhhhh*. "Them vitamins are working wonders already. I feel as strong as a bull—or in my case, a mule. You ain't the only stubborn one here." He elbowed me and took another swig. "Anyone ever tell you you're stubborn before?"

I pretended to think it over. "Nope," I said, shaking my head. "Can't say anyone has."

Joe chuckled. "Bet Mendel would beg to differ," he said, referring to my best friend, Emery Phillips. Joe only knew the boy genius by his middle name, Mendel. In fact, he knew everyone in my life by a pseudonym, except for Jared Wells, my kind-of boyfriend whom I had kind-of introduced to Joe once.

"Ha! Compared to Mendel, I'm as stubborn as a . . . a . . . cotton-tailed rabbit!" That was the most docile critter I could come up with.

"He still got everybody fooled at your school?"

I squirmed. Me and my big mouth. Why had I ever told Joe anything about anyone from my *normal* life?

Before answering, I took a moment to categorize what Joe knew and what he didn't know, in order to avoid revealing too much once again.

He knows that exposure to an undisclosed substance in the laboratory of Emery's mother Serena had mutated me last October, resulting in ultra-enhanced senses, super strength and speed, and skin that can turn rock-hard. He also knows that I have the ability to learn fight moves just by watching them, and to heal from almost any injury, which might make me immortal.

I grimaced. I tried to avoid thinking about immortality.

But he doesn't know that Serena's experimental gene therapy, Formula 10X, created the strange retrovirus I'm infected with.

Formula 10X was a concoction of animal DNA with an Assassin kicker. Assassin had been a top-secret biological weapon that Serena and her former employer, criminal mastermind Arthur King Sr., had been developing for the military fifteen years earlier, until Serena had pulled the plug on the project.

Then there's the Phillipses moving into the house across the street from mine, where Serena searches for my cure, while Emery, a fifteen-year-old college graduate, poses as a ninth-grader and attends school with me, obviously.

But he doesn't know Emery's dad Gavin is a secret agent for the CIA.

On second thought, I couldn't remember ever mentioning Gavin to Joe. That was the problem with sharing pieces about my life with someone I shouldn't. I was having trouble remembering which pieces I'd shared.

So Joe knows squat about Gavin, but he does know my family finally learned the truth about me.

How could I not have told him that? Keeping my family in the dark had been very hard for me.

And he doesn't know there are others like me.

Well, sort of like me. The mutants who Arthur King Sr. had created fell more into a monster category. One of his experiments, Raul Diaz, and I had practically ripped one another to shreds before King had escaped and crawled back into whatever hole he'd been hiding in. He was most likely still there, creating more abominations.

"Yes, he does," I answered at last. "No one knows Mendel is a genius, and *I* don't know how he can stand it. He has to be bored out of his mind, especially in our science class. He could teach it, after all! He does have a degree in microbiology—"

I stopped talking and pressed my lips together for safe measure. At least keeping them closed would prevent more foolishness from escaping. Why couldn't I just shut up?

"Green Eyes, you ain't got nothing to worry about," Joe assured. "Your secrets are safe with me. Besides, who's going to listen to an old ex-con like me, anyway?" His eyes dropped to the newspaper in my hand. "There's more than just them," he said.

"What do you mean?"

"There's street folk missing, too. Been disappearing for a long while now." His troubled gaze moved to the water bottle he held. "I know folks move on, but not these. Mason, Doc, now Lady Jane—they was regular fixtures out here."

"Lady Jane? The woman with the cat?" I asked, picturing the young woman with matted hair and haunted eyes. I'd crossed paths with Jane on my midnight jaunts every so often. Hidden in the shadows, I'd watched her dote on her smoky-gray cat, Cleo. Cleo had looked well fed. No doubt Lady Jane would sooner feed her cat than herself.

Joe nodded, watching the water he swirled in the bottle.

"She really loves her cat," I said.

"Never lets Cleo out of her sight. But the other night, Cleo was wandering through Occidental Park, yowling for Lady Jane."

"Did you tell the police?"

"Na." Joe watched the water spin around and around. "When you got nothing and no one, you're invisible."

At a loss for words, I watched the liquid swirl in the bottle, too. The water splashed against the brand name etched in the plastic in bright lavender with beams shooting out from each letter, like an explosion of light:

Luminous.

Chapter 2

The Mask Comes Off

I leapt through the window of my second-story bedroom around two a.m. I could have walked through the front door, since my nighttime activities were no longer a secret. But I preferred coming and going through my window. Bad habits are hard to break.

On my way to bed, I pulled off my mask, sweatshirt, and shoes, discarding them on the floor. I crawled underneath the covers and fell into a deep, dreamless sleep. The back of a hand slapped me awake in what felt like only moments later.

"Chazz," I groaned, pushing his hand away. It sprang back like a bungee cord, nailing my nose. It's like the kid was made of rubber.

"Why do you keep crawling into my bed?" I complained to my sleepy, six-year-old brother.

I knew why. He felt safe with me. Whether or not he wanted to admit it, Chazz was afraid that someone would discover my secret and would hurt our family in order to get me. I hated that he had this fear, but, as Gavin put it, fear keeps us on our toes.

Chazz whistled a snore.

Groaning, I pulled a pillow over my head.

~~~

"Who'd you save last night, Cassy?"

I pried my eyelids apart. Chazz's cute, round face hung over mine, red hair poking out every which way. His big green eyes were eager.

"No one."

His face fell in disappointment.

"But I did stop a robbery."

His mouth turned up into a huge smile, revealing a new gap where a bottom front tooth had been. He was too cute for words.

"Did the Tooth Fairy come?"

Chazz rolled his eyes, shaking his head. The song "Who Let the Dogs Out" suddenly blared from my alarm.

"There is *no* Tooth Fairy," he stated, offended by the mere suggestion there was. He hopped out of bed. "I'm going to tell Daddy what you did. He'll be so proud!"

"That's debatable." I yawned as he darted into the hall. "And there is a Tooth Fairy!" I called after him.

Adding a "woof, woof," with the song, I slammed down the snooze button.

My parents weren't exactly thrilled with my crime-fighting shenanigans. In fact, it took some convincing from Serena and Emery just to get them to give me permission to work off excess energy in the dead of night. My parents still couldn't wrap their heads around the fact that a girl who could give Jackie Chan a run for his money and leap a car in a single bound wasn't all that vulnerable.

~~~

I got ready for school, then went down to the kitchen.

"Mornin'," I greeted my family and Dad's cameraman, Ben Johnson. With his mocha skin, wild corkscrew hair, and happy amber eyes, twenty-four-year-old Ben was one of my favorite people in the world.

"Hey, Cassy Girl." He gave me his infectious grin.

"Good morning, sweetheart." Dad gave me a disapproving look.

My twin, Nate, gave me the *shame, shame* gesture, rubbing one forefinger over the other.

I gave *him* a glare.

I glanced over my shoulder at my mom, Elizabeth, who was standing behind our white-marble-topped kitchen island, meticulously spreading cream cheese on a bagel as though it were the most interesting task on Earth. *Uh-oh.* Chazz had obviously brought them up to speed on my heroic deed before Ben had arrived. Thank goodness he'd come over early this morning. Otherwise, I'd be getting an earful.

"Bagel?" she offered with a side of forced smile.

"Thanks, Mom." I took the bagel and sat down at the table with the males, wondering if I was the only one who could feel the tension collecting in the air like dust particles. It was almost palpable. It isn't like my parents were *uninvolved bystander* types. They were good people. They just worried about me.

Ben didn't appear to sense anything amiss, and he continued to relay the latest Lake Washington Monster sighting. At least that's what believers in the outlandish, such as Ben, had dubbed the recent events at the lake, despite the conflicting details.

A few weeks earlier, a couple had claimed a serpent-

21

like creature had slithered under their speedboat, and another woman had described seeing a mermaid the week prior. The latest sighting had been made by another boater, who'd allegedly seen a silvery creature with a stark white mane, before it had submerged into the depths.

"A *mane?*" Nate repeated, raising his eyebrows. "You mean like on a *horse?*"

"What else, Nate?" Chazz answered for Ben, flipping up his palms in exasperation. His fingertips and teeth were coated with cream cheese.

Ben chucked a wadded-up napkin at Nate. "Don't be so closed-minded."

"*Moi?*" Nate aimed forefingers at his chest. "I'm, like, the opposite of closed-minded, or else I wouldn't believe in the Seattle Shadow."

Dad glanced up from his laptop to give Nate a look. Behind me, I could feel admonishment rolling off Mom in waves. Nate liked living on the edge.

"Nate, dear," Mom said, in a super-sweet voice, "would you like orange juice?"

Nate, you are in so much trouble, I sang in my head, smirking around the bagel lodged in my mouth.

Glancing at Mom, Nate straightened up in his chair. "Uh, no. Thanks, Mom."

The sounds of "Soul Sister" suddenly sang from Ben's cell. He looked at the text and grinned.

"Cool!" His thumbs punched out a reply. "Drake, this is Leroy. He's flying in tomorrow."

"Is he making an episode about The Lake Washington Monster?" I guessed.

Leroy Rays was the host of the hunting show *Big*

Game. After a run-in with a supposed Sasquatch—me—he had started another cable show: *Monster Hunters*.

"Yep!" Ben beamed and sent his text. He lived for supernatural stuff.

"I look forward to seeing him." Dad's crystal-blue eyes combed the news on his laptop. With his golden-blond hair, clean-cut features, and million-dollar smile, he looked every bit the successful news broadcaster. "We'll have to schedule an interview with him. Cassidy and Nate, you might be interested in this."

Dad started a video and turned the laptop around so everyone at the table could see the screen. The footage rolled from a still of Jared's dad, Owen Wells. He stood next to a man a bit taller than he, with deep-set eyes, a cleft chin, and a weather-beaten complexion. On the other side of the man stood a girl my age. She was gorgeous and exotic-looking. She had bronze skin, almond-shaped eyes, and a beautiful head of raven hair. Her dark, silky locks shone even on the laptop screen.

The man introduced her as his stepdaughter Ashlyn. "Patrick Grimm, Owner/CEO of Luminous Water" flashed at the bottom of the screen as he talked about some charitable work his company was doing for the homeless. Grimm had a Southern accent, and the more I looked at him, the more I pictured him in a flannel shirt, gripping an ax like Paul Bunyan. Seemed to fit him better than the swanky Armani suit and tie he wore.

"What's Jared's dad doing there?" I asked, noting that Ashlyn looked like she wanted to crawl under a rock. I could hardly blame her. I wouldn't like a news camera in my face, either.

"He's Patrick Grimm's lawyer," Dad responded.

"So he's making sure his client minds his p's and q's," I guessed, studying Jared's father.

Jared had his father's dirty-blond hair, angular face, and athletic build, but that was where the similarities ended. Where Jared was noble and trustworthy, his father was a snake. He'd left Jared's mom Eileen when Jared was three. That was all I knew about him. Jared rarely talked about his dad.

~~~

As was our routine, I texted Emery that Nate and I were leaving for school as I collected my stuff from my room. By the time Nate and I ambled onto our front porch, Emery was waiting at the end of our English Tudor's front walk. That morning, he wasn't alone.

"Hey," Nate called to Emery and his father, jogging ahead of me.

I lingered behind. Gavin and Emery noted me doing so, with identical amused expressions.

Emery was the spitting image of his father. The same jet-black hair, black, intelligent eyes, milky complexion, and chiseled good looks. The only thing six-foot-four-inch Gavin had on Emery was four inches and muscle mass, both of which I had no doubt Emery would one day match. As it was, he wasn't one of those tall, scraggly high school boys. Emery was mature beyond his years, in more than just physicality.

Emery and Nate were in the midst of exchanging high-fives when I finally joined them on the sidewalk. Gavin smirked.

"You were busy last night, Cassidy," he remarked.

I shrugged. "Just in the right place at the right time."

"You've made a habit of that," he observed.

Unlike my parents, Gavin didn't mind my protecting public safety. More accurately, he didn't mind me exercising my abilities. My superpowers fascinated him. I could practically see the gears turning behind his eyes, which would often become calculating as he watched me perform one of Serena's physical tests, or when Emery and I would playfully spar in their family's basement. Sometimes Gavin joined in—but, with him, the fighting wasn't for fun. He would give it all he had, executing every lethal move he knew, and he was extremely innovative.

Once, during sparring, he had swiped a hammer from the floor and hurled it at me. I'd caught it by the handle. As Serena scolded him for the dirty trick, he'd just leaned against a support beam, catching his breath, and stared at me. Sweat was beading on his forehead; behind, those gears turned and turned.

"So, how's the remodeling going?" I asked to change the topic. So I'd intervened in another crime. Big deal. I motioned to a dump truck piled high with dirt and the white van with "Marathon Construction" painted on the side.

The "remodeling" was more like Bruce Wayne's construction project when he'd had the Bat Cave built. Right now, the Marathon workers—with the help of shovels, wheelbarrows, and a jackhammer—were digging out a secret room, which would eventually serve as a laboratory. They also were digging a tunnel underneath the street to connect our two basements. That way, we could go back and forth between our houses without witnesses. The secret laboratory also would act as a safe room, if worse came to worst.

Frankly, I didn't know if this project was legal, even though Gavin had obtained building permits. We didn't ask how, just like we didn't pump him for information about the Marathon Construction workers. They were a shady-looking crew. Nate and I had decided that whomever they really worked for must have owed Gavin a big favor. But we kept our theories to ourselves.

About a month earlier, Dad had queried Gavin about them when he couldn't stand it any longer. Gavin had looked at him squarely and warned, "Drake, don't ask." And Dad didn't. Where government operatives are concerned, it's best to keep questions to oneself.

"It's coming along," Gavin answered vaguely, a typical Phillips. He cast a glance at Emery and Nate. "You boys can grab a shovel this afternoon and help speed things along."

"Sounds like a blast," Emery remarked cheekily while he checked his email on his cell.

"Whoa! Wait a sec." Nate held a hand up and eyed a wheelbarrow, as though someone had had the gall to scrawl his name across the mound of dirt it held. "You mean, *we* should haul dirt?" He flipped his thumb between himself and Emery. "No offense, Gavin, but you're missing the obvious. Think speed, strength, and *not* boy."

"Wimp," I said.

"No argument there, if it gets me out of shoveling."

"Well played, Nate," Emery ribbed as he punched out something on his cell's keypad.

"You're a master at shoveling, son, and I don't mean

dirt." Gavin gave my twin a playful dope-slap. "I'll see *you* after school. Bye, kids."

Gavin crossed the street to their Victorian and asked one of the workers, Cristiano, a husky, shifty-eyed man who was unloading an air compressor from the van, "How about a cup of Joe?"

"No, thanks. I'm good." Cristiano grinned and waved a bottled water at him.

His smile was a bit of a surprise. Cristiano was hardly the smiling type.

"Hey!" Miriam Cohen called from her porch, two houses down from mine. "I thought I'd missed you!"

"Run," Nate advised Emery.

I backhanded Nate's chest. He made an *umph* sound, as though I'd knocked the air out of him.

"Careful," he said, rubbing his chest. "I'm delicate."

His poking fun at Miriam's obsession with Emery was getting old. But, as she bobbed toward us, I couldn't imagine why Emery wasn't enthralled with her. Dark, smooth curls bouncing off slender shoulders, dazzling smile on an animated and classically beautiful face, cobalt-blue eyes that glistened like deep seawater—How could any boy resist her?

"When are you going to admit that you're madly in love with me?" she brazenly demanded of Emery, probably waking up a few neighbors in the process. She squeezed his cheeks between her hands, creating fish lips and causing his black-framed glasses to lift on his nose.

I nodded. Yes, if in Emery's shoes, I could resist her, too.

~~~

I locked gazes with the most beautiful set of chocolate-brown eyes in the world—limpid, soulful, and fringed with thick, black lashes. My heart thumped like a rabbit.

Jared's sculpted lips curled at the corners into his slow smile. I had spent long hours lost in daydreams about what it would be like to kiss those succulent lips.

"He's looking at you like he wants to gobble you up, like a coconut pie," Miriam observed, and not quietly at that.

Chuckling, Jared continued to his table across the room, while Emery said under his breath, for my ears only, "And you wonder how I can resist her?"

I glanced at him, stumped. I couldn't recall ever asking him that.

"Coconut pie—*yum*," Dixon Pilchowski butted in, giving me a lecherous look. His toady, Rodrigo Perez, sniggered.

I glared across the table into Dixon's mean, smug face, furious that he'd made me blush.

His mocking eyes slithered to Emery. Crossing his arms over his broad chest, he leaned back in the chair and attempted to stare Emery down. All at once, Dixon became uncomfortable and glanced away. Typical bully.

Ever since Emery had humbled him for threatening Miriam, Dixon had been scared spitless of him. Everyone in the school knew about the incident, including Mr. Levy, our science teacher, whom I'd become convinced was inherently evil. A well-intentioned teacher wouldn't assign the five people involved in conflict to the same table. It was as though he'd tossed a lit match into a barrel of gas and sat waiting for it to explode.

Mr. Levy had come to dislike Emery almost as much as he obviously despised Dixon, who must have represented every bully who had ever made Levy's personal high school existence miserable.

His resentment of Emery was apparent in his thin, pinched face, which perfectly matched his sour disposition. His reasons why weren't as clear-cut, however. I'd assumed that he'd sensed Emery was brighter than he let on. Just *how* bright would have probably blown Levy's mind.

The bell rang, and right on cue Dixon slouched in his chair, setting his jaw and tucking clenched fists into crossed arms. Levy had trained him well. Dixon would remain in that position, not speaking, unless Levy decided to humiliate him.

I peeked over my shoulder at Jared. He gifted me his breathtaking smile. I never grew tired of that smile.

"Blackwell . . ." Mr. Levy began roll call.

Reluctantly, I turned back around. When Jared had transferred into my class for our second semester, I'd been ecstatic. Then Levy seated him at the table farthest away from mine. Like I said, the man was pure evil.

After roll call, Levy walked to the front of the room—in his odd, crabby, hunched-over, shuffling way—and grimly peered at the open textbook in his hands. Jerking up his head of stringy hair, he scanned the room, planning an assault. His thin lips turned up into a quivering smile; his hostile gaze rested on Emery.

"Mr. Phillips, you do realize that when you are absent, it is your responsibility to be prepared for class upon returning?"

Emery had played hooky the day before so he could

track down a delinquent client for bail bond agent Riley O'Shea, his employer and former college mate. When Emery wasn't keeping an eye on me or pretending to be a regular teenager, he often did skip tracing for her.

Emery gave Levy a cocky grin. "Yeah."

My stomach tightened. The dislike being mutual, Emery dumbed himself down even more for this class, just to set Levy off. You'd think the old sourpuss wouldn't have been worth his effort. But I've learned that, genius or not, a fifteen-year-old boy will behave like a fifteen-year-old boy.

"Since you have familiarized yourself with the chapter, as I observed you doing while entering the room—"

"Busted," David Hsu whispered behind us.

I squirmed in my seat. Emery was in the habit of doing assigned reading while walking between classes. He thumbed through pages so rapidly that it had become the source of a joke among our friends. No one believed he was really speed-reading. I knew better.

"—Perhaps you could tell us which revered scientist is known as the Father of Microbiology."

"Er, Einstein?"

Miriam giggled and reached around me to pinch his arm. "You're naughty, Emery *Mendel*."

Laughter rippled through the room. Our classmates caught on, teasing:

"I wonder who it is, Emery *Mendel*?"

"Emery *Mendel*, I'm clueless, too."

"Emery *Mendel*, didn't you read the chapter?"

"Silence!" Levy shouted. His puckered face displayed outrage, but his beady eyes gleamed with satisfaction.

I sighed, seeing another detention in Emery's near future.

"Mr. Phillips, as your classmates *perceptively* deduced, you did not read the chapter. Since you are unable to find time to prepare for class, I need to create an opportunity for you—in detention, *this* afternoon."

"Sounds fair."

Mr. Levy's gloating expression faded. "Let us see if your tablemates are better prepared." He glared at the back of Dixon's head. "Mr. Pilchowski, please turn around in your seat."

Dixon mouthed a profane word and twisted around.

"Mr. Pilchowski, which protozoa can be distinguished by their unique slipper shape and by the cilia that surround them?"

"Paramec–"

"Incorrect," Levy cut him off.

Emery tensed.

I considered the answer. "Paramecia" sounded right. The soft murmurs around me agreed. But Levy's harsh expression dissuaded challenges.

His eyes skirted to the other side of the room. "Miss Ling, define 'sporozoa.'"

Yue Ling visibly gulped and glanced helplessly at her tablemates. As she opened her mouth to speak, Emery's deep voice resonated, and it was his true voice—incisive, confident, and mature—not the voice he had adapted for his act. "If 'paramecia' is wrong, what is the correct answer?"

"Mr. Phillips, I did not see your hand–"

"If it isn't 'paramecia,' what is it, then?" Emery repeated calmly.

Levy stared at him, speechless.

I tapped my foot nervously, glancing sidelong at

Emery's composed face. He always drilled in how critical it was to be discreet. What was he doing?

The ticking of the clock echoed over the SMART Board. An anxious tension collected in the air, as everyone became uncertain of what to do or where to look, with the exception of Emery. His steady gaze didn't waver from Levy.

"Class, take out a piece of paper for a pop quiz," Levy ordered, taking his revenge.

No one protested.

As the sound of clicking binders and rustling paper filled the silence, Mr. Levy shuffled to his desk, picked up a bottled water with an unsteady hand, and took a long drink.

"Dude, that was cool of you," Dixon whispered to Emery.

Emery looked at him squarely. "You were right, Dixon," he stated matter-of-factly.

Dixon nodded, then looked at Rodrigo and snatched his pencil.

Smoothing a piece of paper, I attempted to calm myself. The scene had driven a wedge of icy fear into my heart. Emery had revealed himself. Screw-ups were my department, not his. His removal of the metaphorical mask confirmed a whispering terror that tormented me every night while lying in bed, waiting for sleep to come after racing around Seattle.

This charade of ours won't last forever.

When the jig was up, what then?

Emery slid his sheet of paper in front of me. He had written*: I was wrong to let the pretentious windbag get to me. The mask won't come off again.* He pulled the paper back and scribbled over his note.

Levy tossed the plastic bottle he had drained into the wastebasket. He twisted off the top of another, took a swig, and then read the first quiz question.

Pens and pencils sailed across paper, except for mine. I hadn't even heard the question, as my eyes stared at the spot where "mask" had been written on Emery's paper.

Was his word choice a coincidence?

At one time, I would have presumed so. But we'd had too many coincidences.

Fear wasn't my only nightly tormenter. Guilt was equally persistent. Emery wasn't normal, and I knew why. And every day I regretted the promise I'd made Gavin to keep my mouth shut about it until he felt his son was ready for the truth.

Arthur King Sr. had experimented on my friend when Emery was young, and had changed him.

Somehow.

Chapter 3

Three Down, One Who Knows

"Levy's class was intense," Jared said, breaking the silence.

We were walking to his mom's apartment after school to get his stuff and feed the pets. Eileen was on a business trip, so he was going to hang with us for the weekend.

I had fallen into deep thought about Levy's class, too. Emery acting out of character had thrown me. Sure, what Levy had done to Dixon was wrong. And, yes, the pompous jerk should have been called out for abusing his authority. Emery had a strong sense of justice. But he wouldn't normally act so rashly. I expected *me* to make stupid decisions, not him. Emery dropping his act had been a rude awakening. He was subject to mistakes, too. After all, he was only human.

Maybe . . .

Having fought King's mutants, I couldn't comfortably presume Emery was completely human. I had no clue how King had tinkered with his mind, or why he would have. Gavin hadn't felt obliged to fill me in when he'd sworn me to secrecy.

"Uh, Cass? Did you hear me?"

"Yes!" I blurted so abruptly that Jared jumped.

"Man," he said with a laugh. Bending over, he pressed

his palms to his thighs and laughed more. He found almost everything I did funny, especially the odd stuff.

"Sorry. I didn't mean to yell. I was sort of lost in my head."

"No worries," he said, trying to catch his breath. "You just took me by surprise." Grinning ear-to-ear, Jared straightened up. He put me in a light chokehold and grated his knuckles over my scalp.

"Well, that's romantic!" I protested, squirming free. I smoothed my mussed hair and attempted *a look*. It failed utterly, earning me more chuckles from Jared.

"Is this better?" He wove his fingers into mine, taking me by surprise.

We started walking again, hand-in-hand. An elated smile split my face, making my cheeks feel ready to crack.

"Let's try this again," Jared said, smiling at my smile. "Levy's class was intense."

"Uh-huh." His palm was toasty warm. Our hands fit together perfectly.

"'*Uh-huh*?' That's all you have to say?"

"No. I like this." I swung our clasped hands up.

The last time Jared had held my hand was when he'd told me I was special to him. He had shared his feelings for me with my dad, too. Dad thanked him for being honorable, then informed him that Jones kids weren't allowed to date until they reached the age of sixteen.

"Me, too." Jared returned. His smile tightened, and I felt his fingers loosen. Bummed, I assumed he was recalling his talk with my dad, too. He probably figured holding hands was barred. Safe guess.

"I'm getting the feeling you don't want to talk about Emery," he teased as my hand fell from his.

"That *was* intense." I balled my lonely hand and shoved it into my sweater pocket. "Levy needed to be challenged. He is a total jerk! So is Dixon, but no one deserves to be degraded like that."

"Agreed."

I could see on Jared's face that he was evaluating whether to share more of his thoughts on the incident. He wasn't one to blurt out whatever sprang into his head.

"What are you thinking about?" I prompted.

"This hilarious thing happened at Cherry Street last night," he eluded, changing the topic to the coffeehouse where he played guitar.

I knew that wasn't what had been on his mind, but he didn't claim it to be. And he wouldn't. Jared never lied.

~~~

"Hi, Athena," I cooed at Jared's cat. She was curled up on the sofa, which was bathed in sunlight filtering through the picture window.

Jared locked the front door.

The building had been built in the early 1900s, so the apartment had all the cool architectural details common to that era—high ceilings, elaborate moldings, oak floors. I found it charming, eclectic, and homey, especially furnished with Eileen's antique shop finds.

The calico had cracked an eye open when I'd spoken to her, then let it slide shut again. It had taken some effort on my part to get her to warm up to me. Due to odd reactions from other animals since my mutation, I had come to realize that I didn't smell human anymore. I usually

36

didn't care what animals thought of me, but that wasn't the case with Athena. She was Jared's cat.

The first time she'd encountered the new me—the old one, she didn't give a rip about—she hissed and ran away, as if in mortal danger. Jared had been stunned by her reaction. I'd felt humiliated, and scared. I didn't want him to think there was anything wrong with me. But by sneaking her cat treats and patiently petting her, I eventually gained her trust. A few times, we had trapped one another in unblinking stares, and I'd felt some sort of weird mind-meld initiate. That had been my cue to look away. I didn't want to know what would have happened if we'd kept it up.

"How about you feed Athena, and I'll feed Killer? Unless you'd rather feed Killer?" Jared flashed a grin.

Killer's future meals chirped in Jared's room.

"Ha! The only thing I'd do with Killer's *food* is set them free."

"So I'll feed Killer then." He tugged my hair and headed down the short hallway to his room.

I walked through the dining room to their adorable galley kitchen, with a black-and-white checkerboard floor, mint-colored cabinets, red countertops, and 1950s reproduction appliances. Entering their kitchen felt like being time-warped to *Leave it to Beaver*. There was a faint odor of meals from the past that only I could detect, though probably Athena could, too. It was as though ninety years of food preparation had seasoned the room.

After a long, savoring breath of the comforting kitchen aroma, I filled Athena's food bowl with kibble and gave her fresh water. Then I walked to Jared's room, where I took another long, savoring breath that ended in a sated smile. The room smelled of him: exquisite.

"What are you smiling about?" He dropped a cricket in his tarantula's terrarium.

"Nothing." I swiped up a goalie mask that I had almost stepped on and tossed it onto his unmade bed. "You need to clean your room."

"Look who's talking!"

"You're right. My floor is my dresser, too. Oh, listen to them!" I motioned to the jar, from which Jared was in the process of fishing out another cricket. "They're pleading for their lives!"

"Not for long." Jared wiggled his eyebrows and dropped another cricket to its death.

"You're heartless!"

"A guy's gotta eat."

There was a knock at the front door.

"Mrs. Carmichael," Jared predicted.

Mrs. Carmichael was a widow who lived a couple of apartments down. She kept Eileen and Jared in ample supply of homemade baked goods and motherly advice.

"I hope she's bearing gifts of warm chocolate chip cookies," I said, glimpsing one of his soccer shoes thrown on its side near the window. The cleats were packed with mud and grass. That explained the earthy smell in the room.

"Me, too." Jared handed me the jar. "Don't feed him too many. He's starting to get cricket belly."

"Charming. And no worries."

With distaste, I set the jar next to the terrarium just as Jared left the room, leaping over a pile of clothes on his way out. I would never want a pet that required live food.

"You'll have to make do with what you've got," I told Killer, bending over to peer at him through the glass.

Hanging out in his shallow water bowl, Killer appeared not to give a hoot about the crickets hopping all around. "Not hungry, eh?" I tapped the glass. The spider didn't flinch.

The front door opened. "Can I help—"

There was a fast movement of feet.

"Wha—" Jared gasped. A sharp smacking sound cut him short.

My heart leapt to my throat. I ran to the bedroom door and peeked out.

A rough-looking man with sunglasses bolted the front door. Another thug had an arm around Jared and a hand clamped over his mouth. I could see a red welt forming on Jared's cheek where he'd been backhanded. A third man held a gun on him.

Jared began to struggle.

The gunman cocked the pistol.

Glaring at him, Jared stood still.

Think, think! I willed my brain, my heart hammering against my ribs. *If I go out now, Jared could be shot. All that creep has to do is squeeze the trigger.*

A shudder shook my body. My head swam. This could not be happening.

THINK!

My frantic eyes latched on to the hockey jersey wound around my shoe. It had gotten caught on my foot when I'd run to the door.

"Tape him," the gunman ordered.

I yanked the jersey over my head.

"You have your old man to thank for this—"

I swiped the goalie mask off the bed.

"When you play with fire—"

Pulling on the mask, I dashed to the door and looked out. The thug in the sunglasses was wrapping duct tape around Jared's wrists while the other thug held him still. Jared's mouth was taped shut. I gripped his hockey stick leaning against the wall.

"—*you* don't decide when to stop playing."

I prayed the gunman would uncock the weapon and lower it. He didn't, keeping it trained on Jared. The thug binding Jared squatted down to tape his ankles together, while the other, wearing a sordid smile, held him still.

The gunman approached Jared. "Shame. You're a good-looking kid."

"No!" I screamed and shot out of the room.

Swinging around, the gunman released the trigger.

My eyes slowed the speeding bullet. I saw it coming and could have avoided contact, but the thug in sunglasses distracted me. His hand dove for a gun tucked into his waistband. My skin hardened as the hot metal tore into my left shoulder, stopping the bullet's progression. I launched forward, swinging the hockey stick back and into the gunman's chest. The stick snapped in half, and the gunman crumbled to the floor, his head smacking against the wood.

Without pause, I seized the thug who'd been going for his weapon. I grabbed him by the throat, lifting him off the floor and throwing him. He flew into a hutch that displayed Eileen's prized fine china. China and glass shattering, the hutch toppled over and pinned the man underneath. His sunglasses sat cockeyed on his face, and blood streamed from glittering shards sunk deep into his right cheek. It trickled over his drooping lips and splashed on the floor.

The man who held Jared released him and stumbled

backward, his vile smile gone. I came at him in a flying kick, ramming my foot into his gut. His body curled around my leg, the impact propelling him backward. He took out a rocking chair and side table, sending the lamp and ceramics on top crashing. He rolled on the floor in agony, gripping his stomach, and squealed like a frightened pig.

I sprang at the creep, pulled him to his feet, and brought my fist into his face. Cartilage cracked under my hand, and blood spurted from his nose, splattering my face through the mask. I could taste it on my lips.

His eyes rolled into the back of his head. I released his collar, and he collapsed into a heap at my feet.

I spun around, prepared for another attack, but found only sprawled bodies, overturned furniture, broken glass, blood, and Jared. He was on his knees, his chest heaving, his round eyes full of shock . . . fixed on me.

My heart sank.

Jared was terrified—of me.

Chapter 4

Damage Control

"Everything is going to be okay, Jared," I choked out. He just stared at me with those wide, shocked eyes.

Pulling off the hockey mask, I brushed away tears and noticed blood smeared on my fingertips. Shame flooded me. I was an animal.

Turning my back to him, I walked to the entryway and shakily set the blood-splattered mask on a table, and then gathered the corner of my sweater under Jared's jersey to wipe my face. The room was silent, save for Jared's labored breathing behind me, and the crickets chirping down the hall.

Outside the apartment, doors opened and anxious voices inquired:

"Did you hear a gunshot?"

"Crashing?"

"Where did it come from?"

"This floor?"

Nearly rubbing my skin raw, I released my sweater, drew in a ragged breath, and braved a look at Jared.

Still on his knees, he hadn't moved an inch.

"You don't need to be afraid," I assured, tears pooling again. I moved toward him, haltingly, raising my hands to show him that I meant no harm. "I won't hurt you."

A police siren wailed in the distance.

I got down on my knees next to Jared, pinched the corner of the duct tape over his mouth, and carefully peeled it away, avoiding eye contact. Slow, warm tears rolled down my face.

The siren was closer now. Another fired up.

"Someone called the police," I surmised in a choked whisper. "I need to call my dad."

Jared looked around him, wearing a lost expression, as I fished my cell from my jeans pocket. His dazed gaze settled on the bloodied, unconscious thug sprawled a few feet away. My hands shook so badly from the spiked adrenaline and fear that I could barely open my contacts.

"Dad," I wept into the phone when he answered.

"Cassy, what happened?"

The doorbell rang.

"Jared, are you home?" Mrs. Carmichael's tense voice called from the other side of the door. She rang the bell again, holding it down.

My hand flew over his mouth. He gasped into my palm. The speed with which I had moved surprised him.

"*Please* don't answer her," I pleaded in a whisper.

Wide eyes staring into mine, his head bobbed.

While this was going on, Dad had been anxiously repeating my name and asking if I was hurt. I suppressed a bitter laugh. He was worried that *I'd* been hurt?

"Wait, Dad," I whispered into the phone. I hated the way Jared was looking at me, like I'd materialized from his worst nightmare.

Dad stopped talking. His panic practically poured from the receiver.

When Mrs. Carmichael pattered on to the next door, I released Jared's mouth. I gave him an apologetic look, then told Dad: "Something bad has happened."

"Where are you?"

I composed myself enough to explain the awful, awful situation. That isn't to say there weren't tears. They cascaded over the brim of my eyes like Niagara Falls. Why wouldn't Jared stop looking at me like that?

"The men are unconscious?" Dad asked, fear edging his voice.

"Y-yes," I wept.

"Don't let them regain consciousness. Do you understand what I'm saying?"

"Y-y-yes." I was to knock them out if they started reviving.

"Stay calm. I'm in the car now. Gavin and Emery will be there within minutes. Cassy, do not let anyone in the apartment *and* do not let anyone leave."

"K-k-kay." Jared and these men were my prisoners.

"Everything will be all right. I'm coming. I need to hang up to call Gavin."

"B-bye, D-dad."

"I'm coming, sweetheart," he repeated and disconnected the call.

I dropped my face downward, cradling it in my hands. Why did this have to happen? What would happen next?

I heard the police cars pull up outside. The sirens stopped.

"They're here," Jared said in a hollow tone.

Shocked to hear him speak, I flung my head up and almost clocked him in the nose. Noticing blood still smeared on my palms, I quickly wiped them on my jeans.

"It'll be all right," I echoed what my dad had promised.

Jared didn't reply.

I wiped my wet cheeks and moved behind him to free his hands.

"Help is on the way—but it's not the police," I clarified, the words spilling over one another. "We can't let them come in, okay?" I couldn't undo the tape with my trembling fingers, so I resorted to teeth. "*Please* act like nobody is home when they come to the door." I bit down on the tape and jerked my head to tear it, knocking a couple of teeth loose in the process. No big deal. They'd heal. "The police are in the building—" I pinched the tape on either side of the tear I had made, tasting fresh blood in my mouth. "I can hear them knocking on doors, downstairs—" I ripped the tape down the center. "You're free."

Jared brought his arms to his chest and absently massaged his wrists as he plopped down on his backside. I tested my teeth with my tongue. They were solidly rooted again, healthy and whole.

"I'll get your feet," I offered, unable to take his silence.

"Ohhhhhh," the nearest man groaned.

In a flash, I'd grabbed a handful of his hair and slammed his face into the floor. Judging by the crunching noise, I'd busted his nose. His body went limp again.

"Oh God," Jared gasped.

I whipped around.

Hands raked into his hair and eyes wide on the gunman, Jared's face displayed an expression one would expect to see on the witness of a grisly murder. He rocked slightly, back and forth. I'd traumatized him. Utterly traumatized him.

"My dad told me to," I explained, scooting up to him on my knees. He squirmed backward, recoiling when I touched his upper arm. I dissolved into tears again. "I won't h-hurt you. I don't want to hurt a-anyone. Don't you understand? I had to. They c-can't s-see me."

My cell phone vibrated on the floor. I didn't remember dropping it.

I flipped it over and read a text from Emery: *I'm here. I'll knock 3x.*

"Oh, thank you, thank you, thank you." I gave my cell a slobbery kiss.

There were three firm raps on the front door.

I ran to answer it, wiping my face on the jersey sleeve. My eyes met Emery's, and I threw my arms around his neck, hanging on to him as if for dear life. He carried me into the apartment, dangling off him like a Christmas ornament, and closed the door.

"Everything will be fine," he whispered into my hair, hugging me. Then he grasped my arms to extract them from his neck.

"Cassidy, we need to work quickly." Emery set the locks on the door. "The police are almost through the first floor." He turned around to assess the situation.

"Jared, it is a matter of life and death that you remain silent," Emery ordered. He lifted the gunman's head off the floor to determine if he was truly unconscious. Jared winced when he let the man's head fall to the floor. "It won't be long before the police are at your door." He lifted the next man's head, scrutinized him, and let go. "Do not make a sound," he repeated, his eyes moving to the thug trapped beneath the hutch. He didn't bother checking him. "Cassidy, give me a rundown."

I did what he asked, with surprising calmness. During my recap, Jared silently freed his taped ankles.

"Give me the jersey," Emery instructed, after rapidly processing the information. I blew out a relieved breath. He already had a plan. "Leave through that window." He pointed to the dining room window. "There is only a walkway between buildings. You are less likely to be seen. I'll give you my backpack, since I won't need—"

"She's been shot," Jared spoke up.

I jerked my head toward him, surprised to hear his voice. He had moved to the sofa, where he sat with elbows on his knees, hands in his hair, doing some processing of his own.

Emery turned his head from Jared to me. His eyes narrowed on my left shoulder. I glanced down at the bullet hole. I had forgotten about being shot until Jared mentioned it.

"I forgot. My skin is hard," I apologized, gripped with shame again. My skin was numb, and felt like it was cinched over bone. How could I have not noticed until now? "Because of the bullet," I added needlessly to Emery. He knew from experience that a bullet deadened my nerve endings so I felt no pain.

Inserting this new data into his mental calculation, Emery slid his backpack off his shoulder. It was filled with a gadget for almost every situation. He set it on the dining room table, unzipped it, and removed latex gloves.

"Put these on," Emery ordered, handing them to me.

Jared stared at him as though Emery were a mirage.

"I know you're in shock, Jared," I tried to console him as I tugged on the gloves. Emery rummaged through the backpack. "I get it. You haven't seen Emery like this before. But this is the real him."

Jared's bewildered eyes snapped to me. I wished I'd just kept my mouth shut.

"Where are the police?" Emery asked me. He pulled out a switchblade.

The look on Jared's face made it impossible to answer, let alone concentrate enough to hear anything outside the apartment.

"What are you going to do with that?" he demanded of Emery.

Emery flipped the blade out. "I said to not speak," he reminded Jared.

"Like hell!" Jared lurched off the sofa.

I stepped in front of Emery. Jared plowed into me, bouncing backward as if hitting a cement wall. My hands shot out, grasping him by the biceps so he wouldn't tumble to the floor. He gaped at me, speechless.

"I won't hurt her," Emery assured calmly, although I did detect irritation in his voice. He produced a bottle of cleaning solution from the backpack. "We need to get the bullet out of her and lodged where it would logically be." He took a small package of white cloth handkerchiefs from the backpack. "Cassidy's life will be in grave danger if evidence doesn't measure up or is left behind. Jared, you are to do *exactly* what I tell you." He flipped a chair around for me. "Cassidy."

I sat down. Emery picked up the knife and ordered

Jared: "Watch these three." He gestured toward each man with the blade. "Speak up if any of them start to come to."

Emery hooked the collar of my V-neck shirt with a finger and eased it over the bullet wound. The metal butt protruded from my shoulder like a cork in a wine bottle, thick blood burbling around it.

"Hold your shirt back," Emery said.

I collected the fabric, watching Jared. Confusion, fear, and panic mingled on his face.

"Don't watch," I forced out around the lump in my throat. I didn't want him to know what a freak I was. He had seen enough already.

Emery wedged the tip of the knife under the bullet. Jared's eyes grew even wider with horror, but he didn't intervene. My cheeks burned with humiliation. Why hadn't he listened to me?

"She can't feel this," Emery assured and repeated his order. "Turn around and keep an eye on your assailants."

As Jared complied, I wondered if Emery had told him to do this to save me from additional embarrassment. *No*, I decided, as the bullet popped free. *He's just being efficient.*

"Jared, listen carefully—" Emery said as he slid on latex gloves. "You and I were alone in the apartment, in your room." He doused a handkerchief with the cleaning solution. "You answered the door and were attacked. Seconds later, I came out, in the mask, swinging the hockey stick." He meticulously cleaned the bullet. "*I* took these men out. *Me.* Put your hand out, Cassidy." He dropped the bullet into my palm and walked toward the gunman. Now I knew why he'd asked me to wear gloves. "As I was freeing you from the duct tape, I called my dad." He stepped over the thug and faced Jared's bedroom, evaluating. "He is out front now, waiting for me to text him to come in. We were in shock, not thinking straight, and were afraid to leave the apartment. Not an implausible reaction for the average teenager. Cassidy, come here."

While I did what he asked, Emery continued talking. "When the police arrive with my dad, I'll do the talking. You nod and confirm everything I say. Do *not* offer any information. Cassidy, that picture—" He pointed to a print at the entrance to the hallway, of a Victorian girl holding a kitten. "Throw the bullet through it, full force. A nine millimeter bullet would travel approximately 650 miles per hour when fired, so don't hold back."

"In front of Jared?" I whispered.

Emery threw up his hands in exasperation, and motioned to all the reasons around us why I shouldn't still care about what Jared witnessed.

"Time is of the essence," he reminded, stepping back to give me space. "Jared, do not move from that spot."

Pulling my arm back, I threw the bullet with all my might. It pierced the kitten, leaving a clean hole in the glass, and traveled through the wall. I could hear it break through the other side, whiz across the dining room, and strike the opposite wall. Obviously, I hadn't hit a stud.

I couldn't even look at Jared.

Emery secured my arm and pulled me to the dining room table. Peripherally, I glimpsed Jared, rooted to the spot where Emery had told him to stay, blinking at the bullet hole through the kitten.

Emery slid off his hoodie. "Put this on," he ordered, handing it to me.

While I did what he asked, he doused another handkerchief with solution.

"Our goal is to not draw attention," he explained, and cleaned my face.

Heat flowed into my cheeks. The evidence of my violence was still on my face?

Emery tugged the hood over my head, snapped off my gloves, and ordered me to tuck in loose hair. He tossed the gloves into the backpack, along with his gloves, the switchblade, bloodied handkerchiefs, cleaning solution, and Jared's bullet-torn jersey. His tension was mounting. He'd obviously sensed the police were closing in, and he was right. I could hear them approaching down the hall.

"Here—" He shoved the backpack at me and pointed to the window again. "Go!"

"I'm sorry," I said to Jared. He looked as though he were in another world.

Dashing to the window, I shoved it open, made sure the coast was clear, and then jumped, without a backward glance to see if Jared was freaking out.

What did it matter anymore? The damage was done.

Chapter 5

The Truth Hurts

I was an utter wreck. In our family room, I rested in my mother's arms while Serena rubbed my back and offered words of consolation. Across the sectional from us, Chazz huddled next to Nate, watching me with great concern. Even at six, Chazz understood our family would be in danger if Jared told the police the truth.

Dad had called an hour earlier from outside Jared's apartment building, which he'd been about to enter under false pretenses. The cover story was that his neighbor, Gavin, had called him about the attack, since my parents were responsible for Jared this weekend. Fortunately, the police hadn't been able to contact Eileen, since she was somewhere over the Atlantic Ocean. They'd also had no luck tracking down Mr. Wells. He hadn't gone into his office that day, and wasn't picking up his home or cell phone. This gave Dad, Gavin, and Emery an opportunity for damage control—and to convince Jared not to expose me.

However, Mr. Wells's unavailability did bring up a concern. Those goons had showed up at Jared's apartment because of something his dad was involved in. So where was he?

"Guys, I think we're overreacting," Nate piped up. "I mean . . . this is Jared."

"You didn't see him, Nate." I plucked another tissue from the box. "You didn't see *me*. He was terrified."

"Don't fret, dear," Serena soothed. "Gavin will contain the situation."

Contain? I certainly didn't like the sound of that.

~~~

At 7:18 p.m., Dad's Volvo pulled up to the curb in front of our house. Spying Jared in the front seat, I let the curtain in our living room window drop. Police statements had taken longer than usual, perhaps due to another report of a missing person, a Candace Something-Or-Other. I'd been too distraught during the news broadcast to pay much attention to her name.

Dad had updated us in his last phone call, saying that the three thugs were in the hospital under police guard. As far as he knew, they'd declined to talk until their lawyers arrived, the thought of which filled me with unspeakable fear. What if they'd overheard us talking? What if they knew a girl named Cassidy had pummeled them?

I sat down in the wingback chair slanted toward the foyer and listened to Gavin's SUV pull up across the street. The doors on Dad's car closed.

Jared, don't hate me. Don't be afraid of me.

"Come with me, Jared," I heard Gavin summon.

I resisted getting up to look out the window.

"We'll be right over." Dad sounded weary.

Footsteps came up our walk. I recognized them as belonging to Dad and Emery. I would know the sound of their footfalls anywhere.

Keys jiggled in the deadbolt. I forced air into and out of my lungs. The front door opened, and Dad stepped into the foyer.

"We're home," he called, not noticing me sitting in the dark. It was the first place Emery looked.

Mom walked briskly from the kitchen, entering the foyer while drying her hands on a dishtowel. The boys trailed her. They'd been playing Xbox in the family room, decompressing.

"Where's Cass?" Dad asked.

Locking the front door, Emery didn't speak up.

Before Mom or the boys had a chance to answer, Dad swiveled his head to the living room, as it suddenly occurred to him where I might be.

"Cassy?" He flicked on the light. Concern reshaped his tired features when he saw me. "I'm sorry for being so vague on the phone," he apologized as he approached me. "Jared was in the car."

"Does he hate me?" A tear tumbled down my cheek. Knowing the danger I'd put my family in was unbearable.

"No. Of course not." Dad got down on his knees in front of me and wiped my wet cheeks with his hands. "He doesn't hate you. How could he? But he is very confused. I explained as much as I could in the car, but we have more to talk about before you can see him." He gathered me in his arms. "Everything will be fine. Jared just needs time to sort through everything."

"That's right." Mom stroked my hair. She and my brothers had followed Dad. Chazz looked scared out of his mind. This had to stop.

"I'm okay," I lied, pulling out of Dad's hug. "Chazz, it'll all work out."

He didn't appear to buy it.

Dad smiled. "It will." He patted my knee and stood

up. "Your mom and I will be back soon." He motioned to her with his head that they were going to the Phillips's, where Gavin and Serena were probably coercing Jared into silence. This was a nightmare.

Emery had watched the scene with hands shoved deep in his pockets. After the door closed behind my parents, he pushed off the living room's entryway molding where he'd been leaning.

"I'm famished," he announced. "What do you have to eat?"

~~~

"You're probably wondering what happened after you left," Emery remarked between bites of casserole.

He hadn't said a peep while Nate dished him up a plate and I scrounged around the pantry for a can of soda.

"Ya think?" I couldn't help myself. I popped open the soda and placed it before him.

"Dude, you're being cruel," Nate chided.

"I'm not trying to be." Emery wiped his mouth with a paper napkin. "I'm gathering my thoughts."

"Well, are they *gathered* yet?" I couldn't help myself, again.

"I deserve that," Emery agreed and launched into his account. "When I texted my dad the 'go ahead,' he approached the officer securing the building and told him that his son had called from his friend's apartment, where they'd been attacked, but managed to overpower their assailants. He brought them to the apartment, where I answered the door, *distraught*. We played our parts perfectly, sparking no suspicion, and Jared did as instructed, agreeing with everything I told the police and keeping his mouth shut otherwise.

"The police weren't able to contact Jared's parents, so they wouldn't allow your dad to drive him to headquarters for a statement. You can imagine how chancy leaving him alone with the police would be. My dad persuaded the officers to let me ride with Jared. Luckily, the police at the station were able to contact Jared's grandfather in Ohio. He gave permission for him to be released into your parents' custody."

"Where is his dad?" Nate asked what had been bothering me.

Emery shrugged.

"Maybe the bad guys got him," Chazz said just above a whisper, his eyes widening.

"Chazz, why don't you watch TV?" I suggested.

He glared at me. "I'm not a baby," he scoffed, puffing out his chest. Whipping his nose up and away from me, he addressed Emery, deepening his voice. "Do you think the bad guys shot him like they were going to shoot Jared?"

Oh, this had to stop.

"Don't worry, Chazz. No one was going to shoot Jared," Nate stated as though he knew this for a fact.

Chazz scowled.

"He had a gun," he challenged.

"They were just looking for Jared's dad, *end of story*," Nate insisted.

"Back to what I was saying," Emery continued, not wanting to back up Nate—who hadn't even been there. If he had, he would know the possibility of Jared getting a bullet between the eyes had been highly probable. "Obviously, Jared and I weren't able to corroborate our stories in the squad car, and we weren't sure what he would disclose out of our presence. I did worry that he would rat Cassidy out. Thankfully, he proved me wrong."

"Why would you think that?" Nate demanded, offended for his friend.

"Why *wouldn't* you think that?" Emery countered.

"Because that's not Jared!" Nate shot me a fiery look. "You're awfully quiet! Shouldn't you be all worked up, defending him?"

"You weren't there, Nate," I bit out.

"I'm mad at all of you!" Chazz screamed, shaking his fists. He stomped out of the room.

"Chazz," I called after him, but he ignored me.

"Oh, man!" Nate barked a humorless laugh. "This sucks."

"Sums it up," Emery agreed.

Chazz turned up the volume on the family room television, seeking his revenge. He had *SpongeBob SquarePants* on. Guess he wasn't feeling overly reckless.

"Dude, there's pie in the fridge," Nate gave Emery his peace offering.

"Sounds good."

While they wolfed down apple pie, I paced the kitchen.

"Cass, sit down," Nate urged. "You're stressing me out." He belched pie.

"Emery, did Jared talk about me?" I blurted. I wasn't going to ask, but not knowing was killing me.

"There wasn't an opportunity."

"What about before your dad brought the police to the apartment? There was time then!"

"Cassidy, sit," Nate commanded. "You're putting my stomach in knots."

I was at the table and in the chair next to Emery in a flash. Emery didn't flinch at my speed, though Nate practically jumped out of his skin.

"Are you trying to make me puke?" he demanded.

"Stop feeding your face!"

"Stop being agro!"

"Both of you cool it," Emery ordered. "Cassidy—"

"What?" I bellowed.

He grabbed my face between his palms. *"Calm* down." His eyes bore into mine. I glared daggers into his. "You're not angry with me," he stated, unmoved by my fury. "You're angry at the situation. To answer your question, we did not discuss you because Jared was in shock."

My rage dissolved. "Is he afraid of me?"

"Cass," Nate protested. Even he knew Jared was afraid of me.

I pulled my face loose from Emery's grip and averted my gaze. I had embarrassed myself enough with all the waterworks. I wouldn't cry again. What was done was done.

"Why don't you trust him, Emery?" I asked, controlling my voice.

"Jared isn't a member of your family, nor mine. He is a crush, Cassidy. That's it. What happens if he loses interest in you, if there is another rift, or if you date and break up?"

"I keep my mouth shut."

I jolted upright in my chair. How could I have not heard, or smelled, Dad and Jared come into the house?

Holding Athena, Jared stood stoically next to my dad. Chazz had trailed them into the kitchen. The tears I had just sworn off once again filled my eyes. There was no fear in Jared's steady gaze.

"Hi, *kitty-kitty*," Chazz cooed, petting Athena.

"Her name is Athena," Jared told him, flashing a gentle smile. He looked at me again. "Can we talk?"

"Y-yes," I stammered and scrambled to my feet. "But privately—if that's okay?"

He smiled. "Of course it is." His eyes moved down to Chazz. "Would you watch Athena for me?"

While Jared handed over the cat, I took the opportunity to swipe a quick sleeve across my eyes. It would be okay, after all.

Chapter 6

No More Lies

Jared shut the attic door behind us, and we made our way up the stairs in silence. Near the top, it occurred to me that I hadn't switched on the lights. I'd been so nervous that I'd forgotten he didn't have night vision, too.

"Can you see?" I asked mid-step and glanced back at him.

He stared at me without squinting, indicating that he could see. "Yeah," he confirmed with a shy, sweet smile. "Thanks to the full moon." He gestured to the two large skylights soaking the open space in natural and urban light.

"Just checking. Sometimes I forget not everyone can see in the dark as well as I can," I explained awkwardly and began ascending the steps again, grateful that Jared couldn't see my blush in the dimness. This would be a difficult talk.

Stepping onto the landing, I looked from one side of the attic to the other, uncertain where to go. Jared made the decision for me.

"Over there." He walked past me to the large gymnastic mat. I would have chosen the sofa on the other side. Jared didn't always do the predictable thing.

He plopped down dead center on the mat and stretched out on his back. Hands folded under his head, he gazed at the night sky through the skylight. I lingered at the mat's edge, nudging it with my foot.

The corners of Jared's mouth curled. "Cassy, join me."

I reclined next to him. He stared at the skylight, thinking. Once I had situated myself, I directed my gaze upward, too.

"Wow," I said with wonder. It wasn't often stars were visible in Seattle.

"I know. It's amazing."

"Believe it or not, I've never done this before." My eyes bounced from twinkling star to twinkling star. "And this window has been here for, what, three years?"

"Longer than that. We were in sixth grade when your house was remodeled." Jared rolled his head to me, his hair swishing against the vinyl. I watched him peripherally with a galloping heart. He studied my profile for several seconds before speaking. "I'm sorry, Cassy."

"You're sorry?" I asked incredulously, turning my head toward him. Our faces were inches apart, which didn't do a thing to calm my pounding heart. "What for?"

Jared rolled to his side. "I made you feel bad about yourself, and for that I'm very sorry." His gaze lingered over my hair splayed across the mat. "I don't know what to say." His fingertips traced my hairline. I couldn't breathe. "Those goons . . . you . . . Emery . . ." He gently tucked loose strands behind my ear, his fingertips brushing my skin. "It was like a dream."

"Like what?" I was having trouble listening to what he was saying.

He smiled. "A dream."

I cleared my throat. "*Dream*? More like a nightmare," I said, picturing the bloodied faces of the thugs. Nothing kills a romantic buzz like remembering that you're lethal. "Are you afraid of me?"

His fingertips traveled down my jawline, delicately, as though I were made of fine porcelain. "No." His smile twisted devilishly. "But Emery scares the crap out of me."

I sputtered into laughter.

Jared busted up, too, and soon we were rolling on the mat, hugging our guts, and laughing so hard that no noise emerged.

"I'm being serious," Jared insisted at last, his voice hoarse from laughing. I was still trying to get my laughter under control. "I always knew something about him was off. But I didn't see *James Bond* coming."

"James Bond with a two hundred IQ." I hiccupped, and we cracked up again.

"A two hundred IQ—seriously?" Jared questioned when we got hold of our laughter again.

"I don't know, but it wouldn't surprise me. Did our parents tell you about him?"

"About Emery being a child prodigy and graduating from Wallingford University last spring?" Jared gave me a wry smile.

"Yeah, that." I chuckled, feeling embarrassment creep in. "You probably think we're all super strange."

"Not strange—unreal."

"Oh." I didn't know if I liked that.

"Don't take that negatively. You're still Cassidy Jones, the girl I've been in love with since I was, like, ten."

"Ten?" I asked skeptically.

"Yeah, ten. The only difference is now you can beat me at arm wrestling."

"Yeah, right. I'm no threat beyond that." I regretted the words as soon as they came out. What was I doing? Did I *want* Jared to be scared of me?

Better safe than sorry.

"Don't do that, Cass," Jared said, tracing my hairline again. His touch sent what felt like a tingling electric current over the surface of my skin. "Don't even think about trying to push me away. You are Cassidy to me, no matter what."

"That's a miracle in and of itself, considering what you saw."

"I saw you save my life. If you hadn't been there, I might not be here now."

"Don't say that." I grabbed his precious face in my hands, fiercely. "I love you, too."

"You do?" His eyes drank me in.

"Yeah, since I was *nine*."

"You always have to one-up me."

We grew sober then, fixed in one another's gazes. I wanted to prove that I loved him, and knew exactly how. "I want to tell you something that I have never told anyone."

I summarized the night Emery and I stormed King Pharmaceutical to rescue my dad and Serena. After describing the three ninjas and the weapons they wielded, I came to the part I had never confessed to another living soul. "The throwing-star ninja came at me in this jump-kick. My brain imprinted his kick, so I was able to counterattack with the same move. My heel rammed into his face, and I could feel cartilage snap, pushing his nose off to the side of his face. It was disgusting."

Jared nodded, synapses firing behind his serious eyes.

63

"While all of that was going on, it gave the nunchuck ninja a chance to attack. He hit my head with nunchucks and shattered my skull. At least that's how it felt. The pain was indescribable."

Jared slid his hand over mine; his gaze intensified. "What happened then?"

"I died."

He stared at me, as if having trouble packing the information into his grey matter. "You *died*?"

"Yeah, died—as in croaked, kicked the bucket, bought the farm." I let out a nervous laugh. I was about to tread on sacred ground and reveal an experience I had vowed to keep to myself forever. "That isn't what I wanted to tell you, though. I was just leading up to my secret. I had one of those *near-death* experiences—you know, when the person feels their spirit leave their body and sees a beckoning light?"

"You saw God?"

"Yes." I fell silent.

Absently, I traced the graphic on his T-shirt with my forefinger as I assembled my emotions. Talking about this was more difficult than I'd anticipated. "I wanted to keep floating up. But I couldn't. All at once, it felt like this force grabbed my inner core and yanked me downward, right back into my body. What scares me most—I'm going to cry."

"It's okay." Jared's fingertips caressed my cheekbone. "Cry."

"No. There's been enough crying for one day. What scares me most is an endless life, where I have to watch everyone I love die. There! I said it."

Jared enveloped me in his arms, and I snuggled against his warm, solid chest, relishing his steady heartbeat thumping in my ear. I could have stayed like that forever.

"Don't worry about what might or might not happen," he encouraged thickly.

"Stop!" I protested. "You're going to make me cry. They probably didn't tell you about my emotions. Up and down, to extremes. It's crazy!"

"Are you trying to say you being emotional is new?" he teased.

"Yes!" I nestled my chin on his chest so I could see his face. Much to my surprise, his eyes were moist with tears. "Look what I did to you! Your eyelashes look like wet flower petals."

"Just what every guy wants to hear."

"Well, they look beautiful. You're beautiful, inside and out."

"Thank you. And ditto." He laughed at himself. "That was lame." His fingers returned to the task of tucking hair behind my ear. "But in all seriousness, your secrets are *always* safe with me. And as far as you know, Mrs. Phillips could find a cure tomorrow."

"She could. But she won't." Before Jared could argue, I rushed on. "There's something I need to show you. Come on."

As I stood up, a mixture of disappointment and relief played over his face. It was good to know our intimacy hadn't affected only me. My legs felt like gelatin.

I led him to the sofa and switched on the desk lamp.

"Have a seat." I rummaged through the top drawer. "I want you to see why the bullet didn't get past my skin." I found what I had been searching for—sewing scissors.

When he saw the scissors in my hand, Jared's curiosity became alarm. "What are you going to do?"

"I told you—show you why I'm bulletproof." I sat next to him. "Don't move. Don't try to stop me," I repeated the instructions Serena had given me when she performed the same test. "Do *not* stop me," I reminded for safe measure and flattened my palm, aiming the scissor's tip dead center.

"Whoa! Wait—" Jared grabbed my hand that held the scissors.

"That's just what Emery did *after* Serena had told him not to."

"You've done this before?" Jared stared at me like I was off my rocker.

"This is how I entertain myself when I'm bored," I joked.

Jared didn't think it was funny.

"It'll be fine." I smiled at his sweet, anxious face. "I won't get hurt. But it won't work if you stop me again. So just watch. Don't move a muscle."

He concentrated on the scissors targeting my palm, worry lines creasing his forehead. My smile expanded. Jared was too adorable.

I dropped my arm; the scissors plunged. Apparently due to Jared's adorableness, my brain didn't register *danger*. My skin didn't harden like I'd planned. The scissors ripped into my flesh, activating pain receptors. I yelped. Blood gushed into the deep wound. Only then did my skin turn rigid, numbing the pain.

"No," Jared gasped.

I blinked at the scissors sunk into my palm, blood welling around the blades, pooling in my palm. Jared reached for the handles to save me from myself, but before he could get hold of them, I yanked the blades loose.

"That wasn't what I had intended at all," I apologized, feeling a faint throbbing around the cut. Jared pressed the edge of his T-shirt into the gash.

"W-why?" He groped for words, completely rattled.

"Your cuteness distracted me. I feel like a *complete* idiot."

"Your voice—" Jared assessed my face. "You don't feel pain?"

"Of course not. Can't you feel how hard my skin is? It's like a rock, but won't be for long. Hurry and look, before you miss it."

"Look at what?"

"Where I stabbed myself." I pried his hand from my palm. He stared at me in shock, experiencing my strength firsthand. "Look," I urged.

He forced his eyes to the wound, or what remained of it.

"Dang. It's nearly healed," I observed, disappointed. The ravaged flesh had almost closed.

Jared gaped at my hand. "I can't believe it," he said. He took hold of my hand to examine it.

"My skin is normal again, too. Did you feel how hard it was?"

Not appearing to have heard me, he rubbed away blood, searching for the wound.

"You won't even find a scratch. But if you touched my hand three seconds ago, it would have felt like a rock. We could do the test again. Just don't distract me this time."

"Stab you?" Jared asked, flabbergasted at the suggestion. "I don't think so. Never again."

"It's no big deal—" I began, but switched gears when

Jared's expression told me it most certainly was a big deal. He just didn't get it. "Well, at least you saw my rapid cell regeneration at work. Now you get why I'm hard to kill, with the exception of—" I retracted from broaching the subject of Raul Diaz, a.k.a., Silver Tooth.

Due to our similar genetic makeup, Diaz's venom was my only mortal weakness, thus far. But Jared didn't need to hear that right now. He had enough to sort through. What had happened on the *Enchantress* was a story for another day.

"With the exception of what?"

"I'll tell you another time. Do you know what's going on with your dad?"

"No." His face betrayed his anger, embarrassment, and worry. "But my guess is he owes someone money for a gambling debt, or he pissed off one of his lowlife clients."

"Oh." I didn't know his dad had a gambling problem.

"I'm sorry about what happened," Jared apologized.

"You have nothing to be sorry for. Don't think about what could have happened. Think about what *did* happen. I was there."

Rage flashed in his eyes. "I can't help but think—what if it had been my mom at home instead? What would they have done to her?"

"Well, she wasn't. So don't even go there. Everything happens for a reason. It wasn't a mistake that I was with you, or that you saw what you saw. I'm glad you did. I don't want to keep any secrets from you."

"I'm glad, too." He smiled, though his eyes simmered. His father had brought those creeps to their door. That was a lot to cope with.

I heard footsteps coming down the hall below us.

"My dad is coming," I told Jared.

He listened and shook his head, not hearing my dad.

The attic door creaked open.

Jared grinned. *"Now* I hear him."

"Cassidy," Dad called as he climbed the steps.

"Yep. We're here, and I didn't traumatize Jared too much."

Dad came into view. Surprise sprang onto his face. Eying the blood smeared at the bottom of Jared's T-shirt, he offered him the phone handset. "Your mom," he explained.

"Any word from my dad yet?" Jared asked.

Dad shook his head regretfully.

"He'll call soon." I gave Jared's shoulder a reassuring pat. Of course, I didn't believe he would. I couldn't shake the image of Owen Wells wearing cement boots at the bottom of Lake Washington.

"Hi, Mom," Jared said into the handset.

Eileen's frantic voice flowed through the receiver.

"Mom, it's okay—*I'm* okay." Jared placed an elbow on his knee and cradled his forehead in his palm so we couldn't see his face. "No one can find Dad. Do you know where he could be?"

My dad motioned for us to give Jared privacy. Then he spied the scissors on the floor. His mouth dipped with disapproval.

"A demonstration," I whispered as he swiped them off the floor. A bit of my blood had stained the Berber carpet. Mom was going to have a fit.

Dad raised his hand for me to say no more. By the deepening of the lines on his forehead, I guessed he had a massive headache coming on.

Chapter 7

What's Eating Emery?

The next morning, Eileen was flying somewhere over the continental US on her way home, and there still had been no word from Jared's dad. Authorities had learned that his law partners and the staff at Cooperstein, Scolla and Wells hadn't been in contact with him since Tuesday, due to his being on vacation. The vacation was news to Jared.

During breakfast, conversation was kept intentionally light, as we avoided the previous day's events and speculations about Mr. Wells's whereabouts. The phone rang as I forked the last spoonful of veggie scramble into my mouth. My dad's scrambles were to die for.

Chazz jumped from his chair and bolted for the phone as though we were going to race him to it. No one moved a muscle. We all knew Chazz would get it.

"Hello!" Chazz's head bobbed vigorously as he listened to the caller. He pulled the phone from his ear and ordered with an air of importance: "Cassidy, Serena wants your blood—*now*."

I cracked a smile over Serena's protest of the usage of "now." That had been Chazz's touch.

"Well, you heard him," I said, rising to my feet. "I have to go *now*. Guess that means you're doing the dishes, Nate."

He chucked a wadded napkin at me, which I let nail my face. It was the least I could do.

"Want to come?" I invited Jared. "You might as well see what my housecleaning duties for Serena entail."

~~~

"Let me guess," Jared said as we crossed the street to the Phillips's. "You don't vacuum or mop floors."

"Sometimes I do." I waved at Cristiano. He smiled around the bottle of water he was chugging and waved back. "Wonder what's made him so happy lately?" I mused in a lowered voice to Jared. "He never smiles."

"The construction worker?" Jared inquired. He discreetly studied Cristiano, who was assisting a coworker named Briggs in removing a beam from the van. After yesterday, Jared had caught on that nothing was as it seemed, even the Phillips's remodeling.

~~~

"Knock, knock," I called from the front door threshold.

"Come on up," Gavin called from upstairs.

Jared and I moved aside so Briggs and Cristiano could carry the beam inside the house. The four other workers must have been in the basement, shoveling dirt or something. Cristiano flashed us another smile as they walked by. If his breath hadn't indicated differently, I would have suspected the bottle I'd seen him gulping from contained something other than water.

71

"Are you in love, Cristiano?" This was the next logical explanation.

Jared stifled a snicker.

Briggs and Cristiano hooted, their feet crunching along the plastic that was protecting the hallway floor.

"Only with himself!" Briggs ribbed.

"I can't believe you asked him that!" Jared whispered, grinning, as we jogged up the stairs.

"Well, he looks like he's in love." I touched the stair rail and immediately pulled my hand back. There was a thick coating of dust on it, just like there was on every flat surface of the house, due to the construction. "I seriously don't know how they live like this," I remarked, wiping my filthy palm on my jeans.

"About Cristiano," Emery called from the spare room at the top of the stairs, having overheard my question. "You do know what killed the cat."

"Curiosity," I answered. We stepped up to the landing. "Now it makes perfect sense why I'm curious."

We veered left into the spare room. Jared's eyes roamed the thirteen-by-thirteen-square-foot space.

"Welcome," I said with flourish, shutting and locking the door, "—to the temporary laboratory of the world-famous geneticist, Professor Serena Phillips, and headquarters to the finest spy on Earth, Gavin Phillips."

"You're making me blush," Gavin teased from his desk. His eyes scanned the screen of his laptop. A live feed of the inside and the outside of the house streamed in each of the eight blocks on a large monitor mounted over the desk. Gavin had hidden the cameras so expertly that even I'd had a challenging time locating them.

"I'm the consigned lab technician," Emery said from behind the steel cart, where he'd prepared for the blood draw. He held up a syringe with a sinister smile. "And the spy's *zealous* interrogation assistant, when *persuasion* is necessary."

Serena clucked her tongue with disapproval as she prepared a slide for her microscope.

"Ha-ha." I slid Jared a concerned look. "He's kidding, you know."

"Oh, *am* I?" Emery wiggled his eyebrows.

"Psychoactive drugs are rarely necessary," Gavin chimed in. "My suspects usually break when Emery lectures them on the mathematical odds of their success."

"Which I don't understand. Who doesn't enjoy probability theory?" Emery shook his head as though dumfounded, and then patted the medical exam table. "Come, Cassidy. Let's settle the question that has been eating at Jared's mind these last seven months: What exactly *is* Cassidy doing at the Phillips's house?"

My jaw dropped. Emery was in rare form.

"You have my permission to deck him, Jared," Gavin said.

"Do I?" I managed a smirk.

Emery grinned at my crimson cheeks. "You haven't asked permission before. Jared, if you only knew what I deal with."

"I've got a good idea," Jared joined in.

"What is this? The 'Harassing Cassidy' hour?" I tried to sound playful. Serena, with her usual tact, utterly defeated my attempt.

"You've embarrassed Cassidy," she reprimanded the

boys. "Take note of the widening blood vessels in her cheek tissue."

"Noted," Emery goaded.

I shoved him with my shoulder.

"Jared, it was nice when he couldn't be himself around you," I retorted as I hoisted my backside onto the exam table.

"I like this version better," Jared joked. At least, I think it was a joke.

"It's my preferred version, too." Emery tied a tourniquet around my arm.

"You have so many," I quipped. "How do you keep track?"

"Jared, get used to this," Gavin contributed. "Cassidy is like the *sister* Emery never had."

I noticed how he emphasized "sister." Then I noticed the tightness of Jared's smile.

"Yeah, he is almost as annoying as Nate," I added hastily to further derail Jared's thoughts from the track they were on. He was obviously reading more into our bantering than he should. "How's the remodeling coming along, Gavin?"

As he felt around my elbow joint for a juicy vein, Emery let his grin subside.

"The crew is making progress," Gavin answered, congenially and vaguely.

"Oh," I said, unsure why he didn't want to share more details in front of Jared. Jared knew Gavin was a CIA operative, Emery was a genius, and I was a mutant, after all. Why would the future Batcave be a secret, then?

Emery inserted the needle. Blood flowed into the syringe.

"How often do you draw her blood?" Jared asked, watching with fascination.

"Whenever ordered." Emery jerked his head toward his mom. He was acting really strangely.

After the blood draw, Serena conducted her usual examination, which Jared watched with fascination, too, peppering her with questions about the virus. She answered him in excruciating detail, obviously not sharing Gavin's and Emery's reluctance.

"Oh, Jared, this reminds me," I said as Serena flashed the beam from her ophthalmoscope into my eyes. "Did you notice my eye color changed?"

Jared stared at them with confusion. "When?"

"Like, over two months ago. I just woke up one morning and they were this jade color. Can't you see the difference?"

He narrowed his eyes on mine. Serena examined my ears.

"They look the same to me," Jared said a moment later.

For some reason, his not seeing the difference disappointed me.

"Why did they change color?" he addressed Serena.

"We don't know," Emery butted in. He sat behind his mother's laptop at the opposite end of the lab table, inputting data from her notes. "She'll ask you about the freckles next. I *can* tell you why those vanished."

I motioned at my nose to show Jared where the spray of freckles had been.

Jared smiled. "You don't need to," he told Emery. "Rapid cell regeneration." His smile flipped into a frown as he studied my nose. I could see on his face the very moment he remembered my freckles. "How did I miss the freckles?" he asked himself.

"Way to go, Sherlock," Emery jeered.

"Don't be rude!" I rebuked him. I was sick of his attitude.

Emery's head jerked up in surprise. I glared at him.

"I didn't mean to be ru—" Jared cut his apology short when he realized the dirty look was aimed at Emery. "You were talking to Emery?"

From the corner of my eye, I saw Gavin turn around in his chair. Puzzled, I wondered why he and Serena weren't jumping down Emery's throat.

"What did Emery do, dear?" Serena inquired. "Did he say something under his breath?" She gave her son a look.

"Guilty as charged," he said and directed his attention back to the laptop.

I stared at him, baffled. It almost seemed as though his confession were a lie, like he hadn't made the remark at all.

"Stop provoking her," Serena ordered, placing her stethoscope on my chest. "I'm about to listen to her heart."

"Oh, you'll find this interesting," I enthusiastically said to Jared. I wasn't about to let Emery's weird mood put a damper on mine. "My heart beats more slowly now, like forty beats per minute. A healthy heart doesn't have to work as hard. If you listen, it sounds like I'm dying—"

"*Shh,*" Serena shushed me with a frown.

When the exam was finished, I led Jared to the world map pinned to the wall next to Gavin's desk.

"All these thumbtacks are where Lily White has struck." My forefinger hopped from tack to tack. "Gavin is tracking her, trying to figure out if there's a pattern with her heists." I glanced at Gavin. His mouth held a small smile on his none-too-pleased face. What was his problem?

"Well, we should go," I said to Jared with feigned brightness. "Bye, everyone."

We left, and I shut the door behind us, resisting the urge to slam it.

"This is going to be a problem," Gavin whispered when we were halfway down the stairs.

"She's listening," Emery warned him, not bothering to lower his voice. He was really getting on my nerves.

"SPD classed the two new missing persons filed yesterday in this last hour," Gavin changed the subject. "The media will be notified soon."

Gavin had hacked into the Seattle Police Department's computer system, I deduced, assuming that he had been reading a confidential police blotter.

The missing homeless people Joe had told me about leaped to memory. I toyed with the idea of going back upstairs to tell Gavin about them, but decided against it for now. Why give Emery another opportunity to take potshots?

Chapter 8

Odd Encounter

"Cassidy!" Leroy Rays boomed as Jared and I entered my house.

On his feet in one second flat, Leroy scooped me up into his huge arms and turned me in a full circle around the living room. It didn't take me aback in the least, even though I'd only met him once before.

Everything about the big-game hunter was excessive—size, energy, personality, voice, and movements. You wouldn't think he could sneak up on anyone or anything. However, I knew from experience that he could be quite stealthy. Otherwise, he wouldn't have managed to shoot me with a tranquilizer dart last November.

"How are ya, girl?" he inquired with a Texas twang and a Texas-size smile, setting me on my feet.

He had blue eyes, a shaved head, and a blond handlebar mustache growing down the sides of his mouth. He was wearing his standard ensemble from both of his cable shows, *Big Game* and *Monster Hunters*—combat boots, a mustard-colored T-shirt, and camouflage pants that clung to the muscles roping his large legs.

Before I could answer, he shoved a young, pretty blonde woman at me. "Cassidy, meet my niece, Jenna

Wade."

As Jenna and I shook hands, Leroy added, "Jenna is my producer for *Monster Hunters*."

Ben caught my attention. Seated next to Dad on the sofa, the cameraman couldn't take his eyes off Jenna. Chazz sat on Ben's lap, and Athena was curled up on Chazz's.

"Nice to meet you, Cassidy," Jenna said with enthusiasm. "I'm *so* excited to be here! Aren't the Lake Washington Monster sightings thrilling?"

Dreamy-eyed, Ben sighed. This was a match made in heaven.

I introduced Jared to them. As Leroy practically pumped his arm off in a hearty handshake, our front door burst open and Bobby Neigh stumbled into the foyer. Startled to see everyone in the living room, he hastily smoothed his mop of brown curls and struck a pose that he thought would make him look cool. It had the opposite effect.

"Hey." He lifted his chin and smoothed his hair again.

I swallowed a laugh and glanced at Nate, who was sitting on the stone hearth of the fireplace. My impish twin winked at me. Obviously, he had texted Leroy's "biggest fan" that the cable show star was at our house.

Bobby strutted into the living room.

"Leroy, this is our friend, Bobby Neigh," Dad introduced, careful not to show his amusement. The rest of us didn't bother.

"Hey," Bobby said again, and casually offered his hand to Leroy, who took it and gave Bobby's arm the same treatment that Jared's had received. After shaking Jenna's dainty hand, Bobby discreetly massaged his bruised arm, wincing, and parked himself next to Nate. He'd probably have to ice his muscles tonight.

Leroy settled his hulking body back into the wingback chair that he'd jumped out of when Jared and I had arrived. Then he launched into an animated account of every creature from myth and legend that he'd pursued since a five-foot-five Sasquatch had propelled him into a tree and opened his eyes. Sea serpents, werewolves, hobgoblins, dragons, little green men from outer space, and now—

"The Lake Washington Monster." Leroy rubbed his big palms together, as though he were about to dig into a juicy T-bone. Like Ben, he lived for the outlandish.

"We have an interview scheduled with eyewitnesses at three o'clock," Jenna's tone betrayed her own breathless excitement. Her ever-present smile leapt to Dad. "I hate to rush things along, but we should do the interview soon."

"Absolutely," Ben answered for Dad. "We've chartered a boat on Lake Washington for the interview. We thought filming where the sightings happened would be cool." He stood. "Come on, I'll drive!"

"Awesome!" Jenna hopped to her feet, too.

She and Ben will have the cutest and happiest kids.

"Can I come with?" Bobby asked.

"By all means," Leroy boomed.

"Right on!" Bobby pumped his fist in the air.

"Why don't y'all come along?" Leroy invited. "Unless Ben chartered a rowboat." He hooted at his own joke and slapped Ben's back, causing Ben to stumble forward.

"There's plenty of room." Dad sought out Mom's gaze.

Smiling, she nodded her approval.

The doorbell rang, which only I could hear over all the boisterous chatter.

"I'll get it," I shouted, but no one appeared to have heard me.

I jogged to the door and flung it open. My heart stopped. Owen Wells was standing there, smiling at me.

"Hello, Cassidy. Sounds like I'm missing all the fun."

It took me a second to find my voice. "Dad!" I finally screamed.

The chatter ceased. Unable to peel my eyes from Mr. Wells's quizzical face, I could hear Dad walking briskly toward me, and everyone else following to see what was up.

"Owen," Dad said, standing next to me. "Please come in."

Now why hadn't I thought of inviting him in?

"Dad!" Jared squeezed between us to hug his dad.

"I'm sorry," Mr. Wells said. "Thank God you weren't hurt."

Gavin and Emery came out of their house. I figured Gavin had seen Mr. Wells drive up on his live camera feed.

"Where have you been?" Jared pulled back from his dad. Outrage had replaced relief, and rightly so.

Mr. Wells appeared to be paying more attention to everyone crowded in the foyer than to Jared.

"Let's discuss this inside," Mr. Wells suggested with a miry smile. I really did not like the man. He looked over his shoulder, sensing Gavin's and Emery's approach.

"Please come in." Dad said again and tried to remove my hand from the doorknob. When he couldn't budge it, he cleared his throat to get my attention.

I released the knob, and Dad opened the door more widely. Feet in the foyer shuffled backward as he did so.

"Drake, how 'bout we go ahead of you guys, and get set up?" Ben offered thoughtfully.

"Sounds good," Dad agreed.

Ben patted Jared's tense shoulder. Mr. Wells noted the gesture. His eyes hardened, though his smile never wavered, as our guests filed past him.

"Dude, go with them," Nate said to Bobby. "I'll come down with my dad."

Conflicted, Bobby glanced between Leroy and Mr. Wells.

"Later," he said, choosing the big game hunter.

If he'd had knowledge of Jared's attack yesterday, no doubt his decision would have been different. Bobby's nosiness and loose lips almost surpassed our neighbor Mrs. DeAngelo's, which was saying a lot.

Mr. Wells entered the foyer. He frowned when Gavin and Emery followed. His scowl whipped into a plastic smile as he eyed Gavin. He clearly didn't like the look of him. The feeling was obviously mutual.

Dad shut the door. "Owen, this is Gavin Phillips and his son Emery. Emery was with Jared when the attack occurred."

Mr. Wells had the decency to appear concerned.

"Gavin, Emery," he acknowledged, adding to Emery, "I understand from Jared's mother that I owe you a debt of gratitude."

That's it? I thought with disgust. *He has nothing more to say, like, "I'm sorry your life was put in danger due to my dirty dealings"?*

"Glad I was there," Emery replied tersely.

Gavin didn't say a word.

"Kids, why don't you go into the family room?" Dad suggested. He glanced at Emery to let him know that included him, which wasn't necessary. Emery knew he fell into the kid category with anyone unaware of our ruse.

~~~

Huddled with Emery, Nate, and Chazz on the sectional in our family room, I listened in on the conversation taking place in the living room. I repeated what was being said in a whisper to the boys.

After relaying everything that had happened since he'd opened his front door to three goons—with my dad adding in minute details here and there—Jared demanded, in an acidic tone: "So where've you been, Dad?"

"On a much-needed sabbatical." Mr. Wells sounded as though he were pleasantly unaware of Jared's rage.

I bristled. Didn't he even care that his son could have been killed?

"A *sabbatical*?" Nate questioned. At the same time, Jared spat out: "Care to elaborate?"

Mr. Wells laughed.

"His dad just laughed," I hissed to the boys, astonished. What the heck was wrong with him?

"You and your mother are cut from the same cloth," Mr. Wells said. "You even sounded like her just then."

The living room fell silent. I took the opportunity to digest what I'd heard. Jared's dad was completely bizarre.

"I want to deck him," Nate whispered.

"What a jerk!" I said.

"He's mean," Chazz agreed, a little too loudly. We shushed him while I refocused my attention on the living room.

"I can't talk to you," Jared said.

"Sit down, Jared," Mr. Wells ordered.

I heard Jared stalk across the room.

"Jared's leaving," I whispered, and started to stand.

Emery caught my arm. "He needs space. And we need *you* to listen."

Consigned, I sat down and concentrated. We all heard the front door slam.

"Owen, I think it would be better if I talked to him," Dad said. "Gavin has some questions for you."

"Fire away, Gavin," Mr. Wells said in a cavalier tone. I could tell he was indignant about Jared blowing him off. But what did he expect?

My dad closed the front door behind him as he pursued Jared. I pictured Mr. Wells resting an elbow on the sofa headrest, cupping the side of his head in his palm and wearing a smug expression on his face as he and Gavin sized up one another.

"But first," Mr. Wells said, "mind telling me how anything concerning my son and myself concerns you?"

"Did you miss the part about *my* son having to save *your* son's life?" Gavin's tone caused the hair on the back of my neck to stand. There was no way Mr. Slimy Lawyer hadn't picked up on the fact that he was dealing with a very dangerous individual.

Mom cleared her throat.

"I'm sorry, Elizabeth," Jared's dad said, not sounding

sincere at all. "I didn't thank you for watching over Jared. I'm certainly grate—"

"*Owen*, have you contacted the police?" Gavin cut him off.

"My next stop." The way Mr. Wells spoke made me think he was smiling.

"Who were the goons who held a nine-millimeter to your son's head?" Gavin interrogated, going for shock value.

"I don't know."

"Who hired them?"

"I don't know *who* they are."

"Who'd you piss off, Owen?"

Mr. Wells chuckled derisively. "Who haven't I pissed off? I *am* a defense attorney."

"Why'd you double-cross Ariel Vilvary?"

There was a moment of silence. I imagined the men staring at one another. Finally, Mr. Wells *tsk-tsk*ed. "It appears I'm already talking to the police. Did you forget something, detective? Like reading me my Miranda rights? Show me your badge."

"I'm not a cop. Just an angry parent who can type keywords into Google. Your client, Ariel Vilvary, is a local crime lord—"

"*Alleged* crime lord, and *former* client—"

"Did he fire you?"

"I chose not to represent Mr. Vilvary anymore."

"Why?"

"Because I didn't *feel* like it."

"*Hmm* . . . .Doesn't seem like a man like Vilvary would take kindly to that."

"A bit of advice, *Gavin*. Cut back on the television. In the real world, when a businessman such as Mr. Vilvary has a lawyer who decides to terminate the relationship, he simply finds a new lawyer—"

"And may *terminate* his former lawyer in the process."

"Cute," Mr. Wells replied dryly.

"Let's go through the facts. Fact one, three armed men showed up at your ex-wife's apartment. Fact two, they told your son that they were there to settle a score with you. Fact three, they are represented by Yesler, a top law firm. Who's cutting the check for Yesler, Owen?"

"Got me. Why don't you *Google* it?"

"Next time my son might not be around to swing a hockey stick."

"There *won't* be a next time."

"I think he's standing up," I whispered to the boys, who were on the edge of their seats—quite literally. If Nate had moved a fraction of an inch more, he would have slid right off the cushion and onto his backside.

"I apologize for any distress Gavin may have caused you, Elizabeth. I'm indebted to you and Drake. I had planned on taking Jared with me—"

"I wouldn't advise that," Gavin interjected.

"However, in light of his reaction, I think he'd prefer to stay here," Mr. Wells continued as though Gavin hadn't spoken. "When does Eileen's plane arrive? She neglected to give her flight information in the multiple hysterical messages she left me."

"Which brings us back to—where have you been, Owen?"

"Don't take this personally, Gavin, but go to hell."

I replaced "hell" with "Phoenix." Chazz gasped anyway.

"She'll arrive in a couple of hours," Mom answered quickly. "Drake and I plan to pick her up. We've invited her and Jared to stay with us until it's safe."

"Thank you, but it *is* safe."

"You sound awfully sure of yourself, Owen," Gavin continued to provoke. "Did you strike a deal with the devil?"

"I only know the devil by reputation. But instinct tells me you two are well acquainted," retorted Mr. Wells. "It's been amusing, Gavin. Elizabeth, I have a gift for you. I'll be back in a moment."

I released a long breath and sank into the cushions. "He's headed for the front door."

"Good work." Emery patted my knee and stood up.

My brothers scrambled after Emery. I peeled myself off the sectional and caught up with them. Gavin and Mom stood on the front porch, watching Mr. Wells saunter to his silver Porsche.

"I'm sorry for putting you through that," Gavin was saying to Mom when the boys and I entered the hallway.

"No need to apologize. I've never liked him. However, I haven't witnessed him behaving so callously before. It's as though he doesn't care."

"He doesn't care—because he isn't afraid."

"You've lost your touch," Emery teased, clamping his hands on his dad's shoulders. "I'm disillusioned. Getting under that cheesy veneer should've been child's play."

"My *oh-so-humble* son, that is no veneer. I couldn't

rattle the man because that wasn't a ballsy act. He has absolute confidence that he has control of whatever he has mixed himself up in."

Mr. Wells lifted a case of bottled water from the Porsche's trunk.

"What is he doing?" Mom asked.

Mr. Wells turned on his heels to face us, gripping the water and wearing a smile.

"Looks like he's giving us *water*," Nate observed, equally dumbfounded.

Jared's dad was a tool.

"This isn't your average bottled water," he informed us as he lumbered up our front walk. "No gimmicks, no calories, no added sugar. Just your daily recommended vitamins and minerals—perfect for a growing boy." He winked at Chazz. "The electrolytes will make you feel like a million bucks. Nate, will you take this, please?

"Elizabeth, thank you." He hugged Mom's stiff shoulders and then offered his hand to Emery. He ignored Gavin completely. "Thank you, again, for your bravery yesterday."

He released Emery's hand and smiled at me.

I glared.

"Cassidy, you grow more beautiful each time I see you."

I wanted to stick my finger down my throat.

"Tell Jared I love him and will call later." He nodded a farewell and turned on his heels. Aware of his audience, he stuffed his hands into his pockets and sauntered down our walkway, as though he were strolling down a sunny country lane. I almost expected him to start whistling.

"He really likes that water," Chazz said.

Despite my disgust, I laughed. Only Chazz would interpret that deadbeat's indifference as love for his client's bottled water. At least I figured it was his client's water.

"Bottled water sure makes up for being a *jerk*," I commented to everyone on the porch. Jared's dad closed his trunk.

"Cassidy—" Mom began to scold, but then stopped. How could she argue?

"Dang, this is heavy," Nate grumbled about the water. His back arched from the strain. "Take it." He handed me the water and shook out his arms.

Glancing down, I looked at the packaging closely for the first time. *Luminous* was printed in lavender across the plastic covering.

Yep, it's his client's water. I remembered Joe had been drinking the same brand. He had said he'd gotten it from the soup kitchen, and Mr. Wells's client had donated water to local homeless shelters. I couldn't recall his client's name, but did remember his stepdaughter's. *Ashlyn*.

Guess he keeps cases on hand for lame peace offerings, I thought as Mr. Wells sped away in his fancy car.

Chapter 9

Boys are Territorial?

No one was in the mood to join Dad for his interview with Leroy when he and Jared returned to the house fifteen minutes after Mr. Wells's odd departure. That isn't to say Jared wasn't in need of distraction. Xbox was his diversion of choice, which my brothers happily obliged him in.

The boys feverishly worked the controllers, taking out their aggression on the screen and fighting their way to new levels. Amid the explosions and exchanges of gunfire with spidery alien invaders, I curled up in the corner of the sectional, watching Jared more than the game. My heart ached for him.

"Jared," I said softly, sitting up.

"Hmmmmm?" His fierce gaze didn't leave the battlefield.

I leaned in toward his ear. "Are you okay?"

"Fine." His thumb punched a button on the controller. *Boom!* The battleground erupted into a fireball.

I settled back into my corner and texted Emery.

Any new info?

He and Gavin had gone home to see what more they could dig up on Mr. Wells and Ariel Vilvary. Gavin was positive that the local gangster was behind the attack.

At least they're being proactive, I thought, waiting for Emery's reply. I longed to be with them, researching and chiseling out a plan, but I didn't feel comfortable leaving Jared.

Emery texted back: *Nothing compelling.*

I scratched my chin, thinking. *The FBI didn't have anything?* I typed, but thought better of sending the text. The FBI could have been monitoring our cells for all I knew. Deleting the characters, I plucked out: *Did you talk to Riley?*

Riley was a bail bond agent, after all, and an ex-convict. It was totally conceivable that she could have information about Vilvary that law enforcement wouldn't have.

Emery texted back: *Check. No leads. Come over?*

I can't. Keep me posted, I texted, frustrated. I hated sitting around like a lump.

"Guys, I'm getting a snack," I announced. "Want anything?"

"No thanks," Jared answered, eyes on the game. My brothers didn't bother responding.

I entered the kitchen, whining to Mom, "I *hate* video games. How can they even stand looking at the screen?"

Leaning over a magazine at the kitchen island, she smiled at me.

I wondered how she could look so happy, with everything that had been going on.

"Funny you should mention it," she said. "I'm reading an article about that very thing: why males become more addicted to video games than females." She paused to take a swig of bottled water.

I parked my backside on the stool next to hers.

"Apparently, special computer imaging shows that the part of the brain that generates feelings of reward is activated in males when playing games, especially games in which territories can be gained—"

"Boys are territorial? I hadn't noticed." I picked up the bottle of Luminous she had already drained. "So it's good water, even though the giver sucks?"

"Uh-huh," Mom answered, taking another drink.

The fact that she didn't chide me for the slam on Mr. Wells surprised me. It was so unlike her.

The doorbell rang.

"I'll get it." I was thrilled to have something to do. As I passed the family room, the boys didn't even glance at me.

I threw open the door to Jared's distraught mother. Her hair was disheveled, her suit wrinkled, and she had dark half-moons under puffy, bloodshot eyes that held traces of smeared makeup. It was shocking to see the usually immaculate Eileen such a mess.

"Cassidy—" She rushed into the house, forgetting her suitcase on the porch. "Where's Jared? Jared!" She called before I could answer, looking around frantically.

Jared bounded out of the family room. Eileen broke down at the sight of him. Her laptop bag slid off her shoulder, tumbling toward the floor. My hand shot out at lightning speed and caught it. Behind Jared, Nate raised his eyebrows at me. Luckily, Eileen was too distracted to notice. I don't think she even realized she had dropped the bag.

Jared embraced his mother. "It's okay, Mom."

She buried her face into his shoulder and sobbed.

My throat tightened with sympathy. Her reaction was more of what I had expected from a parent whose child had been threatened. Jared was her life.

I grabbed the handle of her suitcase. Across the street, Emery stood in his front doorway. Obviously, the Phillipses had seen Eileen arrive.

"We'll be over soon. Call if you need us," he said in a normal speaking voice, knowing I would hear him.

I gave him a thumbs-up and wheeled the suitcase inside.

"I love you," Eileen wept, kissing Jared's face. "I am so sorry."

I closed the front door.

"It isn't your fault, Mom."

"It's Owen's." She spat his name as though it were a foul word. "Has he turned up yet?"

Jared nodded, glancing away from her. "He stopped by a couple of hours ago."

"He *stopped by*?" she repeated, disdain on her face.

"Eileen," Mom spoke up. "Why don't we have a seat in the living room? Can I get you anything?"

Eileen smiled weakly. "Thank you, Elizabeth. A glass of water would be wonderful." She rubbed her throat as though she'd just realized it was parched.

Mom looked at Chazz. "Would you get Ms. Kirsch water, please?"

Chazz bolted, as though fetching a glass of water was a matter of life or death.

We found seats in the living room. My family gave Eileen and Jared the sofa. Nate claimed one wingback chair while Mom sat in the other one and I parked my backside on the arm, which Mom would normally object to.

"I talked to Detective Woodrow on the way over," Eileen told us, wiping her wet eyes. Her other hand gripped Jared's, the white bone of her knuckles shining through the skin. "He said the men who came to the apartment have declined to talk."

"Yes, but the main thing is they are in police custody," Mom pointed out. "Eileen, you should've called. I would have been happy to pick you up at the airport."

"I couldn't wait. The taxi was right there."

Chazz tore into the living room with a bottle of Luminous. "Here!" He shoved the water at Eileen. "It's good for you. It has electricity."

I smiled to myself. Chazz meant electrolytes.

"Thank you, Chazz." Eileen took the bottle with a gracious smile, which evaporated when she looked back at her son. "I'm sorry I wasn't here for you." Fresh tears sprang into her eyes.

"It's okay, Mom. Dad said he's taking care of things."

Eileen barked a cynical laugh. "I bet he is."

Chapter 10

Cunning Slacker

Following an explosive phone conversation with Eileen later that evening, Owen seemed to have fallen off the face of the planet. Well, not completely. He had returned to work. Dad had called his law firm on Monday to make sure.

I felt awful for Jared. I couldn't believe his father hadn't called to check up on him. If I'd been in Jared's shoes, I would have felt like my heart had been ripped out of my chest. But I had no way of knowing what his true feelings were—he avoided the topic of his loser dad altogether.

Mr. Wells also appeared to be the farthest thing from Eileen's mind. However, I knew differently. Kicked back on the attic sofa bed—I'd given up my room for Eileen—I eavesdropped on late-night conversations between her and my mom. I learned stuff that I'm sure Jared didn't know, and, hopefully, never would. He thought he hated his dad now.

I didn't feel any qualms about letting my ears wander where they shouldn't, until Eileen shared details about how she'd discovered her husband was unfaithful. Guilt overruling the busybody in me, I flipped on the television to drown out their voices. If I distracted myself, my ears couldn't roam. The attic didn't have cable, so I had three options: sports, a Spanish program, or the news. Since I couldn't speak Spanish and I hated sports, I went with option three. Breaking news—

another missing person.

That makes eight reported missing people now, I thought, but amended the number to seven, remembering that Anita Harris was no longer missing. She had turned up a couple of days before, safe and sound. In an interview, she claimed to have "taken a break." She had apologized to her family, friends, and anyone else whom her thoughtlessness had hurt. The thing was, she hadn't seemed all that sorry.

Anita Harris wasn't the only missing person to resurface. Joe told me Doc was back after he'd disappeared from the streets six weeks earlier. He'd glimpsed his friend, smiling and appearing "fit as a fiddle" while unloading cases of bottled water from a truck at the shelter. Doc had obviously cleaned up, Joe had said, meaning he'd stopped drinking. I didn't know how Joe could tell just by looking at Doc, but he'd lived on the streets for a long time, and he knew about addiction.

Anita Harris and Doc not being victims of anything horrific eased the fear and sick feeling that each new missing person news report had given me. If nothing bad had happened to them, maybe nothing bad had happened to the other people.

~~~

For three weeks, tension had been palpable in the air—everyone was on edge about the locals who had disappeared. However, as the days wore on, I sensed a shift.

Eyes were less watchful and suspicious, and fewer glances were cast over shoulders. Perhaps I wasn't the only one to lower my guard after Anita Harris's happy homecoming.

But it was more than diminishing public panic. There seemed to be more smiles and laughter everywhere I went, as though chill pills had been passed out like Halloween candy. This should have been a positive thing, but the movie version of *The Stepford Wives* popped in to my head every time complete strangers flashed me oddly sated smiles, as though they were tripping across happy clouds. People were just being too nice.

Of course, our twenty-five-year-old bum of a neighbor, Jason Crenshaw, was the exception. Behind those crafty, hazel eyes of his was nothing nice. Which was my exact thought after school on Monday, when he crooked his forefinger at me to come hither as he sunned himself in a chaise lounge among immaculate flowerbeds that his mother slaved over and he used as ashtrays.

"I'll be right in," I told Jared and Nate, glaring at Jason. Emery was climbing his front porch steps and had missed the summons, just as Jason had planned. Whatever he wanted was between him and me. This thought turned my stomach. I wasn't a fool. I knew I couldn't outsmart the scoundrel.

Jared's eyes followed where my glare was aimed. He put two-and-two together.

"Ignore him," he advised.

"I can't."

"Why not?"

"Because Crenshaw has too much dirt on her and Emery," Nate explained for me, taking the backpack I

97

handed him. Part of me suspected he secretly admired the cunning slacker.

"That sucks," Jared said, sizing Jason up.

Jason reclined in the chaise again, his hands folded behind his sandy-blond head. He had no doubt that I'd obey his command.

"Indeed, it does," I agreed with Jared. "Emery and I totally underestimated him."

Or, at least, I had. Emery had hired Jason to drive us back and forth to Catamount Mountain, where we'd been hunting a tiger and a "metal man." Emery claimed to have known exactly whom he was dealing with, and had even set aside extra money to pay for Jason's pending blackmail. Jason didn't let him down.

"I can come with you," Jared offered.

"Thanks, but he won't say whatever it is he has to say if you're there." I assumed it would be a shakedown for more money.

Jared and Nate went inside the house while I strolled to the Crenshaws'. I tried to give the impression that I wasn't worried. I'm sure Jason wasn't fooled.

What are you plotting behind those sunglasses? I sent him as I entered the pristine yard of the pristine Victorian through a pristine white picket gate. Mrs. DeAngelo watched me from her Dutch Colonial's dining room window next door.

"What?" I parked myself in front of Jason, casting a shadow over his half-naked body. I kept my glare pinned to his smug face, although I had to admit his abs looked better than I'd expected, especially for a former high school football player whose current workout consisted of his moving his thumbs around a video game controller.

Jason waved a lazy hand for me to move out of his sunlight. I could see his eyes were shut behind his shades.

"Aren't you cold?" It was only, like, 65 degrees.

"Won't be, when this irritating black cloud passes." He again motioned for me to move. There was no way I'd budge.

"Get on with it. What do you want?"

"Patience, sugar."

Gritting my teeth, I held my tongue and watched him with hostility as he took his sweet time adjusting the back of the chaise into an upright position.

"There." He smirked and relaxed into the cushion. My disloyal eyeballs admired his chest before I caught myself and flicked them to a rose bush.

"Now, none of that," Jason chided, and I wanted to slap him and myself. Of all people to get caught ogling! "Sir Lancelot is jealous enough," he added, referring to Jared.

My blush deepened, which infuriated me even more.

"It's only a matter of time before he and Slick have a little fisticuff right out there on the stree—"

"What do you *want*?"

"We're talking, Cupcake. It's called a conversation." He trapped a cigarette burning among discarded butts in a cut-crystal bowl, then brought it to his smirking lips. The bowl was probably one of his mother's favorite pieces. He was just that kind of guy.

Exhaling gray death, his gaze meandered to Emery's house. "That must be quite a remodeling project they have going on," he said.

I fidgeted, and Jason noticed—darn it.

"Yeah, it is. The house was a dump."

"Interesting that McCormick sold."

"McCormick?"

"The previous owner of said *dump*. You wouldn't remember him, since you were just a snot-nosed kid in diapers when he lived there." Jason tapped ashes onto the grass.

My mind raced. *Where is he going with this?*

"McCormick, that old coot." Jason took another long drag from the cigarette while looking thoughtfully at the Phillips's house. "He and my dad are still chums."

"Fascinating." I doused my tone with an extra helping of sarcasm to cover my skyrocketing alarm. Gavin never did mention how he'd gotten the previous owner to sell his rental house. "Well, it has been a hoot! But I must be on—"

"This Marathon Construction seems like a proficient outfit," Jason interrupted, as though he hadn't heard me.

I glanced over my shoulder. Cristiano tipped a wheelbarrow of dirt into a dump truck from the top of a ramp. He shot us a smile. What was up with that guy?

"They've hauled a lot of dirt out of the house. Are they tunneling to China?"

I looked back at Jason. His eyes assessed me from behind the shades.

What does he know? Why is he out here, anyway? Spying?

"Yeah, but they ran into some trouble with a T-Rex at the center of the Earth." I prayed that I appeared irritated, but calm. "Any other questions?"

"You've told me all I need to know, Pumpkin."

My stomach plunged. *What had I told him?*

"It's been stimulating, Jason. Truly, it has," I said,

walking toward the gate. "We must do this again sometime."

"Give Slick my regards."

How did he know I was going to Emery's?

"Will do!" I sang and slammed the gate, resisting the urge to break into a run.

~~~

"Hello!" I flashed a plastered-on smile to another Marathon worker wheeling dirt down the hall.

This is out of control! I thought, heading for the stairs. *Who are these guys, anyway? Hit men who do construction work on the side?*

"Emery!" My voice cracked. My feet climbed faster.

He poked his head from the spare room/laboratory/spy headquarters. Oh, geez, this was crazy!

"Everything okay?"

"Dandy." I shoved him into the room and shut the door. "How did your dad get the former owner to sell this house?"

"My dad can be *extremely* persuasive." He socked his fist into his palm.

"Emery, can't you see that boy from across the street has unnerved Cassidy enough?" Serena scolded. She squeezed liquid from an eyedropper onto a microscope slide and looked at us.

"So you were watching Jason and me?" I asked.

"What else would we be doing?" Emery teased.

"This is no time to be funny! Jason was dropping major hints that he had information about how your dad *persuaded* the owner to sell this house."

101

"Don't be dramatic," Serena chided me now. She fitted the glass slide on the microscope's stage. "Gavin had made the previous owner an offer that only a sentimental fool would refuse: twenty-five percent over market value."

"So just money?" I hoisted myself onto a stool.

"*Just* money?" Emery sighed and shook his head.

"Well, you'd better not get too attached to *yours*! Jason is obviously short on cash again, and he's also giving your dad a run for his money in the spying business."

Emery glanced at the security feed on the screen and grinned. "And getting a tan while he's at it, I see. Crenshaw, you multi-tasker."

"This isn't a joke."

"Trust me, I take Jason seriously," Emery assured, peering into a microscope. "I have him *right* where I want him."

I snorted, crossing my arms and legs. My foot flicked with irritation. "He knows that there's something fishy about your remodel."

"And I know that he sells coveted artifacts and jewels from *Gods and Kings* to the highest bidder. Not within the game, mind you. But for cold, hard cash."

"He sells items from that video game to other players for *real* money?"

"Indeed he does. He has created a very lucrative business for himself. You should see his clientele list. Celebrities, politicians, tycoons, racketeers—"

"How do you know this?"

"Explaining how would bore you," Emery eluded. "Jason has remained anonymous through these business transactions, which are in direct violation of *Gods &*

Kings's licensing agreement. If Jason were caught, he'd be banned from the game and would lose his cash cow. You pay a hefty price for items from *Sera, Ruler of the Seven Kingdoms*'s treasure trove."

"So you'd turn Jason in?"

"If push came to shove. But it won't. Jason is well aware that I'm as busy collecting dirt on him as he is on me."

"Collecting dirt," I repeated, watching the tip of the ballpoint pen I clicked go in and out of the cylinder. "That's what Nate just said. Why did Jason call me over, then?"

"He knew he could fluster you, especially shirtless."

Heat rose in my face, and I kept my gaze locked on the clicking pen tip. I sensed Emery's smug smile. Was I that easy to figure out for *everyone*?

"Cassidy, don't worry about Jason. This is just a game we play."

"Well, I wish you'd both leave me out of it." I dropped the pen. "Serena, do you need blood?"

"You don't normally offer," she remarked as she jotted down whatever it was she had observed on the slide. Emery's eyes followed what she wrote.

"You're right. Don't know why I'm being so generous. I'll take that as a *no*." I slid off the stool.

"That can't be right," Emery said to Serena, referring to her notes. He angled her microscope toward him and squinted into the eyepiece. "How could you not see this?" Emery admonished her.

I couldn't believe Serena let him talk to her like that. My mom would flip out.

He took her pen, slashed through her entry, and started

writing his own. Serena didn't protest, or even look miffed. She appeared more worried than anything.

"Is something wrong, Serena?" I asked.

She didn't hear me. She was studying her son's profile.

"There," Emery said as he finished writing. He pushed the journal toward his mother.

Serena drove the worry from her face and read his notes. "You're right. I should have caught this. It is obvious."

Something told me whatever Emery had written wasn't obvious. Something also told me that this had to do with whatever King had done to him.

"Is there something you want to discuss, Serena?" I prodded. She would have to come clean someday.

Serena gave me a strange look. "What an odd question."

"Well, I'm an odd girl," I grumbled, slumping. *Haven't there been enough secrets?*

"Dear, didn't you say you had to leave?"

I frowned at her dismissal. Why did she want me to leave?

"I need help with math first," I fibbed and flopped down on the exam table. I wasn't going anywhere yet.

"Luckily for you, your boyfriend is at the top of our class," Emery pointed out.

I glared at the ceiling. *Does Emery want me to leave, too?*

"I don't have a boyfriend. I can't date until I'm sixteen, remember?"

"Minor technicality."

"I dare you to tell my dad that! And Jared is *not* at the top of our class. *You* are."

"But only you know that."

"Are you going to help me with math or not?"

"When have I not helped you?" he challenged, but I could hear in his voice that he was happy I wanted to stay.

I smiled at the ceiling, happy that he was happy.

Chapter 11

A Scene to Remember

I entered our kitchen the next morning to find everyone in the household milling about, including Ben.

"This is insanity," Eileen said, referencing the latest missing person report. With her teal suit, crisp white shirt, and blonde hair that was swept into an elegant French twist, she definitely looked the part of a fashionable businesswoman. Even her fingernails, sporting a polished French manicure, coordinated with the white steaming mug her long fingers wrapped around.

"Totally," Ben agreed. The rapid rhythm his hands absently drummed on the cherry tabletop revealed his agitation. Being perturbed was highly unusual for him. "I don't get why more isn't being done. Like a curfew or something, especially since these abductions are happening at night."

Helping myself to a slice of toast, I pondered Ben's word choice. Knowing him, he probably thought space aliens were involved in the "abductions."

"Dude, you say that like you think people are being beamed up to the mother ship," Nate voiced my thoughts.

"Show some respect," Ben said, snapping the back of his hand against Nate's chest. "No bodies, no witnesses, no evidence—why discount anything?"

"Good point." Nate popped a grape into his mouth.

Across the table, Jared fixed me in his gaze. I decided I could get used to the view.

But it won't last much longer, I remembered sadly. Jared's eyebrows rose at my frown. He and Eileen were going home when she returned from the business trip that she was leaving for that morning. After a discussion with her ex-husband the night before, she felt confident that she and Jared wouldn't be harassed again.

Only six days left to savor this yummy sight. My teeth tore off a chunk of toast as I stared wistfully at Jared. He appeared ready to laugh. His gaze flicked to my dad, a precaution.

"Mandating a curfew would violate a few amendments," Dad said, unaware that my eyes were devouring Jared as my mouth devoured my toast. "Only under the most extreme circumstances would the state consider setting a citywide curfew."

"Eight missing people in three weeks isn't extreme?" Ben challenged.

And that doesn't include missing homeless people, I thought.

"Believe it or not, no."

"This is insanity!" Chazz copied Eileen's remark.

I tried to hide my smile. Chazz had a huge crush on Eileen.

"Chazz, eat your breakfast," Mom sang from the sink, where she was scrubbing the pan she had cooked the scrambled eggs in. I hadn't realized until that moment how out-of-place her soft humming was, considering the topic of conversation.

"I can't eat these eggs," Chazz stated. "My throat is as dry as the desert." He forced a scratchy cough. He just didn't want to eat the eggs.

Mom giggled. I glanced back at her. That was strange.

"You have legs," Nate told Chazz. "Go get yourself a glass of water."

Chazz coughed more loudly.

"Chazz," Dad began to reprimand, but Mom interceded.

"You're thirsty?" She twisted the top off a Luminous Water bottle and placed it before Chazz. "Drink up." She moved behind Dad and rubbed his shoulders. "Eileen, the spring auction is coming along beautifully."

Mom launched into the auction news with fervor. She really got into helping organize school events, but wasn't normally that peppy in the morning.

"And we get to go on a boat *with* a swimming pool!" Chazz relayed, showing as much excitement as Mom.

"We're hosting another family on the cruise," Mom explained as she planted a kiss on Dad's cheek. Dad glanced at her sidelong in surprise.

"What side of the bed do you think she woke up on?" Nate whispered so low that only I could hear him. At the same time, Eileen said, "That will be a very lucky family. Maybe even us." She elbowed Jared.

I sighed loudly at the idea of going on a cruise with him.

~~~

On the way to Levy's class, I glimpsed Robin Newton

down the hall, flanked by her top remoras, Mindy Ames and Jessica Blanchette.

My stomach tightened, as it always did when I saw Robin, which irked me to no end. Why should I care what she thought of me?

But I did. And it drove me crazy.

Robin hated my guts because I'd broken her nose. It had been an accident, but try to tell her that. And the fact that her arrogant, on-again/off-again boyfriend, Chad Dunham, had hit on me also hadn't helped matters.

"Have you heard from your dad?" I asked Emery, just to make conversation. I wanted to look at him and pretend not to see Robin. Her scent had already invaded my space.

"No, and you know I won't until he gets back."

Gavin had gone on a "business trip" four days earlier, meaning the government had sent him on a covert mission.

"Oh, yeah." I studied the passing locker bank as though it were an awe-inspiring work of art. My nose told me Robin was almost upon us.

"Hey, Cassidy," she said.

I almost walked straight into the lockers.

Robin smiled at me, and it wasn't her usual disgusted sneer. Her smile actually appeared genuine.

"Hi . . . ?" I floundered as she took a swig of water.

"Wonders never cease," Emery teased after Robin and her remoras were out of earshot.

I chuckled. "Maybe Ben is on to something with alien abductions."

~~~

Mr. Levy shuffled to the front of the room, though I noticed he lifted his feet a little higher off the floor, and his face was a little less pinched and sour-looking than usual. I wouldn't say he appeared happy per se. Just less miserable.

"Whoever she is, I hope she keeps giving him big smooches," Miriam whispered to me, but everyone within a twenty-foot radius heard her. Luckily, Levy hadn't, and he jauntily called roll.

"Wonder what else he has in that water?" Rodrigo whispered, making a drinking gesture with his hand.

I slid a glance at the trashcan overflowing with Luminous Water bottles, snickering softly with my tablemates. Miriam released a snorting laugh.

Levy's face puckered. "Miss Cohen, would you care to share what you find so amusing with the rest of us?"

Miriam looked as though she were actually considering it.

I cleared my throat to discourage her.

"Uhhhhh . . . no," she said, much to my surprise. I was positive she was going to ask if he had a flask hidden in his desk drawer. "That wouldn't be such a good idea."

"Miss Jones, would you agree?" Levy goaded.

"W-with her?" I stammered. Why was he picking on me?

"No. With the Maharaja."

"Levy, you prig," Emery said.

"Emery!" shot out of my mouth before I could stop myself.

My outburst startled everyone, except Emery. He stared at me with that inscrutable expression of his, and became engrossed in deep thought.

"You seem quite confused today, Miss Jones," Levy mocked. "I am Mr. Levy."

110

There were a couple of snickers, which died out quickly when other scoffers didn't join in. My face burned bright red.

Satisfied with my humiliation, Levy took a long drink of water, his thin lips curling into a wretched smile around the bottle's mouth.

I loathed him. Absolutely loathed him.

~~~

"Levy is such a jerk," I complained at the lunch table. I hadn't been able to shake off the humiliating scene.

"I know!" Miriam shook her ringlets in agreement.

"Cass, it's no big deal," Jared assured me, again. "He made an idiot of himself, not of you."

"I don't know," I grumbled, twisting the top off the water bottle Mom had packed for me. I took a swig as the degrading scenario replayed in my head.

Nope. Idiot sums it up.

I took another drink. Luminous had a pleasant fruity taste. No wonder Mom was guzzling so much of it. "I can't believe he didn't jump all over Emery."

Across the table, Emery, who'd been rather quiet, stared at me.

"For what?" Miriam asked, confused.

"How could you have not heard him? You sit right next to him!"

Miriam's eyes lit up. "What'd you say?" She shook Emery's arm.

Emery shrugged and glanced around the room, as though bored with the conversation. Everyone was acting so weird lately.

111

"What'd he say?" Miriam demanded of me.

"Nothing, I guess. Must've been hearing things." I took another drink of water. What was up with Emery?

The conversation moved on to the latest and greatest indie bands and then to conjecture about the missing people.

"It's a serial killer," Bren concluded.

Jared's hand sought out mine under the table. I drained the water bottle and noted that Carli stared at where our arms disappeared from view. My chest swelled with pride. She knew Jared was holding my hand. I was the luckiest girl in the entire cafeteria.

"I don't think so," Cheyenne challenged Bren. "Because of that mom who ran off."

"So *all* these disappearances are just a *coincidence*?"

"Wishful thinking," Bobby agreed with Bren.

Jared's thumb gently rubbed the outside of my hand.

"Dudes, I vote for alien abductions," Nate said.

"Alien *experimentation*." Bobby raised his hand high.

"Are you volunteering, Bobby?" Jared ribbed.

I laughed, and tasted my turkey sandwich coming up my throat.

"How hot are these aliens?" Bobby came back.

"Too hot for you," Nate razzed.

My stomach contracted, and it felt like more than just the taste of turkey was about to come up.

"Oh my gosh," I gasped, covering my mouth.

All eyes at the table swung to me. As though I hadn't suffered enough humiliation for one day.

"Cass, are you sick?" Carli asked.

Blushing, I shook my head, but the movement made me gag.

Jared snatched my lunch bag and offered it to me. I waved it off. There was no way I was puking in the cafeteria. No way!

"But you can't be sick," Nate said and shot Emery a worried glance. Emery returned his look with one that warned Nate to think before he spoke. But it was too late.

"Obviously, she can be sick, Nate," Miriam said. Turning to me, she asked, "Do you need to go to the restroom?"

"I'm okay now," I lied. "The turkey must be bad. How do you feel, Nate?"

"Fine."

"I must've gotten a spoiled piece," I said, swallowing a belch. This was awful! But it had to be food poisoning. Like Nate had said, I couldn't get sick.

But can I get food poisoning?

"Give me your water." I reached my hand to Nate.

He slammed his water bottle into my palm, and I drained every drop.

~~~

I could barely sit in my chair during sixth period. It felt like a knife had been driven into my stomach.

"Cassidy, do you feel all right?" Ms. Lake inquired, pausing her lecture.

I swiped away the sweat beading on my forehead. "Yes," I forced through my raw throat. Stomach acid had been shooting up it like balls of fire for half an hour. "Thank you," I managed to add as I gulped down another fireball.

113

"Cass."

I jolted upright and looked around, forgetting where I was for a second.

Leaning toward me, Lena Mistry explained, "You fell asleep."

"Oh." I wiped sweat from my forehead. "Is it hot in here?" It felt like a hundred degrees.

Lena shook her head.

"Just don't give it to me," said Ruben Schelper over his shoulder.

"You're all heart." I dropped my head on the desk.

"Cassidy." A hand shook my arm.

Peeling my eyelids open, I lifted my head. It felt ready to split in half. I'd never had a headache that bad before.

"You have a fever," Ms. Lake told me. Her palm felt cold against my forehead. I shivered.

"That's impossible." The mutant DNA invading my body wouldn't allow me to get sick. "It's food poisoning."

"You need to go home. Go to the nurse's office."

The bell rang. I started at the sound. It seemed like class had just begun.

My classmates headed out the door while I tried to gather my stuff. Ms. Lake helped me.

"Feel better," she said, giving my back a sympathetic pat. I pushed myself to my unsteady feet. Every muscle in my body screamed.

"Would you like help to the office?"

I shook my head, but Ms. Lake ignored my feeble protest. She snaked her arm around my waist, assisting me. Each sliding step sent waves of nausea rolling through my stomach.

My palm smacked the door jamb and I looked up, meeting Emery's alarmed gaze. He ran across the hall from where he had been waiting to escort me to P.E. I broke free from Ms. Lake and stumbled into his arms.

"My god, you're burning up," he said, feeling my clammy face.

Then the turkey made good on its threat.

Vomit fired up my throat like a missile, shooting out my mouth and nostrils. The contents of my stomach splattered Emery, splashing the floor and the feet of unfortunate schoolmates. I collapsed to all fours. Screaming and running feet flashed past me, and the vomit kept coming and coming.

"Are you done?" Emery asked when I'd finally stopped heaving. He was holding my hair with his hand. His other arm, circling my waist, was the only thing that kept me from doing a face plant into the pool of barf.

I nodded weakly.

Emery lifted me into his arms. My head rolled against his chest like a loose bowling ball. His shirt was saturated. I'd gotten him good.

"Emery, take her to the nurse's office," Ms. Lake shouted after us.

"Hang onto my neck, Cassidy," he said, stopping to shift me in his arms to get a better hold. I did as told, burying my sticky nose in his collar.

Walking again, one of his arms released me. I cracked an eyelid open and watched his thumb work the contacts on his cell. He never broke pace.

"Mom," he said into the phone, walking down the wide path our schoolmates made for us, plastering their

115

backs to the lockers. I shut my eyes, not wanting to see the disgust on their faces. I couldn't block out their whispers and snickers, though.

"Come to the school *now*," Emery told Serena, then disconnected the call.

"I'm sorry," I whispered, humiliated beyond measure. I'd never be able to show my face at school again—if I survived.

"You'll be all right, Cassidy." Emery hoofed it down the stairs. "I promise."

Chapter 12

Something in the Water

Mom, Dad, Nate, Gavin, and Jared were gathered around the exam table, worry etched on their faces as they watched Serena poke and prod at me. Seated at the lab table, Emery studied my blood under a microscope.

"Honestly, I feel better now," I reassured everyone for the hundredth time.

And I truly did.

Gavin had returned from his secret mission to find utter chaos at home. Mom and I were arguing in his foyer about my taking a shower before Serena examined me, not to mention Emery's and my revolting appearances. Gavin didn't ask questions, or even act surprised. I figured Serena had given him a heads-up.

I won the argument, and just in the nick of time. Dad arrived with Jared and Nate while I stripped off my disgusting clothing in the Phillips's bathroom. I thanked my lucky stars to be in the shower at that moment, pouring half a bottle of shampoo over my head, getting rid of the evidence of a scene that I had no clue how I'd ever live down.

By the time I got out of the shower and dressed in the fresh set of clothes Mom had brought over, I felt significantly better. My immune system was obviously prevailing over whatever was wrong with me. Now it just felt like I was at the tail end of a flu bug.

"That may be," Serena told me as she pressed her fingers under my jawbone. "But we still need to figure out what happened. Lymph nodes are swollen," she reported to Emery.

"Her TCL is elevated," he informed her, peering into the microscope.

"So she has a virus," Gavin deduced.

"No. This is bacterial." Serena motioned to the males to turn around.

As they followed her instruction, Mom placed her hand on my clammy forehead.

"She isn't as warm," Mom observed with relief. "If it's bacterial, she can take antibiotics."

"She shouldn't have to take antibiotics," Serena began lifting my T-shirt. "That's the concern—" she paused, noticing the angry red rash on my torso, which itched like crazy. I had discovered it in the shower, but felt too embarrassed to mention it in front of the boys.

"Curious," Serena remarked.

Mom looked at my stomach and gasped.

"Don't turn around!" I shouted at the guys. "It's only a rash. No big deal."

"Fever-induced," Serena concluded, feeling under my armpits.

I smiled to myself. That's what I'd thought, too.

"As I was saying," Serena continued to Mom, "the concern is that her immune system didn't overcome the pathogen instantly. Then there's her severe reaction. Yes, her symptoms have improved. Her immune system is fighting admirably. But we are dealing with an aggressive disease—"

"A disease?" Dad interrupted. "Do you think it's contagious?"

"Drake, keep in mind that Cassidy has a unique genetic makeup. What affects her may not affect us. If the general population were susceptible and at risk, we would know by now, considering how quickly Cassidy succumbed." Serena placed the business end of her stethoscope against my chest. "Take a deep breath."

I drew in air, then released it slowly.

"Her heart rate is slightly accelerated, unsurprisingly. But her lungs are clear. You are on the mend, my dear."

"Can I take a nap?" I was suddenly exhausted.

"Sleep is exactly what you need." Serena tugged my shirt down. "Gentlemen, you may turn around. Emery, please straighten your room for Cassidy."

Straighten his room? I thought. Emery was a neat freak. He even made his bed military style. "Why can't I sleep at home?"

"I'd prefer it if you slept here." Serena jammed a thermometer in my mouth. "Elizabeth, please bring over all the food items Cassidy had for lunch, including condiments."

Picturing turkey, I felt my face turn a shade of green.

Serena extracted the thermometer and read my temperature. "You're doing quite well. You'll feel as good as new when you wake up from your nap."

~~~

Fog as thick as blood enveloped me, obscuring my visibility.

"Where am I?" I asked, narrowing my eyes, trying to penetrate the dense gray.

I brought my hand to my face to see dozens of scarlet ribbons tied to my fingers, floating upward. My gaze followed the plush bands ascending to the heavens. The fog melted away to reveal a starlit blue night sky, illuminated by a great glowing moon. Attached to each scarlet ribbon was a human heart, pulsating vibrant colors, each pattern beautiful and intricate. Like snowflakes, no two patterns were alike.

They're souls, I realized, smiling up at the hearts that drifted high above me like tethered helium balloons. Precious souls.

The moon grew brighter, and its white light began to swirl. The hearts began to bounce around, as though caught in a strong breeze. The ribbons tugged at my fingers. Panic grew in my chest.

"Stop!" I yelled at the moon, which had suddenly become a cyclone of light, spinning faster and faster. The hearts, seized by the powerful wind, strained at the ribbons. Strangely, I couldn't feel the wind on my upturned face. The air was still.

Why can't I feel it?

A ribbon snapped, and the attached heart was swept into the vortex, disappearing into the bright light. Another ribbon broke, and then another.

"You can't take them!" I screamed, helplessly watching the ribbons break one after the other. "They're mine! They can't leave me!"

The last ribbon snapped. Tears flowed down my face.

"Take me, too!" I pleaded with the moon, willing it to touch down and suck me into its light. All at once, it became a normal moon again, hanging among stars.

I'm alone.

I fell to the ground in despair, cradling my face in my hands.

The beating of my heart filled my ears as I grieved—strong, slow, and steady, like a person pounding on a drum. The rhythms began to echo, as though other drums had joined in the song. After listening to rhythms multiply, as if hundreds played, I realized the beating wasn't coming from within.

I lifted my head. All around me, hearts pulsated on the dark ground. Some were kaleidoscopes of vibrant colors while others were deformed, ashen monstrosities. These sent a shiver up my spine. They were dead-looking, yet beat as strongly as the beautiful hearts.

There was a tug at my left hand. I looked down and my spirit leapt for joy. A lone ribbon was bound to my ring finger.

My eyes began to rise to the sky. Cold rain slapped my face—

~~~

I yelped and sprang straight up. A sopping wet washcloth plopped onto my lap, saturating Emery's comforter.

"What the—?" I pinched the washcloth by the corner and flung it to the wood floor.

The guilty party stared at me with big, green, unapologetic eyes.

"Mommy said you were sick," Chazz explained.

"So you tried to drown me?" I ran my hand over my wet face. The kid had drenched me. "What are you doing here?"

"We're all here. Serena and Emery are looking for bad stuff in our food."

Dad rushed into Emery's room. He looked at the washcloth and chuckled.

"Thank you for taking care of your sister." Dad mussed Chazz's hair and winked at me. He pressed his palm to my forehead. "Your fever has broken. How do you feel?"

"Wet." I grinned at Chazz. "Good as new, just like Serena said I would be."

Dad kissed the top of my head. "Chazz, will you please tell everyone Cassidy is awake?"

"And not barfing," Chazz added.

I groaned. "Don't remind me."

"Chazz—" Dad picked up the washcloth from the floor. "Please put this in the bathroom sink."

My brother grabbed it and darted off to complete his task, leaving a trail of water droplets behind him.

Dad smiled. "It's just water. It'll dry." He sat on the edge of the bed and pushed back the wet locks plastered to my face. "Chazz really got you good."

"He is *extremely* thorough," I said with a laugh. "Actually, he did me a favor. I was having a weird dream." I drummed up the image of hearts getting ripped away, then shook my head to dislodge the depressing scene. I knew they represented everyone I loved, and ever would love. "Did Serena or Emery find anything in the food?"

"Nothing unusual."

Mom and Serena walked into the room.

"Did you sleep well?" Mom asked, touching my forehead. Her smile widened. "No more fever. You're all better."

Serena felt under my jawbone. "Your lymph nodes are normal, too. You beat the infection."

"Here," Mom said, handing me a bottle of Luminous. "Drink this. You've lost a lot of fluids."

I moaned. "I can't believe I puked at school. *And* all over Emery."

"He's no worse for the wear," Serena said, then ordered: "Do as your mother says. Drink."

Nate poked his head into the room.

"She lives!" he announced, throwing his arms up. "Come on in, dude," he invited Jared. "She's decent, or as decent as she'll ever get."

Jared walked in and smiled at me like I was the most beautiful creature to walk the face of the planet. "Glad you're better. You had me worried."

"Thanks. I'm just happy it wasn't contagious." I took a long drink. The water felt good on my parched throat.

"Only mutants can catch it," Chazz explained, as though he knew it for a fact.

Dad grimaced. He didn't like me being referred to as a mutant.

I pulled the now-half-empty bottle away from my mouth and asked, "Where are Gavin and Emery?"

"Gavin is on a phone call and Emery is in the lab," Serena replied.

I nodded, took another drink, and wondered why

Emery hadn't checked up on me, too. Maybe he was totally grossed out by me.

"I'd like a blood sample," Serena said.

I gulped down the last of the water. "Coming right up." I hopped out of bed like I hadn't been at death's door a couple of hours ago—or *felt* like I was at death's door, at least.

As we all walked into the hallway, we saw Gavin leaving the master bedroom. "How do you feel, Cassidy?" he asked.

"Great. Thanks." I thought of asking whom he'd been talking to, but that was most likely top secret.

"Where are the workers?" I asked, suddenly remembering I hadn't seen them when Emery had helped me out of Serena's car earlier.

"Serena sent them home when Emery called. Apparently, Cristiano didn't show up today. I'll have to look into why." Gavin said the last part more to himself than us.

We filed into the spare room. Emery glanced up from the microscope. Dabs of everything that had gone into my lunch were in a dozen or so petri dishes. He and Serena had been busy.

"You look chipper," he remarked.

As though the word "chipper" was a bad omen, my stomach suddenly turned.

"It smells disgusting in here," I complained, covering my nose. "I'll hate turkey forever—and mayo, and yeast, and lettuce."

"What's wrong?" Emery asked, alarmed. He slid off the stool.

"The smell is making me nauseated."

"Boys, open the windows," Serena ordered.

"Where are you going, Cass?" Dad asked, grabbing hold of my shoulders.

"Lying down."

As Dad assisted me to the exam table, Mom became frantic. "Are you sick? Serena, is she sick? You said she'd healed!"

"Elizabeth, please calm down. Emery, let's get a blood sample."

"Gotta go!" I broke free from Dad and flew across the room, knocking Gavin out of the way. I heard him tumble into the wall as I sped to the hall bathroom. By the time everyone had caught up with me, I was bent over the toilet, vomiting water.

"Why is she sick again?" Mom shrieked, gathering my hair to the back of my head.

Serena clamped her palm to my forehead. "She has a fever again."

"She mentioned the turkey smell. Maybe she was still on the edge," Gavin suggested.

Why did they all have to stand around watching me throw up?

"Privacy," I shouted between heaves.

Everyone left but Serena, my parents, and Chazz, who patted my back and made comforting "*sh-sh-sh-sh*" sounds, like one would soothe a crying baby.

A minute or so later, I was finished.

"Can we go back to the lab?" Serena asked gently.

I nodded and got to my feet. I felt lousy, but not as bad as before.

Back in the spare room, I crawled onto the exam table. Gavin and the boys had cleared out the food samples and emptied the wastebaskets. Fresh air and a few squirts of a floral air freshener covered the vile smells. I could only faintly detect turkey.

Serena stuck the thermometer in my mouth and checked my pulse. Emery prepared a syringe. I stared blankly at the ceiling.

"My right eye stings," I complained around the thermometer. "It feels like something's in it."

The thermometer beeped. Serena extracted it from my mouth. "It's one hundred point six," she reported. "Let's have a look at your eye. Sit up."

Serena peered into my eye. Her face went blank.

"What?" My hand rose to paw at it.

Serena clutched my wrist to stop me. "Emery, give me the ophthalmoscope."

My parents anxiously crowded in.

"What is it?" Mom gasped, covering her mouth.

"What do you see?" I screamed. A shadow crossed over my eye. I screamed again.

Dad put a firm hand on my shoulder. "Stay still," he ordered, staring into my eye. "Serena, it's moving."

I shuddered violently. *I* could feel *it* moving!

Emery shone the bright beam from the ophthalmoscope in my eyes. I blinked in response.

"It has passed through the tissue," he said.

"What is it?" Dad asked. He was rattled, but no one was as shaken up as I was.

"A parasite of some sort," Serena said.

"And it's living in my eye?"

"Cassidy, do not panic. Your immune system will kill it before long," Emery predicted.

"The parasite is probably searching for a way out," Serena added.

"And that's supposed to make me not panic?" I moaned and dropped my throbbing head into my hands. A parasite that's large enough to be seen with the naked eye— just when I thought my day couldn't get any worse. "*Annihilate* it, white blood cells, and don't let it wiggle out my ear."

Chazz whimpered at my appeal.

"Sweetie, are you thirsty?" Mom asked softly. I lifted my face to see the stress on hers. Barfing, eye worms—I certainly was a buzz-kill.

"Thanks," I said dismally, reaching out for the bottle of Luminous.

"The water!" Revelation exploded on Emery's face. He palmed his forehead. "That's the same brand you had at lunch today."

"Yeah."

Mom pulled the bottle to her chest. "Are you suggesting that the parasite was in the water?"

Wow. That's weird, I thought. Mom's strange reaction didn't escape anyone in the room. She held the bottle to her chest as though she were protecting it.

"It's the one food item we haven't tested." Serena held out her hand. "Elizabeth, the bottle."

"Well, that's ridiculous." Mom relinquished the Luminous. "*I'm* not sick."

"You are not Cassidy," Serena pointed out as Emery laid out clean petri dishes on the table. "It is possible our immune system doesn't recognize the parasite as an invader. Boys, please go home and bring back anymore of this—" Serena looked at the bottle, "—*Luminous*." Her eyes skimmed over the nutrition facts. "Gavin, find out what you can about the company."

"Patrick Grimm is the CEO and president," Dad recalled from the interview. "I can help dig up more information. Serena, may I use your laptop?"

Nate, Jared, and Chazz left to fetch our remaining bottles of Luminous, and Gavin and Dad delved into learning more about Grimm and his company. Emery divided the contents of the water bottle into petri dishes, clearly upset with himself for overlooking the water. Serena examined my eyes again.

"I didn't think of sending the water over," Mom confessed, collapsing into a chair. "Why didn't I thought of it?" she asked herself.

"Do you see that worm?" I asked Serena with a shiver.

She switched off the ophthalmoscope. "No. Let's see what we find in the water."

She joined Emery at the lab table, where he was adjusting the lens of his microscope over a petri dish.

"I didn't think about the water, either," I said, attempting to comfort Mom. "It's bottled, so you'd think it would be safe. And it might be. We learned in science all the ways you can pick up parasites. I could have touched something—Emery! I just remembered—"

"Levy has been downing Luminous like it's going out of style," he finished for me. "As has Cristiano," he added for me, too.

"Creeps me out when you do that," I told him. "But, yeah, I was about to mention Cristiano, too."

"Maybe he ingested this parasite and it made him sick?" Gavin thought out loud.

"He has been in a really good mood lately, just like you, Mom."

Slumped in the chair, she stared at me wearily. Either she didn't like the suggestion she could be host to a hideous worm, or resented the idea that she wasn't normally in a good mood.

"Clear," Serena announced and slid another petri dish under her microscope.

"Nothing here," Emery said, also switching out petri dishes.

I could hear the boys coming up the Phillips's front walk.

"I'm going to lie down," I mumbled. "I still feel sick."

I reclined on the exam table and shut my eyes. The boys entered the house. I did feel sick, but I also didn't feel like talking anymore. It had been a long, miserable day.

"What's wrong with Cass?" Nate whispered as they tromped into the room.

"She's just resting," Mom answered in the voice that sounded ten times more tired than I felt.

"Clear," Serena announced. I heard her slide the next dish under the microscope.

"Patrick Grimm was military," Gavin spoke up. "Served in Afghanistan before being discharged—I'll look into that more, if need be. There are no tax records for him the two years following his discharge, until he took over the family business thirteen years ago—Grimm Estates. This was after his father, Christopher Grimm, a real-estate developer, passed away."

"I'm reading about Grimm Estates now," Dad said. "It's a big outfit in Louisiana. Doesn't specify Christopher Grimm's cause of death, however."

"Drowned," Gavin told Dad.

"Nothing," Emery reported about the water he had been examining. "Jared, please pass that flask."

I slit my eyelids open and watched Emery empty the contents of a Luminous bottle into a tall glass flask. Jared opened another bottle and handed it to him. Emery poured it into the flask, too. As the liquids combined, whirling together, the water lit with a burst of light.

"Holy . . . !" Nate shouted.

I shot off the exam table. The quick movement caused vertigo. I slammed my palms against the tabletop, waiting for the spinning sensation to subside. Jared gripped my waist to steady me.

"Are you okay?" he asked.

I bobbed my head, staring in awe at what appeared to be two lightning bugs swimming through the water. Is that what was digging around in my eye?

"What are they?" Gavin asked.

Serena brought her face to within inches of the flask. The flashes of light faded in and out at intervals, reflecting in her eyes.

"Bioluminescent parasitic organisms," she replied, as though bioluminescent parasitic organisms were everyday occurrences.

Emery continued for her: "Parasites that can produce light, most likely by combining the substance luciferin and an enzyme called luciferase."

"Why didn't they glow until they were together?" Jared wanted to know.

I nodded. It was a good question.

"Some bioluminescent organisms start glowing when another of their species is nearby." Emery pulled out a drawer in front of him. "Let's test it."

"They're pretty," Chazz declared, chin propped on the table's edge, enchantment on his face as he smiled at the parasites. He clearly believed that we'd had the good fortune of trapping two magical water fairies, not nasty leeches that could chemically glow.

"Do you think they're dangerous?" Dad asked Serena, his worried eyes flicking from Mom to Chazz.

Fear swooped down on me like a hawk, sinking razor-sharp talons into my heart as I made the connection. Mom had been drinking the stuff nonstop, and she had given Chazz at least two bottles.

Mom didn't react to the question, or even seem to hear it. She was watching Emery pursue a parasite with a pipette.

"It's too premature to determine," Serena replied in her clinical tone. "We have to establish if the organisms are responsible for triggering Cassidy's immune response—"

"It seems highly probable," Dad said, cutting her off.

"These parasites may be harmless," she reasoned.

Emery suctioned the parasite into the pipette. It illuminated the cylinder like a glow stick. The other organism darted around the flask as though aware his buddy was gone.

Emery extracted the pipette from the flask, and both parasites flickered and faded, as though their batteries had died. They became translucent again.

"Bizarre," Nate uttered.

Emery held the cylinder up to the overhead light. "I

131

can't see it," he said, moving the cylinder around, studying it. "Can you, Cassidy?"

I scanned the cylinder and shook my head, unnerved. "No one would even know they're swallowing them."

"You don't—" Mom cleared the emotion from her throat and started again. "You don't think someone intentionally contaminated the water, do you? They can't be in *every* bottle."

"Dad, please get a few more flasks?" Emery requested.

Gavin collected four flasks from a cabinet and set them before Emery and Serena, who poured bottles of Luminous into them. The water was clear in each flask, until a second bottle was added. As the liquids converged, two parasites exposed their presence, lighting up like sparks from a fireworks display.

"One parasite in each bottle," Dad said, distraught. He rammed a hand through his golden hair, yanking it at the roots. "I don't understand the motive."

"A motive may become clear once we learn how these organisms affect the human body." Serena looked at Mom. "Elizabeth, describe how you feel."

"How I feel?" Mom looked like a lost child.

My throat tightened with rage. *What have these things done to her?*

"Since you started drinking this Luminous water," Serena clarified.

Dad put his arm around Mom's shoulder. He pressed his lips together, hoping that would keep his internal battle from creeping onto his face, I supposed. It didn't.

"I've experienced flare-ups of the Epstein-Barr virus

for years," Mom shared in a small voice. "It has been especially bad lately. I'm so fatigued that I can barely get out of bed sometimes."

"Her muscles are sore, even to the touch," Dad added.

Nate and I exchanged surprised looks. How could we not have known this about our own mother?

"But all that went away after I started drinking Luminous—the fatigue, the soreness, the depression, all of it. I have the energy I had ten years ago." Her eyes moistened. Mine did, too. "How do I feel? Healthy, happy, invincible—" Her eyes slid to a bottle of Luminous, clinging to it. Tears rolled down her face. "I feel like if I don't get a drink soon, I'll die."

"Lizzy," Dad whispered, then buried his face in her red hair. We kids hugged her, assuring her she'd be all right. But how could we know?

Mom's hand reached around Chazz's head, and she pulled him to her fiercely. She stared at Serena, desperate. Serena nodded.

I understood their silent communiqué. Mom wasn't scared for herself. She was terrified this parasite would hurt her children.

Chapter 13

I Hear Them Calling

A couple of hours later, we were sitting around my kitchen table, eating pizza and listening to Gavin's plan. He and Serena would fly to the Centers for Disease Control and Prevention in Georgia, where Serena could work in their advanced laboratories and study the parasite with other scientists to determine its risks, if any.

"We know the parasite isn't compatible with Cassidy—" Serena said.

"In other words, mutants," I grumbled, reaching for my fourth slice of pizza. Feeding my face hadn't provided much solace.

"—however, the rest of us—" Serena continued, as though she hadn't heard me.

"Humans," I translated.

"Cassidy," Mom admonished with a sigh.

"—could be another story," Serena finished, daring me with a look to interrupt her again.

I crammed pizza into my mouth.

"The government won't act on presumption," Gavin said. "We need proof. So while Serena is at the CDC, I'll fly up to DC to meet with the appropriate agencies and attempt to get the wheels turning for an investigation. Drake, you'll set up an interview with Grimm. Lead him to believe he's being interviewed for his charitable works. Emery and Cassidy will accompany you, for obvious reasons."

"I might smell lying, and Emery can hack into their computer," I cleared up, talking with my mouth full.

Dad frowned at me. Emery looked amused.

I snagged pizza slice number five from the box.

Once we'd hammered out the plan, Serena warned Mom about withdrawal symptoms, which could resemble those of a substance abuser getting clean. This didn't sit well with Mom, but she took it in stride, vowing to be accountable to us if she weakened and found herself headed out to buy a case of Luminous.

"I've gotta check on Athena," Chazz announced at that point, bored with all of the talking. "She might be up from her nap."

He'd become obsessed with Jared's cat.

"She *surrrrre* sleeps a lot," he said as he trotted out of the kitchen.

"Elizabeth, Chazz doesn't appear to be suffering your symptoms," Serena said in a hushed voice.

I straightened in my chair, hopeful.

Mom's heavy expression lifted. "He only drank a quarter of the bottles I gave him, if that."

"There's a chance he didn't ingest the parasite," Serena concurred.

"And Nate's safe, because I drank his water at lunch," I contributed, and then proceeded to list the names of everyone I had seen drinking the vile stuff.

"This will be difficult for each of you," Gavin interrupted me. "But it's critical that you don't share what we've discovered with *anyone*."

We all nodded. We could do that.

"That means you don't stop anyone from drinking Luminous Water."

"Whoa!" Nate put his hand up. "Wait a minute! Why not?"

I didn't need to ask why we couldn't. I already knew.

"We need more information," Gavin said, confirming my assumption. "Until the government is involved, we don't want to tip our hand. We have no idea the magnitude of what we're up against, nor the motivation behind it. This situation needs to be handled with kid gloves, and with the proper organizations in place to manage a crisis. I have experienced firsthand the catastrophic results of public panic, and witnessed guilty parties get off scot-free when the trigger was pulled too early."

"So we just let people infect themselves?" Jared asked with disgust.

Gavin looked at him squarely. "Until we know what we're up against."

Scowling, Jared nodded and looked away, deliberating. I suspected he was thinking about his dad, who had introduced my family to the contaminated water. I certainly was speculating about Mr. Wells's involvement. Did he know this parasite was in the water, or was he a victim, too?

I was still pondering the thought as I dressed to go out on my midnight run. Then Jared knocked on my bedroom door.

"Come in, Jared."

He opened the door. "How'd you know it was me?"

I smiled. "I can smell you."

He playfully sniffed his armpits, then closed the door behind him. "You're going out?"

"Yep." I put on a black Nike. "I have to talk to Joe."

Jared sat next to me on the bed. "You're going to tell Joe, even though Gavin said not to?"

"Uh-huh." I forced the other shoe on. "Joe doesn't have anyone to look after him. Besides, who's he going to tell?"

Jared nodded, then appeared transfixed by a pair of jeans wadded on my floor while I tied my shoes. His face dropped, as though the weight of the world was on his shoulders.

"Jared," I said, smoothing his hair. "This is a stupid question, considering everything you've been through, but what's wrong?"

"I need to run something by you, since I don't know how objectively I can view my dad," he said, turning somber eyes to me. "Do you think he would intentionally hurt me?"

Rage exploded in my chest at the mere suggestion. I knew I couldn't view his dad objectively, either, but I could see that Jared needed me to. However, I had to be straight up.

"If you want an impartial opinion, you should ask a Phillips, not me. I don't trust your dad. I'm sorry, but it's true. The thought *alone* that he could harm a hair on your head makes me crazy! You don't *ever* want to see me *that* angry, *believe* me."

Jared's mouth curved into the sweetest smile. He caught my cheek in a warm palm and stared tenderly into my eyes. My mouth went dry. I was positive he was going to kiss me. But he didn't.

"Thank you," he said, smiling. "You have no idea how much that means to me. How much *you* mean to me."

His face grew troubled again. His hand dropped from my cheek. Leaning forward so his elbows rested on his knees, fingers intertwined, he frowned at the floor. "I don't trust him, either. But I do trust you. Please don't tell anyone what I'm about to share."

"I won't." I wouldn't ever betray Jared's trust. "You know I won't."

His troubled gaze flicked to me and then back to the floor. "I know." He blew out an agonized breath. "I think my dad has been infecting me with that parasite. You know how your mom described feeling after drinking the water? That's exactly how I feel when I stay with him. I'm happy—*really* happy. And when I go home, I fall into this depression and get sort of desperate to go back to his place. I even take it out on my mom, snapping at her for no reason. And I get these headaches, like Serena told your mom she might get. You know, withdrawal."

I nodded, processing. It was a lot to take in. For Jared's sake, I couldn't freak out and react emotionally. I had to be logical. I had to be Emery.

"Did your dad give you Luminous?" I figured this would be Emery's first question.

"He didn't hand me a bottle. But he could have snuck the parasite into food."

"Did you see him use Luminous while he was preparing food?"

"No. But that doesn't mean anything. Basically, I'm going off the feelings your mom described."

"And your being angry with your dad doesn't help."

Jared winced, which made me feel like a total jerk. Nevertheless, I had to sort facts from feelings, just like Emery did with me.

"Is it possible you felt happy at your dad's simply because you were happy to be with him, and you felt depressed when you went home because you missed him?"

"Sure." He didn't look convinced.

"Your dad might be like my mom, and have no idea what he's drinking. That's probably the case."

In that moment, I believed it was true. Jared's dad had to be a hapless victim, addicted to the good feeling the parasite produced. *He should be warned.*

"I know Gavin said not to, but you can tell—"

Jared shook his head. "No. I can't tell him. As far as I know, he's involved, somehow. If you recall, I had a nine-millimeter aimed at my chest because of him."

"Like I could forget." Anger gave objectivity the boot. Owen Wells was slime. "Maybe the best thing to do, after a day like today, is to get some sleep. And, Jared—"

"Yeah?"

"I've always got your back." I gave his cheek a quick peck. "Get some sleep. We can talk more in the morning."

I stood. Jared caught my fingers and stared up at me with those beautiful, soulful eyes of his.

"Do you think we can pull off being callous, and keep our mouths shut when we see people drinking Luminous?"

"We have to. Gavin knows what he's talking about." I squeezed his fingers affectionately and swiped my ski mask from the nightstand. "But that doesn't include Joe."

I switched off the light and rolled on the mask.

"Get some sleep." I gave him a brief hug, then ran for my open bedroom window, diving through.

139

~~~

When I found Joe, huddled in his box, my heart stopped. He looked awful. I knew it was because of the parasite.

What has it done to him? Is it eating up his insides?

"Joe, are you sick?"

He forced himself into a sitting position, smiling weakly. "Just recuperating. Something's wrong with that vitamin water."

"How'd you know?" I asked with surprise, searching his dark eyes. No parasites were visible—thank goodness.

"How'd I know?" He rubbed his temples, making a face as though they were tender. "I go to great effort to feel bad about myself, but no matter how much I tried, I couldn't feel bad on that water."

He chuckled at his joke, which struck my heart like a chunk of lead. When would Joe cut himself some slack?

"How'd *you* know there's something wrong with that water?" he asked, and I didn't hesitate to tell him.

Joe let out a low whistle, watching me with worry. "Mendel's mother thinks that parasite in you is dead?"

"Yes, she does, or I wouldn't be better. My immune system fought it, but for some reason, yours—a human's, I mean—doesn't recognize the parasite as an invader. Ser—" I almost used Serena's name, then remembered the pseudonym I had dreamed up for her when talking with Joe. I didn't like using real names with him. "Er . . .. Charice is going to go to the CDC to study them with other scientists."

Staring off at something only he could see, Joe

nodded. "I hear 'em calling me. They want me to drink more of that water. They're making me thirst for it."

"Do you mean you hear voices?"

"Not voices. I *feel* it." He tapped his forehead. "I won't weaken, like the others did."

I touched his forehead to make sure he wasn't delirious with fever. Joe wasn't making any sense. His skin was cool to the touch.

"I'm not suffering from fever," he assured me. "I'm at war with this parasite. It won't get the best of Ol' Joe."

"You'll be okay." I prayed my words would be true. "Charice will figure out what it is and what medicine kills it."

"Ain't gonna be easy," Joe predicted. "There's more than meets the eye. It's all connected."

Again, I had to wonder if he was in his right mind. "What's connected, Joe?"

"I'll tell you after I do some investigating."

"What do you mean?"

"I got my suspicions," was all he would say.

Chapter 14

Missing Person

"*Psst*, Cass."

Nate's whisper wrenched me out of sleep. My alarm clock blinked *5:34 a.m.*

"What?" I moaned.

I had crawled into bed only a couple of hours earlier. After I'd left Joe, I patrolled the streets until three a.m., keeping a watchful eye for unsavory characters. You never knew. I could have crossed paths with whoever was behind the missing person cases. As it was, the Seattle Shadow didn't even sniff out a mugging to intercede with.

"Hurry, before they leave," Nate said in one quick breath, then took off.

That was enough to get me moving.

I sprang from the bed, swiped a hoodie from the floor and tugged it on, and caught up with Nate on the stairs. In the living room, Jared peeked out the front window.

"Are they still there?" Nate whispered, eagerly hooking the other side of the burgundy curtain panel with his fingers.

I pulled in close to him and peered outside, too.

Serena and Gavin, toting suitcases, approached a Crown Victoria with tinted windows parked under a streetlight. An alert, burley man in a black suit opened the

142

back passenger door for the Phillipses. Gavin greeted him with a nod.

"That guy looks like—"

"*Men in Black*," Jared finished and wiggled his eyebrows.

Nate practically giggled.

An older gentleman climbed out of the backseat. He had stark white hair clipped close to his scalp, and strong features. He held himself like a highly decorated general.

Nate cracked open the window. "Make use of those ears," he ordered me.

As though I wouldn't.

"Gavin." The general shook Gavin's hand.

"Sir," Gavin returned, confirming that the man was his superior.

"Are they talking?" Nate demanded.

I shushed him so I could listen.

The general smiled at Serena. "You look as lovely as ever, Serena."

"Thank you, Alton," she replied crisply, handing her suitcase to the agent who had opened the door for them. "It's nice to see you," she added as a courtesy. It was clear she was giving him lip service.

"We have a jet waiting at Boeing Field," General Alton informed Gavin as he helped Serena into the car.

"Thank you, sir." Gavin gestured for General Alton to get in next, then climbed in after him. The agent closed the back door and got into the front seat of the vehicle.

"Did I ever say how freakin' cool Gavin is?" Nate stated in awe.

"He is a badass," Jared agreed.

"That must be his boss," I remarked.

"No *dur*," Nate said.

I gave him a swift jab in the upper arm.

"Bully," he teased, massaging his arm as he craned his neck to get one last glimpse of the Phillips's impressive ride.

~~~

It seemed that Luminous was everywhere I looked. Pedestrians passing us on the way to school, drivers taking swigs at stoplights, our schoolmates, school staff—it was an epidemic.

How can we just let them infect themselves?

What kind of people are we?

"Cassidy, think of the consequences," Emery whispered, reading the distress on my face. I had counted ninety-seven Luminous bottles since that morning. How had I not noticed it was everywhere?

"I can't believe I was so blind, either," Emery confessed, in perfect timing with my internal dialogue. It bugged me when he did that.

Robin approached, sporting a smile and a Luminous.

"Hey," she sang.

"Hey," I returned, eyeing the bottle. Now it made sense. The parasite was making Robin nice.

She winked at Emery and took a swig. I didn't like that at all.

"Cassy," Jared called.

Emery and I stopped walking so he could catch up.

"This sucks," Jared whispered in my ear.

"It does," I agreed. Our troubled eyes leapt from Luminous bottle to Luminous bottle.

~~~

My stomach took a nosedive when I spied an evil Luminous perched before Miriam at our table in Levy's class, appearing deceptively harmless. My fingers twitched at my side, ready to grab it and hurl it through the window.

"Don't," Emery warned, realizing I was on the edge of going ballistic. Each time I saw a bottle of that unholy water, I wanted to scream. "I'll take care of it."

As we made our way toward Miriam, Jared crossed the room, looking on the verge of smacking Luminous bottles off the tables he passed.

"Hi, there," Miriam greeted Emery. She brought the water toward her provocative smile. I would have rolled my eyes at her flirting, if they hadn't been occupied with burning twin holes into her Luminous. A couple of inches closer to her mouth and I'd have knocked it from her hand.

Emery slid into my chair, smiling.

"Hey." He took the bottle from Miriam and pretended to drink.

Miriam watched him with delighted shock. This was the first time Emery had reciprocated her endless flirting, or so she thought. What would she say if she knew his only motivation was to protect her?

"Thanks," Emery said with a smile. "I was thirsty."

"Well, it's about time!" Miriam teased, reaching for the bottle. When her fingertips brushed Emery's, he opened his hand. The bottle fell between their chairs, hitting the floor. Water splattered the bottom of their pant legs and shoes.

Miriam squealed.

"Smooth, Phillips." Emery feigned embarrassment.

"You're wet! Here, let me help you." Miriam snapped her sweater from the back of her chair and brought it toward Emery's thigh, intending to dry him off. He caught her hand.

"That's thoughtful of you," Emery said with that toying smile. He backed toward his chair, holding her sweater at bay. "Maybe next time."

"It's a date." Miriam winked a twinkling eye at him.

"Are you two finished?" I pretended to be exasperated. In reality, I wanted to hug Emery for protecting my friend.

"Looks to me like they're just getting started," Dixon remarked.

"Looks to me like class is about to start," I retorted. Then I noticed the pensive woman with mousy brown hair and big round glasses who was sitting behind Levy's desk.

The final bell rang.

"Please be seated," the substitute teacher said, rising. "I'm Miss Prescott."

"*Miss Prescott*," Dixon echoed. He leaned back in his chair and folded his hands behind his head, sporting a brutish smile. He would make this woman rue the day she subbed for Levy.

"There are no lesson plans," Miss Prescott said, stationed behind the desk, fiddling with her hands. "So you can use this time to study for other classes."

"Or nap!" Dixon tipped his head back and whistled a snore.

I rolled my eyes at Miriam. *Oh, yes, Dixon. You're a clever one.*

"Dear Students and Staff," Principal Woolsey's somber voice flowed through the intercom.

Miss Prescott sat down, as though the announcement was her cue, and stared at her shaking hands.

"I share this news with you with a heavy heart. Moments ago, I received confirmation from the authorities. Mr. Levy has been reported missing."

~~~

Mr. Levy's disappearance had put me in a tailspin. It was one thing to hear about a complete stranger disappearing, but quite another to know the victim.

A victim of what? I shuddered at the possibilities.

The school hallways were unnervingly quiet. Spooked whispers, soles of shoes scraping against wood, long faces—it was like walking through a funeral home.

"What do you think happened to Mr. Levy?" I asked Emery, rubbing the goose bumps on my arm.

"Not here." He pointed to an emergency exit that was positioned out of the flow of traffic.

We wove our way through our schoolmates to the secluded spot. Emery swung his back to the wall. This was a habit of his. He liked to keep an eye on what was going on around him.

"A better question is: What's the connection between Luminous Water and missing locals?"

"So you think there's a connection, too?" Emery had voiced my fear.

147

"'In the magical universe, there are no coincidences, and there are no accidents,'" Emery quoted.

"Is that your way of saying *yes*?"

"It's William S. Burroughs's."

"Emery, please don't joke around. If we're right, my mom—" I couldn't finish.

Emery hooked my neck in the crook of his arm and placed a brotherly kiss on my forehead.

"Your mom will be fine," he promised.

I wiped away tears. "Do you think the parasite killed the people who are still missing?"

Emery tilted my face up to his so he could look into my eyes. "There are no bodies, Cassidy," he reminded. "So, no, I don't think the parasite kills its host. Forgive me for being insensitive."

"I forgive you, and it is a good quote. I think everything that's happened to me was meant to be."

"'Let us follow our destiny, ebb and flow. Whatever may happen, we master fortune by accepting it.' Virgil."

I knocked on his head. "How many quotes do you have in there?"

"Do you want me to answer that?"

"No." I grew serious again. "What do we do from here?"

"We go to fourth period."

"You know I wasn't referring to this very instant."

"I do. I just don't have an answer beyond this very instant."

I found his admission discomforting. Emery always had answers.

Chapter 15

The Plot Thickens

After a long, frustrating day of knowing that people were in danger and not being able to do a darn thing about it, I couldn't wait to cut out of my house at midnight in search of a situation that I *could* take control of, like a robbery or a cat stuck in a tree.

But before I could be in the right place at the right time, I had to check on Joe. I discovered him pacing his alley.

"Joe, what's wrong?" I whispered, almost giving him a heart attack.

"Green Eyes," he breathed, turning to face me with one hand clutching his chest. I narrowed my eyes on his dreadlocks. They looked damp. "You're as quiet as a ghost. I was even keeping an eye out for you."

His face looked stricken, as if he *had* seen a ghost.

"Maybe you should sit," I suggested. Joe didn't look well.

He just nodded, which freaked me out even more. I gripped his arm, guided him to the doorway that his box was nestled in, and helped him sit on the top step. He brought trembling fingertips to his head and stared into the void before him, as though watching a disturbing scene in a movie. Something was terribly wrong.

Is it the parasite he swallowed? Panic grew in my chest.

"Joe, do you need to go to the hospital?"

He shook his head. "No hospital. I'll be fine. Just need to sort things out."

"Sort what out?" I touched his dreadlocks. They were damp. "Why's your hair wet?"

"Took a dip in Lake Washington," Joe explained. "The way that vitamin water made me feel wasn't the only thing that riled my suspicion. Doc did, too. His best friend had always been a bottle of Jack Daniels 'fore he came back, and he used to have a limp. Told me once he'd discovered a lump on his leg, but wasn't gonna do nothing about it. Can't go on living forever on the streets, he said. Thing is, he don't limp no more.

"I been spying on him at the shelter, where he's serving up meals and passing that water around to folks. I followed him this evening when he left. He got on a bus and I got in a taxi. Had to show proof I was good for the fare 'fore the taxicab driver would take me anywhere. Thank the Good Lord that Doc got to where he was goin' quick. Only had fifteen dollars on me.

"He got off at a park next to the lake. Not sure of the name. He walked into that park like he was in no hurry at all. I kept my distance, 'specially since we was the only two around. Appeared that way, at least. There was a young lady with long, yella hair waiting for him on the beach.

"Side by side, they made their way into the lake, walked right in and went under. The cold water didn't even bother them none. When they didn't come up for air, I ran out from the bush where I was hiding and went into the water to search for them.

150

"There was no sign of Doc or the lady. Only the moonlight over the water." Joe rubbed a hand over his stubbly face. I had never seen him so disturbed—granted, there was plenty to be disturbed about.

"Do you think they committed suicide?"

"No. I don't. Don't know what they was doing. But I know they didn't drown. I know it in my gut."

"Then why didn't they come up for air?"

"I don't rightly know."

~~~

I went straight from Joe's alley to Emery's house. Even though I could have knocked on the front door—now that everyone in his household knew my secret—I'd grown accustomed to using his bedroom window late at night.

After hearing what Joe had witnessed, Emery took a moment to process.

"We'll search Lake Washington tonight," he announced.

"You mean *I* will search Lake Washington. This could be dangerous, after all."

"No. *We* will." Emery pointed to himself and me. "It's non-negotiable. We'll rent scuba gear this morning and borrow a boat from a marina in the evening."

By "borrow," Emery meant hotwire and steal.

"I'd also like to check out this Doc character. We'll stake out the shelter."

"What makes you think he'll be there? Remember, he and that woman never came up for air." This was my delicate way of pointing out they may have drowned. Joe

151

was convinced they hadn't, but what other logical explanation could there be?

"I'm with Joe on this one," Emery said. "They didn't drown. Doc will be at the shelter tomorrow."

Emery's plan wasn't sitting well with me. His plans seldom did.

"Shouldn't we call your dad before we do anything?" Gavin would probably veto the whole thing. Without a doubt, my parents would.

"My dad has a full plate of bureaucracy right now. Your parents will worry. We'll do this *tú y yo*." Emery pointed to himself and me again.

This was the way he liked it. Just the two of us. The brain and the muscle.

Chapter 16

Monkey Wrench

The next morning while getting ready for school, my BIG mouth and I created a problem, one that Emery wouldn't be happy about.

As I brushed my hair in the bathroom, I told Jared what Joe had witnessed, and about Emery's plan to search the lake. Being an experienced scuba diver, he announced he was coming along, too.

"You can't go," I stated flat out.

Jared watched me in the bathroom mirror, arms crossed, an obstinate expression on his face.

"Why not?" he challenged.

"B-because—" I used the brush to direct the words like an orchestra conductor: "Because . . . you can't!" I went back to brushing my hair, which was my way of saying *end of discussion*.

The corners of his mouth turned up into a determined smile. "You'll have to do better than that."

"Well, you're going to have to take *no* for an answer!"

Jared shut the bathroom door, leaned against the counter, and fixed an amused smile on me. I pretended he wasn't there as I ripped the brush through my hair.

"What's the likelihood of me taking 'no' for an answer?"

"What's the likelihood of me duct-taping you to a chair?"

Jared laughed.

"What? You think I won't?"

"I didn't say that."

"Look, Jared." I shook the brush at him. "This isn't a game, and it's probably dangerous, if the scrapes Emery and I have gotten ourselves into before are any indication! Besides, he knows how to scuba dive—"

"So do I. What about you?"

"N-n-*no*," I sputtered. "*But* I can hold my breath for a *real* long time—"

"If you knew anything about scuba diving, you'd know that's a very bad idea."

"You're making me want to scream!" I declared, but he did have a point. Jared had been diving since he was young, and what kind of trouble were we realistically going to run into? We'd be in fresh water, at the top of the food chain.

"Okay, you can go," I conceded. "Now I'll have two of you to protect! Great! And don't tell Nate—*or* my parents. With you and Emery, my hands are full enough!"

Jared pretended to zip his lips. "You won't regret this."

"I already do!"

~~~

As predicted, Emery wasn't happy with me. At school, when Nate and Miriam ambled off to their lockers and Jared didn't, Emery shot me a frustrated look. He didn't have to ask why Jared had hung behind. He knew me well enough to figure it out.

I opened my mouth to defend myself, but before I could get a word out, Jared stepped between Emery and me.

"I've scuba dived since I was nine, my dad moors a 39-foot yacht, and you can take a look around his place while I borrow the keys," Jared stated in a low voice.

Emery nodded, impressed.

"Welcome aboard," he consented, giving Jared's upper arm a firm pat. Then he motioned for us to leave.

I followed the boys out of Queen Anne High, flabbergasted that Emery had given in without a fight. It wasn't like him. But then again, the yacht made a compelling case.

~~~

Mr. Wells's luxury apartment overlooking Elliott Bay was our first stop. Contemporary furnishings, with lots of horizontal and vertical lines, graced the large, open interior. There were floor-to-ceiling windows, tile floors, and dark, richly colored walls. Jared's father's minimalistic taste was a far cry from his mother's warm, eclectic antique finds. In other words, it was cold and sterile—an accurate reflection of its owner.

"Nice place," Emery remarked, scanning the living/dining room and kitchen combo. He wasn't checking out the décor. He was looking for a computer.

"He calls it the '*chick magnet*.'" Jared made quotation marks with his fingers and rolled his eyes. "Do what you gotta do," he told Emery. "His home office is the first door on the right."

Jared had made no attempt to hide his disgust with his dad. For some reason, that made me sad.

Needing no further encouragement, Emery headed for the hall. In the foyer, Jared flipped over a black-and-white print of old Seattle in a black frame. A key organizer was concealed behind it.

"That's clever," I commented.

"Uh-huh." Jared snapped a set of keys off a hook.

"Does he keep his car keys in there, too?"

"Not usually," Jared replied. He was rearranging the keys to make it less obvious that a set was missing.

"*Sooooo*—" I turned on my heels to the living area. "This is the *chick magnet*."

Jared slammed the key organizer's door.

I winced, expecting to hear the glass shatter.

"In other words," Jared approached me from behind, "a bachelor pad for a wealthy middle-aged man on the hunt for women half his age. Women who like shiny, sparkly things."

"Oh." What else could I say?

"Sorry," Jared apologized. I glanced at him sidelong. He scanned the opulence with distaste. "It's just hard to be here right now."

"I understand." And I did. If I were him, this would be the last place I would want to be, too.

I smiled and rubbed his lean arm. His muscles were tense. "How'd you turn out so well?"

"Trying not to be like him." Jared turned away and stalked to the open L-shaped kitchen, anchored with a huge island. He opened a black-stained pantry cabinet that flanked a stainless steel refrigerator. His fierce expression tempered into surprise.

"I wasn't expecting this."

"What?" I asked, stepping up next to him. The food items were neatly organized on the laminated shelves.

"No Luminous," he pointed out. "I thought it would be packed in here." Relief rolled off him in waves. I realized in that moment that fear had sparked his cutting mood. He was scared for his dad.

"Maybe he stopped drinking it," I encouraged.

"Could be." Jared opened the refrigerator.

I smiled when I saw there were no Luminous bottles in there, either.

"Maybe he figured out there's something wrong with the water," I suggested with a note of hope, just as Emery called for Jared to come to the office.

Jared shut the refrigerator and didn't respond to my remark. It was frustrating not knowing what was going through his head.

We found Emery in the office, studying a wall safe. He held an oil painting that had been hanging in front of it.

"Whoa," Jared gasped.

"That answers my question," Emery said. He propped the painting against the wall. "You don't know the combination. Fortunately, it's a dial lock. Cassidy, come here."

I did as he asked. Emery turned the dial around twice to the "0."

"Tell me when you hear a click," he instructed.

Jared barely breathed as Emery slowly turned the dial and I listened for clicks. Within seconds, we had the safe open.

"Remind me to bring you to all of my safecracking

jobs," Emery teased. He removed a black satchel from the safe and handed it to Jared. "Look through this," he ordered. Then he extracted a stack of files, and fingered through them.

I watched as Jared dug out a variety of velvet jewelry boxes from the bag. The fabric on most of the boxes was faded and worn.

"Family heirlooms?" I asked as we opened the boxes, revealing antique-looking jewelry.

Jared shrugged. "Got me." He opened a black ring box and stared at it.

"What is it?" I shifted so I could see, too. Inside was a tear-shaped diamond ring. Two gold wedding bands lay on either side.

Emotions warred in Jared's eyes. "My parents' wedding rings, I think."

My heart broke for him.

"Your dad kept them?" I murmured.

"Yeah, he kept them. They're worth money." Jared snapped the box shut and tossed it into the satchel, as though the contents were meaningless.

"There's nothing of use for us here," Emery announced. From his tone, one would have thought he hadn't overheard us.

Did his dad keep the rings for sentimental reasons? I watched Jared as he returned the boxes to the satchel. His face had become an impassive mask, which I knew hid pain. *Maybe Mr. Wells kept them as a reminder of all he's lost.*

Emery put the files back inside the safe, arranging them the way he'd found them. Jared handed him the satchel in silence.

Once Emery had replaced the picture, we moved to the guestroom, where Jared slept. Seeing it was only a guestroom was gut-wrenching. Why wouldn't Mr. Wells set aside a room for his son? I didn't have the stomach to follow the boys into the master bedroom, opting to wait in the entry instead, where I spaced out on the picture of old Seattle. I couldn't wait to get Jared out of there.

"Any luck?" I inquired when the boys joined me a couple of minutes later.

"Nope," Jared said without making eye contact.

Emery looked at me, though.

I raised my eyebrows at him as Jared unlocked the door. He gave me his easygoing smile. It wasn't an answer to my unspoken inquiry. It was a "Don't ask."

~~~

"Nice yacht," Emery remarked, as indifferent about Mr. Wells's expensive toy as he had been about his swanky apartment. His eyes scanned the cabin, cataloguing where everything was.

"Where's the gear?" he asked Jared.

Mr. Wells's wet suit, fins, surf boots, and mask fit Emery. Since Jared had his own, we just needed to rent equipment for me, along with scuba tanks. Emery didn't want to use Mr. Wells's.

We walked down the street from the marina to a dive shop.

"You're sure an employee won't recognize you?" Emery asked Jared for the second time.

"I haven't been in there for years," Jared reassured him.

"Everything okay, Emery?" I asked. He appeared at ease, but I could sense his alertness, which had greatly increased in the last thirty seconds or so.

He smiled at me. "Of course."

I started to turn my head to look around, but Emery slung his arm over my shoulders to stop me.

"I can wait outside if it makes you feel more comfortable," Jared was saying as he opened the door, the words trailing off when he saw Emery's arm around me.

Bewildered, I shrugged at him. I had no idea what Emery didn't want me to see.

"It wouldn't," Emery replied and pushed me toward the door. He took the door from Jared and lifted his chin for him to go in, too.

"What's going on?" Jared asked quietly as Emery followed us in.

"Do as I tell you," Emery whispered. Then he said to Jared, loudly enough for the store clerk to hear: "Pete, would you help Claire get what she needs? I'll be right there." He strolled over to a rack of Seattle apparel in front.

"Sure." Jared narrowed his eyes on the front window.

I patted his arm to urge him forward.

While Jared ordered our gear from the clerk, Emery browsed. I kept a sharp eye on him. He stayed at the front of the store, as though he were waiting for someone. When it came time to pay, Emery moseyed back to us, wearing a pair of sunglasses he'd plucked off a display.

"These, too." He handed them to the clerk. "Can you hold our gear for us?"

I spun around to the front. We had planned on taking the gear to the yacht. Why had Emery changed the plan?

Emery cleared his throat. Understanding his cue, I faced the register again. He wanted our backs to the door. Why?

"No prob, man," the guy answered, adding the sunglasses to the sales receipt. "We close at six."

"We'll be back in an hour or so."

Jared took a step away from the counter.

"Pete," Emery stopped him. "Check out the longboards."

Complying, Jared walked to the longboards stacked along the left wall, sliding glances at the door. My heart hammered. Who was outside the store?

"Claire, I'll be right over," Emery said as he handed the clerk three hundred-dollar bills.

I stared at him, torn. He wanted me close to Jared to protect him from whomever he'd spotted out there. But what about him?

I'm taking care of this now. I glared at the door, my hands rolling into fists. *I'll pound whoever's out there into the ground!*

"Go ahead, Claire." Emery smiled. He tilted his head toward Jared. "I'll be right over."

I jerked a nod and chose a route to Jared around racks that put me closer to the front. If anyone came through the door, I would take him down before he even knew what hit him—or them.

"Hey," I said to Jared, eyeballing the door.

"Who's out there?" He held himself tensely, ready to spring into action.

"Don't know."

"Thanks," Emery said to the clerk, pocketing his change. "We'll be back soon." He sauntered toward us, appearing relaxed.

"Sweet boards, huh?" he said. "Ready to go?"

"Yeah," Jared and I agreed in unison.

The store phone rang.

"As you've already guessed, Jared is being followed," Emery whispered as the clerk answered the call. "Here's the plan. Cassidy, we're a couple. When I signal you, run outside with the sunglasses, laughing, like you'd just taken them from me. I'll come out after you. Put the glasses on and pose for a picture, with your back to the street, angle south—"

"Which way's south?"

"Right. There are two men parked in a silver Acura across the street. Do not look in their direction. I'll pretend to take your picture, while actually taking theirs. Laugh, smile, flirt, be goofy—we're having a good time. Jared, you come out twenty seconds after us. Do not react to anything I do. In fact, look annoyed with me. That shouldn't be difficult to pull off."

Emery shoved the bag into my hands and opened the door. "Showtime," he said, pushing me out.

I stumbled onto the sidewalk, almost smacking into a pedestrian, and let out a howling laugh. The woman shot me a dirty look. The laugh caught in my throat.

"Sorry," I apologized, blushing.

She shook her head and continued on her way.

Emery came barreling out the door, not looking like himself at all. Wolfish grin, shiny, infatuated eyes—he drank me in with the same unnerving stare I had caught Chad giving me before. Taken aback, I forgot what I was supposed to be doing.

"You think you're funny," he shouted loudly,

scooping me up into his arms. "You look terrified," he said into my hair. His calm voice didn't match his feverish expression. "Play along or we'll arouse their suspicion. Squeal—you're having fun."

I squealed, as ordered.

Emery set me on my feet with my back to the Acura. "I'm going to put the glasses on your face," he said through his grin, shaking them loose from the bag that I clutched. Obviously, due to my ineptness, he had contrived a new plan.

As Emery slipped the glasses onto my face, I glanced at Jared, who had just come out of the shop. I had to hand it to him. He appeared extremely annoyed.

"You're *so* hot!" Emery declared, stumbling backward as if stunned by my beauty. He whipped his phone from his jeans pocket. "Say cheese."

"Cheese." I struck a pose, which I was sure looked absurd.

Emery snapped picture after picture, angling the phone in different directions, while I did my best to ham it up. I must have done a fairly decent job, judging by the looks passers-by were giving us.

"They're getting suspicious," Emery said through grinning teeth. He was watching the men on his phone screen. "We'd better stop before they decide to get out of the car."

He put away the phone, then hooked my neck in his arm and dropped a lavish kiss on top of my head as he pulled me down the sidewalk. My face burned several shades of red.

"I want to deck you," Jared informed him when he'd caught up with us.

I peeked at him. His deadpan expression proved that he was a better actor than I was. But then again, he wasn't trapped under Emery's armpit.

"I'd want to deck me, too," Emery admitted, beaming for the goons. "We don't want them to know how you feel about Cassidy, since they know where she lives."

"What are you talking about? They followed us from my dad's."

"No. They followed us from school." Emery grabbed my waist and swung me onto a small bench outside a bookstore. "Cassidy, keep your face angled down, like you're listening to me. Don't stop smiling."

He entwined his fingers in mine.

"I watched the security feed from last night before school. A silver Acura drove down our street twice during the night. I didn't see a car following us as we rode the bus, and don't think I wasn't paying attention." His eyes slid to Jared. "Good, Jared. Look anywhere but at them, or us. We're your love-struck friends who are too insensitive to realize we're making you uncomfortable."

"I was watching, too," Jared said. "I've been keeping an eye out since everything happened. I've never seen that car before now."

"My guess is they followed your mom from work—"

Suddenly, Jared did look like he wanted to punch something.

"—These men know what they're doing. Trust me, Jared. We have taken precautions. I'm at fault here. *I* should have seen them before now."

"No, dude. This is on me. My mom and I shouldn't have stayed with the Joneses. What do we do now?"

"I'm working on that. Cassidy, I couldn't see their license plate through the camera. The car they're parked behind, and traffic, obstructed the view. I anticipated this, hence the sunglasses. You'll be able to see their license plate at this height. Keeping your face down, tell me the number."

"You think of everything," I said in awe.

"I try. The number. My neck is getting a kink."

"A-Z-6-8-8-2-I."

"Washington?"

"Yes."

"What are they doing?"

"Watching us and talking."

"Like they're shooting the breeze? Nothing serious?"

"Yes."

"Excellent." Emery plunked down on the bench and pulled me onto his lap.

Shocked, I sat as stiff as a board.

"Relax," Emery ordered with a grin. "You're into me, remember? Sit, Jared."

Scowling, Jared waited for Emery to fish his phone from his pocket before sitting down. There wasn't enough room for three of us, which is why I ended up on Emery's lap, I gathered.

"Don't enjoy yourself too much," Jared growled, squeezing in next to Emery.

I wanted to box his ears. As if this weren't awkward enough!

"Shouldn't we be trying to lose them?" he asked Emery, arms crossed, as he watched pedestrians walk by.

"No point in losing them. They know where Cassidy

lives," Emery reminded, examining the photos he had taken of the creeps. Their windshield had blurred their faces. "We're going to take them out of commission. We can't have them nosing around. My guess is they have standing arrest warrants." Emery began typing a text to Riley's son, Mickey O'Shea, with his thumb. "Cassidy, we're looking at the pictures I took of you, while our third wheel continues to look miserable. Jared, you really need a girlfriend."

"Ha-ha."

"Cassidy, these are pictures of you. Act like it."

I pretended to laugh at shots of me, and even protested, here and there, to make the scene appear genuine. What girl doesn't complain about pictures of herself, right? Emery laughed, too, as he finished the text, telling Mickey what was going on and asking him to run the license plate number. After sending it, he emailed the best shot he had of the goons.

"Now what?" Jared asked.

"Ice cream." One of Emery's hands scooted under my knees and the other snaked around the small of my back. He stood up, taking me with him, as if I were a blushing bride being carried over the threshold.

Heat poured into my face. I felt like a complete dork.

"Emery, couldn't you have just told me to get up?" I scolded, wiggling out of his arms, but remembering to smile.

"What would be the fun in that?" He laced his fingers in mine, yanking me along.

Getting to his feet, Jared followed us, muttering under his breath.

We backtracked to Marianne's Ice Cream. I hadn't

noticed it when we'd walked by the first time. What was wrong with me? Was I totally unaware of what was going on around me?

Jared treated Emery and me to ice cream, even though eating was the last thing I wanted to do. The past fifteen minutes had my stomach in knots.

"I'm sorry, Cassidy, but I'll be too busy to grope you now," Emery joked, lifting a waffle cone packed with Rocky Road to explain why he couldn't manhandle me anymore.

"Dude, you really need your butt kicked." Jared took a slow lick of his mint chocolate chip.

I eyed Emery. "Maybe by a girl." I tasted my cookies and cream, eyes rolling at the heavenly flavor. "Great call, Emery! I needed this."

"It's well earned. Being the object of my affection isn't easy." His cell rang. Emery looked at the screen and nodded. "Turns out the driver missed a court date, and on Riley's dime. Not good for him at all."

"He's a fugitive," Jared said, pumping his fist.

"One who will be apprehended soon. The O'Sheas can run the passenger's license when they pick up—Victor Capaldi," Emery read. "They might get lucky with two bounties. We'd better get back to our bench. How's that for Providence?" he elbowed me.

Walking back, I spied on the goons through my new sunglasses while savoring my ice cream. I would probably fixate on cookies and cream from Marianne's Ice Cream for weeks. Between licks, I reported to the boys what Capaldi and his friend were doing, which amounted to watching us.

"So these guys are just following me. Why?" Jared wondered as we sat back down on our bench.

I sat on Emery's knee, which didn't feel as awkward while eating ice cream, for some reason.

"Could be they were hired to keep tabs on you," Emery said. "Or intimidate you. They're not even trying to hide themselves at this point. It isn't their fault we didn't notice them until now." Out of the blue, he attacked my ice cream, biting into it.

"Hey!" I yanked the cone away.

"That's good." Emery licked cookies and cream remnants off his grinning lips. "Or they plan to grab you when you're alone—"

I stopped eating. "No. That can't be right."

"It can. You just don't want it to be right," Emery pointed out. "Jared, you've only been in public settings, or with the Joneses or us. There hasn't been an opportunity to abduct you without witnesses."

Jared grimaced. "I'm sorry for all the trouble my family has caused yours. If something happens—"

"It won't," I interrupted, adding fiercely: "Between Gavin and me, *no one* will mess with our families."

"What am I? Chopped liver?" Emery grumbled and then tried to sneak attack my ice cream again. I pushed his face away. He chuckled into my palm.

"But why?" Jared wondered out loud. "What would they want me for?"

"Your dad will have to answer that. Regardless, we can't have them lurking around while we're getting prepared for tonight." Emery's cell rang. A grin spread across his face as he read the text.

"Finish your ice cream," he told us. "We'll be leaving in a couple of minutes."

A black SUV with tinted windows came to a halt alongside the Acura, blocking the car in. The hazard lights flashed and electric windows rolled down, revealing stout Riley in a zebra-striped blouse that strained over her ample bosom. Her red hair was teased into a frenzy, and a ton of makeup covered her freckled skin. Burly, redheaded Marty sat in the passenger seat. I wondered if his twin was in the backseat, then glimpsed Marky stroll up the sidewalk to the Acura's passenger door. He was decked out in bounty hunter attire and cool sunglasses. Grinning, he saluted the goons, muscles rippling up his thick arm. The O'Shea brothers were big boys.

Marty gestured for the driver to roll down his window.

"Victor Capaldi!" Riley bellowed, leaning toward the passenger window so she could see him. Riley was very loud, and very Irish. "Fancy meeting you here. Remember me?" She turned her head toward us. Winking a shrewd green eye, she blew a kiss.

Mickey pulled up to our curb in his Jeep Wrangler. The passenger's side window rolled down. He flashed his devilish grin.

"Hey, kids!" he called. "Wanna ride?"

Chapter 17

The Wrong Hostage

"Hi, Mickey," I gushed as I climbed into the backseat of his Jeep. Red hair, freckles, smiling green eyes, roguish grin, Irish accent, charisma out the wazoo—I would be lying if I said I didn't have a *teensy-weensy* crush on Mickey O'Shea.

"Hi there, Cassidy." His face sported that rascally grin of his. "You've had a bit of excitement today."

"A little. Thanks for rescuing us."

"My pleasure. Someone's got to look after this boy." He backhanded Emery's chest, then shot his hand over the seat to Jared. "Mickey O'Shea," he introduced himself.

Jared shook his hand. "Jared. Good to meet you."

"Likewise, although *good* is not how I'd describe Victor's day." Mickey shook his head at the scene across the street and made a *tsk-tsk* sound.

The two goons were reluctantly getting out of their car. There was an O'Shea twin stationed outside each door, ready to chase them down if they ran.

Hands on hips, stilettos striking the asphalt, Riley made her way over to the Acura, her evil eye fixed on Capaldi, daring him to even think about bailing.

"Do they need your help?" I asked Mickey.

"Nah. Besides, I have my own skip to bring in."

Mickey cracked his knuckles, then backhanded Emery's chest again. "Whaddaya say, li'l bro? You in?"

"When am I not? Cyrus?"

"Yep," Mickey confirmed, pulling out into traffic. "Matthew Cyrus *foolishly* used his debit card at the Shell station down the street from his granny's this morning. She's a scary little spitfire. Bad-tempered. Clobbered me with her cane last time I stopped by to inquire if her fugitive grandson was about—"

"Wait," I interrupted, confused. "What are you talking about?"

"Cyrus's cantankerous grandmother," Emery smart-mouthed.

I bopped him on the head.

"Cyrus's granny isn't the only scary little spitfire, I see," Mickey teased and then explained: "Emery is my apprentice."

"What? You mean you're training him to be a bounty hunter?"

"That I am, though he hasn't assisted in the apprehension of a fugitive accused of a first-degree felony, mind you. He *is* a minor."

Jared and I exchanged astonished looks.

"But is it even legal?" I wanted to know.

"To become a bona fide bounty hunter? Sure, if you're eighteen. Twenty-one to carry a handgun. But Emery is an *intern*."

I didn't really see the difference. Intern or not, Emery was helping to capture fugitives.

"Why didn't you tell me, Emery?" I whined.

He tossed his hands up in mock exasperation. "I did."

"When?"

"The night I unveiled the mystery shrouding the O'Shea clan."

Mickey barked a laugh.

"I thought you were kidding!" I protested.

"And that's *my* fault?"

"Yes!" I whacked him again.

"Careful," Mickey cautioned. "Emery bruises easily."

I huffed, crossing my arms. Emery drove me crazy!

"Get me up to speed, kids," Mickey said, changing the topic to a more pressing one. "Who hired ol' Victor? And why?"

"Jared?" Emery said, giving him the opportunity to explain.

Jared told Mickey about the attack at his apartment—or our fabricated version, that is. Mickey didn't display any surprise upon hearing that Emery had taken out two thugs with a hockey stick.

"Jared, who's your dad?" Mickey asked.

"Owen Wells. He's a partner at *Cooperstein, Scolla and Wells*."

Recognition flickered in Mickey's eyes. "I've heard about your dad," he acknowledged, then directed his attention to switching lanes. It was obvious he wanted to avoid elaborating. But Jared wasn't going to let it go.

"What have you heard about him?"

Mickey met Jared's steady gaze in the rearview mirror.

"You're a tough kid," he assessed, looking back at the road. "A bright one, too. That's as plain as day." He made a left turn. "So I'm not going to insult your intelligence. Your old man represents some real baddies in the local organized crime syndicates. He is a coveted lawyer, from my understanding. Now this is making sense. Victor is what you'd call an *associate*, an errand boy, meaning he's hired to do the dirty work. He hasn't been arrested for a mob-linked crime yet, but word gets around."

"Thanks for being honest, man," Jared said. "But I know how my dad got rich—"

I winced at the bitterness in his voice.

"—We think Ariel Vilvary sent his soldiers to put a bullet in my skull, to teach my dad a lesson—"

"Jared, I'm going to interrupt you here." Mickey turned around to look at him, since we were stopped at a red light. "I doubt those thugs were going to kill you. Maybe mess you up. But murder? Unlikely. The point was to scare your dad into toeing the line. Why do you think Vilvary is behind this?"

"My dad said he had *terminated* his professional relationship with him."

Driving again, Mickey let out a long whistle. "Can't imagine Vilvary would take that well. I'm guessing his soldiers aren't talking?"

"Only to their lawyers."

"Do you know their names?"

Jared told him.

"Familiar with them, too. We're here." Mickey parked the car.

We were in an older, rundown neighborhood. Apartment complexes and Craftsman homes, all with peeling paint and unkempt yards, hemmed cracked sidewalks. My eyes locked on an elderly man sitting on a ratty sofa on a dilapidated front porch, smoking a pipe.

"This is depressing," I said.

"Don't let Cyrus's granny hear you say that," Mickey cautioned. He stuffed the stun gun and handcuffs Emery had handed him from a duffel bag into his leather jacket pockets.

"It's like you two have done this a hundred times," I said, watching with relief as Emery removed a stun gun and handcuffs from the bag for himself, too.

Mickey winked at me. "We've got a system."

"Is this guy dangerous?" I gnawed a fingernail.

"No," Emery said flatly. He lifted his backside off the seat to wiggle the Taser into his back pocket.

"How do you know?"

"Cassidy, Cyrus is a petty thief, and not a very good one at that," Mickey reassured. "He doesn't have a history of violence." He unclipped a pair of shades off the sun visor.

"Can I go, then?"

Mickey slipped on the sunglasses, grinning at my request. "If I weren't the upstanding bounty hunter I am, I'd consider it. Cyrus's granny wouldn't dare strike me if I used you as a shield."

"The shades make you look intimidating," I remarked.

"That's the point. I need any edge I can get with Granny. Now you two stay put and keep the doors locked. We'll be back quicker than you can say 'Jack Robinson.'" They got out of the car.

"Who's Jack Robinson?" I asked Jared.

"Got me," he said.

We watched as Mickey and Emery climbed the front steps of a nearby house. There was a shopping cart parked in the gravel front yard.

Mickey pressed the doorbell. Emery's head turned to the side as though he'd heard something.

"Good time to call my dad," Jared said, and opened the contacts on his cell.

"Are you sure you should do that?"

"Definitely."

The front door opened to an irate elderly woman in a housecoat and slippers. She almost came up to the middle of Mickey's chest. Leaning on her cane, she gave Mickey the stink eye. My nerves settled. What trouble could a frail, eighty-year-old woman cause?

"Hello, Jared," I heard his dad answer.

"Hi, Dad."

"Can I call you back? I'm late for a meet—"

"Two goons have been following me. They know where Mom and I are staying."

There was a moment of silence. "Are you positive you're being followed?" Mr. Wells asked in a lawyerly fashion, though I detected angry undertones in his voice.

Good, I thought as I watched Cyrus's grandmother shake a crooked finger at Mickey. *He is somewhat human.*

"Positive," Jared responded, without elaborating. "Be straight up, Dad. What is going on?"

"I don't know who those men are, or why they are following you," his dad lied between his teeth. "I will look into the matter and I *will* end this. Where are you now?"

"With Cassidy," Jared misled. Mr. Wells would assume we were at school.

Cyrus's grandmother let Mickey and Emery inside the house.

"Don't worry, Jared. This *will* be over soon," his

father assured ominously. "Call me if you see those men again. I love you."

"I'll call the police first. Bye, Dad." He disconnected the call without returning the sentiment. I wouldn't have, either.

Suddenly, a man came barreling around the side of the house.

"Let me guess. Cyrus," Jared said.

"He looks dangerous," I said.

Clean-shaven head, a goatee, tattoos covering his neck, a mean face—Cyrus wasn't one you'd want to meet in a dark alley.

He wheeled a left, headed straight for Mickey's Jeep.

"This is too easy," I said, opening my door and bracing it with my arm.

He plowed into the door, bouncing off it. Falling backward, his back smacked into the sidewalk.

"Oh crud," I gasped, jumping out of the car. I didn't think he'd hit the door that hard.

"Wait, Cass," Jared said, opening his door, too.

"Are you okay?" I asked Cyrus, a stupid question considering he was rolling on the cement in agony. I offered him my hand.

"Cassidy, get back in the car!" Mickey shouted, sliding around the corner of the house.

"He's hurt," I yelled back as I helped Cyrus up.

Then he pulled a fast one.

Cyrus wrapped his arm around my neck and yanked me against him, using me as a human shield. I blushed on the spot. If I hadn't been looking at Mickey, no way would I have missed such a predictable move.

Horrified, Mickey stopped dead in his tracks, throwing his hands up. Emery, coming to a halt behind him, appeared ready to laugh. I noted Jared also didn't look overly alarmed.

"Cyrus, use your head," Mickey entreated. "Let her go."

"Back off!" Cyrus held me closer to him. My nose crinkled. His breath was revolting.

"Did your grandma make you tuna for breakfast?" I wiggled in his grip.

"Shut up!" he commanded. "I don't want to hurt her," he told Mickey.

"Of course you don't. *No one* is going to hurt anyone. Let her go, Cyrus, and we'll talk."

"Leave, and I'll let her go in five minutes."

"That's not gonna happen. Let her go *now*."

"No!" Cyrus bellowed, almost blowing out my eardrum.

I'd had enough. I extracted his pinky off my shoulder and used it to maneuver him to his knees.

"Please, please, please," he begged all the way down, in utter pain.

"You took the wrong person hostage," I told him. He collapsed to his knees before me.

Mickey cautiously approached, stunned that I had incapacitated a man who had at least eighty pounds on me. Jared coughed and covered his mouth to hide a grin. Emery didn't even bother to conceal his amusement.

"You certainly don't listen well, *Missy*," Mickey reprimanded me as he took Cyrus's hand from me and roughly forced him to the ground. "And, *you*, Cyrus—do you have a brain in your head?"

Cyrus cursed at Mickey in empty bluster, his cheek being ground into the weeds as Mickey handcuffed him.

Mickey yanked him to his feet. "Lucky you. You get to ride shotgun," he said, shoving Cyrus toward the Jeep.

Emery, Jared, and I climbed into the back. Mickey jerked the passenger seatbelt across Cyrus.

"I'm sorry, Mickey," I apologized in a small voice. I knew he felt guilty.

His features softened.

"No. *I'm* sorry," he confirmed my suspicion. He did feel responsible for what had happened. He shook his head and grinned. "I should have known better. You're female. You're not going to listen." Letting out a laugh, he backhanded Cyrus's arm. "*Whoa-ho-ho!* Wait 'til the boys at the precinct hear a hundred-pound *girl* took you down!"

The look on Cyrus's face was nothing short of horror. "You ain't tellin' *nobody*!"

"Aren't I?"

"Um . . . one hundred thirteen pounds," I corrected softly.

Mickey, Emery, and Jared burst into laughter. Cyrus was not amused.

"I stand corrected," Mickey declared, wiping mirthful moisture from his eyes. "A hundred-and-*thirteen*-pound girl brought you to your knees by twisting your *little* finger back." He started the car. "A heartless girl, I might add, being that she paid no mind to your begging for mercy."

"I never begged for mercy!"

"Oh no? My partner back there got it all on his cell phone," Mickey fibbed.

"You taped it?" Cyrus sputtered. "Not cool, man!"

"Neither is taking a hostage. Where am I dropping you kids off before Cyrus and I run our little errand?"

Emery told him the street where the dive shop was located.

All the way there, Mickey harassed Cyrus about how he'd broadcast the non-existent video on YouTube, predicting it would become a global sensation within days. From there, he mused about submitting it to *America's Funniest Home Videos*, too, and inquired if we knew what the cash prizes were, as he pretended not to hear Cyrus's whiny pleas and threats.

~~~

Mickey dropped us off at the Acura, which had been abandoned. Apparently, the O'Sheas got lucky with three bounties today. I assumed that if the passenger had had a clean record, he would have left in the Acura.

After we lugged six tanks and my dive gear to the yacht, Emery took off for the homeless shelter to see what he could learn about Doc while Jared gave me scuba diving lessons. We couldn't go with Emery, since there was a possibility Joe would be spying on Doc, too. Joe had met Jared before and would probably figure out my identity if he saw me with him.

Jared gave me a tutorial so detailed that I wanted to bash my head into the yacht's table repeatedly. But before his thoroughness could drive me to such extremes, Emery returned with food.

While we chomped chips and sipped sodas, Emery gave his report. Doc had been helping prep for the shelter's dinner shift, while a man who he assumed was Joe browsed a used clothing store adjacent to the dining hall. He described Joe to a *T*, right down to his grungy Seahawks jacket.

Emery had fed the shelter's manager a story that he was conducting research for a paper for school, and got permission to interview the staff and volunteers. The manager was happy to comply. Emery didn't learn much from Doc. However, he did observe his happy countenance, which we had learned to be associated with the parasite. Although this observation wouldn't hold up in court, it was still a connection. A man who had disappeared, and then resurfaced six weeks later, was now joyfully passing out Luminous Water bottles at the shelter.

We cracked open our second round of sodas and launched into a debate about whether to let my parents in on our plan. Emery had already decided not to tell his parents—until we had useful information.

"Why bother them with conjecture?" he reasoned.

After hashing out the pros and cons of enlightening my parents, we also collectively agreed not to involve them. Best case scenario: my mom would freak and my dad would insist on coming. Worst case: they'd forbid us from going, which would cause a major problem, since Emery would follow through with his plan regardless.

Eventually, we geared up and took the yacht into Elliott Bay. The actual scuba diving went well. It felt like how I imagined flying would feel—floating weightless, free—and breathing through the regulator came naturally. It was like inhaling clean country air, which, frankly, surprised me. I'd been positive that sucking in the breathing gas would make me hyperventilate. Not the case. The biggest challenge was remembering *to* breathe. I actually had to think about it, and would forget from time to time.

Whenever Jared noticed that air bubbles weren't escaping my regulator, he would have a hand-signaling fit, rolling his hand slowly for me to breathe, and to do it "sleepily" in order to conserve oxygen.

Emery left the scuba diving instruction and monitoring to Jared. I figured he wasn't overly concerned about my messing up—if I ascended too quickly and ruptured an eardrum or lung or whatever, I'd just heal. But tell that to Jared.

Chapter 18

Deep, Dark, and Dangerous

W e did something we hadn't done before. Emery drove us to the marina.

"I can't imagine how much trouble we'd be in if you got pulled over," I fretted. We were cruising down Queen Anne Hill in his dad's SUV, a little after eleven p.m. "Or if our parents knew what we are about to do!"

"Relax, Cassidy. They won't." There wasn't a smidgen of doubt in Emery's voice. How could he always be so confident?

"Besides," Jared chimed in from the backseat. He rapped his knuckles on the window and grinned. "Tinted glass. No one can see who's in the car."

"And I *won't* get pulled over." Emery flipped on the blinker and made a right turn. "But if they try, I'm fairly certain I can outrun the authorities in a high-speed chase."

"Ha-ha," I said while Jared actually did laugh.

My ill ease didn't diminish when we were safely parked at the marina. A sense of calamity grew with each step toward the yacht, as though I could smell doom swirling around us in the cool, salty air. The eerie mist rising off the dark water of the bay contributed to the bad feeling. We had been so focused on getting to this point that we'd neglected to discuss exactly what we hoped to find.

182

People?

Isn't that what we were looking for? People in Lake Washington?

A shiver scurried up my spine.

~~~

I sat with Jared as he drove the yacht. Emery organized and checked our gear in the cabin below.

"I haven't gone through the locks before," I said. We were waiting, sandwiched between two barges in the narrow chamber of the Hiram M. Chittenden Locks, for passage from the salt water of the Puget Sound to the fresh water of Lake Union and Lake Washington. The water was rising, as fresh water poured into the chamber, bringing us level with the lakes.

"When did you learn to drive a boat?" I rambled on, not giving Jared a chance to comment on my previous remark. I rubbed the cool skin of my cheeks, nipped at by the night air, and surveyed the dark clouds threatening to release a torrent of rain.

"When my dad bought this yacht, about two years ago."

"Two years? Why didn't you tell me about it before?"

He shrugged, eyeing me. "Are you nervous?"

"A little. I don't know why." I fidgeted in the seat. "I'm the last person who should be. Are you?"

"Not really. What are we going to find down there, anyway?"

"Probably nothing," I agreed, hoping we were both right.

~~~

"Do you think those are fish?" Emery asked Jared. They were studying some squiggly lines toward the bottom of the depth-finder screen.

For the last half hour, we'd been searching the area where we assumed Joe had seen Doc and the woman go into the lake.

My eyes dropped to dark water below, squinting, trying to penetrate the black. I couldn't see very deep. Overcast skies hid the moon and stars, leaving only the artificial glare that emanated from the 520 Bridge that linked Seattle and Medina as the greatest source of light. I estimated we were around a mile away. The misdirected beams from the bridge didn't touch the darkness surrounding us, nor did the residential lights that dotted the shores on either side of the lake.

"Could be, but they're not moving much," Jared pointed out. "Since we're looking at a sunken forest, they could be tree branches." He frowned with frustration. "Don't know why my dad didn't update the equipment before remodeling the inside. If this was a new depth finder, we'd know exactly what we're seeing at seventy-one feet."

"Well, let's find out." Emery gave Jared a pat on the back.

I smiled. I liked seeing them friendly.

The golden moment was fleeting, though. Within seconds, my mouth had flipped back into a frown. That feeling of foreboding had returned full-force, chiseling away at my brain.

~~~

While Jared lowered the anchor, Emery and I went down to the cabin to change into our wetsuits.

"So his dad spent a ton of money making all of this look state-of-the-art, but doesn't bother with the equipment?" I remarked, glancing around at the fancy-schmancy cabin with disgust.

"Remember his dad's taste in women." Emery pulled his hoodie off.

"Superficial, like him."

"Your gear is next to the bed." Emery ignored my snide remark. Instead, he turned his back to me and faced his gear, neatly organized across the table. Apparently, he was done discussing the subject. I wasn't, however.

"Doesn't it make you happy to have your parents?" I tossed my jacket on the bed and peeked over my shoulder at him. Glimpsing the knotwork circle tattoo on his broad shoulder, I jerked my head forward. I had expected him to have on a Neoprene shirt, like the one he had bought me when we'd picked up our rentals from the dive shop.

"I've always been grateful for my parents," he answered, seemingly oblivious of my discomfort. I could tell by his voice that he was taking off the sweats that had covered his board shorts.

Blushing, I fought the urge to peek again.

"Me too," I blurted out, then concentrated on getting into my wetsuit as quickly as possible.

So I find my best friend attractive—what's wrong with that? I reasoned, wiggling my leg into the snug material.

185

Emery worked quietly, too, which made me wonder if he was aware of my thoughts. The very idea caused a blush to burn up my forehead and into the roots of my hair.

"*Burrrrr* . . . this is chilly," I remarked of the wetsuit, which was still damp from my earlier lessons. I hoped filling the silence would bust up the tension building in the air. It was so thick that I could almost taste it. "You know I'm talking about the wetsuit, right?"

"Uh-huh," was all Emery would say, which made me even more self-conscious.

Why isn't he talking?

The yacht blasted backward. Being in the process of forcing my other leg into the wetsuit, I lost balance and did a face-plant into the bed.

"What the . . . ?" I said, pushing my leg through. I sprang to my feet.

"He's finishing anchoring," Emery explained, working the wetsuit over his torso. Catching myself staring again, I gave my face a sharp smack and pivoted to the bed.

What is wrong with me?

"Oh," was the only thing I could think to say. I punched my right fist through the sleeve hole.

"How's it going?" Jared called from above, interrupting the awkward silence that had once again fallen over the tight quarters. He climbed down the ladder.

"Good," I lied, trying to zip the wetsuit. Putting the stupid thing on hadn't been that difficult earlier.

"I'll get it," Jared offered, lifting my hair. He pinched the zipper slider and smoothly pulled it up my back.

I cleared the embarrassment from my throat.

"Thank you." I turned around to face Jared. Looking

into his eyes, a tsunami of guilt crashed over me. The corners of his mouth curled into his slow smile that I loved so much. I felt even worse.

"You're welcome," he said, tugging my hair.

While Jared walked to the built-in leather sofa where his gear had been laid out, I braved a glance at Emery. He stared back at me, wearing his standard relaxed expression, and his wetsuit and hood. I suspected he had finished dressing while I'd been wrestling with my wetsuit. Why hadn't he offered to help me, like Jared had?

Because he caught me staring at him.

Horrified, I busied myself with my hood.

~~~

"Cass, what do you do if you lose your regulator?" Jared quizzed as he double-checked the pressure gauge on my scuba tank.

"She'll hold her breath until we ascend," Emery gave a smart-aleck answer on my behalf. Grinning at this cleverness, he checked his own pressure gauge.

The awkwardness between us had dissipated once we'd escaped the claustrophobic cabin—or it had for me, at least. I was positive the mortification had been one-sided.

"If I did hold my breath, trapped air would expand in my lungs and would probably burst my eardrums, or give me *the bends*, even if I ascended just a little," I quoted Jared and stuck my tongue out at Emery. Jared had chewed me out earlier for holding my breath during our practice. He fretted about my safety like a mother hen. "Which, by the way, would heal—"

187

"After causing insurmountable pain," Emery interrupted.

"Nothing compared to having your skull cracked with nunchucks." I gave him a smug look. "To answer your question, *Jared*: I capture my regulator by sweeping the cord thingy with my arm, like this." I demonstrated.

"Don't let her fool you, *Jared*. She'll hold her breath, even at the risk of rupturing eardrums, or her lungs. You didn't mention lungs," Emery said to me. I rolled my eyes. To Jared, he added, "She rarely does what she's told."

"Correction: I rarely do what bossy boys tell me to do, but I'll do whatever you tell me, Jared. Really, I will."

"*Hmmmmmmm* . . . Somehow that doesn't breed a ton of confidence," he joked, then inhaled a quick breath from my regulator to make sure the air was flowing properly. "Speaking of ruptured eardrums, whenever you feel pressure building, clear your ears by swallowing, moving your jaw—"

"Or pinching my nose and blowing. I know, I know. Now, stop worrying. I've got this."

"No doubt. But humor me. Let's go over 'Bruce Willis Rocks Action Films' again—"

He had no clue how close I was to discarding the stupid gear and just diving in.

~~~

After Jared felt confident that I wasn't going to drown myself or risk bursting something, he and Emery did buddy checks for equipment, and we were finally ready to go. Emery turned on the dive light tethered to his wrist and went in first, taking a giant step off the platform and disappearing into the dark water.

He bobbed, cleared his mask, and sank back under. Icy fear slid through my stomach. I didn't want him floating in that dark water alone.

Jared motioned for me to go. I didn't hesitate. I turned on my dive light, extended my leg, and dropped into the lake, the chill of the water only touching the exposed skin of my face. Instinctively, I wanted to hold my breath, but forced myself to inhale the breathing gas—deep, even breaths, just as Jared had taught me. The mask instantly began to fill with water, so I swam to the surface and lifted the mask to empty it, as I continued to breathe through the regulator.

Jared bobbed up next to me, cleared his mask, and gave me a thumbs-up. I nodded. Deflating our BCD jackets—which Emery called "glorified life jackets"—just a little, we exhaled slowly and sank below the surface, then swam to the anchor chain where Emery waited for us.

Emery held his wristwatch under his dive light, noted the time, and gave us a thumbs-up. It was strange not to be able to hear him, or hear anything for that matter, other than my own breathing through the regulator. The inhalations sounded like Darth Vader's ominous breathing; the exhaling of bubbles looked and sounded like I was trapped inside a fish tank filter.

There was still enough light from the surface for some visibility, but below us, the heavy chain sank into what appeared to be a bottomless black hole.

But it isn't like we're in Puget Sound, where there are creatures big enough to eat us, I reminded myself, recalling

Jared's warning: *What's down there isn't dangerous; it's the getting back up.* I moved my jaw around to clear my ears. *This is a piece of cake*—I breathed out and sank more. Emery and Jared, only feet away, sank, too. *Especially compared to swimming across the Puget Sound without a tank, BCD jacket, or wetsuit, and in the dead of winter, and I never once popped my ears*—

Suddenly, pitch black enveloped me. I froze. The absence of light was abrupt, as though we'd crossed a definitive border into a frightening new universe. My cockiness escaped with the air bubbles streaming past my face—bubbles I could hear and feel, but not see anymore.

The boys angled their dive lights downward, continuing to sink.

Keep moving, I commanded myself, releasing air from my BCD jacket so I could catch up with them, which also proved my inexperience. I began sinking as though I had suddenly packed on twenty more pounds.

Emery caught me in his beam and grabbed my arm as I started to pass him. Jared appeared at my side. He pressed the button on my BCD jacket, giving it a hit of air, and *voila*! The additional twenty pounds melted away.

Jared asked if everything was okay with a thumbs-up. I nodded, feeling like a complete idiot. Then he pinched his nose to remind me to clear my ears.

Emery pointed down. We emptied our lungs and continued into oblivion.

I can't forget anything else. I wished I'd paid more attention to Jared's tutorial.

As we sank, Jared kept his beam aimed below us, watching for obstacles, while Emery and I swept our beams over the darkness that ravenously swallowed the light. Blackness pressing in on the cylindrical beams, our dive lights pierced about ten feet into greenish water and abruptly disappeared, as though the light had been chopped off with a hatchet. I could push my vision out another twenty feet beyond where the light beams reached. I almost didn't want to know what was out there.

My Darth Vader breathing, the darkness, the jolting shock of seeing fish caught in our beams, the building pressure that made me feel like a giant hand was slowly crushing me like a soda can—this was, hands-down, the creepiest experience of my life. It was like watching a deep-sea horror film, except for the fact we weren't watching. We were living it.

Forty-three feet under water, I noted, checking my depth gauge. I cleared my ears again. My gaze followed Jared's beam down. I had hoped to see the lake floor littered with fallen trees, not a bottomless pit.

Only another twenty-eight feet to go . . .

Inhaling slowly, I pushed down rising panic. I had to keep my wits. Otherwise, Emery or Jared could get injured trying to help me.

My dive light beam spotlighted a tree, standing erect and limbless, covered in algae with water critters darting in and out of it. An underwater hotel. Another ravaged tree trunk appeared, and then another. We had entered the sunken forest.

Emery brought his hand into his beam and held up five fingers and then three to let us know we were almost at the bottom, not that he needed to. Jared's beam had collided with a thick tree trunk lying across the muddy lake floor. He had cautioned me about not touching the bottom or the trees. Doing so could damage the delicate aquatic ecosystem. Plus, the lake floor appeared deceptively solid. The mud would swallow me like quicksand if I tried to stand on it.

Emery hovered over the humungous tree trunk that Jared had spotlighted. The anchor was sunk into the lake floor next to it. He checked the depth gauge on his wrist, then motioned for us to swim left, into a cluster of rotting trees that rose from the mud like skeletons.

Of course this is where Emery would want to search, I thought, as the beam from my light grazed crooked branches that reached out like sinister fingers, long strands of algae hanging from them like streamers.

Decorations left over from a party for the dead, skittered through my mind as I followed Emery deeper into the dark, drowned forest. My beam uncovered twisted, corroded metal, debris from a shipwreck or a plane crash.

Wonder if there were survivors? I shivered. I couldn't get out of there soon enough.

Don't psych yourself out. There's nothing down here but rotting trees and fish. My eyes caught movement from the left corner of my mask. Heart in my mouth, I swept my beam toward it. Something ducked behind a tree.

It's just a fish, it's just a fish, I chanted in my head. Gasping in breathing gas, I turned my dive light off and on three times to signal the boys, and then swam toward the spot where I'd seen movement. It occurred to me that was exactly what all stupid characters in slasher flicks do: investigate, instead of running for their lives.

Just a fish, just a fish, just a fish . . .

A man moved from behind the tree into the open. I screamed, sending a barrage of bubbles up my face.

He didn't disappear when the bubbles cleared, as I'd prayed he would. Sebastian Romero, the missing owner of Champion Health Clubs, hovered over the lake floor like a phantom, staring back at me. His dark hair moved with the water, and he wore a purple T-shirt with his club's logo, Speedo warm-up pants, and no shoes. Green algae wrapped around his toes. His toenails were long and chipped, as though he hadn't cut them for weeks.

He breathed water in and out, studying me, as if contemplating what to do. Emery's and Jared's beams struck his face. Squinting, Romero raised a hairy arm to shield his eyes from the light. Then he tilted his head to the side, as though he were listening to something. His eyes wandered to the right.

Petrified, my eyeballs trailed his gaze. A scream stuck in my throat. Mr. Levy floated half a dozen feet away, barefoot, arms and legs crossed, like a genie from a bottle.

Levy stared back at Romero, showing no signs of recognition, or concern about our presence. His thin lips puckered, as though he and Romero were talking, and he didn't like what Romero had to say.

I allowed my eyes to move from them to a female and another male who had emerged from hiding, too. I thought I recognized the woman as one of the missing people from the news, but I wasn't sure. How could I be sure of anything at that very moment?

Mr. Levy's head pivoting on his pencil neck grabbed my attention. His gaze fixed on an object behind me.

My spine stiffened. Whether Levy's reaction tipped

me off or some internal alarm did, I knew danger was afoot. Instinct kicked in.

I swung my leg around, pushing it through the resistance with everything I had. My knee connected with a solid object, propelling it away.

Emery whipped his dive light around, catching a chubby, balding man in a polo shirt and khaki pants tumbling backward through the water. He disappeared into the recesses where the light couldn't reach. From the darkness, another female emerged.

I blinked, and in the split second it took for my eyelids to spring open again, her face was inches from mine. Caramel-colored locks slashed around her strong features, the ends getting battered by the bubbles escaping my regulator. Low eyebrows over almond-shaped eyes gave her a sinister appearance. Her assessing eyes were familiar, although, in my fear, I couldn't place where I had seen them, or her, before.

Another male floated next to her. Peripherally, I saw other faces that Emery and Jared's beams swept over, confirming we were surrounded. The boys instinctively drew closer to me, reconfiguring in a back-to-back triangular position, so we could better defend ourselves. All the while, I couldn't break the unrelenting stare of the woman, whom the beast within me recognized as the leader of these aqua people.

A growl rumbled deep in my throat, releasing a mass of bubbles.

Curiosity shone in the woman's intelligent, golden orbs, as though she'd perceived me to be more than human, too. Her gaze briefly evaluated Emery and Jared, then rejoined mine. Her lips curved with amusement. We were threats that she believed would soon be eliminated.

Dream on! I brought the dive light down on her skull.

There was a mass of bubbles as the aqua people attacked, their injured leader retreating. I had hurt her, but not badly. The water had cushioned the violent blow.

I threw my fists through the water, using the dive light as a weapon, fending off clawing hands that attempted to rip away our regulators and masks.

Emery and Jared fought blindly, for the most part. Thankfully, their martial arts skills enabled them to anticipate and block strikes. I caught fists flying at them, too, but couldn't move fast enough to protect the boys fully. There were just too many of the creatures.

The ruckus stirred the sediment, obstructing vision further, and I panicked as I lost sight of Emery and Jared among flying limbs and flashes of enraged faces, exposed by the dive light beams.

If these people don't kill the boys, fighting them will, I thought, as Jared's warnings of water pressure tumbled through my head. *I have to get them out of this—NOW!* I grabbed two aqua people by the hair, cracking their skulls together.

All at once, the aqua people withdrew, forming a loose circle around us.

I released the two people I had rendered unconscious. Their bodies sank like deflated balloons. The water began to settle, and I looked around anxiously for the boys. Jared was a few feet away, heaving breaths, his dive light dangling from a hand, positioned for a fight. Emery was nowhere in sight.

Emery!

Their leader entered the circle. Blood flowing from the gash on her head, she raised her arms, extending them toward the surface, and looked up, as though worshipping a sun god. Her hands began spinning faster and faster, becoming a blur and melding into the water. The motion climbed up her arms until two whirlpools shot from her arm sockets, like unrelenting tornadoes, thrashing through the filthy water. Her chin dropped, and her gaze seared us. Leaping at Jared, I grabbed hold of his BCD jacket as the whirlpools converged, sucking us in. Spinning wildly, I held him, wrapping legs around his waist, feeling the powerful vortex pull at him, trying to tear him away from me.

I won't let you go, I vowed, clamping my eyelids shut to try to quell the insane dizziness. It felt as though my guts were being ripped out. The building pressure in my ears was unbearable. If I was feeling this much pain, I couldn't imagine what Jared was experiencing.

Emery! Where are you?

Cassidy . . .

My eyes popped open to swirling mud. I had distinctly heard Emery's voice.

I'm drowning . . .

NO! Unwinding my legs from Jared, I threw our bodies diagonally against the twisting current and kicked my legs like pistons. I thought I wasn't making progress, but the vortex spit us out, firing us through the water like bullets disengaging from a gun barrel. We plowed headfirst into mud.

Help me . . .

One arm around Jared, I kicked and clawed my free

hand through the thick muck until we popped free from the sludge. The water was so dirty that I couldn't see a thing. It was like being caught in a sandstorm.

Emery, where are you?

Here . . . His voice sounded weak in my head.

I frantically swam through the dirty water toward where I thought I'd heard Emery's voice, towing Jared, who had become alarmingly still.

I'll die if anything happens to either of them.

The sediment began to settle, and I made out a floating silhouette. I prayed it would be a tree limb as I fumbled my dive light at it. My heart sank when the beam revealed a scuba diver trapped underneath a spidery branch, face-down.

Emery wasn't moving.

Chapter 19

Melding of the Minds

The sight of Emery's lifeless form left me immobile.
This cannot be happening.

Jared struggled against me. My despairing eyes fell to his face. He stared back at me with alarm as he fought to break free from my vice grip. I thought he was panicking, until he pointed at Emery. I snapped out of the shock.

Jared wants me to let him go so I can get to Emery faster. Why am I still here?

I released Jared and shot through the water. Tears of relief cascaded over the brim of my eyes when I saw air bubbles escaping Emery's regulator, flowing around his dangling head. Unconscious, he miraculously hadn't lost his regulator. He was breathing. He was alive.

But maybe not for long.

I tugged Emery free from the branches and turned him over, shining the dive light on him. His face was as white as a sheet, his eyes closed. His chest rose and fell rapidly with quick, shallow breaths.

We have to get him to the surface!

Before I had a chance to react rashly, Jared swam under Emery, wrapping his right arm beneath his, and inflated Emery's BCD jacket just enough to get him into an upright position, while holding Emery's regulator in his mouth so he wouldn't lose it. When Emery was vertical, Jared vented a little air out of the BCD jacket, so he and Emery wouldn't ascend too rapidly. He motioned for me to come up with them at the same speed.

I prayed fervently during the excruciatingly slow ascent. It frightened me beyond words to see Emery unresponsive, his head flopped against Jared's temple.

It will be okay. It will be fine. Please let it be fine.

I directed the dive light beam down and moved the beam around the sunken forest. There was no sign of Levy, Romero, the aqua people, or their leader. Agitated sediment was the only evidence that they'd been there at all. Fortunate for them, because in my present state of mind, it was difficult to predict how I would react, especially if I saw *her.*

I'll make her pay, my feral side growled. The small voice of reason that usually corrected any violent declarations had the good sense to keep quiet. However, it did risk murmuring: *Why didn't they finish us off?*

There was a disturbance in the water. I directed the beam back up to Emery and Jared. Emery's body convulsed, his eyes rolling to the back of his head. His arms thrashed the water. Jared released Emery's regulator and held him tightly from behind.

"No!" I screamed into the regulator and reached for Emery.

Jared shook his head for me to stop. I clamped my hands to my skull and squeezed.

Emery cannot die!

And he can't lose his regulator! I resolved.

I ignored Jared's order to stay away and swam up to

Emery. His desperate hands grabbed at me, but he could tear me apart, for all I cared. He wouldn't lose his regulator. I pressed my hand over it.

All at once, Emery went limp. The seizure had ended. Jared nodded at me, and we began moving upward again, more slowly than before. I kept my hand on Emery's regulator, wishing I could just see his eyelids flutter open, those twinkling coal orbs look at me. I would've given my life for that.

We passed the definitive border from pitch black into scant light, and Emery stopped breathing. My frenzied hands motioned to Jared, alerting him. His thumb pressed the valve on Emery's BCD jacket, and they rose swiftly. I assumed Jared had decided decompression injuries could be fixed; death couldn't.

Don't think that way, I commanded, choking on my tears. Water rushed into my mask, sweeping away the pool of tears that had collected at the bottom as we broke through the surface.

Jared ripped the regulator from his mouth.

"Take him," he gasped at me.

Rain pounded the lake. I collected Emery, looping my arms under his armpits. Jared tilted Emery's head back to my shoulder, pinched his nose, pressed his mouth to his, and breathed in. I felt Emery's chest expand against my arm, the air released. A breath didn't follow.

"Have to get him onboard," Jared gasped and brought his mouth to Emery's again. Rain pelted us as he continued mouth-to-mouth while I swam Emery to the yacht fifty yards away.

I threw my fins onto the yacht's deck. "What do I

do?" I shouted at Jared, hauling Emery's dead weight up the ladder. His mouth hung open. His skin was blue. Shaking from head to toe, I pulled him underneath the overhang, out of the rain.

"Get the tank and jacket off." Jared's face was calm and focused.

My trembling hands managed to work the clasps. Jared pulled off his mask, dropped down next to Emery, and took off his mask, too. Tilting Emery's jaw up and pinching his nose, Jared breathed air into his mouth. Emery's chest rose.

"Check for a pulse," Jared ordered. He sealed his mouth over Emery's again, then blew.

I searched Emery's neck.

"Nothing," I sobbed.

Straightening up, Jared placed his palms on Emery's chest, elbows straight, and began chest compressions. I gently clasped Emery's cold face in my hands and brought my ear to his purple lips.

Breathe, I prayed, listening.

" . . . ten, eleven, twelve," Jared counted under his breath.

I pressed my lips next to Emery's, whispering against his icy skin, "breathe."

"Cassidy, move." Jared pushed my head away, repositioned Emery's jaw, and began mouth-to-mouth again.

I snapped.

"Breathe, Emery!" I yelled, leaping to my feet. Seizing Emery's tank off the deck, I ran to the edge and hurled it into the lake.

"I will find you, and I will kill you!" I screamed at the water, completely out of my mind. I ripped the hood off my head, yanking my wet hair with it. Rain hammered my face. "Do you hear me? I WILL KILL YOU!"

Emery gasped a breath. I spun around. He hurled, just as Jared rolled him to his side, having anticipated Emery would throw up.

Seeing Emery alive extinguished my fury. Dissolving into tears, I ran to Emery, skidding up to him on my knees, and hugged his head, burying my face in his wet hair, paying no mind to his vomiting or weak protests. Emery was alive. That was all that mattered.

"Cass, we need to get him down to the cabin. He needs oxygen," Jared said with a labored breath as he removed Emery's fins.

"Are you okay?" I demanded, grabbing hold of his face. Why hadn't I noticed how pale Jared was before?

"Fine." He waved off my concern. "Can you carry him?"

Emery was already pushing himself up. "I can walk."

"You will not!" I ducked my head under his arm, grabbed his waist, and stood, bringing Emery to his feet with me. I reached to help Jared up, too, but he was already walking toward the ladder, his back heaving.

"Jared, what's wrong?" I asked anxiously, tugging Emery along with me. "Are you having trouble breathing?"

"I'm fine," he insisted, climbing down the ladder.

"You don't sound *fine*! Is it your lungs?" The boys were breathing and moving, but that didn't mean they hadn't sustained decompression injuries.

"I'm fine," he stated again, helping Emery down the ladder.

"You are not *fine*!" I gripped my hair by the roots and pulled hard in frustration, and jumped into the cabin the moment Jared had cleared Emery away from the ladder.

"Where's the oxygen?" I snarled, landing in a squat.

"Calm down," Emery croaked as he lowered himself to the bed. He looked awful! "Everything will be fine."

"If I hear that word one more time, I'll scream!"

Emery gave me a weak but stern look.

Jared opened a lower cabinet in the kitchen area. "Here, man." He tossed Emery a hand towel to wipe his mouth. "Are you doing all right?"

"Yes. You?" Emery fell back on the bed and closed his eyes.

"I'm good," Jared said, rummaging through the cabinet.

I stood there, helplessly looking from boy to boy, then made haste for Jared.

"Can I help?" I asked in a carefully controlled voice. I had to stop freaking out, even as the beast still growled for me to dive back into the lake and lay waste to the woman who had tried to murder us.

If I ever see her—

Stop!

"Here, I'll take that." I grabbed the emergency oxygen tank from Jared's hands. I contemplated helping him stand, but figured he'd just wave me off and tell me again that he was fine.

"Let me help you," I offered Emery, seeing he was in the process of sitting up. He suffered my assistance. What was it with these boys not wanting my help?

Jared's arm hooked my neck. "Thank you for rescuing me," he said, resting his cheek in my wet hair.

"Thank you for saving Emery. If you hadn't been there . . . " I couldn't finish.

"Thank you both," Emery said, slumping forward. "I need a moment to think."

"No. You need oxygen," I insisted.

"That you do," Jared agreed and turned on the tank. I slipped the mask over Emery's mouth. He rolled his bloodshot eyes at me.

"Now lay back and breathe." I shoved him into a reclining position.

"I've gotta get us out of here before we have unwanted visitors," Jared announced.

My feral side leapt with joy at the prospect. Cassidy mentally kicked the beast down.

"I'll keep an eye on Emery," I told him.

"Sounds good," Jared said, unzipping his wetsuit. "Cass, hand me my clothes."

I did, then turned back to Emery. As he inhaled through the mask, his eyelids fluttered shut.

"He's just resting," Jared assured.

"He needs it." I bit my lip, fighting back tears. If Jared hadn't performed CPR, we would have lost Emery.

"He's going to be okay," Jared reassured again, coming up behind me and squeezing my shoulders. I turned around and hugged him tightly.

"I love you, Jared," I choked out.

"I love you, too." His voice was tender, but edged with anxiety. "Cass, I need to get us out of here."

I nodded and released him.

"Call me if you need anything," he instructed as he climbed the ladder.

The engine powered up. Emery dozed, and I fretted over the fact that he was still wearing his soaked wetsuit.

"Emery, want to get into dry clothes?" I whispered.

He didn't respond.

I folded the other half of the comforter over him, snagged a pillow, and crawled across the mattress to situate it under his head. Lying on my side, I rested my head in the palm of my propped arm and watched Emery's chest steadily rise and fall, rise and fall. The image of Jared giving him chest compressions would haunt me forever.

"I love you, Emery," I whispered.

"Love you, too," he murmured into the oxygen mask, not opening his eyes.

I tucked the comforter underneath his chin. Then I stretched out on my back and stared at the teak ceiling, rewinding the scene at the bottom of Lake Washington over and over again.

The parasite obviously mutates its host into aqua people, I surmised, picturing the human Mr. Levy downing a Luminous Water bottle. My thoughts raced to his reaction to the other aqua people, who had appeared with their leader. He wasn't happy to see them. *Why?*

The yacht slowed down. I assumed we were at the locks. Crawling off the bed, where Emery slept soundly, I climbed up to the cockpit. Jared cut the engine. We were the only vessel waiting for passage into Puget Sound.

I wrapped my arms around his neck from behind.

"Cass, what the heck just happened?" he asked.

I knew he had been doing what I had been doing—playing the disturbing scene over and over again in his head.

Water began to drain from the chamber.

"It seems like a bad dream right now. Doesn't it?" I rested my cheek on his shoulder and combed his wet hair back with my fingers. "They're like something out of a horror movie, but they're not. Look at me, the mutants King made, Lily White . . . If we're possible, so are they. The parasite mutated them into something. I don't know what they are, other than evil. They didn't think twice about trying to kill us."

"We were in the right place at the wrong time," Jared said. "It wasn't about us. It was a showdown between them."

"I was thinking the same thing. We were just an irritation that their leader wanted to eliminate."

"We were more than that. We were a threat. If we lived, we'd tell the world about them. She thought we were dead, and we would have been if it weren't for you."

"I'm going to be sick," I hissed through my teeth, feeling rage ignite.

I pressed my forehead into Jared's shoulder, released a slow, calming breath. I wouldn't lose control again.

"I'm sorry for losing it like that," I apologized. I felt ashamed.

"You were afraid for Emery. So was I."

"I didn't mean it, you know, what I yelled. I wouldn't kill her." *At least I don't think I would.*

"I know." Jared's voice displayed no doubt. This bothered me. He should doubt me. I couldn't be trusted.

I'm dangerous, and becoming more dangerous.

Jared powered up the engine.

"I'm going to check on Emery," I told him, leaving with my dire thoughts.

Emery was still asleep. His breathing was strong and steady.

He's recovering. I sighed with relief and gathered my clothes. In the tight bathroom, I wiggled out of the wetsuit and the Neoprene shirt and shorts, cursing under my breath each time I whacked a body part against the porcelain sink or wall. Back in jeans and a T-shirt, I slipped on my sweater and untangled my wet locks with my fingers.

My ears picked up Emery moving in the next room. The oxygen tank turned off.

"You okay?" I asked, opening the bathroom door.

He stood up, looking groggy.

"Yes. Thank you." He examined me. "Good idea. Be a sport and help me out of this wetsuit."

I didn't hesitate, nor did I have the same feelings I'd had earlier, when he'd put on the wetsuit, which seemed like eons ago. We didn't talk as I helped him shed the wetsuit and pull a hoodie over his head. When I handed him his jeans, the yacht slowed down.

"Have we gone through the locks?" Emery asked, stepping into his pant legs.

I glanced away. "About ten minutes before you woke up."

"We're in the marina," he deduced. "Good. We have a lot to discuss."

"When Jared was giving you CPR, I sort of lost it and threw your tank into the lake," I confessed, flooded with familiar shame.

"So?"

"So, I'll pay for it."

The yacht came to a stop.

"No, you won't." Emery patted my cheek. "Thanks for caring enough to go beast."

"You always know the right thing to say!"

"Unlike you, I appreciate your beast. Jared and I wouldn't be here if the beast hadn't emerged to protect us."

"I don't want to think about that." I waved away the suggestion of them dying, and took a deep breath, fighting the threat of tears again. "What happened to you down there?"

"I'd like to know, too," Jared chimed in as he came down the ladder.

"I was thrown into a tree, or so the throbbing spot on the back of my head tells me. I don't remember exactly." Emery's gaze sprang to my face, as though he'd suddenly recalled something.

"What is it?" I asked.

"Let's sit," he said.

Emery plopped down on the built-in L-shaped leather sofa. I sat on the other side, diagonal to him. Jared plunked down beside me. Emery stared at me as though he were working a complex math equation in his head.

"Why are you looking at me like that?"

"I heard you call me. How is that possible?"

"You mean on the surface?" Jared asked, confused. "You were passed out, but could have heard us talking."

"No," Emery answered him, his eyes drilling into mine. "I didn't hear your voice, Jared, and not Cassidy's *actual* voice, either. I heard her speak, here." He tapped his forehead, not breaking our stares. "You asked me where I was."

"And you told me you were drowning."

Emery's expression grew intense as he slipped mental

puzzle pieces into place. I already had. Obviously, I had a new ability. What the heck was I evolving into?

"You're telepathic?" Jared asked me, incredulous.

I shrugged. I really had nothing else to say, and if I tried to talk, I might just start bawling again. I didn't want to be telepathic. How much would it take to scare everyone off who was privy to my freakishness?

"Cassidy, have you ever heard anyone in your head, aside from me?" Emery questioned.

"No," I choked out. *Darn it. Don't cry.*

"Tell me specific instances where you heard me."

"When I was lost in Elliott Bay."

"I heard you, too. I've heard you often, actually. I thought it was my imagination." He raked his hands into his damp bangs, computing.

"So you *can* read minds?" I deduced.

"What?" Jared asked, appearing uncomfortable with the notion. I knew it would scare him. I wouldn't like the idea of anyone crawling around in my head.

"Relax." Emery gave him a disarming smile. "I can't *read* minds. But there is some kind of psychic connection between Cassidy and me."

"Great!" Jared joked, but was clearly bothered. "You're *exclusively* telepathic."

Emery smirked. "Bites, doesn't it?"

Jared barked a laugh. "And I saved you, *why*?"

"Because you can't fight who you are," I said ironically. When didn't I have to fight what I was?

"Cassidy, rest assured, I catch only snippets of your thoughts, here and there," Emery clarified. "And I don't *audibly* hear your voice—"

"Well, I hear yours. How can we be telepathic at all?" The question was out before I could stop it. I averted my eyes to my fingers, fidgeting in my lap. I already knew *how*. When would I learn to just shut up?

"And why would only *you two* have this connection?" Jared added. I truly wished he hadn't.

"Haven't you figured out yet that I'm . . . *unusual*," Emery teased Jared. "In all honesty, I don't know. Do you, Cassidy?"

I looked up and met his scrutiny. "Like you said, you're unusual." I managed a smile. Now wasn't the time to tell Emery about his dad and King's conversation, not in front of Jared. Whatever King did to him, it was probably responsible for this connection between us.

"I also heard you call Mr. Levy a prig," I deflected, and almost mentioned his rude comment to Jared in the lab, before thinking better of it. Emery hadn't said the dig, he had thought it. "Oh, and the time I was about to attack Robin in the cafeteria, when she was hitting on *you*!" I jabbed Jared's ribs with my elbow.

"Me?" he asked, taken aback.

"Yes, you! And you know the situation I'm referring to! The little witch kept taunting me, and I was *this* close to, I don't know—punching her, flinging her across the room, ramming a sandwich into her foul mouth. I started to get up from the table, but then I thought Emery yelled at me to stop."

"I did, *in my head*." Emery chuckled at the memory. "I had just consigned myself to tackling you to the floor when you sat back down."

"Because you yelled at me!" I laughed, too, despite the unsettling disclosures and my shameful lying.

Why did I promise Gavin to keep my mouth shut? Emery will never forgive me.

"Don't take this personally, but I'm weirded out," Jared admitted.

"You and me both. So, let's not digress any further," Emery suggested, ending the conversation, which was okay by me. I wasn't much liking the fact that he could catch even a fragment of my thoughts.

What if he caught a snippet when we were getting into wetsuits?

Stop thinking about it!

Oh, this was scary. *All romantic thoughts are hereby banned.*

"Back to our discovery in Lake Washington," Emery went on, seemingly unaware of my internal dialogue.

"Aqua people," I offered, to divert my mind more than anything else. Of course, now that I had banned fantasizing, reminders of specific daydreams fired through my head, one after another.

"Aqua people," Emery repeated. "A cute and adequate description for this new species, for now. Obviously, we had landed smack dab in the middle of a tussle between them."

"Cassy and I thought so, too," Jared said. "We weren't the problem. Levy—or whatever he is now—and his friends were."

"I agree. It was bad timing on our part."

"You were probably unconscious when their leader unleashed her power," Jared said. Then he explained what had happened.

"That's disturbing," Emery remarked. His eyes settled on me.

I stared back, wide-eyed, wondering if he'd caught a bit of a classic Jared daydream that I was mentally batting away. It had flown into my mind from nowhere. I hadn't fostered that romantic scene for months.

"We need to go," Emery announced abruptly, standing up. "I have to get my parents up to speed ASAP. Gather everything. We can't leave behind any trace that we've been here. Jared, we can refuel the yacht later today. Take care of your wetsuits and BCD jackets. I'll collect other gear and rentals. Cassidy, straighten the comforter."

"How about I gather everything?" I said. Emery still looked pale.

"I'm fine," he assured, looking slightly perturbed.

I bit my tongue. I hated the word "fine" now.

While fixing the damp comforter, I discretely observed Emery as he put scuba masks and fins back precisely where he'd found them. As a test, I allowed a couple of banned fantasies to play through my head. His focused expression showed no indication that he'd heard them. Despite this fact, I still blushed from head to toe.

Chapter 20

Flesh, Bone, and Fallible

"Oh, crud," I groaned as our English Tudor came into view. It was 3:34 a.m., and the living room lights were ablaze.

Nate had called Jared's cell phone as we were walking out to the marina parking lot. My brother had woken up and discovered Jared was missing. He checked my room, and saw I was gone, too, but didn't want to assume Jared and I were together, since I went out to exercise every night. So he'd called Jared, who then gave my twin a brief overview of what had occurred, quietly, in case there were any prying ears about. I could have told him there weren't.

When they hung up, I thought that was that. Nate would rather eat a bucket of dirt than be a tattletale. But, obviously, my parents had found out. Not completely surprising, since I knew—from listening in on the marina parking lot conversation—that Nate hadn't been as conscious about the volume of his voice as Jared had been about his.

"Ready to face the firing squad?" I asked the boys as Emery pulled up to the curb in front of his house.

"You'll have to endure the initial tongue-lashing alone," Emery said, killing the engine. "I have to talk to my parents."

"They'll understand, Cass," Jared assured.

"We are talking about my mom and dad, right?" But even as I said this, I knew I was being unfair. My parents did nothing but understand.

~~~

"Did Nate tell you what happened?" I called out from the foyer. I couldn't see my parents yet, but I could feel their anger radiating from the living room.

Bring it on. I geared up for a fight as I shut the door.

A few more steps revealed the frowns I'd anticipated. My parents were so angry that they hadn't even bothered to get up from the sofa to chew me out, opting for stony silence instead. All this stress couldn't be good for people their age.

"Yes," Dad finally answered austerely. "I've made Gavin and Serena aware of your latest stunt. They weren't surprised. Wish I could share the feeling." He gestured for us to sit, which Jared and I promptly did. We exchanged looks; his guilty, mine indignant.

"We understand why you didn't tell us," Mom said, playing her wounded card. But there was no way I would feel guilty. And why should I? We were trying to get answers—answers that could help her.

"Nevertheless, it hurts," she said, dropping her long-suffering gaze.

"Look," I said. "You can't take this personally—"

"Cassidy, I have no patience for mincing words right now," Dad warned. "You didn't tell us because you didn't want us to stop you."

"Yeah, I didn't want you to stop me! Do you have any idea what is going on here? We're not stupid kids sneaking out to a party or something. *Lives* are at stake! Correction: *humankind* is at stake! We're trying to get answers, and I'm best equipped to get them. Not you, because you can die. *I. Can't. Die*. As it is, Emery almost did!"

Shock raced across their faces. I could almost hear Jared inwardly groan. He had sensibly not told Nate about Emery's near brush with death. But I was too mad to parse information. My parents had to get a grip!

Silence saturated the room after my revelation. You could almost hear a pin drop. My temper cooled.

Dad leaned forward on his knees and folded his hands thoughtfully, considering his words. It was something I could admit, especially in that moment, that I needed to learn to do.

His solemn eyes met mine. They looked so weary.

"This isn't easy for me," he confessed, making me feel even worse. "I'm doing my best. The need to protect you supersedes, regardless of your abilities. It's difficult to stop being a father—"

"I don't want you to, Dad."

He smiled. "I won't—not ever. However, I will give you room to be what you have always been: a hero. If for nothing else, so you'll allow me into your world. I realize I can't fully comprehend what you have experienced, and *are* experiencing, with these changes, but please let me in—let *us* in. Your mother and I could surprise you."

"Of course I will." I couldn't believe Dad had called me a hero.

"Thank you." His loving gaze held mine. "I also

realize you are well aware of how tragically this evening could have ended, and almost did. Despite Emery's confidence, he is flesh and bone, and fallible. And Jared, in case it has escaped your notice, so are you."

"Yes, sir," Jared said quietly.

"I know, too, Dad," I admitted. "Trust me, I'm angry with myself. I shouldn't have let them come with me." *How could I have been so foolish?*

"I didn't give you a choice, Cass," Jared reminded. I opened my mouth to object, but he dove right into an apology. "I'm sorry I put you in a bad position." He looked my parents in the eyes. "I'm sorry I put all of you in a bad position."

"Thank you, Jared," Dad said. "And don't think I don't understand your need to get answers. Your father is involved with this, to some degree."

Surprised by Dad's bluntness, I peeked sidelong at Jared to gauge his reaction. He took the truth like a man, just as my dad had given him opportunity to do.

"I know he is," Jared agreed. "Thank you for understanding, Mr. Jones."

"Drake," Dad corrected him. "If you ever need to talk, I'm here for you."

"I appreciate that, Drake," Jared said, regarding my dad with respect. I couldn't help but think about all his father was missing out on.

Dad smiled at him and then looked back at me. His mouth flattened into a stern line.

"Regarding your previous statement, my dear daughter: No, you shouldn't have gone along with Emery's plan. Don't challenge me on this," he warned, as I began to open my mouth. "I know Emery, and this undertaking has his name written all over it. He is brilliant, yes. But he is also a fifteen-year-old boy who takes tremendous pride in exerting his independence, which at times has blinded him to the foolishness of his actions. At the very least, he should have told Gavin. That would have been the responsible thing to do."

"You're right." I could make no bones about it. We had to stop being stupid kids.

"Let's make a pact. You don't hide anything from us, and we will discuss the situations that arise like adults." Dad glanced at Mom.

She nodded her approval.

My gaze lingered on her, as a whispering fear that had been chipping away at my brain piped up: *This parasite is in her. Will she be the next missing person?*

If she disappears, I'll know where to look for her, I comforted myself. The poor families of the missing people came to mind. How relieved would they be to know their loved ones were safe and sound at the bottom of Lake Washington?

I considered this. *Maybe relieved isn't the right word.*

"Deal, Cass?" Dad asked.

"Deal," I agreed, and then proceeded to make good on my word, sharing all that had transpired since the night before last.

There were moments during the account when I suspected my parents regretted the bargain they'd made with me.

When I finished the play-by-play, Dad released a long breath that whistled between his pursed lips. His golden-blond hair stuck out every which way from repeatedly running his hands through it as I had talked. It looked like he'd styled it with a fork. He'd wanted the uncensored truth. He got it.

"The reporter in me wants to pick up the phone and call our news team," he confessed. "The public should be alerted, regardless of liability. But that is emotion speaking. Where is the solid evidence?" Dad stood up and paced the room, deliberating out loud. "Missing locals alive in Lake Washington. Ludicrous, to say the least, and three teens are the only eyewitnesses—my daughter being one. What could the repercussions be, if Cassidy's name slipped out to the media? Or for running the story prematurely?"

"Is it cool if I answer that, Drake?" Jared asked.

"Please."

"Guilty parties would be tipped off, evidence destroyed, and maybe this would ruin the chance for a cure," Jared projected. "And if Cassidy *or* Emery are linked to any of this, the wrong people might put two-and-two together. Plus, you didn't see what happened down there. Cassidy didn't hold back."

I eyed Jared, wondering how I had appeared during the attack. Clearly not very human.

"My thoughts exactly," Dad said, pointing at Jared. "Nothing can be done, not yet. I have to talk to Gavin. Emery is probably on the phone with him now." He swung around to the foyer and suggested, as he made haste for the Phillips's house, "Why don't you three try to get some sleep?"

"Like that's going to happen," I called after him.

~~~

After two very sleepless hours passed, my dad returned home. I considered heading him off on his way to his room for an update, but dismissed the idea. He was exhausted, and needed what little sleep he could get for the Patrick Grimm interview, looming late morning. He definitely had to be on top of his game.

However, after I'd eavesdropped on my parents' whispers for several minutes, I changed my mind.

I shrugged into a robe as I made my way to their room and rapped my knuckles lightly on their door.

Dad answered it. "You're up?"

"How could I sleep?"

"I'm with you," Mom agreed, shuffling up. She had dark circles under her eyes, and her face was scrunched in pain. I wondered if she was still experiencing Luminous withdrawals.

"You okay, Mom?"

She smiled faintly. "Just a headache. Let's talk in the kitchen. Coffee will help."

"Coffee sounds like a plan," Dad agreed.

In the kitchen, while filling the coffeemaker with water, he explained. "Apparently, the CDC's microbiologists are dumbfounded by this parasite. According to Serena, there is no classification for the species. She says the parasite is elusive. They haven't been able to find it in infected mice. They suspect the parasite attaches to brain tissue and the brain cavity—"

Mom scraped at a scratch in the cherry wood with her fingernail. Her thoughts appeared to be elsewhere.

"My unscientific interpretation of what Serena has shared is that the parasite can cloak itself, like it does in water. It'll be interesting to see how she'll introduce your experience into their research without revealing the actual occurrence." Dad joined us at the table, studying Mom with concern. "Lizzy, why don't you try to get more sleep?"

Mom shook her head, wincing. She obviously had a headache. "What is Gavin going to do?"

"Yesterday, two CIA agents *illegally* posed as King County health inspectors. In other words, this isn't a government-sanctioned investigation. Gavin pulled some strings, called in favors. They didn't find anything incriminating at Luminous Water's plant, however. Water samples they'd collected were sent to Serena. She hasn't received them yet. Unfortunately, the burden of proof lies on her and her team. The CDC has to provide evidence that the parasite is harmful before an investigation will be launched."

"That is so lame!" I blurted.

"Completely," Mom agreed. "The parasite is in the water, one in each bottle, and when they're put together they glow like Christmas lights! Isn't that enough *evidence* for an arrest and a product recall?"

"I know, Lizzy. I'm frustrated, too." Dad suddenly appeared almost a decade older than he had a minute beforehand. "We bear the weight of damning evidence that can't be shared without putting our daughter's life at risk."

"Well, that makes me feel great," I grumbled. "Maybe we should stop being so selfish and come clean. It's only my life, compared to thousands, if not millions."

"It's more than your life, and you know it," Dad replied.

He was right. Anyone who unlocked the magic combination and recreated my virus would rule the world.

An army of me—that's a frightening thought. Almost as frightening as the army Arthur King is probably building.

"Ignorance is bliss," I said in reply to Dad. "Did Gavin tell you what's next?"

"He's flying home later today to brief the Seattle Police Department. Since there is no evidence of any crime at this time, local law enforcement will investigate. Gavin believes they'll handle the case as a HAZMAT situation, a hazardous materials incident."

Dad's cell phone rang. He picked it up from the table and handed it to me. "My glasses are upstairs," he explained.

I read the text. It was from Emery.

"Emery is on his way over," I told my parents, rising from the table to let him in.

I opened the door. He looked exhausted, too. "Long time no see," I greeted. "How are you feeling?"

"Good as new," he whispered, entering the foyer. "Where's Jared?"

"In bed. Why?"

Emery motioned for me to keep my voice down. He obviously didn't want me to wake Jared.

"Your parents?" he asked.

"In the kitchen. What's happened?"

Emery gestured with his iPad for me to follow him to the kitchen. "Did Jared call his dad about the men following him?"

"Yes. When you and Mickey were getting Cyrus. Why?"

Without answering me, he entered the kitchen.

"Good morning," he greeted my parents. "I'm assuming you haven't seen the breaking news yet?"

"What now?" Mom asked with alarm.

Emery swung a long leg over a chair and sat down. "Ariel Vilvary and his bodyguard were found dead."

My insides curled. "What?"

"Where?" Dad asked, taking the iPad that Emery handed him.

"In Vilvary's swimming pool. They were drowned."

Chapter 21

Interview with the Enemy

To get more details, Dad called the reporter at Channel Five News who was covering Vilvary's death, while Mom and I watched the report again. The segment didn't mention any gunshot wounds or fatal blows to the head, just that both men had apparently drowned.

"When Jared called his dad from Mickey's car, his dad said he would take care of things," I told Mom and Emery.

Mom released a slow, haggard breath, scrubbing her face with her palms. Emery stared at me, thinking. I had a good idea what was churning through his head. But was Owen Wells capable of murder?

Dad hung up with his colleague. "Drowning appears to be the cause of death," he informed us. "From what Charity learned, there were no visible wounds or injuries that could have caused death."

"Meaning both men were drowned while conscious and not disabled," Emery clarified.

"Jared's dad must be one of *them*," I concluded, feeling sick. Maybe he hadn't been among our attackers last night because he'd been busy killing his former client.

"From what we've witnessed, I'd say there's a strong chance," Emery agreed.

"*Shh*," I cautioned, before anyone else could contribute. "I hear Jared. He's coming."

Full of dread, I dropped my forehead to the tabletop, shutting my eyes. How would Jared take the news? My ears followed him and Nate through the hallway and down the stairs, whispering so as not to wake anyone up, clueless about the coming shock.

"Why's everyone up?" Nate asked with alarm as they entered the kitchen. "What's wrong with Cass?"

I couldn't bear to lift my head. I just wanted to shrivel up and blow away. My heart broke for Jared.

"Please sit down, boys," Dad requested solemnly.

Jared pulled out the chair next to me. His arm brushed mine as he sat. I straightened up and found his hand under the table, but couldn't bring myself to look him fully in the face. His palm was moist. He knew bad news was coming.

Dad broke the news, and a torturous silence ensued. Jared squeezed my hand and finally cleared his throat.

"Vilvary and his bodyguard—they were the only victims?" he asked.

The guilt edging his voice shattered me. Jared felt responsible for the deaths of the two men, which meant he believed his father was a murderer.

"To my knowledge," Dad answered.

I peeked sidelong at Jared's profile. His face was deadpan.

"Keep in mind that the cause of death is a presumption at this time," Dad went on. "Autopsies could reveal more."

"Like poison," Nate interjected.

"It doesn't matter how they died." Jared stood. "If it's cool, I need some time alone."

"Of course," Mom said, eyes full of sympathy.

I captured Jared's dangling fingers. He pulled his hand away.

"Thanks for telling me." Jared turned to go.

"Don't call your father," Emery ordered.

I wanted to smack him.

Jared shot Emery a glare over his shoulder.

"I wouldn't do that," he said coldly, then left the room.

"Dude, that was heartless," Nate chided Emery in a whisper.

"So is murder."

I started to get up.

"Cassidy, give him space to work this out," Mom advised.

I nodded, then sat back down. Why did everything always have to be so terrible?

"We're jumping to conclusions," Dad pointed out. "We only have the details that have been released to the media. Vilvary had a substantial enemy list. Plus, we don't know for certain if he had hired the men who attacked Jared and followed him. His involvement is complete conjecture."

"That's right." I breathed a sigh of relief. "Gavin drew the conclusion that Vilvary was involved in the first place— based on complete conjecture. And Mr. Wells denied it, remember? He said Vilvary had no issues with him. Maybe his death *is* a coincidence."

"We'll know soon enough. I'm sure Vilvary has security cameras," Emery said. Then he steered the conversation toward matters he deemed more critical. "Drake, we need to go over your approach with the Grimm interview, especially in light of last night's events."

"Events," I muttered. Only Emery would describe his near-death experience as an "event."

~~~

Dad, Ben, Emery, and I headed for the Luminous Water offices a little after ten a.m. Jared and Nate had gone to school. When Dad had suggested that Jared stay home, he politely declined, pointing out, "No one will be following me anymore. Vilvary is dead."

Dad didn't argue. Despite his earlier encouragement, he believed, as we all did, that the threat had been eliminated.

"So, Serena found some kind of weird parasite in Luminous Water?" Ben summed up. My dad had shared selective information with him.

Ben didn't know specifics about the parasite, its link to the missing people, or that said missing people were now slumming around the bottom of Lake Washington. He also didn't know the aqua people were most likely behind the Lake Washington Monster sightings. The missing locals, the sightings, and the parasite—they'd all come together the moment Mr. Levy came out of hiding, floating in the water like Aladdin's genie.

"Yes," Dad confirmed from the driver's seat. "The interview is a cover. The goal is to determine if Grimm is aware that there is a parasite in his product, without mentioning the parasite, of course."

"And you're not just coming out and asking him *why*? You are a reporter, and that is what reporters do."

"There's an investigation the public is unaware of,"

Dad explained vaguely. Ben also didn't know Gavin was CIA. "We don't want to compromise it in any way."

"Understood," Ben said. He shivered and made a face. "Glad I never tried the stuff."

You have no clue, Ben, I thought.

"Drake, if you don't mind my saying, you look like you've been hit by a semi," he observed.

"It was one of those nights," Dad replied dryly.

Glancing out his window, Emery hid a smile behind his hand.

I scowled at him, not seeing the humor in giving my poor dad another one of "those nights."

Dad pulled into the business complex where the Luminous Water offices were located, an uninspired white building lined with tinted windows.

Luminous Water was on the fifth floor. We entered the reception room, and the cheerful smile of a young male receptionist greeted us. Recognizing him, I almost tripped over my feet. He hadn't looked so friendly clawing at my face seventy feet underwater.

"May I help you?" he twanged.

I peeked at Emery. With a pleasant expression, he gave his head an almost imperceptible nod, indicating that he recognized the receptionist as well.

"Yes, hello, I'm Drake Jones from Channel Five News. I have an interview scheduled with Patrick Grimm."

Emery stepped on my toe. Understanding the signal, I hiked up my gaping jaw and forced my eyes to glance around the room, as though admiring it. My thoughts were so scrambled, I wasn't even sure if I could remember how to walk.

"Great to meet you, Mr. Jones. My name is Josh," the aqua man introduced himself. "I'll let Patrick know you're here." Smiling, he said into the phone, "Hey, Patrick. Drake Jones is here . . . Will do." He hung up and explained, smiling his almost-too-pleasant smile, "Forgive the informality, Mr. Jones. We're like family at Luminous Water."

I felt my jaw slacken again. Family? Guess that was one way to put it.

"That's wonderful," Dad replied. I was glad he didn't know the truth about Josh. Otherwise, he might be acting as weird as I was, studying a handy brochure about water treatment as though it were the Declaration of Independence.

"You're lucky," Dad added.

"Don't I know?" Josh agreed and stood. "Patrick is a great boss *and* a great guy. You'll really like him. Follow me, please."

As we trailed him into a hallway, he gestured to the camera perched on Ben's shoulder. "I see you're the cameraman."

Before Ben could answer, a smiling woman stepped out of an office. My heart skipped a beat as I recognized her, too.

"Hey, Mary Jo," Josh greeted her, then directed his toothy grin toward Emery and me. "Are you Mr. Jones's kids?"

"She is. I'm not," Emery answered with ease. My tongue appeared inoperable. "We're doing a career thing in one of our classes. Mr. Jones was cool about us following him around."

"Sounds like fun." Josh gave me a strange look.

I ducked my head to hide my face. What if he recognized me? The scuba mask and regulator had concealed our faces, and the hood had covered our hair, but who knew what abilities these human hosts had?

"Well, here we are," Josh announced and knocked on an office door. PATRICK GRIMM, PRESIDENT AND CEO was etched into a brass plate mounted to it.

"*Entrare!*" Patrick Grimm responded. I remembered his voice from the news broadcast.

Josh pushed open the door.

Smiling, Grimm rose from a sleek black-lacquered desk topped with a thick slab of glass.

My eyes narrowed. He had to be one of them, too. However, there was no way to tell. So far, all the aqua people I'd seen appeared like any other human, until they were submerged in water.

"Hello, Mr. Jones." Grimm rounded the desk to shake Dad's hand. "It's a pleasure to meet you. I'm honored you'd interview me for *In the Spotlight*."

"The pleasure is all mine, Mr. Grimm." Dad shook his hand. "I appreciate you making the time. Please, call me Drake."

"Only if you'll call me Patrick."

"I look forward to learning more about Luminous Water, especially your numerous charitable acts. Patrick, this is my cameraman, Ben Johnson."

"Nice to meetcha, Patrick," Ben said, shaking hands.

"Likewise, Ben. Did you go?" Patrick indicated to Ben's X-Games T-shirt.

"I did! It was awesome! You?"

"Nah, haven't had the chance. But it's on my bucket list, along with a zillion other things. I've seen the world a few times over, but can't seem to get enough of all it has to offer."

"I know what you mean," Ben said and then aimed his grin at Emery and me. "Patrick, this is Drake's daughter, Cassidy, and our friend Emery."

"Hmmmm . . ." Patrick rubbed the cleft on his chin, attempting to give us a suspicious look, which his grin utterly defeated. "Playin' hooky, huh? Not that I'd throw any stones. I cast a line in ol' Mr. Disick's pond more than I ever saw the inside of a classroom." He let out a hearty laugh, holding his thumb and forefinger slightly apart. "Maybe that's a *slight* exaggeration."

"Watch him," a woman's voice warned in a Southern drawl. "He's apt to do that."

I turned around with everyone else, and fire suddenly blasted through my veins. The beast lurched from the recesses of my mind, howling and bloodthirsty. *IT'S HER!*

Emery's fingers dug into my wrist.

I glared at the woman through slit eyes. A growl rumbled deep in my throat.

Emery increased the pressure.

I shook the haze from my head and swallowed the growl. *No, I will not thrust my foot into her gut,* I told myself, unclenching the fist connected to the wrist that Emery was squeezing the tar out of. *No matter how much I want to.*

"—And beware of his big fish stories," the woman continued, seemingly unaware of my severe reaction to her. "He used to catch bass *this* big in Mr. Disick's pond." She held her slim arms wide, as her long legs on high heels clicked their way toward Patrick. "When I was ten, I believed him."

She pulled up alongside Grimm. Her lips, defined with liner and lustrous lipstick, held a coquettish smile. Her caramel-colored hair was immaculate, but I envisioned it wild, thrashing around in the water, across the sharp edges of her face. Her neat hair revealed a pronounced widow's peak that resembled a spear, which I had missed last night. I wanted to pluck it from her forehead, strand by strand.

Grimm caught her cheek with a kiss, then draped an arm around her shoulders. "Meet my partner-in-crime and the gullible recipient of my tall tales—"

The woman snorted and slapped his stomach.

"—The beautiful and brilliant Constance Grimm, undeniably my better half."

"Well, if you insist," Constance teased and turned up the wattage of her smile. She had the whitest teeth I'd ever seen. "Wonderful to meet you, gentlemen, and my lady." She slightly bowed her head to me.

Dad, Ben, and Emery returned the sentiment and shared their names while I worked the corners of my mouth up into a rigid half-smile. It was like stirring a stick in setting cement. I had never met such a spirited woman in my life, and under normal circumstances, I could have smiled at her playfulness. But these were far from normal circumstances. She had tried to murder Emery and Jared!

Was it her or the parasite that had tried to drown us?

Is there even a "her" left in there?

That was something to consider. Was the real Constance Grimm no more than a vessel now? Did *she* have any control over her mind?

"And who might you be, pretty lady?"

Constance's voice knocked me out of my thoughts. I shifted my eyes, which had drifted to her thick brass choker and up to her golden, almond-shaped eyes. Her daughter had inherited her eyes. That's where I'd seen them before.

"Cassidy Jones." The words sounded oddly hoarse.

"Well, pleased to meet you, Cassidy." Constance scrutinized me. Her smile didn't waver, but I could see that something about me bothered her. Maybe I wasn't the only one who recognized eyes.

"I'm envious. I've always wanted red hair. I've been a redhead twice in my life, but could never pull it off."

"Red?" Patrick feigned confusion. "I recall *orange*."

"Stop!" Constance gave him a little shove. "He's been giving me a bad time for years. We grew up together."

"And she wouldn't have a thing to do with me all through high school. Broke my heart." Pouting, Patrick patted over his heart, as though trying to console it. "I blame her for my enlisting in the military the day after graduation."

"*Patrick Grimm*, you know full well that had nothing to do with me!" Constance protested, wagging a finger in his face. "He'd been accepted to Duke, but thought that college would cramp his style. He wanted freedom, to see the world. So what did he do? Join the United States Army." She rolled her eyes.

"Yes," Patrick conceded, good-natured. "I was a lost pup for a long, long time. When my term was up, I left the Army so quickly that heads spun. Then I aimlessly wandered this grand country of ours until I found my way back home to Connie. She'd come to her senses by then, and realized I was the man for her. The rest, as they say, is history."

"Yep, that's it, Drake. Guess y'all can pack up and go home now." Constance winked. "I won't hold you up anymore. Good luck getting straight answers from this fine specimen of a man. In all honesty, I couldn't be more proud of anyone. Patrick is an inspiration—a visionary—as you will soon see for yourself. Give Josh a holler if you need anything. Again, wonderful to meet y'all."

Constance left the room.

I stared at the doorway she had disappeared through, trying to get my mental bearings. My instinctual reaction to her, and the lively, warm woman who had just treated us as though we were neighbors, had my mind spinning in a cyclone of contradictions. At least the confusion had tempered my feral side. I wasn't seething with murderous hatred—for the moment.

I redirected my attention toward Patrick, who was chatting with Dad and Ben as he helped them organize the room for the interview.

What is in there with him? I wondered.

Emery, are you freaking out as much as I am? I sent him. When I didn't hear his response in my head, I glanced at where he leaned against the wall next to me. He watched the men, giving no indication that he'd received my transmission.

"Cassidy, honey, why don't you wheel my desk chair back there?" Patrick suggested when he noticed Emery and me standing in the back, while Ben fitted him with a microphone. He and Dad sat in the identical leather chairs angled interview-style. "Emery, there's a conference room a few doors down on the left. Grab a chair for yourself."

"I will. Thank you, Mr. Grimm."

"Patrick, young man."

"Patrick," Emery amended with a smile.

I didn't need telepathy to know what he was thinking. Unbeknownst to Grimm, he'd given Emery permission to snoop around.

"Don't get lost," I teased Emery in a whisper as he pushed off the wall.

He winked a twinkling black eye at me.

As I fetched Patrick's plush chair, I realized, with some surprise, that I hadn't told my parents about the odd connection Emery and I shared. It had slipped my mind, in light of the aqua people. I wondered if Emery had told his parents. I somehow doubted it.

"By the way, Patrick, Josh gives your company a good first impression." Dad fiddled with the microphone clipped to his collar. "He's a nice young man. Is he also from your hometown?"

"Yep, as are half of my employees."

Owen Wells's scent curled up my nose. My muscles tensed. What was *he* doing here?

"Really? Then why did you start Luminous Water in Seattle, and not in Louisiana?"

I tucked a hair behind my ear, listening to his feet tread against the carpeted hall. They were quick, purposeful steps, as though he were in a hurry for a meeting. He greeted a woman named Samantha.

"I decided to launch Luminous here on the recommendation of a family friend, a snake of a lawyer who was a rotten kid, too. To this day, he can't own up to being second-fiddle on the basketball court." Patrick spoke more loudly as Mr. Wells drew near, as though he somehow knew he was in the hallway.

"That's because you cheat," Mr. Wells responded, strolling into the room. The addition of his voice startled Dad and Ben. He gave me a cursory glance and then redirected his attention toward the men.

Patrick hooted. "Speak of the Devil! Whatcha doing here, ya ol' *benchwarmer*?"

"To make sure you don't discredit the Luminous Empire," Mr. Wells teased. Sighing, he crossed his arms. "Of course, the only way to ensure that won't happen will be to gag you."

"Love ya, too, brother." Patrick grinned at Jared's dad.

Their bantering tangled my emotions further. It was so—human. They appeared to genuinely care for one another, and seemed in total control of their own minds. But then again, so had Constance and Josh.

"Actually, this is business, not pleasure, though I always take pleasure in watching Patrick stick his foot in his mouth. I have documents we need to go over," Mr. Wells explained to Grimm. "But it can wait. Mind if I crash the party, in the meantime?"

"Crash away! Ya always do anyhow. Cassidy, could you get another chair? And maybe find Emery while you're at it? *My* left must be *his* right."

In other words, Emery was taking too long to get a chair. I had to agree.

"Okay." I managed a fleeting smile for Mr. Wells. As I started around him to get out the door, he rocked back on his heels to block me, making it appear unintentional.

"You and Emery are both here?" he queried, looking at me squarely.

"We're here for a c-class project." I wanted to slap myself for stuttering. I was sure smooth. "Jared isn't in our class."

His eyes narrowed. I could feel my cheeks redden. Why did I mention Jared? He hadn't even asked about him. "Jared is at school today?"

I nodded. I didn't trust myself to speak.

"Frankly, I'm surprised, after what happened yesterday. You must have been scared," he baited.

I shrugged, glancing over my shoulder at the three men. Grimm watched us.

"I can't believe his mother would let him go to school."

I swung my eyes to Mr. Wells. "She isn't in town." I heard the bitterness in my voice. He heard it, too. I could see on his face that it shocked him.

Without responding, he moved aside so I could get by him. In the hallway, I bent over, clasped my kneecaps, and drew air deep into my lungs.

"What happened?" Emery whispered, pushing a chair toward me.

I straightened up and looked at him, afraid to speak.

Someone could be listening.

These aqua people might have enhanced hearing, for all we knew. Grimm had known Mr. Wells was coming down the hall.

"We need to get another chair," I said.

Concentrating on me, Emery nodded. He set the chair against the wall and motioned for me to follow, leading me to the conference room. Once inside, he pulled me into an embrace.

"In case you're right and the offices are bugged, or they can hear us," he explained. "There's a security camera behind me. It's live."

I peeked at the camera over his shoulder. The little red light was on. How weird was that?

"There was a camera in each office I wandered into looking for the conference room," Emery continued. "The camera in the reception room came on when Josh announced our arrival. Grimm must have turned them on then. I'm sorry for hugging you like this. But standing around whispering would heighten their suspicion. Sneaking off to snuggle won't. What upset you, aside from the majority of this staff trying to drown us?"

"The majority?"

"I recognized three other employees, in addition to Constance and Josh."

"You said 'heighten their suspicion.' You think they're suspicious?"

"I think they are wary, and for good reason. They are trying to hijack human bodies. What happened in Grimm's office?"

"Jared's dad is here, and he *is* suspicious. He asked why Jared was at school today."

"He was feeling around to see if Jared suspects he murdered Vilvary," Emery concluded. "He knows Jared wouldn't go to school unless he believed the threat was gone. Did you sense he knows about the yacht?"

My breath caught. I hadn't thought of that.

"Don't worry, Cassidy. If he does, he'll believe the cover story."

The cover story was that Jared had met a college girl at Cherry Street Coffeehouse and took her for a joyride in the yacht. In my opinion, it was a weak story.

"*Don't worry?*" I repeated. "Look where we are, and who or *what* we are surrounded by."

"It'll work out. It always does," Emery reassured. "We'd better get back in there."

As we each lugged a chair into Grimm's office, where the interview was in full swing, I couldn't come up with a single scenario in which this particular situation would work out.

Chapter 22

Dominance Display

We left the Luminous Water offices and headed toward the company plant so Ben could get footage for the segment. Patrick Grimm had bowed out from accompanying us, citing a meeting he couldn't miss. He appeared quite disappointed by this, and assured us that his plant manager, another friend from his hometown, would take good care of us.

Once we had piled into Dad's Volvo, Ben said, "Patrick and Constance are over-the-top, but I didn't pick up any bad vibes."

I made a mental note not to trust Ben's "vibe" barometer.

"They may not be aware of the parasite," Dad granted.

I glanced at Emery. Was it possible that my dad had fallen for their act? After all, he was missing critical information: Constance and most of her staff had tried to drown us.

Emery shook his head.

I shrugged, flipping my palms up. Was he saying, "No, your dad is savvy," or, "No, your dad doesn't get it"?

He grinned and looked out his window, leaving interpretation up to me.

I huffed. *A lot of help you are.*

Emery kept staring out the window.

Did you catch me ogling you on the yacht? I dared.

Emery didn't even flinch.

Thank heavens that failed, I thought, slowly exhaling and sinking into my seat. Why would I take a risk like that? Was I completely nuts?

~~~

The tour of the plant revealed nothing, other than more friendly aqua people. If I hadn't recognized a couple of faces from the previous night, I would have thought they were just normal human beings.

The whole way home, I fidgeted in my seat, anxious to enlighten Dad about *what* had been entertaining us for the past three hours. If only Ben hadn't been with us.

Relax, Emery would mouth to me periodically during the drive—to which I'd roll my eyes to and readjust my backside on the seat. How could I relax? Grimm aimed to take over the human race.

"Finally," I muttered under my breath when Dad turned down our street. Ben had been rambling for ten minutes about alien parasites being studied in top-secret military labs.

"I'll put down a hundred bucks, *right now*, that within a week Luminous Water is shut down and you never hear another peep from Serena about parasites again," he predicted passionately. He looked back at Emery. "No disrespect to your mom, dude. She'd only be following the orders of the powers that be."

"None taken," Emery assured. "And you're probably right."

240

I was out of the car before Dad had come to a complete stop. Instantly, my eyes were drawn to Emery's front door, which was opening. There were no Marathon workers that day, so I knew it was Gavin. He was home now, and had seen us drive up on his monitor.

"Gavin!" I hollered. I shot across the street, up his front walk and porch steps, and lunged into his arms, not caring one iota how odd my actions would appear to Ben. I was so relieved he was back. He'd know what to do.

"That bad, huh?" he asked.

"You have no idea," I said, my feet dangling over the ground. Gavin was a mountain of a man.

He set me down and watched Emery say goodbye to Ben. "I'm taking it my son hasn't told me everything about last night?"

"I don't know what he told you."

"Only what he *thought* I needed to know," Gavin replied, his eyes fixed on Emery crossing the street. "That boy is too much like me."

"Hey, Gavin!" Ben shouted from his Explorer, waving.

Gavin smiled at him and lifted his hand, then locked his eyes on Emery again.

Ben drove off and Dad headed our way, cell phone to his ear. I assumed he was calling Mom. She had told us that morning she had an auction meeting and would take Chazz with her. Weird how normal life continued on, despite it all.

"How much time do we have?" Emery inquired.

"Plenty. I won't brief SPD until the morning." Gavin's gaze shifted to Dad. "How are you, Drake?"

"Puzzled," Dad answered, climbing steps. He looked

at me. "It was the Grimms, wasn't it? They attacked you last night."

My dad was sharper than I'd given him credit for. "Patrick wasn't there, but Constance was," I told him. "She was the woman who shot whirlpools from her arm sockets."

Emery considered this thoughtfully. Gavin watched him.

"You didn't see this, did you?" Gavin deduced. His eyes narrowed on his son. "Why is that?"

"I was unconscious," Emery admitted, then walked into the house.

Gavin gave Dad an exasperated look, and Dad responded with a sympathetic one. I was glad they had one another to commiserate with. Having kids like Emery and me couldn't be easy.

~~~

We sat around the kitchen table, joined by Serena on Skype. Emery and I discussed which of the Luminous employees we'd encountered at the bottom of Lake Washington the previous night.

"Guess this clears up the Lake Washington Monster sightings," Gavin surmised.

"Yeah, there are no mermaids," I agreed, picturing Constance's caramel hair being battered by air bubbles from my regulator. Would I ever forget that image, or the one of Emery convulsing in the water?

Gavin studied me. "Cassidy, why don't you tell us what happened last night from your perspective, since we've only received a secondhand report." He gave Emery a pointed look.

"What is this?" Serena asked with alarm. She tried to move around on her end to see her son through the camera. Gavin aided her by angling his laptop at Emery.

A grin twitched at Emery's mouth. What was wrong with him? *His parents were going to be furious with us.*

"Emery got knocked out and Jared had to give him CPR," I blurted.

Serena gasped in horror. "Underwater?"

"Yes, *underwater*. I didn't see how. I found him caught under some branches. He had a seizure on the way up, then stopped breathing about twenty feet from the surface. Jared brought him up slowly so he wouldn't get more injured than he already was, and started CPR on him as soon as we got to the top. He kept it up as we swam Emery to the yacht. I got him on board, and he still wasn't breathing, so Jared did chest compressions and mouth-to-mouth—" I stopped talking to wipe away a tear. I hadn't realized I was still so shaken up.

Serena grew pale on the screen, and Gavin didn't move. Emery wore a humble expression. This was the first time he'd heard the details of his rescue. I don't think he'd fully appreciated how traumatizing the event had been for Jared and me.

"We owe Cassidy and Jared a great debt," Gavin said quietly.

"And I owe an apology," Emery added, meeting the eyes of everyone at the table. "I'm sorry for taking matters into my own hands and risking our lives. It was foolish."

A sob escaped Serena. She turned from the screen, covering her face with her hands. Emery appeared shocked by her anguish. But what did he expect? She was his mother.

"Sweetheart," Gavin said in a pained voice, his fingertips touching his wife's weeping image on the screen.

"I am so sorry, Mom," Emery apologized again. "Don't cry. Obviously, I'm fine."

Gavin grabbed Emery and pulled him fiercely into his arms.

"This has to stop," he whispered, smoothing his son's hair with his hand. He kissed his temple.

Dad put his arm around my shoulders to comfort me. This did have to stop. Emery and I couldn't selfishly worry our families like this anymore. We had to grow up.

"I know." Emery's voice had grown thick. He leaned back to look his dad in the eyes. "I give you my word." He forced his eyes to Serena's stricken image on the computer screen. "I give my word, Mom. No more acting alone without consultation."

"I'll tell if he tries," I vowed.

"Cassidy, I gave my word," Emery protested.

"Okay, he won't. He gave his word." Emery's word was gold. "I'm sorry, too. I'm going to admit something. I go along with Emery's schemes because I think I can defeat anything. I can't, especially these aqua people on their own turf. Like I told Emery and Jared, they're like water gods. What Constance did was pure magic. How is it possible? How are *they* possible?"

"We have a theory." Serena turned to the camera, dabbing her wet cheeks with her sleeve, composing herself. She clearly didn't want to discuss her son's near-miss with death anymore. The idea would ravage any parent.

"There is a phenomenon in nature that we refer to as coevolution, in which two or more interdependent species reciprocally alter one another's development. The yucca moth and yucca plant are an example of this. The plant's shape has reformed so that only this tiny moth can pollinate them; the moths, in turn, lay their eggs on the yucca flower. Their larvae grow in the ovary and eat the yucca seeds. This is a *mutualistic* relationship. Then consider the garter snake and rough-skinned newt, an example of *predator and prey* coevolution. Newts produce a powerful neurotoxin in their skin. Through a series of genetic mutations, the garter snake has developed resistance to the poison. Now, our case may be an example of *host and parasite* coevolution. The change occurs at a molecular level, reordering the genetic code of the host—"

"Mutating them into another species?" Dad interrupted, disturbed, just as we all were.

"Yes, with a similar genotype of the parasite. As you already know, this parasite is an unprecedented organism— complex, unrivaled, and extremely puzzling. We can't trace its genome to any life-form that originated on this planet."

"Whoa, babe!" Gavin held his hand up. "Are you suggesting this is extra-terrestrial?"

"At this time, we have no other theories."

"Have you filed a report yet?"

"We will in a few hours."

"So the window of opportunity is rapidly closing," Gavin concluded, and explained to us, "Local law enforcement will handle this as an *Unusual Occurrence*. Seattle Fire Department will be first responders, while SPD provides perimeter containment and evacuation of the Luminous Water plant. Where it goes from there depends on what first responders find, which we know will most likely be nothing. But *none* of this happens until I pass off the investigation into SPD's lap tomorrow. Once the CDC's report is filed, however, the FBI will step in and could screw up *our* black-bag job."

"Yes," Serena concurred. "You'd better utilize Cassidy while you can."

Dad held up his hand in a *whoa* gesture. "*Black-bag job? Utilize Cassidy?*" he repeated with an emphasis that meant no one would utilize his daughter for anything.

"Drake, Cassidy's abilities give her an advantage no one else in this investigation has," Gavin reasoned. "I have to get her into that plant for a closer look, before there is no access—"

"So you want to obstruct a police investigation by conducting an illegal one on your own?"

"There is *no* investigation until tomorrow," Gavin fired back. "I know how these investigations go, especially when everyone and his mother gets involved, which *will* happen when the CDC files that report. Cassidy is our best chance of blowing the lid off this thing *quickly.*"

I glanced between the two men, leveling one another with a look, wondering if I had a say in the matter. I'd be lying if I said Gavin's confidence in me hadn't stoked my ego. His praise alone made me want to run headlong into whatever direction he pointed.

"This is *not* your decision." Dad lashed the words like a whip. "You are *not* her father."

"And Cassidy doesn't go anywhere without me," Emery informed, crossing his arms stubbornly, getting in on the dominance display. If any more testosterone was released in the kitchen, I'd grow a mustache.

"*Yoo-hooooo.*" I waved my arms over my head. "I *am* in the room and the decision should be mine. Dad, I know I'm only a minor, but I can also flip a car with my bare hands. So let's not lose sight of what's going on. A freakish, *maybe alien*, parasite is invading people and mutating them—"

"Rapidly," Emery added. "My mom didn't drive this point home. We are not witnessing traditional coevolution. In fact, classifying these human mutations as coevolution is a stretch. What we're seeing has never been documented before. The mutation is instantaneous—once the parasite population reaches a specific level, that is. That's the other aspect. The parasite population in a host has to reach a particular level before mutation occurs. Until that time, it's a symbiotic relationship between host and parasite."

"What does that even mean?" I protested.

"The parasite lives in the host covertly," Emery explained. "However, at this stage, the parasite and host are *separate* living organisms, until the parasite population hits a specific number. *My* theory is that the host and parasite eventually incorporate, becoming one. Of course, there is no substantial evidence of this—*yet*. It's pure speculation.

"In regard to the tipping point, the parasite population has to be somewhere in the hundreds, if Levy's Luminous Water consumption is an indicator. Remember, one parasite per water bottle. And if the parasite could reproduce in the host, missing person reports would be in the thousands, which is also conjecture. The parasite's inability to breed is a hypothesis, that is."

"And Elizabeth and Chazz would be among them," Dad said in a hollow voice, apparently not hearing Emery's disclaimer.

My skin crawled. This was too horrible for words.

"But can it hurt Mom and Chazz now that they're not drinking the water?" I could hear the fear in my voice. "If they don't add any more parasites to the population, they'll be okay, right?"

"We don't know," Serena said, pulling no punches.

My dad banged his fist on the table. I jolted, startled. I had never seen him hit anything before.

"Dad, are you hurt?"

"No," he said through gritted teeth.

I stared at the angry red flesh on the outside of his hand, but kept my mouth shut.

"What *is* the plan?" he asked Gavin. Rage flashed in his eyes, but he was consigned. He would agree to whatever Gavin proposed.

"We'll search the Luminous Water plant tonight," Gavin said. "You and Emery will do vehicle surveillance. Cassidy—my asset—and I will be running point."

"What's an asset?" I asked.

"An agent—you are my agent, my secret weapon."

I smiled, despite the circumstances. That was pretty cool.

"You have *two* assets." Emery held up two fingers with a determined look. "You know I can handle myself, Dad."

"Yes, you certainly proved that last night," Gavin retorted.

Wanting to head off any more conflict, I backed Emery up. "I *know* he can. Plus, our telepathy gives us an edge."

Dad, Gavin, and Serena stared at me like I was speaking in Hungarian.

"Your *what*?" Gavin spat out.

I placed my hands on my hips and glowered at Emery. "I knew you wouldn't tell them about our mental telepathy!"

Emery spluttered into laughter, spraying spittle across the table.

"But I didn't tell you guys, either," I apologized to Dad, sheepish. "I sort of forgot about it, with everything else going on."

Dad glanced between Emery and me, and asked, as though afraid to hear the answer, "Cassidy, what are you talking about?"

"As if things couldn't get more *Twilight Zone*," Emery managed between laughs, elbows on the table, shaking his head pressed into his hand.

I assumed he was embarrassed, but he would just have to deal with it. Our parents had a right to know.

After I explained what had happened, which Emery allowed me to do without interruption, that old familiar silence settled over the room.

"Emery, can you *hear* Cassidy in your mind?" Serena inquired. She didn't have that excited, mad scientist glow that she typically had when discussing my freakishness.

"Cassidy hears my voice in her head; I don't hear hers," Emery answered without elaborating.

"It's me, Serena," I said. "Not him. It's just *another* ability."

"Cassidy, have you read other people's minds?" Dad asked in a strained voice. One more surprise and his brain might blow a gasket.

Gavin shifted in his chair, clearly unsettled by the

revelation, and understandably so. What spy would want to be around someone who could siphon top secrets from his cortex?

"No, only Emery's," I quickly clarified for Gavin's sake. "But it isn't like I can read his mind per se. I can't control it, meaning I can't hear his thoughts at will, or transmit mine to him—"

"Oh?" Emery lifted an amused eyebrow. "What *transmissions* did I miss?"

"This isn't exactly like telepathy," I prattled on, pretending not to have heard Emery. I patted my cheeks, which suddenly felt hot. "And I have a theory about that, I mean, about how Emery hears my thoughts, or *thinks* my thoughts, since he doesn't hear my actual voice in his head, like I do his—which, by the way, he'd only thought, or picked up, in moments of, er . . . mmmm . . . " I searched for the right word, " . . . duress. I think, somehow, my brainwaves barge into other people's minds, or things—" I wasn't ready to talk about my connection with furry critters, so I switched tracks again. "My brainwaves open up this *mental line* of communication, just like a phone line." I nodded with satisfaction. I liked that.

The adults stared at me with blank faces. Emery was thoroughly amused by my floundering about. I knew I wasn't making any sense.

"Just stop it," I scolded him, quickly explaining to our parents. "We weren't mentally communicating just then. Emery is giving me a funny look because this whole thing embarrasses him. But it isn't like we can help it!—So, as I was saying, when this mental line is open, thoughts can be received both ways, like in a conversation. I bet everyone could hear me, if their brains were as pliable as Emery's—"

"*Pliable*?" Emery's eyebrows shot up. "I take offense at that."

"Well, how else am I supposed to say it? You have exceptional brainwave reception?"

"Oh, this is too much," Serena exclaimed, exasperated. "Cassidy, you don't understand what brainwaves are. They are not electromagnetic radiation—"

"Well, obviously they are!" I interrupted, even though I had no idea what electromagnetic radiation was, or brainwaves, apparently. I jabbed my finger in Emery's direction. "Because he can hear my thoughts!"

"Let's address that." Dad rubbed his forehead, wrinkled with confusion and worry. It resembled a topographical map of a mountain range. "Why can only Emery hear your thoughts?"

"Oh, I don't know!" I threw my hands up and frowned at Gavin. If he and Serena had just come clean with Emery, this would all make sense right now.

Just then, my cell rang. I fished it out of my pocket, glad for the interruption.

"It's Jared," I told them, and quickly answered. "Are you okay?" I asked. I had a really bad feeling.

"My dad called," Jared said. "He wants me to spend the weekend with him."

"No!" I jumped to my feet. "You can't! Did you tell him you can't?" I looked from alarmed face to alarmed face, explaining, "Jared's dad wants him to spend the weekend!"

"Who's with you?" Jared asked. His voice was so calm that I wanted to scream. He didn't need to answer my question. I already knew. He had told his dad he would.

"You cannot stay with him!" I shouted, not answering him.

"It's Gavin. He's with you," he concluded eagerly. "Let me t—"

"Your dad knows about the yacht! He might even know it was *us*!" *And he might even be one of them!* "Dad, Gavin—" I looked at them desperately. "Tell him he can't go!"

"Cassidy, put Gavin on the phone," Jared said. At the same time, Gavin held out his hand for my cell. I practically threw it at him.

"Tell him he can't do it," I pleaded with Gavin as I sat down. There was only one reason Jared would want to talk to a CIA agent. He planned to spy for the spy.

Gavin shifted his eyes to Dad and said into the cell, "What do you propose, Jared?"

I let my head drop to the table like a free-falling weight.

Chapter 23

Unsettled

"**Y**ou're a minor," Gavin reminded Jared, but he said it more for himself. He leaned forward in our wingback chair and rubbed his forehead. "Without a legal guardian's permission, the CIA can't wire you."

"The CIA can't," Jared persisted. "But you can."

I heaved a frustrated breath and glanced at Mom, sitting next to me on the sofa, wringing her hands. Jared sat on my other side.

Throughout the conversation, I'd wanted to grab him by the shoulders and shake some sense into him. Learning that his father was a longtime friend of Patrick Grimm's hadn't deterred Jared, and neither had Dad's attempt to scare him by disclosing that we suspected his father also might be mutated. Jared hadn't batted an eyelash at this, but the determination had hardened in his face like cement. He would spy on his dad, with or without our help.

My eyes skittered left to Dad, in the other chair, and then to Nate, perched on the fireplace hearth next to Emery. Dad and Nate were as unsettled by Jared's wild scheme as Mom and I were. But I didn't bother gauging Emery. I already knew he was cool with it. After all, he had spied on his dad when we'd thought Gavin worked for King.

"Yes, we can," Emery answered for Gavin, then asked

his dad: "Can you get a hidden camera in a button, or something along those lines?"

"It's already on the list." Gavin tapped his temple.

"Eileen has to be told," Mom insisted.

"Told what, Lizzy?" Dad posed, looking as conflicted as she was.

Mom's expression lost resolution. Bringing Eileen into the loop would mean we'd have to reveal information that my mom was unwilling to divulge—namely, that I was a mutant.

"My mom would think we're all crazy," Jared said. "Then she'd call my dad."

I nodded in agreement. Eileen lived in the *real* world, where people you knew weren't secret agents, and mutants were a far-fetched Hollywood creation. Without a doubt, she would call her ex-husband to try to get to the bottom of things.

"We have to keep in mind what we're up against. Humanity depends on it," Emery reminded, resorting to dramatics. He would do and say whatever it took to get everyone onboard. "We need concrete evidence of criminal activity, and evidence that this parasite is harmful. Jared is in a unique position. Don't let his age be a factor, nor his lack of experience. Civilians are used by law enforcement to gather evidence against suspects every day. Let's move forward on this—before more people get hurt."

"Are you sure, Jared?" Dad tried one last time.

"I am."

Nate patted Jared's shoulders with respect. I still wanted to shake them.

"Then we have a lot to do," Gavin said, ending the

debate. He looked at his cell. "I'm running out of time to call in favors and get what we need." He stood up. "Emery, you do your thing. Hack into whatever database you can to see if you can dig up anything we don't already know about Grimm, the Luminous Water plant, and his residence. Drake, why don't you poke around, too? Jared, call your father. Tell him you're going to hang out with friends until the early evening, or whatever you think won't spark suspicion. Hold him off from picking you up until eight p.m. Chazz, come here—"

Our heads twisted to the foyer. Chazz slithered from behind the wall on his belly. He stared at Gavin with round, surprised eyes.

Earlier, Mom had come home while Dad was busy taking Jared and Nate out of school, following Jared's phone call. After getting the lowdown, she had given Chazz a bowl of cheese puffs and told him to watch television while we talked. The evidence of his snack was dusted across his face and smeared on his shirt, which apparently had served as a napkin.

Gavin grinned at him. "Well, come on. I have a job for you."

"*Teen Titan*s is over," Chazz explained, galloping up to Gavin.

"So you decided to hone your spying skills." Gavin scooped him up into his arms. "You'd make an excellent field agent. Not even your sister detected you."

Chazz beamed.

"Your assignment," Gavin said, his finger bouncing from Jared and me to Emery and Nate, "is to keep them out of trouble." He dusted off Chazz's cheesy cheek, then set him down. "We'll reconvene here at six p.m. sharp. Emery, prep Jared and set his cell up with GPS. That'll be backup. He'll be wearing a tracker, too. Drake and Elizabeth, I'll give you a call when I've gathered everything we need. Call me if you run into an issue with Owen."

The door shut behind Gavin and we all stared at one another for a beat. Then Chazz warned, bouncing his finger at each of us kids, just as Gavin had done, "I've got my eye on you." Following this notice, he wheeled around and trotted out of the room, calling, "Athena! Where are you— *kitty, kitty, kitty?*"

"X-ray vision," Nate joked, giving us an exaggerated wink.

Chapter 24

Deception

"It feels like we're in a police movie," I whispered, then realized there was no need to hush my voice. Who would overhear me inside a soundproof surveillance van?

It was 7:15 p.m. Gavin had returned an hour beforehand with the van and spy gear for Jared—a jean jacket that housed a hidden camera, wireless transmitter, and tracker. For extra insurance, Jared also wore a seashell pendant necklace that concealed another camera and transmitter. The jacket was cool, but the necklace was lame, something a boy our age wouldn't be caught dead in. When I pointed this out to Gavin, he brushed off my concern.

"Jared can be a trendsetter," he'd said.

Still, no teenage male would wear it.

After conducting an equipment check in the house, Gavin, Emery, Dad, and I, outfitted in black, went out to the van. Gavin had parked it several houses down the street, opposite the direction Mr. Wells would be coming from. Gavin and Emery began the process of getting cameras set up and testing Jared's equipment from its current distance. Dad and I watched them work from foldout captain chairs, which were black like the rest of the van's interior.

"Gavin, the people who owe you favors own cool

stuff," I commented, admiring the state-of-the-art panels that were loaded with dials and switches.

"I make sure of that," he replied as he adjusted a dial.

Dad's mouth turned up into a cursory half-smile. His eyes narrowed on two of the three monitors that had just turned on, displaying our street outside the van.

"Emery," I said.

"Yes?" His fingers flew over his laptop's keyboard.

"We could've used this set-up a time or two." I flashed Dad a grin that I hoped would calm him. Dad was torn. He didn't like leaving Mom and my brothers alone for even a few seconds with Owen Wells, but he had to be in the van, ready to roll, when Owen left our house with Jared.

"Why would we need this, when we have our buddy Jason?" Emery joked.

"What is it with you? Do you enjoy having a thorn in your side, bleeding you dry?" I returned.

"Shall I answer that for you, son?" Gavin joined in.

I peeked at Dad to see if we were offering him some comic relief. No such luck. Apparently he didn't find Jason Crenshaw's shakedowns entertaining.

"We're online," Emery announced. A shaky image of our fireplace mantel filled his laptop screen and the third monitor, which displayed slightly different views since footage was being filmed from two different cameras hidden on Jared. He was obviously pacing the living room.

"And we have audio," Emery said. "Can you hear me, Jared?"

The image of our mantel jolted. Emery's voice coming through Jared's hidden earpiece had startled him.

"Guess you can." Emery grinned. "I'm turning down the volume. Is that better?"

"Yeah. Thanks," Jared's voice flowed through the van's speakers. The room spun on the screens, capturing blurry images of my mom and brothers in the living room as Jared pivoted on his heels, facing the foyer now.

"Jared, it all looks good—audio, visual, GPS," Gavin assured him. "The street is clear. I'll let you know when your dad is coming, so calm down about that. Take a deep breath, and let's run through everything again."

Jared continued to pace as he and Gavin reviewed cover stories, what to say and what not to say, and backup plans in case of equipment failure. Dad and I sat silently, while Emery worked on his laptop. Jared's cameras filmed the rest of our family sitting on the sofa like lumps, too. Part of me was itching to get on with this. I hated feeling useless.

On the monitors, headlights swung onto our street. Dad stiffened, and I blew out the breath I'd been holding in. Mr. Wells's Porsche rounded the corner.

"Is it?" Dad whispered, unable to see the vehicle clearly.

"Yes," I confirmed.

"Your father is here, Jared," Gavin told him.

"He's here," Jared repeated to my family.

Nate nodded, wide-eyed, and Mom shooed Chazz from the room. Chazz let out a howl of protest and threw himself on the floor.

"Chazz, what are you doing?" I shouted at the screens as Mom and Nate jumped to their feet, scolding him. Nate tried to pick Chazz up, but Chazz grabbed a leg on the coffee table and kicked at him.

"They're going to blow this!" I couldn't believe Chazz was having a tantrum when so much was at stake.

259

"I'd better get over there," Dad said, starting to stand.

"Stay put, Drake," Gavin ordered. "You can't bring attention to us. Give them a moment. They'll pull themselves together. Jared, tell Chazz I'm giving him an assignment: Keep watch for other cars from the attic window until he sees you and your dad drive away."

The second Chazz heard Jared say "assignment," the kicking and screaming ceased. He climbed to his feet, rubbed his runny nose, and listened intently, bobbing his head. Before Jared had finished talking, Chazz shot off for the stairs, and not a moment too soon. Jared's dad had just parked in front of our house.

"They did not need that," I said to Dad, exasperated, as we watched Mom straighten her hair, trying to compose herself. "Come on, Nate, wipe that irritation off your face," I willed, while Gavin told Jared that his dad was coming up our front walk. I'd been so frazzled by Chazz's behavior that I hadn't even taken time to evaluate how Jared was holding up.

Mr. Wells didn't appear to be agitated or suspicious as he walked briskly to our porch. He didn't even look around as he ascended the steps and rang the doorbell. My gaze cut to the monitors that displayed our foyer as everyone got into position. My mom headed down the hall to the kitchen, where she'd give the impression she was coming from when Nate answered the door. Jared sat at the hall tree, preparing to put his shoes on.

"Hey, Mr. Wells," Nate greeted in an impressively easygoing voice. Jared gave us a great view of the Nikes that he tugged on, and our oak floor.

"Hi, Nate," Mr. Wells returned.

We could see on the monitors displaying outside images that Nate pulled the door wider for him to come in. Jared's cameras showed his fingers tying shoelaces.

"Elizabeth, how are you this evening?"

Mr. Wells entered our foyer. Dad's nervous fingers drummed the arm of his chair.

"I'm fine. Thank you. So, you and Jared are spending the weekend together?"

I tensed. Mom's tone sounded more challenging than inquiring.

Jared sat up, showing us everyone in the foyer. Mr. Wells didn't appear taken aback by Mom's tone, thankfully.

"We are. I'm looking forward to it." He smiled at Jared. My muscles tightened. There was something about the way he'd looked at Jared that I didn't like. "Ready?"

"Yep." Jared stood.

"I'm not," I muttered to myself.

~~~

"Jared, we have to talk this out," Mr. Wells said.

His voice streamed through the van's speakers while the hidden cameras on Jared filmed the back of the metro bus in front of them. The Porsche cruised down Queen Anne Boulevard, a couple of vehicles ahead of us. Up until that point, they had exchanged only a handful of words. Judging by Jared's accelerated heart rate, which I could hear through the transmitter when I concentrated, he was nervous. Understandably so, since as far as he knew, the man he sat next to wasn't entirely his father anymore.

"Jared's heart is pounding," I whispered to everyone in the van.

Gavin placed a forefinger to his lips, reminding me to keep quiet. He had plugged in a headset to the van's console to communicate with Jared. To avoid confusing Jared with multiple voices, Emery had switched off our end of the audio, but turned up the volume so that Dad, who was driving the van, could hear the conversation in the Porsche, too.

Gavin had ordered no talking among us, unless necessary. Apparently, he didn't deem a report on Jared's heart rate necessary.

"Jared?" Mr. Owen repeated sharply when Jared hadn't responded.

"What do you want me to say?" Jared fired back. He whipped around to his dad, the camera catching surprise on Owen's face. I could only imagine the inner turmoil Jared was experiencing.

The surprise melded into annoyance. Mr. Wells returned acidly, "How about we start with what you were doing with my yacht?"

"Oh, no," I whispered.

Gavin leaned forward, concentrating as he prepared to feed Jared lines if he froze up, or forgot the cover story.

"Crap," Jared groaned. Over the transmitters, his voice came across like he'd been busted, just as he and Emery had practiced.

Emery smiled and gave Gavin a thumbs-up.

"Look, Dad, I'm sorry. I just figured you'd say *no*."

"Darn right I'd say *no!*" Owen shouted, flicking Jared a glare. "I'm so furious with you—I'm at a loss of what to say! Tell me what you were doing! And no jerking me around!"

"I won't!" Jared yelled back. "Okay . . . okay. I won't," he said, more calmly. "I met this girl at Cherry Street . . ."

Mr. Wells's expression softened into amusement.

"She goes to the UW, and she thought I did, too. I don't know why. Guess she thought I looked older . . ."

"And you didn't clear up the misconception," Mr. Wells finished for him, wearing a cunning grin.

"Why would I? She was hot. Really hot!"

Mr. Wells laughed. He had fallen for the lie.

"Somehow it came up that you have a yacht. She wanted to go out in it. Sorry. Obviously, I wasn't thinking with my head."

Emery grinned. I tossed him a dirty look. That last part was *so* his touch.

"What about Cassidy?"

"What about her?"

Mr. Wells chuckled. "You're right. What she doesn't know won't hurt her."

I noted Dad's jaw tighten in the rearview mirror. Owen Wells was scum.

"I know you've eaten, but I haven't," Mr. Wells said, not pursuing the subject of Jared two-timing me, probably because it was insignificant to him. "So, if you don't mind, I'm going through Deluxe."

"Go for it."

Gavin muted the headset. "Drake, park at the 7-11," he instructed, then switched the headset back on and praised Jared, using his codename.

"Nightcrawler, you're doing great. We'll be parked at 7-11. Avoid looking in that direction."

263

The Porsche turned into the burger joint's parking lot. Dad drove past Deluxe and pulled into the 7-11 next store.

After Mr. Wells got his food, he parked the car to eat. By this time, Dad had joined us in the back of the van. Jared sat hunched down in his seat, giving us a great view of his knees pressed to the Porsche's dashboard. Owen returned to his cross-examination.

"So you *borrow* my yacht to impress . . ."

The cameras filmed glimpses of the phone charger cord that Jared spun.

"Will you stop that?" Owen grumbled. His hand caught the cord and jerked it away from Jared. "Her name?" he pressed.

"Sheila."

"Does Sheila have a last name?"

"I never asked."

Mr. Wells chuckled. "Like father, like son."

"Just shoot me now," Jared retorted.

"Don't be a wiseass. French fries?"

"No, thanks."

They were quiet for a minute while Owen ate his food. I heard him slurp soda from a straw. Then he laughed.

"You're going to force me to interrogate you, aren't you?"

Jared sighed. "What *else* do you want to know?"

"Show some respect. If I had talked to my father like that, he'd have backhanded me. Sit up like a *gentleman* and look at me."

The cameras moved upward and settled on Owen's irate face. If Jared's goal was to force his father to explode, he was well on his way to succeeding.

"What do *I* want to know?" Owen scoffed, tapping his chin as though thinking the question over. "Hmmmm . . . Let me think . . . How about . . . where did *you* take *my* yacht?"

"Out in the Sound."

"The Sound?" He stared hard at Jared. "Not Lake Washington?"

My breath caught. *He knows!*

"Criminy," Dad muttered.

"Yeah, the Sound." Jared's voice didn't betray him. He had to be freaking out. His dad knew about Lake Washington, which meant he knew about *them*!

"Ask him *why*," Gavin prompted Jared.

"Why?" Jared asked.

"When did you go out?" Mr. Wells demanded, ignoring the question.

"Why do you want to know?"

"Answer me," Owen said with a piercing look.

"Do not provoke him," Gavin instructed Jared. "Answer him."

"Last night," Jared said.

"What *time* last night?"

"Around six," Gavin fed Jared.

"Around six."

"And Drake and Elizabeth let you go?"

"The cover story," Gavin directed.

"No. They thought I was playing guitar at Cherry Street," Jared answered his dad, not missing a beat. "I met Sheila there. She drove us to the marina and dropped me off at the Jones's afterwards. *There!* Are you happy?"

"Appears I missed my opportunity to have *the birds and the bees* talk," Owen joked.

I *really* hated him.

"Whatever. Your burger is getting cold."

Mr. Wells lifted the burger to his mouth. "We'll go for another round after I polish this off."

Jared sank into his seat, giving us a view of his knees again, and released a long breath in an attempt to calm down. Gavin turned off the headset so Jared couldn't hear us.

"Owen won't win any Father of the Year awards," he remarked.

"And he doesn't have any delusions of that," Emery added.

"He doesn't believe Jared," Dad remarked tensely.

"Yes, he does," I said. I had no idea where Dad had gotten that idea. Mr. Wells had totally fallen for Jared's story.

"*No*, he doesn't," Emery confirmed, and Gavin nodded.

"But he said—You saw him—" I argued, rewinding their conversation and the footage of Mr. Wells's face in my head. "He didn't look suspicious, and Jared did a good job! He just sounded like a kid who had gotten caught. That's all."

"Jared did an excellent job," Gavin agreed. "Owen knows more than he is letting on. He dropped a noose around Jared's neck, hoping he'd hang himself."

Dread oozed through my stomach. I cut my gaze to Jared's knees. "Did he—did Jared hang himself?" I asked Gavin.

"That depends on what Owen knows."

~~~

"Uh, where are we going?" Jared asked his dad. I fumbled out at the same time: "He—Mr. Wells—passed the street to his apartment!"

Jared turned to look at Owen. His father's face held a small smile.

"I'm introducing you to an old family friend," he answered casually, keeping his eyes on the road.

My stomach flip-flopped.

"Here we go," Gavin said, assuming as we all had that Owen was taking Jared to Patrick Grimm. "Emery, bring up the building plans for Grimm's residence again."

I pressed my hands over my pounding heart and glanced at Dad. His furious eyes met mine in the rearview mirror. Was Mr. Wells serving his son up to Grimm?

"Who?" Jared's voice pitched with alarm. I winced and prayed his dad hadn't noticed.

"It's a surprise," Mr. Wells replied. Quickly glancing at his son, he gave him a disarming smile. "Relax, Jared. Trust me. He isn't the bogeyman."

"Trust *you*? Seriously, with everything that's happened lately?"

"Fair enough. Any more barbs you'd like to throw my way?"

"Whatever," Jared muttered, then turned forward again. The cameras angled toward the passenger side of the car. I concluded he was looking out his window, trying to sort through the distressing turn of events.

"Why?" I fretted. "Why is he taking him to Patrick Grimm?"

"We'll find out soon enough," Emery said, plucking

away at his keyboard. "But I'd guess he isn't making a social call."

"Shouldn't we stop him?"

Emery's eyes scanned blueprints on his laptop. "Why would we do that?"

"You're so . . . *callous*," I spat with a measure of shock. Sometimes I didn't feel like I knew Emery at all. "Dad?" I beseeched the one person who might put an end to this madness.

Conflict on his face, Dad opened his mouth to speak. I waited for him to tell Gavin enough was enough and we had to rescue Jared. But the words never came.

In the rearview mirror, I watched his eyes narrow on the road in resigned frustration. "We have to stop this, Cassidy," he said. "Jared will be safe. Gavin knows what he's doing."

"Cassidy, we won't let anything happen to him," Gavin promised.

I looked at him squarely, fire burning in my belly. I'd make sure of that.

Chapter 25

Alpha

Tall iron gates pulled apart, giving entrance to a stone driveway that looped through a lush lawn, gradually curving up to a sprawling mansion that boasted arched windows and natural stone veneer. Beyond the ostentatious home, I could see the dark, lapping waters of Lake Washington sparkling in the moonlight.

The Porsche drove through the gates, which immediately closed behind it, snapping together like jaws. The bluesy tunes flowing through Jared's transmitter created eerie background music, as though the scenes on our monitor were part of some Alfred Hitchcock film. Mr. Wells had turned on the car radio, selecting the jazz station, when Jared had grown quiet.

"Nightcrawler, She-Ra and I will be close by," Gavin assured Jared through the headset, using our codenames in case our signal was picked up. Dad parked the van in front of Grimm's neighbor's house. "Cable will instruct you from this point on. You're doing great. We've got your back."

Gavin slipped off the headset and handed it to Emery. "Any security guards?" he asked Emery. He rolled his ski mask on. I'd donned mine five minutes beforehand.

"So your friend's loaded?" Jared observed, breaking the silence in the Porsche.

269

Dad squeezed between the seats to join us in the back. Gavin pulled a sling holding a semi-automatic gun onto his shoulder. He had other weapons tucked inside concealed holsters.

"Patrick has done well for himself," Mr. Wells confirmed. "He's looking forward to seeing you again. Last time he saw you, you were about three."

"Negative," Emery answered his dad, studying a live satellite image of the property.

"Did you hear that?" I asked. "Jared met Patrick Grimm before."

No one appeared to have heard me. I guess it wasn't earth-shattering information anyway.

The van's monitors, displaying footage from the cameras in Jared's jacket and necklace, showed him climbing out of the car.

"Nightcrawler, walk to the other side of the vehicle. Pretend to look around, turn a slow one-eighty," Emery instructed.

Dad hugged me. "Please be careful."

Gavin and Emery scrutinized the panoramic view Jared gave us of the estate's front grounds. I tapped my foot with impatience.

"Stop," Emery told Jared.

The image on the screen paused on a cluster of trees.

"What do you think?" Emery consulted Gavin.

Bending toward the screen, Gavin squinted. "Zoom in."

"For heaven's sake!" I exclaimed, exasperated. "I can see it fine. You're looking at a bush, not a person. Let's go!"

Gavin snapped up his other gun, a Glock something-or-other. Dad slid the van's side door open for us, sticking his head out and looking both ways to make sure the coast was clear. We already knew it was, thanks to the van's cameras. Before Dad had a chance to give the go-ahead, I squeezed past him and hopped down to the sidewalk. We had wasted enough time.

Gavin stepped down next to me, and we booked it to the stone wall that enclosed Grimm's estate. We had decided in the van to scale this portion. There were trees on the other side that would give us some cover.

At the wall, I cupped my hands, creating a step for Gavin.

"Clear, Hawkeye," Emery told Gavin.

"Copy that," Gavin whispered in response.

Gavin planted his foot into my palms, and I lifted him up. He gripped the top, hoisted himself over the wall, and disappeared. Leaves rustled on a limb he'd grabbed to climb down. I looked up and down the street for good measure. Not a living soul in sight. Luckily for us, the homes were spread out and the street wasn't a main thoroughfare.

Gavin landed with a soft, solid thud.

Taking a few steps back, I took a running leap, caught the top of the wall like a pommel horse, and flipped up into a handstand. Balancing, I assessed the area below, making sure Gavin had moved out of the way and that I wouldn't land in a blackberry bush or something. Seeing an open landing spot, I allowed my straight legs to drop the fifteen feet into a back flip. My feet planted in redwood chips.

"Nightcrawler is inside," Emery reported. "A housekeeper let them in."

271

"I smell dogs," I whispered to Gavin.

Squatting down, Gavin nodded and asked Emery, "Do you have a visual on dogs?"

A pause, and then: "Negative."

"Copy that." Gavin motioned with his gun for me to follow him.

Once we'd reached the tree line, we commando-crawled across the lawn to an elegant marble fountain that had three scalloped tiers. The sound of the ever-flowing water pouring into the large basin was mesmerizing. While we'd made our way to the fountain, Emery had kept us updated. The housekeeper had taken Jared and his father down the far west corridor to a set of double doors, located on the right side of the hallway. She'd opened the doors to a den, where Patrick, Constance, and Ashlyn waited and were now greeting Jared.

"Two rottweilers have been let out from the back of the house," Emery warned.

Gavin groaned. "I hate rotties. You don't know they're there until they go for your throat. Upside, they won't bark and alert anyone." As Gavin said this, he unhooked a holster on his calf where he had a knife stashed.

"You're going to kill them?"

"Only if they try to kill us first," Gavin replied, peeking over the fountain and watching for the dogs.

"Nightcrawler, after you shake hands, make a casual three-sixty. I want to see what's around you," Emery instructed Jared, not flipping off the transmission for us. He wanted us to hear what was going on in the house. "Good. If you saw or heard anyone else in the house, aside from the Grimms and the housekeeper, clear your throat."

There was a pause. Then Emery said, "He hasn't seen bodyguards or any other staff members. The dogs are headed toward you, on your three o'clock."

I pointed right at the house, asking if that was the side Emery was referring to. Steely-eyed, Gavin nodded and placed an index finger to his lips for me to stay quiet. He pulled up into a crouch, like a black panther preparing to spring. I followed suit.

"The dogs see you," Emery calmly informed. "They're running at you, full throttle."

Emery didn't have to tell me the dogs had seen us. I had heard them break into a run, their sharp nails scraping the cement driveway.

Gavin took the safety off his gun and checked his knife again. Before he could get into position and put an unlucky dog in his crosshairs, I sprang to my feet and stepped out into the open. I hadn't anticipated their size. Rottweilers are huge!

"Stay down," I commanded Gavin in a guttural voice that I barely recognized, my eyes locked on the dogs.

Snarls escaped through bared teeth as powerful legs carried the dogs over the grass, muscles rippling up their shoulders. My skin reacted to the threat, turning granite-hard.

The rottweiler on the left lunged at me. I caught it by the jaw in one hand, twisted around, and slammed it into the grass on its back. Down on one knee, I pinned its throat to the ground with one hand as the other dog jumped on my back. I could feel it trying to bite into my shoulder, but its teeth couldn't get a grip on my skin.

I reached around with my free hand, grasped a handful

of spiky hair and loose skin, and flipped my attacker onto its back, trapping it by the throat next to its friend.

I stared into the stunned dark eyes of the first dog and growled. The dog relaxed, resentfully submitting to me. Cutting my eyes to the other dog, I growled again. It blinked at me, as though unable to believe its predicament, but made no effort to challenge my authority. I was the alpha.

"Stay," I ordered them in that strange, guttural voice. From the corner of my eye, I could see Gavin watching me. The ski mask concealed the shock that I was sure had claimed his face.

The dogs stared at me with noble pride. They had too much self-respect to whimper and curl their tails between their legs, as Jason's dog Princess had done when I'd forced her into submission. I would have to watch these two. One sign of weakness on my part, and they'd take advantage.

"Nice job with the dogs," Emery praised in such an easygoing manner that he made me giggle. The rottweilers' eyebrows shot up their foreheads, as though they were trying to determine if this was their opportunity to tear me to pieces. They tested the waters with low snarls. I tightened my grip on their throats.

"My last run-in with rotties didn't go as smoothly," Gavin admitted.

I made a mental note to ask him about that later.

"Status?" he asked Emery.

"Exchanging pleasantries," Emery reported. "The Host is praising Nightcrawler's father for forming their illustrious business and finding the plant's facility."

"Sounds like a setup," Gavin observed.

"Without a doubt," Emery agreed.

Gavin squatted next to my beta dogs and me. "Should we duct-tape them?"

"No need. They'll stay put. Won't you, boys?" I shook the skin on their necks. If looks could kill.

"Then tell them to *stay* and let's go. The door they were let out of is probably unlocked," Gavin pointed out.

An unlocked back door, and only a housekeeper and a couple of dogs—the Grimms didn't appear overly concerned about home security.

"That won't be necessary," Emery piped up. "The Host offered to give Nightcrawler a tour of the plant, then instantly invited his pretty stepdaughter along."

"How could Nightcrawler refuse?" Gavin commented, eyeing the second story of the five-car garage.

"Beauty is a powerful weapon," Emery agreed. "And she is *potent*."

My nostrils flared. Ashlyn was gorgeous, but give me a break.

"The Host called for a car," Emery informed. "You'd better head back."

The lights on the garage's second story turned off. I figured that was their driver's living quarters.

"Do your magic," Gavin instructed me.

I stared hard into the dogs' eyes. "Stay."

They didn't flinch as I released their necks, nor when I moved away. The dogs didn't move even when Gavin and I reached the trees. For safe measure, knowing they could hear me, I ordered from behind a tree, "Stay."

"Impressive," Gavin remarked.

A smug smile twitched at my mouth. What can I say?

It was sort of cool being the alpha to a pair of vicious rottweilers.

A limousine rolled up to the front of the mansion. The Grimms and their guests filed out of the house. Ashlyn was more beautiful than I'd remembered.

Potent, I thought, spellbound. Fascination shifted into offense when I observed her coyly admiring Jared.

Smiling, he said something to her. Ashlyn burst into a giggling fit.

What did he say to make her laugh like that? I fumed.

"*She-Ra*," Gavin barked in a whisper.

My angry eyes snapped to him.

He aimed his finger at the wall. "Let's go."

I muttered under my breath, then sprinted for the wall, leaving Gavin in my wake.

~~~

The conversation in the limousine wouldn't have raised any alarm if we hadn't known the truth about these people and their evil plot against humanity. Patrick and Owen bantered like old friends, with Constance releasing a good-natured zinger now and then. Ashlyn talked Jared's ear off, rambling on and on about her private school, friends, the places she'd traveled to, and whatever else popped into her pretty little head.

Jared had barely gotten a word in edgewise, not that he even tried. I knew his attention was divided between Ashlyn's incessant chatter and the adults' conversation, as he analyzed veneers and theorized about the real motive of this tour. He probably wasn't even aware that Ashlyn scoped him out whenever he looked away from her. However, I did note—with much despair—that her prattle had lulled his heart rate into a normal range. If Grimm's plan was to use his stepdaughter to lower Jared's defenses, it was working.

~~~

"Drake, make a right," Gavin instructed, a couple of blocks from the Luminous Water plant. A right would take us in the wrong direction. To me, he explained, "We know where they're headed. No reason to chance being spotted."

"Uh-huh," I agreed, while thinking, *No duh.* My expression must appear perpetually confused—the Phillips family always seems to feel the need to explain the obvious to me.

"I'm pulling in here," Dad called back, cranking the steering wheel and turning into a parking lot.

"So who's your favorite band?" Ashlyn asked Jared in a breathy voice.

"Doesn't she ever shut up?" I complained.

"Queen," Jared absently answered her.

I smiled at how distracted he sounded. With a face like hers, Ashlyn probably wasn't accustomed to not getting a boy's full attention.

The monitors panned from her, past the Grimms' faces, then settled on the corner of the left back window of the vehicle, which I assumed Jared was looking through, trying to determine where they were. Not that he would know anyway. We were far from our stomping grounds.

"*Queen*?" Ashlyn repeated. "What do they sing?"

I snorted a laugh. *Really?*

"Ashlyn," Patrick gasped in mock horror. The cameras moved toward Grimm. Patrick placed a hand over his chest as though the chatterbox's ignorance had put him on the verge of a heart attack. "How can you *not* know the best rock band of *all time*? Jared, you'll have to educate her later—"

I ground my teeth.

"—Well, we're here. Luminous!"

"And here we go," Gavin said, calling to Dad. "Drake, let's roll."

We pulled out onto the main road again. The monitors showed the limousine passengers climbing out of the vehicle.

"Now, it may not look impressive," Patrick said as Jared gave us a look around him. The Luminous Water plant consisted of a square cinder-block building, a white warehouse, a garage, and a parking lot lined with cypress trees. There were a few other cars in the parking lot, too. I guessed they belonged to janitors. Lights were on behind the closed mini-blinds covering the two windows that flanked the door.

"*But*—" The cameras swung to Grimm's grinning face. He fixed oddly twinkling eyes on Jared. "—the magic is inside."

~~~

Dad pulled up to the curb outside the plant. By that point, Jared, Owen, and the Grimms had entered the building. Masked and ready to go, I reached for the door handle.

"Wait," Gavin ordered, holding up his finger. His eyes were on the monitor.

Puffing a frustrated breath, I obliged, and didn't ask *why*. They were inside the plant, and neither satellites nor Jared's cameras had showed any security guards roaming the grounds. So *what* were we waiting for?

"Cool," Jared remarked. The group had walked inside the large room where the water was bottled. It was called the production room, I remembered from our earlier tour.

"Walk ahead, as if in awe, and make a slow three-sixty," Gavin instructed Jared.

"This is *awesome*," Jared exclaimed, seeming truly amazed.

As he turned a circle, the cameras caught Ashlyn, who looked around with a puzzled expression on her face, trying to see what Jared found so fascinating about the production room.

"Isn't it?" Patrick agreed. Conveyer belts, stainless steel equipment, and stacks of crated water flashed by on the monitors.

He sounds genuinely proud, I thought.

"Nightcrawler, ask where the water comes from," Gavin said.

"Where does the water come from?" Jared asked Grimm.

Patrick's smile widened. He seemed pleased by Jared's interest, and I was becoming more confused by the millisecond. Maybe this tour was only a tour?

"Great question!" Grimm praised. "We extract the water from an underground natural spring."

Gavin told Jared, "Keep eye contact with him and

casually fiddle with the pendant on your necklace. Direct the camera at Mermaid."

The live camera feed on the monitor shifted to Constance, who blandly watched her husband as he explained the water filtration process.

"Now at Fixer," Gavin told Jared.

Owen's face filled the monitor. He wore a look of impatience; his eyes restlessly moved around the room before settling on the pendant.

"Does he know it's a camera?" I whispered.

"No," Dad answered in a low, enraged voice. "That look on his face is called guilt."

"He's avoiding eye contact with Jared," Emery confirmed. He glanced at his dad. "Convinced?" he asked.

Gavin switched off the headset so Jared couldn't hear. "Something's about to go down," he agreed. "Cassidy, put on the tactical pack."

His tactical pack was similar to Emery's "bag of tricks," except Gavin's gear was military-issued.

Gavin turned the headset back on. "Nightcrawler, She-Ra and I will be close by. Keep the Host talking. Cable will feed you questions and instructions." Gavin pulled off the headset, rolled on his ski mask, snapped on his gun holster, and collected the assault rifle from me, slipping the sling over his shoulder.

"Ask how many gallons of water they produce a day," Emery told Jared as Gavin and I hopped out of the van. Dad closed the door.

Gavin rushed for a cypress tree. As I trailed him, a familiar scent wafted up my nose. Alarmed, I came to a halt on the sidewalk and drew in a deep breath to make sure I was smelling correctly.

"*She-Ra*," Gavin hissed from the cypress tree.

I held up a finger for him to wait a moment as I concentrated, mentally shifting through the thousands of scents whirling around in my nasal cavity, pinpointing one: Joe's scent.

What is he doing here?

"Joe is here," I whispered to Gavin, running up to him.

"Joe?"

"Yeah. *Joe.*" I scanned for him. He wasn't anywhere in sight. The faintness of his scent implied that he was no longer outside. "His scent is old. He might be inside."

Gavin informed Emery. "She-Ra says Joe was here. Do you have a visual?"

"I'd tell you if I did. She-Ra, track him. I'll keep you updated on Nightcrawler."

"But—" I began to argue.

"Copy that," Gavin cut me off. He motioned for me to proceed with tracking.

Emery will tell us if Jared's in trouble, I reassured myself as I followed Joe's scent with Gavin close behind. *I can get to him in seconds flat.*

My confidence waned, however, as Joe's scent led us behind the plant, farther and farther away from Jared. It became full-blown fear when we rounded a warehouse corner to see an abandoned-looking building edging a shallow field of dirt. A section of the barbed-wire fence that marked the two properties had been cut away, and a trail had been worn through the weeds on the other side of it.

Why did Joe come out to this building?

The possibilities made me shudder.

Chapter 26

Ruthless

"Stringer, find out what you can about the property we're approaching," Gavin said to Dad in a low voice. He surveyed the area through the night-vision goggles that he'd slipped on at the warehouse. The adjacent property and building were dark. Security lights from the plant didn't reach that far.

"Do you hear anyone?" he asked me.

"No." I was totally stressed. Where was Joe?

We entered the property where the barbed wire had been cut away and coiled back, and followed the trail. The weeds had been worn down to the soil from foot traffic. The dead silence was getting to me. If anything bad had happened to Joe, someone would pay.

"An Ester Burkhart owns the property," Dad informed us. "From what I can see, the building isn't currently being leased."

"Copy that," Gavin said, stepping over a wide, rusty pipe. Moving ahead, he motioned for me to stop walking, then peeked through his goggles around the corner of the building, gun held at the ready.

"Clear," he reported, then slipped from hiding.

No kidding it was clear.

"Gavin, no one is around here," I assured. He paused before a window.

"Just in case, better to not announce our presence by going through the front door." He stuck his hand out. "My pack."

I slid his tactical pack off my back and handed it to him. All the while, Gavin's eyes swept the area.

From the pack, he fished out glasscutters and a suction cup. He attached the suction cup to the window. "Hold this," he ordered.

I took hold of the knob, and Gavin proceeded to slice through the glass with the blade, starting at the bottom of the frame and cutting along the edge. When he'd reached the initial cut, he instructed, "Now pull the glass out, *carefully*."

I gave the suction a little tug. The glass didn't budge. So I exerted a bit more force into the next tug, which proved to be too much. The glass came popping out of the frame and disengaged from the suction. Trying to grab the glass, it sliced through my palm. I let out a yelp as the glass shattered against cement.

Gavin winced at the sound of the breaking glass, then looked at my hand, which appeared to be almost split in half.

"Criminy," he whispered, digging through his tactical pack. "Does it still hurt?"

"No," I said, blushing. How could I have done something so stupid? "Not anymore. Sorry."

Gavin produced a roll of gauze from the pack and seized my hand, his intended medical care interrupted as amazement filled his eyes. The wound had started closing. He had never seen me heal before.

"Unbelievable." Gavin's head jerked up, and he

looked around as though he'd suddenly remembered what we were doing there.

"Status?" he asked Emery as he blotted blood off my hand.

"Unchanged. From our end, the disturbance wasn't detected. Is She-Ra good as new?" Emery inquired.

"Affirmative," Gavin replied, stuffing the soiled gauze into his pack. I felt like such a moron.

"Any sign of Joe?" Emery asked.

Gavin gestured toward the window, asking me to explore the inside with my senses.

Concentrating, I listened, hearing nothing more than urban noise and crickets, although I could smell Joe.

"I can smell him, but don't hear him."

The dead have a scent, too . . .

Don't think that way!

"Is his scent stronger?"

"Yes."

"He's inside," Emery deduced.

"Yes," I confirmed, watching Gavin direct a little wand through the window. It sent a red beam bouncing around the room. A dusty desk and file cabinets suggested it had been an office once. "There are other human scents inside, too. I don't recognize them."

"The motion detector isn't armed," Gavin informed. He stuck his head through the opening, cocking his head up. "But the window frame is wired."

"You mean with an alarm system?" I asked.

"Yep." Gavin dropped his rifle and pack into the room. He climbed through the window.

After he'd collected his weapon and pack and cleared

out of the way, I dove through the window, catching the filthy carpet with my palms, and flipped up onto my feet. I inhaled deeply, and Joe's scent wafted up my nose.

I opened my mouth to call him. Gavin held up his hand for me to wait.

"Find him first," he whispered. He poked his head out the door, looking from side to side. "No security cameras. Let's go."

We crept out into the hall, floorboards creaking under our weight. The forgotten building was old—real old—and spooky. Cobwebs and pests claimed the corridor, and it felt as though eyes were watching us from the abandoned rooms. The building was lifeless, save for Gavin's heartbeats and the rapid heartbeats of the many rodents in residence. The rhythmic hammering echoed in my ears, like tiny people pounding on even tinier drums.

Joe's scent grew stronger, and a new human heart joined in the chorus, along with some cautious breaths.

A relieved smile stretched across my masked face. Joe's shoe soles lightly scraped the floor in an open doorway down the hall. Apparently, Gavin and I weren't as stealthy as we'd thought.

"Joe," I called softly, knowing he'd heard us and was trying to get in a position to see who was coming.

His breath caught.

Gavin tapped my arm, warning me to keep quiet.

"It's okay," I told him. Aside from an army of mice and the two of us, Joe was the only other warm-blooded creature currently on the first floor—or so said my ears and nose. "Joe, it's me. *Green Eyes.*"

He poked his head out from the room, squinting. I let

out a delighted yelp and ran to him, throwing my arms around his neck.

"Thank God, you're not hurt!" I gave him a squeeze.

"You're a sight for sore eyes." He pulled back to get a look at my eyes, which probably resembled two black holes in the dim light filtering in through the window. But I could see his brown eyes just fine. "I knew you'd come."

His eyes flitted to Gavin, widening. I glanced over my shoulder and totally understood Joe's reaction. Gavin's Herculean physique filled the doorway. He looked quite menacing.

"Joe, this is . . . uh . . ." I had no idea how to introduce Gavin. As a secret agent? *Mendel's* father?

"Hawkeye," he introduced himself, saving me the trouble.

"It's a codename," I felt the need to explain. How ridiculous did Hawkeye sound?

Gavin held out his hand. Joe shook it.

I loved it when people I loved met, regardless of the whole w*orlds colliding* thing.

"Pleasure to meet you, Hawkeye," Joe said and then circled a lean index finger around his own eye area. "Military?" he asked of the night-vision goggles.

"Former SEAL. I still have connections to get gear. What are you doing here, Joe?"

"Followed my friend Doc." Joe lowered his voice. "There's somethin' fishy going on. Underneath us."

Gavin and I automatically lowered our gazes to the floor. *Underneath us?*

"I'm guessing Green Eyes told you about me, and about the homeless folk disappearing, and that Doc was one of them?"

"She has."

"I followed him here the other night. Jimmied a lock after he come in. I saw him turn off the burglar alarm, and knew that was my chance." Joe glanced at me. "That young gal with the yella hair I told you 'bout, she was with him."

I nodded, wondering if his "yellow" was the same as my "caramel," and if he had seen Constance. He did say "young," but our interpretation of young would be different, too.

"When I got inside here, they were nowhere around. Then I noticed muddy footprints going down the hall. I followed them to an elevator, but I went up the stairs instead, not wanting to tip them off. Figured they'd hear an elevator running. But I didn't find no sign of them, or anyone else. So I come back down here and found a place to hole up and wait.

"Maybe a couple of hours passed before I heard the elevator power up again. It was coming up, though, not down. Thing is, there's no stairs leading down to a basement, at least that I could find. Looks like there might've been once, in the stairwell. But a wall's been built up over it.

"Doc, the young gal, and another man came out of the elevator and left the building. I been here since, fixin' to find a way to open that elevator. Buttons don't work. It's one of them keypad set-ups. A couple more folks come through here and went down the elevator. I couldn't get close enough to see what numbers they punched in on that keypad, though. Doc's gal and an Asian fella are down there now. Been there since sometime late afternoon. I don't have a wristwatch," Joe added apologetically.

"Joe, you've been here since last night?" It was the first thing to pop into my head. I hated the thought of him being alone in this dark building, especially with aqua people traipsing back and forth to the elevator. What would they have done to Joe if they'd caught him?

"Yes. But I got food and water—always keep something on me. And *this*." He reached behind him and picked up a crowbar leaning against the wall.

Gavin grinned. "That's how you jimmied the lock."

"Wasn't anticipating a crowbar would come in so handy," Joe said, returning the smile.

"Then why'd you have it with you?" I asked.

"Green Eyes, I'm a sixty-eight-year-old man spying on folks that're obviously up to no good. I need to protect myself."

"Absolutely," I agreed. Joe only knew that Doc and the young woman had gone into the water and didn't resurface. He had no clue how complicated this was. "But now I'm here to protect you."

"We'll look out for each other." Joe shook the crowbar.

"Cable, status?" Gavin asked Emery.

Joe lifted his eyebrows at me questioningly.

"We have ear buds," I explained, tapping my right ear. "Hawkeye's talking to another . . . uh . . . *operative*."

Joe nodded, and Gavin rolled his eyes. I assumed this meant I shouldn't have called Emery an operative, but what was I supposed to say?

Emery shared that the plant tour was still in progress and that Stringer was busy searching for building schematics.

Gavin replied with his standard, "Copy that," then asked Joe to show us the elevator.

Joe removed a flashlight from the pocket of his Seahawks jacket. "My reading lamp," he called the flashlight, then flicked it on. He really had come prepared.

He led us down a long hallway and hung a left.

"Notice the walls," Gavin pointed out as we trailed Joe down another hall.

They were scraped and gouged.

"Heavy equipment came through here," Gavin explained. "We're not the only ones with a big construction project going on."

Joe stopped before a set of dinged-up, gray elevator doors. The doors were huge, and installed horizontally, not vertically.

"That's weird," I said. I cocked my head to the side so they looked upright. "It's like they were put in wrong."

"It's a freight elevator." Gavin studied the keypad next to three black buttons. He frowned. "Do-able, but we're too exposed here. Joe, show us the stairwell."

Joe led us down a few more halls, taking us farther from the main corridor, where the freight elevator was located. Gavin appeared pleased by this more secluded area. When we reached the stairwell, Joe opened the door and motioned for us to go in first. Straight ahead, a flight of cement steps shot up to the second story. Walls closed in on either side of us. Gavin examined the wall to our left, tapping his knuckles along it.

"New construction," he said. "This wall was recently built over the stairs to the lower level." He took off his goggles and handed them to Joe. "I'll trade you," he said and collected Joe's flashlight. "Joe, keep a lookout. She-Ra, hit the wall, right here." He rapped his knuckles against the spot he wanted me to punch.

"Won't that make too much noise?" Joe challenged, worry on his wrinkled face. He slipped on the goggles.

"Depends on the quality of construction." Gavin gestured for me to commence.

Stepping up to the wall, I willed my skin to harden, pulled my fist back, and rammed it into the drywall. It smashed through the wall like a sledgehammer, clear through to the other side. That answered the question on the quality.

I yanked my hand loose.

Gavin grinned. "They just don't build things like they used to." He set the flashlight on the floor so the bright beam smacked into the ceiling over us. Then he took hold of the drywall, ripping off a chunk. In seconds, he and I tore a passageway through the wall, with minimal noise, while Joe watched the hallway. Fluorescent light flowed into the exposed dark stairwell from what I assumed to be a slender, vertical window on the door below, like the one Joe was peering through as he stood watch.

"Joe, we can take it from here," Gavin said. "Get off the grounds pronto, in case all hell breaks loose."

Joe shook an obstinate head of dreadlocks. "If all hell breaks loose, I aim to be at the center of it." He wagged a finger at Gavin. "Don't judge on appearances, son. That would be a mighty big mistake on your part."

This earned a grin from Gavin.

"I plan on seeing this through," Joe reiterated. He pointed his crowbar at the opening we'd made. "No more wasting time. The longer we stand here arguing, the more likely all hell *will* break loose."

"Agreed. Do you know how to handle a nine-millimeter?"

"Yes, sir," Joe answered, to my surprise.

Gavin removed a spare gun from the holster concealed under his jacket and handed it to Joe. "Cable, we're proceeding to the lower level. Status?" Gavin squeezed through the opening. Joe motioned for me to go next.

"Unchanged," Emery replied, which meant the tour continued and nothing had occurred that had raised an alarm. This was good news, at least. Maybe we'd find answers before the tour was over. Emery and Jared could keep Grimm occupied with questions for hours.

Cautiously, we moved down the steps. The door's vertical window showed no one in the hall, and I couldn't hear any talking or movement other than our own. That didn't mean anything, however. Unlike the wall we'd ripped down, the original masonry and fire-rated doors were topnotch, and effectively blocked airflow from the adjoining basement level. Any noise would have to be rather loud in order to hear it in the stairwell, until the seal between the door and doorframe was broken.

"Doesn't make a lick of sense why they'd block up an emergency exit," Joe whispered. "Power could go down, or the elevator could break down, or there could be a fire. Then they'd be trapped down here."

"There must be another way out," Gavin agreed. He peeked out the window into the hallway. Then he flipped to the other side of the window to check out that view. "Clear," he announced. "She-Ra, I'm going to crack the door open. Listen."

He turned the metal doorknob and eased it open. The sound of flowing water filled the space. It sounded like a river.

"What is that?" Joe whispered, slipping off the goggles.

"No clue," Gavin said, then urged me: "Listen."

My ears detected a rumbling from machinery. I also could hear a faint conversation between two people.

"There's a man talking to a woman, probably the two people Joe saw. The man has an Asian accent. They're talking about something called 'The Rogue.' That way." I pointed right.

"The water is coming from the left," Gavin judged, correctly. "Focus on that direction."

Underneath the echo of water and machinery, I picked up something odd: a female humming a song. Closer to us, leisurely footfall struck the linoleum. The scent of the approaching person grew stronger.

"Someone is coming," I whispered. "From the left."

Gavin nodded and let the door close almost completely. "In a hurry, like we triggered an alarm?" he whispered.

"No." I listened. "He or she is moving really slowly, like they're distracted and not paying attention to where they're going." No sooner had I said this than the person's pace picked up. I opened my mouth to tell Gavin, but then I heard a vibrating noise. The person stopped walking.

"Give it a rest, *babe* . . . *gripe, gripe, gripe, gripe, gripe, gripe* . . . " a man grumbled loudly. I knew what he was doing in that moment.

"He's texting," I whispered. "Fighting with his

girlfriend is my guess. And I think he's listening to music, too." I'd drawn the conclusion based on the volume of his voice and the cadence of the "gripes." They were muttered in rhythm to a song.

"Gotta love technology," Gavin replied, pleased. His sly smile revealed his plan. This distracted man, with tunes pounding through his ears, wouldn't even know what hit him.

"Joe, when I give the signal, open the door," he instructed, handing the doorknob over to Joe. Gavin moved to the other side of the window, peering around the edge so he could see the man coming.

"He's walking again," I whispered.

Gavin gave a sharp nod. "I have a visual. Joe, on my signal. She-Ra, stand down. This one is mine."

I slunk back into the shadows while Joe and Gavin pressed themselves on either side of the doorway. Barely breathing, Joe gripped the knob. The fingers on his other hand twitched at his side, as though warming up for a brawl. Gavin flipped to Joe's side of the door, bending his knees.

In the window, I glimpsed a head of shaggy brown hair angled over a cell phone. The man's hair hid his face, but I could see his thumbs adeptly punching out a text. By his appearance, voice, and quick texting, I guessed he was young, and I could hear the song he listened to now. Muse's "Uprising."

Gavin signaled to Joe. Joe swung the door open, and Gavin sprang at the man, slamming him to the floor with such brute force that the back of his head bounced off it. His baby face twisted in pain and shock, and I noted patches of acne and a pierced eyebrow and lip. He looked to be about eighteen or nineteen.

"Ooooooo," the boy groaned, his eyes attempting to focus on Gavin.

Gavin gathered him by his Led Zeppelin T-shirt to haul him into the stairwell and out of sight, but the skin on the boy's neck appeared to ripple, like agitated water in a pond. The collar Gavin held sliced through the boy's neck, which didn't lose form. It was as though his neck was solid and fluid at the same time.

Joe gasped.

Gavin pulled back his fist and drove it into the boy's jaw. His knuckles glanced over the surface of the boy's skin, leaving droplets of water in the blow's wake. The shocking sight brought to mind how water looks when a rock is skipped across the top. The disengaged droplets drew back to the boy from midair, as though a magnet attracted them, melding back into his skin, which suddenly appeared solid again. The injured boy was clearly having trouble controlling whatever his power was. What would he have unleashed, if he hadn't been hurt?

Gavin wasn't going to find out.

He dragged the nearly unconscious boy to a sitting position, clasped a strong hand on his forehead, and slammed his head into the floor. The boy's eyes rolled up into his head, and he lay under Gavin's straddling legs, limp as a rag.

I stared at the violent scene, stunned. I had been at the center of violence more times than I cared to remember, but witnessing brutality was a whole other animal.

"She-Ra, take him," Gavin commanded in a hoarse voice, appearing slightly shaken.

I gathered the boy in my arms and carried him into the

stairwell, depositing him gently on the floor. Gavin shut the door behind us. Nausea slid through my stomach. What did Gavin plan on doing to him now?

"Poor kid," Joe said, smoothing the unconscious boy's disarrayed hair. "What is he?"

"We don't know," Gavin responded, peering out the window. "Status?"

"They're preparing to leave the facility," Emery reported. He hadn't made a peep during the ambush. "The Host claims to have something interesting to share. I assume they're headed your way."

"Why didn't you tell us until now?" I screeched.

Gavin gave me a sharp look.

"I don't care if they hear me," I said through my teeth, glaring at him. "Jared isn't stepping one foot inside this building!"

"Your Jared?" Joe asked. Then he shook his head, as though trying to gather his thoughts, and fixed me with a stern look. "Green Eyes, don't act rashly. Follow orders, or this could go bad for Jared."

"I won't do anything stupid," I growled.

Or would I?

Letting Joe handle me, Gavin squatted next to the boy, evaluating him. "I'm taping him, for all the good it'll do. She-Ra, my bag."

"He'll be out for a while," Joe predicted, smoothing the boy's unruly mop again.

I handed Gavin his tactical bag.

"For our sake, I hope you're right. Because this won't hold him for long." Gavin removed duct tape from the bag.

After taping the boy's mouth, Gavin turned him onto

his belly. Then he wound tape around his captive's wrists with a proficiency that implied he'd done it many times before. I watched quietly, with an anxious, heavy heart. Listening to music, arguing with a girlfriend—all totally normal for a teenage boy. Looking at him, there had been nothing that suggested he was anything other than that, until his flesh became a watery substance.

There has to be some of him left in there, I reasoned, as Gavin finished taping his ankles together. He stuffed the duct tape back inside his tactical bag. *A mind-controlling parasite wouldn't care about rock music, or girls.*

His mouth a straight, ruthless line, Gavin contemplated the boy. I grew more afraid for him.

Joe touched Gavin's shoulder. "He's had enough. We'll be outta here 'fore he can cause any trouble."

Gavin nodded, rubbing his forehead. "Status?"

"They haven't left the plant," Emery replied. "Nightcrawler and I have managed to delay them."

Despite the horrific situation, a smile tugged at my lips. *Maybe Grimm will become so exasperated by Jared's constant questions that he'll forget all about whatever he has planned down here . . .*

What is going on down here?

"We need to assume anyone we encounter is like *him*," Gavin said as he patted the boy down for weapons. He extracted a handgun from the boy's waistband. "He would've used this." He looked directly at me, then stuffed the handgun into his empty holster. "We strike them before they can strike us. Surprise will be our only advantage."

Gavin put on his tactical bag and recovered his gun, which he had holstered prior to attacking the kid. Eyeing him, Joe collected his crowbar and the gun Gavin had given him from the floor.

I could see that Joe recognized that Gavin had experienced and seen things most men hadn't, and never would, which earned him a level of respect, although Joe would keep a sharp eye on him, regardless. So would I.

I loved Gavin, but I knew he was capable of anything.

Chapter 27

Battle of the Species

G avin told me to find the source of the water. Joe trailed me, with Gavin keeping watch of the rear, his gun in position, even though I'd assured him that I could only hear the hummer, whom we were headed toward, and the man and woman, who were in the opposite direction, deep in conversation. Their voices sounded garbled, like those of the adults in the *Charlie Brown* cartoons. I didn't dare fix too much attention on them and risk compromising my senses and possibly missing a threat.

"They've left the plant," Emery informed.

I came to a halt.

"Keep moving," Gavin commanded in a low voice. "The Host is bringing Nightcrawler to wherever this water is coming from. We need to be in position when they arrive."

Half a dozen questions fired through my head, such as *Why don't we just stop them before they enter the building?* However, I refrained from asking them. I had to trust Gavin.

Emery will tell us if Jared is in danger, I consoled myself, getting a whiff of a familiar scent.

"I smell a cat," I whispered to Gavin and Joe.

"Cleo?" Joe asked.

"I'm not sure."

"Who's Cleo?" Gavin demanded.

"Lady Jane's cat. She's a friend of Joe's, and she's missing, too."

"Do you smell Lady Jane?" Gavin asked.

"No," I confirmed, watching Joe. A certain clairvoyance had settled on his face. Joe didn't look as though he liked the truths that were materializing behind those sad, wise eyes of his.

"Keep moving," Gavin ordered me again.

I led them down another hall, stopping at the end. The sound of running water echoed behind two double doors about fifty feet from us, in what I assumed was a very large space.

"The boiler room," Joe guessed.

"Let's see." Gavin stepped past me.

"Wait," I said, grabbing his arm. "The woman isn't humming anymore."

"Is she walking?" Gavin asked. He moved in front of me, his gun trained on the doors.

I listened and smiled. "Can you hear that?"

Alert, Gavin and Joe shook their heads.

"She is so loud, I'm surprised. She's *sleeping*, and snoring up a storm!"

"Are you positive she is alone?" Gavin asked.

"Yes, she is," Emery answered for me. "The Host and his party are headed your way. I'll let you know when they enter the facility."

My stomach clenched.

"Where are they now?" I asked, breaking protocol. My dad suddenly sprang to mind. With only Emery communicating with us, I had forgotten he was there, too, watching and listening to everything that was going on. No doubt he was sick with worry.

"Dad, everything is okay," I assured.

Joe's eyebrows lifted at the word "Dad."

"Affirmative, She-Ra," Emery answered, sounding perturbed. "Proceed."

Gavin motioned for Joe and me to wait. Gun poised, he moved quickly and stealthily toward the doors. The door on the right was slightly ajar. Plastering himself against the doorframe, he peered inside. His eyes and chin dropped, indicating that the room was lower than the floor we were on. He waved for us to follow, then slipped through the opening, careful not to touch the door, in case it creaked and woke the woman.

I scurried across the hallway with Joe close behind, stepped through the door, and threw my hands over my mouth to stifle a scream. Joe gasped behind me.

How could anyone have been prepared for this?

Twenty feet below looked like a set from a sci-fi film—only this was real, terrifyingly real.

Two trenches cut across the cavernous cement room. The right was streaming with clear water that dropped off abruptly and poured into a wide ground-level drain. The left was a pool of glimmering, bright-white light. Zillions of bioluminescent parasites had to be swimming through that water. The twinkling water traveled up through two thick glass tubes that were sunk into the parasite-infested stream. One glass tube ran to a large steel machine that resembled an industrial furnace. The other connected to an identical machine mounted next to the first. Eight thinner glass tubes shot out from the other side of each machine, and the conduits carried the water through the cement wall.

In these tubes, the water was clear. At first, I thought the machines had filtered out the parasites, until a vision adjustment revealed that the sixteen glass tubes had been sectioned off at a water bottle length. The parasites hadn't been removed. They had been distributed, one per section of each tube, so they wouldn't glow.

Speculating where the tubes went from here wasn't necessary: the contaminated water was being piped to the Luminous Water plant.

Between both trenches sat an old woman in a rocking chair. White head thrown back, wire-rimmed glasses cock-eyed on her wrinkled face, gray cat curled on her lap, and a knitting project tucked at her side, she whistled snores. I was almost positive the cat was Cleo.

Lined end-to-end between the snoozing woman and the glowing stream, were twenty glass pods. Clear water spewed from a spigot into each enclosed tank, showering upon a human form, one per pod, submerged in parasite-infested water. The twenty humanoids looked very much alive, moving and looking about, each rolling around like a baby in amniotic fluid. They breathed in the water and parasites like oxygen, seeming to exhale more parasites than they inhaled. The twinkling parasites darted in and out of the prisoners' ears and nostrils, swarming around their faces in eerie frenzies of light. Thick glass tubes extended from the backside of each pod, feeding the glowing white pool.

What are they doing to these people?

An insistent tap on my shoulder freed me from my initial shock. I glanced at Joe's disturbed face, and he pointed at Gavin, who was already halfway down the metal stairway, setting a foot lightly on each step, carefully distributing his weight so as not to make a sound.

Joe and I followed his lead. I focused my attention on each step as my foot met it, concentrating on the descent to give my rattled state of mind a reprieve. Maybe when I looked up again, the horrible tanks would be gone.

At the bottom, Gavin jerked his head toward the back of the stairs, where a large discarded steel water tank lay on its side. We scampered behind it and peeked over the top. Snores continued to rip from the woman's throat.

"In that first tank, that's Z," Joe whispered tightly.

"Another missing friend?" Gavin deduced as he filmed the horrific scene on his cell. "What about the others?"

"Couldn't see them clearly coming down. Z's tank is blocking the view now."

Z stopped turning in the slow circle he had been making and stared in our direction, as though he'd heard his name. He exhaled a shimmering cloud of parasites.

"He heard us?" Joe croaked out.

"I don't know," I whispered back. "Is that Cleo?"

"Looks like her."

The cat stretched on the sleeping woman's lap. Z's head cocked to her. A toothy grin broke out across his face.

"Hey, Cleo," he said, bubbles and parasites escaping with the words. He tapped the side of the tank, trying to get her attention. Cleo yawned, uninterested, and curled up to go back to sleep.

"He's aware," Gavin hissed, astonished.

"And not afraid," Joe added. "Z wants to be there."

"They've entered the building," Emery told us.

Just then, a bearded man burst through the surface of the trench containing clear water, as though he'd swam in with the current. Standing up near the edge, he closed his eyes and tilted his head to knock water from his ears, then ran his hands over his hair, pushing it from his face. He wore jeans and a flannel shirt, and appeared to be in his late thirties.

"Doc," Joe whispered.

Gavin nodded and kept filming.

A woman emerged right after Doc. It took me a moment to recognize her with wet hair. Her large eyes fell on Cleo. A bright smile lit her face.

"Cleo!" she exclaimed with delight, startling the old woman out of sleep.

"Nearly gave me a heart attack," she scolded a smiling Lady Jane, who swam to the edge of the trench.

"Sorry, Ester," Doc apologized, hauling himself out of the water. "See, I told you, Jane. Cleo's safe and sound."

"They're headed toward the elevator," Emery informed.

"I'm emailing footage," Gavin whispered to Emery.

My heart sped. Why would Patrick bring Jared here?

Jane scooped her beloved pet off Ester's lap and cuddled Cleo to her wet bosom, despite the cat's yowls and struggles.

"Oh, you stop that, missy," she chided playfully, tapping the cat's nose. "It's just water. Our kind likes water. Mama missed you."

"Well, Thomas," Ester addressed Doc. She took the arm he'd offered her to help her out of the rocking chair. "You managed to bring another one to their senses. Welcome, Rogue! Did I hear Thomas right? Your name is Jane?"

Jane nodded happily, nestling her cheek into Cleo's fur. "Jane Charlotte Altman."

Ester cackled. "It's a pleasure to meet you, *Jane Charlotte Altman*. They're pleased to see you, too." Ester gestured behind her.

My eyes followed to where she'd motioned. I couldn't see around the first tank that held Z, but he waved at Jane, grinning.

Jane waved back. Her smile traveled down the row of tanks. "It's good to see everyone again," she said to Doc.

"They exited the elevator," Emery reported. "A male and female greeted them. Safe to assume the male isn't the one you've taken out of commission."

Doc placed his hand on Jane's shoulder. "See? They're happy. Doing their part, just like I said."

"You'll do yours, too, won't you, Jane?" Ester asked.

I wondered if her *part* entailed being sealed in a tank filled with parasites.

Jane's face fell. She glanced longingly at the channel that she had emerged from. "But I want to be out there," she said like a child yearning to go outside and play.

"We all do, dear. It's where we belong. But we have a job to do."

"Yes, they told me—in *here*." Jane touched her temple. "We are to *assimilate*," she pronounced carefully, looking at Doc for confirmation that she had said the word correctly.

He nodded, smiling.

"That's right. *Assimilate*," Ester said. "We must ensure our survival. And it is *you*, dear. Not *they*."

"Yes. They said—I mean, *I* know Patrick Grimm named us. We didn't have one before."

"Not in the human language," Doc concurred.

"They're headed your way," Emery warned.

Gavin stopped filming and emailed the latest footage to Emery.

Pallid, Joe watched Jane stroll down the row of tanks and greet each occupant by their first name. I tried to process everything that we'd heard and witnessed thus far.

Jane had used the word "assimilate," which I thought meant to incorporate, or absorb, and then touched her temple. Doc referred to the human language as though he were talking about another species.

Gavin put his cell away and freed the semi-automatic rifle from its sling.

"You ain't hurting nobody," Joe hissed at him.

"Think again." Gavin disengaged the safety. "I won't let anyone *get* hurt. Primarily Jared."

"They're almost here," I whispered, hearing Patrick's jovial voice.

"They've entered the corridor," Emery concurred.

Gavin motioned for the three of us to duck down lower.

"Now, Jared, don't let what you're about to see alarm you," Patrick said in an easygoing manner. "Your dad and I will explain everything. But brace yourself for a shock."

"You'll have to trust me, son," Owen said, and I pictured him clasping Jared's shoulder in a fatherly, reassuring way. My fury ignited.

The doors swung open.

"Good evening!" Patrick boomed.

Above us, I saw him throw his arms up animatedly through the landing's metal grids.

"I've prepared Nightcrawler for what he's about to encounter. He knows you're close by," Emery reported as Doc and Ester returned Patrick's greeting. "He has been instructed to get the entire room on film, especially the *aquariums*."

Gavin didn't dare give his standard "copy that," with Grimm and Co. rattling down the steps. Jared hadn't uttered a word as he took everything in.

"Jared—" Patrick grasped his shoulder in the way I had pictured his father doing. Watching them, Owen appeared ill at ease. "Please meet Mrs. Ester Burkhart and Tom Granger—"

The woman who owns this building, I remembered.

Gavin rested his rifle on top of the tank, putting Grimm in its crosshairs.

"—And it appears Tom has brought in another Rogue. My fair lady, allow me to introduce myself. I'm Patrick Grimm."

The Asian man glanced over his shoulder, giving us the first view of his face. Scrutinizing him, Gavin swore under his breath.

I touched his arm.

He stared at me for a beat, thinking. A resigned expression crossed his face. He'd come to some sort of a resolution.

"Cable," he whispered, peering through the rifle's scope again. "Bring in the Mother Ship. ID the Chinese perp."

I assumed Serena was the "Mother Ship."

Grimm released Jared's shoulder in order to offer Jane his hand. Owen moved closer to his son—in case he made a run for it, I guessed. The Chinese man and a young blonde woman appeared ready to tackle him, too.

Jane shook Grimm's hand eagerly. "Good to finally meet you, Patrick." Her expression became sheepish, and a blush crawled across her cheeks. "I shouldn't have said *finally,* like it was your fault. I'm sorry I ran from you."

Grimm bestowed a warm smile. "None of us want to be cooped up on land. But you are forgiven, pretty lady. And you are?"

"Jane. I'm Jane."

"Well, Jane, you are home now." He clasped his other hand over hers. "You'll never be without one again. And it looks like someone else is happy you're here, too."

Patrick released her hand to tickle Cleo under the chin.

All the while, Owen watched Jared with great concern. Constance kept an alert eye on him, too, frowning. Apparently, his calm demeanor had befuddled them.

"Jane, please meet my beautiful wife, Constance."

Constance pulled her eyes from Jared and smiled at Jane. Patrick gripped his shoulder again. With a plastered-on smile, he shrewdly studied Jared, who stared inscrutably at the captives.

In turn, they observed him as though he were the curiosity.

I willed Jared to show some fear. His composure had triggered suspicion.

"Tell Nightcrawler to look afraid," I whispered to Emery.

Gavin released a frustrated breath over my talking out loud.

"He is just trying to maintain," Emery surmised. "Telling him to do anything right now could cause him to unravel."

"He's scared out of his wits," Joe said, confirming Emery's deduction, even though he hadn't heard it for himself.

Gavin made a *psst* sound for us to keep quiet.

Of course he's scared, I continued in thought. *So is Joe. So am I. And probably even Rambo here next to me is, too.*

"I am Dr. Boquin Fan," the Chinese man introduced himself in a soft voice, bowing his head slightly to Jane.

"Dr. Boquin Fan, chemist and CIA research scientist," Emery added.

"Criminy," Gavin muttered. "One of our own."

"The Mother Ship says reinforcements are on their way. Don't say I didn't tell you so." Emery didn't sound happy at all.

Their? Reinforcements? Maybe Serena wasn't the "Mother Ship" after all.

"Try to be in my shoes for once," Gavin grumbled under his breath. "When?"

"Approximately fifteen minutes."

Gavin's eyes flicked to me and then back to the scope.

"Dr. Fan made all of this possible." Patrick motioned around him with his free hand while keeping Jared's shoulder hostage with the other.

Constance, Owen, and the blonde woman, who had introduced herself to Jane as Kiera, exchanged looks as though they were communicating telepathically. There wasn't a doubt in my mind that they had this ability. Owen nodded and moved his gaze back to his son.

"She-Ra, when I order you to leave, *do it*," Gavin said between his teeth, tracking Grimm with the rifle. Patrick propelled Jared toward the tanks by the shoulder.

"Copy that," I whispered, with every intention of doing what *I* thought right, when *ordered*.

"You see, we couldn't reproduce before Dr. Fan," Patrick said, touching hands with the captive in the third tank through the glass. "We were dying out."

Ashlyn had taken Cleo from Jane, and now held the cat face-to-face with the captive in the fourth tank and playfully *meowed*. I had to wonder what planet she was from. Jared shot her a disturbed glance, then his eyes cut back to Grimm.

"We?" Jared's voice sounded normal, not even the slightest detection of a tremble.

"We were trapped for centuries, beneath miles of rock." Grimm stared dreamily into the tank, either ignoring or not hearing Jared's question. "Many of us had died, and we couldn't procreate, or escape. Our situation was bleak. We were on the verge of extinction, until the drill bit from an oil rig emancipated us. Everything changed in that moment, *and* when a couple of rednecks threw me down an embankment . . ." He chuckled. "My smart mouth always did get me into trouble." His expression grew reminiscent. "I still remember how beautiful they were that night, in the lake—" His fingertips trailed along the glass as his eyes stared into the past. "They reminded me of forest fairies dancing around my fingertips in that cool water, casting their spell. I was mesmerized and knew that I'd found something special. Or they found me—had *chosen* me. Then I chose Constance."

He turned his head toward his wife and smiled tenderly.

"As I mentioned, there weren't many of us left. We couldn't reproduce, multiply. There's an organic compound not found on Earth that is essential to our ability to breed. But as mankind has proven, time and time again, nothing is set in stone. If you require a substance that doesn't exist in nature, find yourself a good chemist." He gestured toward Dr. Fan. His gaze returned to the tank. "Our second chance flows here, through our brothers and sisters."

Jared cleared his throat. "So you're saying—these people are your incubators?"

My hand silently smacked my mouth in horror. Of course, that's what they were! Hatcheries! These poor people were *breeding* the parasites!

"Jared, you say that as though I'm a villain!" Grimm exclaimed, laughing. "Look at them—" His hand made a sweeping motion to the line of tanks. "Does it look like anyone is here against their will? Our brothers and sisters are not prisoners. See—" He lifted the lid on the tank he was closest to. "It isn't locked. They can lift the lid and leave any time they want. But they won't, because they are selflessly giving us the greatest gift of all—life."

"Why here? Why did you come to Seattle?"

"I fell in love with the area when I visited your mom and dad. You were just a toddler. The majestic mountains, the lush green, the big blue sky when it opens up—it's breathtaking. And then, these beautiful bodies of water—we can survive in fresh or salt, but we prefer fresh."

"How did Dr. Fan make this happen?"

Grimm fixed Jared with a stare that caused my blood to run cold. A smug smile lifted the corners of his mouth.

"You have your dad's smarts." He flashed a smile at Owen. "And his cunning. You're asking logical questions, but they are the *wrong* questions."

I tensed, preparing to spring. Joe prayed under his breath.

"Okay, then," Jared said, undaunted. "If you want me to ask questions in the right order—What are *they*?" He pointed at the tanks, looking Grimm square in the eye. I couldn't breathe. "What are *you*?"

"We are—" Grimm flipped his palms in the air.

"Luminous," they all said in unison, even the people in the tanks.

Hair prickled on the back of my neck. I had never been so creeped out in my life. "Dear Lord," Joe whispered.

Dark silence dropped over the room as Jared backed away from Grimm. Those behind him moved as well, widening the circle, giving him space but keeping him trapped. His horrified gaze snapped from face to face, finally meeting his father's.

Tears flooded my eyes as I could see the terrible truth slam through Jared's mind. I watched his shock transform into pure rage.

"What did you do to my dad?" he thundered, launching at Grimm.

Ashlyn pushed her palm toward the channel of clear water. Seeing her move, Owen thrust his palm toward it, too. Water flew from the channel as though struck by a powerful force, rushing toward their extended arms, striking their palms and reforming instantly into high-pressure streams. Ashlyn directed her palm at Jared, blasting her stream at him; Owen aimed his hand at her stream, intercepting it. This all occurred at mind-boggling speed.

"Ashlyn!" Grimm shouted in a reprimanding tone. Ashlyn's and Owen's two streams collided, like water discharging from battling fire hoses. The crushing collision forced both streams high into the air over Jared.

Shaking off the surprise, I snapped into action, springing up. Joe threw himself over me, knocking me to the floor. In doing so, the crowbar that he'd held in a death grip struck the tank like a gong.

The sound of pulverizing water ceased.

"It's not time," Joe whispered, staring into my eyes. "They can't see you coming."

"We know you're there," Grimm sang, feet moving our way.

As Joe began to stand, his stern gaze warned me to not interfere.

"Don't move," Gavin ordered me under his breath.

I bit my bottom lip and complied, fighting the instinct to yank Joe down and out of harm's way. But he was right. They couldn't see Gavin or me coming, not if we wanted to stand a chance. Joe was the logical sacrifice.

"I'm coming out." Joe moved around the tank slowly, hands up in surrender. "I don't mean any trouble."

"Joe?" Jane said brightly. "You're not one of us." Her voice had lost its thrill.

The aqua people recognize one another, I deduced, anxious to peek over the tank. Gavin held up a finger to wait, anticipating my impulse.

"Lady Jane, I'm your friend, you know that. I was worried about you, and Doc. That's why I followed him here."

"You shouldn't have done that, Joe," Tom spoke up.

Are they going to hurt Joe? I looked at Gavin desperately.

He shook his head and mouthed, "Only on my signal."

"Joe, as you can see, there was nothing to worry about," Grimm said in an amiable tone.

"No, sir! That's not what I see," Joe responded fiercely. "I see plenty here to worry about. Those are our friends in there, Doc! There's Mike, Javier, Z—how can you be a party to this?"

"Joe, you don't know what you're talking about. We had no life, no purpose—"

"And now y'all are fish hatcheries! But those ain't fish. What are they? Some kind of aliens from outer space?"

"Clear," Emery informed.

Gavin peeked over the tank. I scrambled up and followed his lead. All eyes were on Joe, who stood before Grimm, glaring at him, mad as a hornet. Jared watched on, pale, wet, and deadpan, sandwiched between his father and Constance. Sheepish, Ashlyn skulked over to him.

"I'm sorry," she whispered to Jared as Joe raged on.

"What do you do when you're done with these folks? Make *them* into fish food?"

Jared ignored Ashlyn, keeping his angry gaze fixed on Joe. An injured look claimed her face, and she shifted her eyes to Joe, too.

Patrick grinned at Joe. "Old man, you're full of spit and vinegar."

Joe regarded him coolly. "Do me the courtesy of answering my questions, *Patrick Grimm*, before killing me, or sticking me in one of them tanks."

"You were back there spying, Joe. You know full well

our brothers and sisters can climb out anytime they want. Just like your friend Doc here did. When he felt it was time to give another the privilege, he climbed right on out, didn't you, Tom?"

"We have choices, Joe," Doc said. "Our own free will."

"That's right!" Patrick swiped his palms together and pointed at Joe. "Free will. That's why we're in Lake Washington, night after night, trying to reason with the Rogue. Jane knows. When she was assimilated, she joined the others to run wild, doing her own thing. And this puts us *all* in danger. Don't kid yourself. I could eliminate the threat. Hunt down our rebellious brothers and sisters and *force* them to comply. But I don't, and won't.

"Our goal is to be obscure, to blend in, to assimilate and return to our old lives, undetected. We hadn't anticipated what unhappiness and the feeling of being trapped pre-assimilation would result in: Luminous taking to the water and throwing caution to the wind—"

"The missing locals," Jared spoke his thoughts out loud, which I knew were speeding a million miles a minute behind his poker face.

Patrick turned to him. "Yes, the missing locals who hated their miserable lives so much so that they refused to go back to them. There hasn't been an issue with the vast majority. Most new Luminous don't miss a beat in their daily routine, have never roused suspicion, and continue to be upstanding citizens. We have Luminous in very esteemed and powerful positions: doctors, lawyers, politicians, pillars of society—"

Oh my gosh. How many of them are there?

314

"But you already know about the Rogue, don't you, Jared?"

Jared forced confusion into his expression. "Know what?"

"*Ah-ah-ah-ah*—" Patrick wagged a finger at him. "Time to come clean, young man. Your dad gave you the chance earlier, and you fibbed."

Tensing, Jared glanced at his dad. Owen avoided his gaze.

"Jared, we know you took my yacht onto Lake Washington and that you went diving with another male and a female," Owen said as though he were giving a deposition. "We know you had an encounter with a few Rogues and our search party—"

"Oh, you mean your *peace* party, *Luminous*," Jared mocked.

I cringed. How I wished he hadn't done that.

"Good. So we're beyond denial," his father continued dispassionately. "We need the names of the two individuals you were with."

"I told you, I don't know."

"You told me you took a girl on my yacht. You said she was named Sheila, and you met her at work. But you failed to mention a second person, and that the three of you went diving and had an altercation in the lake. Their names, Jared."

"Is this why you were MIA when Vilvary's goons stuck a gun in my face? Were you being *assimilated*?"

Owen regarded his son neutrally. "I have been a Luminous for most of your life."

Jared gasped as though his father had kicked him in

the gut. His face crumbled into despair. Regret invaded Owen's veneer. I covered my mouth to close it. I had never seen a more devastated expression on anyone's face than the one Jared wore.

"I know this is a lot to digest," Owen said. His eyes pleaded for forgiveness. "I'm deeply sorry you had to find out this way. It wasn't my intention—"

"You've been infecting me with those *things*," Jared accused through his teeth.

"I have always wanted what's best for you—"

"Enough!" Constance stormed. "Owen was being humane with you!" she yelled at Jared. "Take my word on it, boy! You want to take assimilation *slowly*. The mortality rate skyrockets otherwise. Your father—yes, *that* is *your* father—didn't want you to experience the pain he had. The pain alone can kill you." She got right into Jared's face. "Stop sniffling and feeling sorry for yourself. Tell me *who* she is—*what* she is."

I couldn't see Jared's face around Constance's head, but I could hear the reckless smirk in his voice.

"Her name is Sheila."

"Sheila *what*?"

"I never asked for her last name."

"I'm done!" Constance announced, throwing her hands up. She stomped a few feet away, whipped around, and pushed her palm toward the parasite-infested pool.

A glowing, serpent-like spiral shot from its center into the air, twisting toward the group as though taking stock, planning an attack. Suddenly, it dove like a striking cobra, straight at Jared.

A primal scream tore from my throat, and I leapt over

the tank in a blind rage. I hit the floor in a run, flinging Kiera and launching Dr. Fan with a sharp-kick to the chest. Through my red haze of fury, I saw the column of water swallow Jared whole and swing toward the pool.

Screaming again, I reached for the wet flannel collar of my next obstacle. Doc had rushed in front of me to protect Constance. Gripping his collar, I snarled and brought my knee up. My knee connected, but not with anything solid. The sensation reminded me of crawling across my Aunt Lucy's waterbed.

Doc smiled around gritted teeth and brought a very solid fist down on my skull, getting a surprise of his own and a few broken bones.

"Oh, God!" he screamed, cradling his broken hand.

A bullet flew past Doc and struck the upper arm that Constance used to control her water serpent. The bullet made a splattering sound upon entry, as though it had hit a bucket of Jell-O, and sailed right out the other side of Constance's shoulder.

Displaying no pain, she glanced down to where the bullet had entered. Irritation crossed her face as she took notice of the damage done to her tailored dress. She lowered her hand to touch it, and the water serpent holding Jared dropped as though it were an electronic toy and the batteries had just run out. Shimmering water splashed high into the air when Jared hit the pool.

A waterspout shot past Constance like a lightning bolt. I swiveled my head around to see that the water came from Grimm's palm, targeting Gavin.

Gavin dove to the side, narrowly avoiding being hit. The metal landing shook as armed men garbed in black SWAT armor filed through the door.

Compliments of the Mother Ship, I thought as General Alton's face flashed in my mind's eye.

"Well, what do we have here?" Grimm asked in an amused tone, redirecting his palm to the landing.

The other Luminous attacked, their palms summoning water from the channel and blasting streams toward the SWAT team. The SWAT team responded with gunfire. Within seconds, the room was a blur of water, bullets, shattering glass, and screams. All I could think of were my friends.

My frantic eyes spotted Jared and Joe amid the chaos. Joe was helping Jared out of the pool. Bullets struck the tank in front of them. Joe shielded Jared from raining shards of glass and water as a Luminous jumped to his feet, leaping from his demolished pod, emitting a fierce war cry.

I launched myself toward Jared and Joe, but my foot was lassoed by a powerful vortex, whipping me through the air and flinging me into the center of the channel. I hit the water and was instantly sucked to the bottom, at least fifteen feet down, coming face-to-face with Constance. Her golden eyes ignited, hair moving with the excited water around her face like Medusa's snakes. Over us, the battle raged.

Die, she mouthed, raising her arms.

Even in my adrenaline-induced beast state, I understood she had the advantage. The water was her element; she ruled it. I couldn't drown her, or strike her, not with her ability to reform her flesh into a watery substance. I wasn't sure how to defeat her, other than to tire her out. Maybe distracted and weakened, she couldn't employ her rotten tricks. So I shot over her, then under her, and kept her turning in circles as she tried to capture me in her cyclone arms.

After several wild laps, an opportunity presented itself, and a swift kick into her backside proved my theory was spot-on. My foot connected with a solid rump and sent Constance whiplashing through water, her whirlpool arms becoming flesh and bone again.

A lethal grin broke across my face. She was mine.

A body plunged through the water like a torpedo. Ashlyn landed in a squat on the bottom and sprang up, aiming her head at my stomach. I smirked. Silly girl, she was about to knock herself out. Ramming her head into me would be like diving into an empty swimming pool.

Arrogance getting the better of me, I held my arms out, welcoming her to hit her deadly target. The next thing I knew, I was spinning wildly, as though trapped in a washing machine drum—all the while, acutely aware of Ashlyn's presence nearby. I couldn't see her; I couldn't see anything as I turned in endless circles. But I felt her, could sense her all around me, trapped in her unbridled fury.

Faster and faster I turned. My brain felt as though it were sloshing against the sides of my skull, and my stomach was being propelled into my throat. This would certainly result in death if I couldn't escape Ashlyn's vortex. There had to be a way. She had to have a weakness. We all did.

But before there was time to explore the chink in her armor, her vortex lifted. It took me several moments to shake off the residual effects of being spun so violently, and to get my bearings. When I did, I discovered I was alone in the water. The battle overhead had quelled.

I swam to the surface and popped my head out of the water, seeing sprawled law enforcement agents, strewn guns, puddles, scattered broken glass, and bullet casings.

Unscathed, the Luminous stood amongst them, surveying the damage.

"Look what they've done," Z moaned mournfully, kneeling on one knee while scooping up a handful of water.

I glimpsed Gavin about a hundred feet away, pushing himself off the floor, choking up water. My eyes desperately sought Jared and Joe.

"They murdered them!" Z howled, just as I spotted Jared near the pool, drenched, wet hair hanging around his face, elbows locked, his palms pressing against a still form.

Joe!

I lurched out of the water, leaping over downed men, and ran past Patrick and Constance, who appeared to be consulting telepathically, and skidded up to Jared and Joe. There was so much blood!

"No, no, no, no, no," I sobbed, pressing my hand on top of Jared's, over the bullet wound. Blood oozed between my fingers. "Joe, Joe, Joe, can you hear me?"

Gray pallor, eyes shut; he didn't respond.

"We need help!" I screamed. My dad appeared at my side.

"Don't talk," he ordered desperately.

He was worried about someone hearing me? How could he worry about me when Joe was dying before our very eyes?

"We have to help him," I choked out, glimpsing Emery helping his father up.

"Paramedics will be here soon," Dad promised. "Jared, keep pressure on the wound."

"He pulled me from the water, then covered me with his body," Jared explained in a haunted voice, as though

Dad had asked him how Joe had gotten shot. "He sat up, pointed to a place he thought was safe, and a bullet hit him." His tears fell to the blood-soaked white Seahawks jacket. "Come on, Joe. You can make it."

He is too far gone—
No, don't think that way!

"Joe, fight," I pleaded. Grimm's words about the Rogue ran through my head. Unhappy people who had found their escape in the depths of Lake Washington. Would death be Joe's escape? "For me, Joe, please. Please, fight for me."

"You have to get out of here," Emery said, hanging over us, his voice calm and cool. "You, too, Drake—*now*."

"Can everyone just stop worrying about me for once?" I screeched. "No! I'm not leaving him." *Joe won't die alone!*

"Think this through—" Emery started to argue, but then the water in the pool began to lift. Emery's head jerked toward Grimm, whose palm had risen.

Water began to twist into a huge waterspout, producing wind.

"Get down!" Emery shouted, and we threw ourselves over Joe.

I tried to cover them all, protecting them from flying shards of glass, bullets, and forgotten firearms—everything that wasn't nailed down—pulled into the violent, rotating air. I could feel debris strike my back and bounce off, getting sucked up into the cyclone. Daring to crack open an eye, I watched Grimm direct the swirling water over his head with a slow swooping motion of his arm, and into the channel. The wind abruptly stopped, and I lifted my head. Not a drop of water was left in the pool.

Grimm removed what looked to be a remote control from inside his sports jacket. He punched a few buttons. Looking at his cool expression, one would think he was calling a buddy to chat, and not standing in the center of wreckage and bleeding, injured men.

"My good people," Grimm said in a loud, reverent voice. "We wish you no harm. You were doing your job, protecting your species, just as we were protecting ours. You have one hour to vacate this building before it goes up in smoke. There is no use looking for the bomb I've just armed. Don't waste time. Survive."

As if this were a cue, the Luminous made their way toward the channel. The injured members of the SWAT team watched them, making no attempt to intervene.

Hearing the metal steps rattle, I looked at the stairs to see the boy Gavin had beaten and duct taped. His and Gavin's eyes briefly met. He touched his bruised jaw, then pointed at Gavin, a warning that he would not soon forget what Gavin had done to him.

One by one, the Luminous jumped into the clear water. The parasites had followed the current out.

"We are not monsters," Grimm announced. He looked straight at me.

Ashlyn dropped into the channel, followed by her mother.

Owen stepped up to the edge.

"No, Dad!" Jared cried, his hand still pressed firmly on Joe's wound.

"Come with us," his father called.

"Come with you? How? I can't! Where are you going?"

"We are the future!" Grimm thundered.

Owen smiled sadly at his son. "I love you," he said, then jumped in.

Jared's face fell.

"We are *your* future."

With those parting words, Grimm stretched his arms over his head and dove into the channel.

Chapter 28

Shackles

Twelve hours after he'd been shot, Joe had pulled through surgery but hadn't regained consciousness.

He'd lost a significant amount of blood, but the doctors were hopeful he'd have a full recovery.

I glanced around the hospital room, apprising Gavin, Emery, and Jared. They wore the trauma we'd all experienced on their tired, somber faces, along with the knowledge that this was far from finished.

Dad, who had somehow convinced hospital administrators to allow us to keep a vigilant eye on Joe, had left about two hours earlier. My mom and brothers had stopped by to check on us, and Gavin had been in and out, conferencing with the "Mother Ship," and covering our tracks. In the chaotic aftermath of the battle, Dad and I had been able to quietly disappear after assisting the injured CIA agents out of the building.

Following the ambulance that carried Joe, we'd listened to the emergency radio broadcast of the explosion as we watched black smoke billow in the distance. Thankfully, there had been no casualties.

We are not monsters. Grimm's words echoed through my head as I examined Joe's heart monitor, the waves on the screen dipping up and down like the waters of Puget Sound.

We are the future.

We are your *future.*

Not if I have anything to say about it, I growled in my head.

Jared's cell rang. I looked at him. My heart sank, seeing his despair. He had barely spoken a word, but his eyes said it all. He had been shattered.

"It's my mom again," he mumbled. "I'll be right back."

I opened my mouth to ask if he wanted company, but the slight shake of Emery's head stopped me. After Jared was gone, Emery shared more of his theories, just as he had every other time Jared had left the room.

"Infecting the general populace was phase three of their mission," he projected.

"Which is to take over the world," I interjected. The Kings, Lily White, the Luminous—why was there always someone trying to take over the world?

"What else?" Emery agreed. "Phase two had been to infect Seattle's homeless population in order to breed in this particular region. They chose the homeless so they could stay under the radar. If a missing person report was filed for a homeless person—which most likely wouldn't happen—the case would be shoved to the bottom of the pile."

The invisible people, I remembered Joe saying. I looked at him sadly. *Wake up, Joe. You're not invisible to us.*

"In this particular region?" Gavin repeated. "You think they've infected other areas?"

"They had an office full of Louisiana transplants, most of whom were from Grimm's hometown."

"So phase one was infecting targeted victims," Gavin said.

"And there's no way to tell if people are Luminous until they're firing water from their palms," I added, feeling queasy. I wasn't sure if the ill feeling was due to the Luminous threat, or the fact that I hadn't eaten since dinner the night before.

"Are you sure about that, Cassidy?" Gavin asked. "There isn't *any* physical trait? Could you pick up anything telepathically from them?"

I shook my head. "Apparently, they're on a different frequency than dogs, cats, and *him*." I gestured toward Emery. "They look like any other human, and smell like any other human, if that's what you were getting at."

"Jared will be back any moment," Emery predicted, abruptly impatient. "The original *breeding ground* has to be located. It's probably in Grimm's hometown."

"Maybe that's where they've all gone." I pictured the devastation on Jared's face when his father had disappeared in the channel. How could he have left his son like that? Then again, the real Owen had left Jared long ago.

"Believe it or not, Emery, the CIA is a step ahead of you." Gavin yawned and scrubbed his exhausted face. "This is a government investigation now. In other words, stay out of it."

"When you put it like that," Emery retorted, "how can I not?"

Gavin shook a finger at him, lowering it as Jared returned.

I cleared the guilt from my throat. Why were we excluding Jared from the conversation, anyway? It was more than being sensitive to his feelings, I knew. Hadn't he earned a place on our team?

"Um, how's your mom?" I asked awkwardly.

"She's at LAX," Jared answered, sitting down. "She'll be home in a few hours." That was all he had to say on the subject.

I examined his guarded expression, wondering if he suspected we were leaving him out of the loop. It triggered another dose of guilt.

Enough of this, I decided. "Jared, Emery thinks—"

"—Joe is coming to," Emery finished for me.

"That's a cheap trick—" I started to scold him.

Then Joe's eyelids twitched.

"Joe!" I grabbed his hand, relieved and frightened at the same time. The jig was up. Joe was about to see more than just my green eyes. "Can you hear me?"

His eyelids fluttered open. Tears misted mine.

"Green Eyes," he said in a hoarse whisper, trying to focus on me.

"Yes." I dashed a tear away. "My name is Cassidy. Cassidy Jones."

His lips lifted into a smile. "You're as pretty as a picture, just like I reckoned you'd be."

"And this is Emery Phillips—*Mendel*," I introduced, excited. "And Gavin, his father, but you know him, too—Hawkeye. And you already know Jared."

Jared gave Joe a distant smile. "Glad you're okay, Joe." He cleared his throat a little, as though it had constricted, and averted his eyes. I wondered if he felt ashamed about his dad.

"You're a brave young man," Joe whispered, his sage-brown eyes brimming with sympathy. "Everything will be just fine, Jared."

Jared nodded quickly, hoping that would end the

condolences. I'd noticed Joe hadn't delivered the statement with his usual conviction. His words were meant to be comforting, nothing more.

"Oh, Joe, I have good news!" I gushed, wanting to shift the focus off Jared. Plus, I was eager to see how Joe would receive the opportunity. Knowing what I knew about him, I figured he'd politely decline the invitation. But I wasn't about to let him.

"Let me, Cassidy," Gavin said. He smiled at Joe. "Joe, it's going to take a while for you to recover. We have an extra bedroom—"

"Thank you kindly, Gavin," Joe cut him off. "But I'll be fine."

My eyes welled. I knew Joe would turn Gavin down.

"Oh, Joe." I had forgotten all the arguments I had formulated over the hours. "Joe, *please*." I couldn't see him go back on the streets.

Joe took my hand. When I looked at him, I saw tenderness there.

And then I saw the shackles break.

"Gavin," his gaze moved toward Gavin as he squeezed my hand. I swiped away the single tear that had slipped down my cheek, suddenly a happy tear. Joe had finally ended his self-imposed sentence of homelessness and loneliness. "Do y'all need a cook?"

"What do you cook?"

"Cajun."

"Gumbo?"

"I make a *mean* gumbo."

Sinking deep in his chair, arms crossed, Gavin just grinned and nodded.

Chapter 29

Secrets

"I have a year-long family membership for the EMP . . ." the auctioneer announced. He added a few details that I didn't pay attention to, then launched into his chant. "Who'll give me a hundred dollars, now two, who will give me two . . .?"

My eyes moved from smiling face to smiling face at our table—my family, the Phillipses, Jared, and Eileen. I marveled at how normal we all appeared, dressed up, eating, laughing, and having a grand old time. It was as though worlds hadn't been rocked, lives hadn't been shattered, and we lived blissfully free from the knowledge of a new threat against the human race.

For the night, Gavin was just an accountant, Emery was a typical ninth-grade boy, I was human, and Jared was happy. He played the part well. His joy seemed genuine, and at the moment, his biggest challenge in the world appeared to be getting the napkin football he'd folded to go between the goal posts Nate made with his index fingers and thumbs across the table. No one would have guessed the many dark secrets concealed at this one table, behind our bright smiles.

My eyes traveled around the room, taking in the other happy faces. What were their secrets?

That they're Luminous? I examined an attractive woman in a shimmering dress who was nibbling at a slice of red velvet cake as she chatted with her tablemates. As far as I knew, she could be one.

Doctors, lawyers, politicians, pillars of society.

The city could be swarming with Luminous. There was no way to know.

Of course, the burning question was: What about the people who hadn't been completely assimilated, including my mom?

Will the parasites remain dormant in them? Serena had concluded they would. *But does the parasite have more control than we realize?* I fretted, studying Mom.

Mom chatted with Eileen, appearing untroubled and in complete control of her mind. Feeling my worried gaze, she looked at me and smiled. I worked the sides of my mouth into a smile, too. Tonight was not the time to torment myself.

The threat of more Luminous casualties had been greatly reduced. Ester's building and the Luminous Water plant had burned to the ground, and the government had issued a sweeping recall of the contaminated water. Subsequent news reports claimed that a potentially harmful bacteria had been detected in the bottled water during a routine safety test. It was a pale shade of the truth.

There had been a public outcry that first week as Luminous Water was pulled from stores and vending machines. Many consumers experienced withdrawal symptoms. There had been a handful of other missing person reports filed during that time, too. I figured these were the unfortunate people who disregarded the recall and consumed their last flat of Luminous Water. According to Grimm, they were unhappy hosts choosing a new life, a new aquatic existence.

Which brings me to Cristiano.

He had returned to work a couple of days after the explosion, apologetic and moodier than he'd been in recent weeks. Emery said his excuse had been a family emergency, which he hadn't elaborated on. I didn't believe Cristiano, of course. He had to be one of them.

After school that day, I studied him from our living room window, waiting for him to slip up and give himself away as he tossed scraps into a dump truck. As far as Cristiano knew, he was alone and there was no one around to witness the truth. But he remained a normal man, just doing his job.

Maybe Cristiano is only human, I thought as Dad raised his paddle to bid on whatever auction item was up for grabs. *Maybe I should stop thinking about all of this right now.*

Jared's football struck my forehead, confirming that thought.

"Ow!" I complained, rubbing my forehead.

Jared flashed his beautiful grin, the merriment reaching his eyes.

"Having fun?" he inquired. He appeared to be on the verge of laughter. I marveled at how he could be so carefree. Like Emery, he obviously possessed an ability to compartmentalize that I didn't. The heavy stuff always hung directly in front of my face.

"Loads." I shot the football at him. I could at least *try* to put thoughts of impending doom on the backburner for a couple of hours.

331

"Ah, we have a very special item on the table now: a six-day Caribbean cruise on the Sovereign Luxury Cruise Line for a family of up to four members, with the host of *In the Spotlight*, Drake Jones, and his lovely family. Who'll give me one thousand, now two, who will give me two . . ."

Gavin raised his paddle.

"Two-thousand-dollar bid! Now three thousand, will ya give me three?"

Across the room, Robin Newton's dad put his paddle in the air.

"Dad!" she shrieked in horror.

I couldn't blame her. I was pretty horrified myself.

The auctioneer pointed at him. "Three-thousand-dollar bid! Now four thousand, will ya give me four?"

"Gavin, put your paddle in the air," I screeched, gesturing wildly for him to bid.

Emery laughed.

Ruben Schleper's mom's paddle went up.

"Four-thousand-dollar bid!"

I breathed a sigh of relief. Ruben Schleper, I could handle.

"Now five thousand, will ya give me—"

Robin's dad's paddle went up again.

"Are you insane?" she yelled and tried to grab the paddle. He maneuvered it out of her reach, a determined look on his face. He aimed on winning.

"I got five thousand!"

"I want to go on a cruise with Drake Jones!" Mr. Newton told her, loudly and unabashedly. I wanted to crawl under the table for her.

"Now six thousand, will ya give me—"

"Gavin!" I pleaded.

"Cassidy Claire," Mom scolded.

"For heaven's sake," Serena said, seizing the paddle from her husband. Very primly, she raised it.

The auctioneer pointed at her. "Six-thousand-dollar bid! Now seven thousand, will ya give me seven thousand?"

No paddles went up.

"How about six thousand five hundred? Six thousand five hundred? Six thousand five hundred? Would you go six thousand two hundred fifty?"

Smugly smiling, Serena slapped the paddle against Gavin's chest.

"Six thousand two hundred fifty? No? Then six thousand is going once, going twice—"

"Ten thousand dollars!" Mr. Newton called.

Robin released a savage howl.

"I got ten thousand dollars! Eleven thousand, eleven thousand—"

"Gavin!" I begged.

He let out a whistle and placed the paddle down. "Too rich for my blood."

"Ten thousand five hundred, ten thousand five hundred—"

My desperate gaze shot to Emery.

"Ten thousand two hundred fifty—"

"Why are you looking at me?" he asked.

I swiped Chazz's dinner roll and threw it at him.

"*Hey!*" Chazz complained. "I was saving that."

"Ten thousand dollar bid to the gentleman in the Hawaiian shirt!"

Grinning and nodding his head, Mr. Newton gave my

dad two thumbs up while his daughter went on a rampage. I dropped my head to the table miserably. I couldn't believe I had to go on vacation with Robin Newton.

~~~

"Do you think you and Robin will buddy up in a cabin?" were the first words out of Emery's mouth when I crawled through his bedroom window later that night.

The next thing he knew he was being slammed on his bed and beaten savagely with a pillow.

"You think you're funny?" I demanded, whacking him.

Curling into a ball with arms sheltering his head, he laughed and shouted protests.

"This is the *most* terrible thing that has ever happened to me!" I declared, pummeling him with every word.

"The *most* terrible?" Emery managed.

"Practically!" I flopped down next to him, jammed the pillow under my head, and stared up at the ceiling. Peripherally, I saw him turn to his side to study my profile.

"This has been a weird night," I told him.

"A weird three weeks."

"A weird seven months." I shifted to my side and smiled into his eyes. "I always think of glittery black coal when I look into your eyes."

Emery puckered his lips. "Does coal glitter?"

I laughed. "Well, if it did, it would look like your eyes." The evening crowded my thoughts again. "You know what I find strange?"

"No. Tell me."

"How normal we all appeared tonight. No one would have guessed we have so many secrets."

"Everyone has secrets. Just not as interesting as ours." Emery flicked my nose, coaxing a smile out of me.

"Well, I don't have any from you anymore—thanks to our brain connection! I wonder why I can tap into your thoughts and no one else's."

"Have you tried?"

"You know me. What do you think?"

Emery grew serious. For several moments, he absently raked my hair across his pillow, deliberating.

Concentrating on his face, I attempted to extract the thoughts firing off behind his serious eyes, to no avail.

I chuckled, and those black orbs focused on me.

"Yep, I suck as a telepath. Maybe Spock had it right." I stuck my fingertips on his forehead and mimicked the blank expression Leonard Nimoy always wore when reading minds on *Star Trek*. Emery stared back at me, just as blankly.

"Shoot. No mind melding," I joked. "You must have thrown up some kind of mental shield. So much for digging out your deepest, darkest secrets." I sighed.

"I have a great comeback for that, but I'll resist," Emery said without an ounce of humor tinting his voice. "Are you sure you want to know my deepest, darkest secrets? There's one in particular I have in mind."

I nodded against the pillow.

Emery smiled. "Your head is indicating yes, but your *wide*, terrified eyes aren't as confident. Think about it, Cassidy. You don't have to make a decision right now."

He started to sit up. I tugged him back down.

"Oh no, you don't! There is *no* way you're getting out of this. Tell me."

"Promise me what I'm about to share never leaves this room."

"No one else knows?"

"No, and I want it to stay that way. It's critical that it does."

"It will." There wasn't a chance I would betray Emery. "I swear I will tell no one."

"You have it wrong. I am not a mere receiver of your thoughts. Yes, you and I have a telepathic connection. But I lied. I don't hear only your thoughts."

"You can read other people's minds?"

"Like I told you before, I catch snippets of thoughts out of the blue. Most are so vague that they're cryptic. There's no frame of reference to help me know what the person is thinking about specifically—unless it's obvious, of course. I hear just a smattering of words."

"Um . . ." I searched for the right way to phrase this. "Do you think you'll ever get a handle on this, so you'll know *exactly* what the other person is thinking about?"

Emery gauged me. "I don't know. Perhaps. You're confirming why no one else can know. You're frightened of me."

"*Me* frightened of *you*? You can only read minds. I can crack skulls." Emery didn't laugh, so I granted him: "You're right. This isn't funny. I'm sorry for making light of the situation, which I only did because, as you already know, the idea that you can invade my private thoughts scares the heck out of me."

"And rightly so. Now imagine how the CIA agent I live with would feel."

"You'd be a national threat."

"Plus, everyone aware would be afraid of me."

Emery was right.

"No one will know," I vowed. "But you will tell me if you ever, um, get better control of your ability, right?"

"You'll be the first to know." A sly look came into his twinkling eyes. "By the way, thank you."

"For what?"

"Figure it out."

"Do I want to?"

"Probably not," he said. His grin faded. "There's more."

"Another secret?"

"This secret starts with an apology. I'm sorry I've let you wallow in guilt about what King did to me as a kid."

My heart stopped. "You know?"

"I know he experimented on me. But I don't know the specifics, or why. I just have flashes of memory."

"Do your parents know you know?"

"No." Emery didn't elaborate.

Why wouldn't he tell them that he knew and alleviate *their* crushing guilt? Guilt had consumed Gavin for years, fueling his drive to bring King to justice. And if Emery told them, maybe they could help him understand *why* they had allowed King to hurt their son.

Instinct warned me not to tread on this particular ground, though, or risk Emery clamming up. Besides, Emery wasn't cruel. He had his reasons for keeping his parents in the dark, and he'd share his motives with me in due time. I'd make sure of that.

"What do you remember?" I asked gently.

Emery rolled onto his back and looked at the ceiling. "King's face, bright lights, pain, and the faces of other children."

Chapter 30

Endings and Beginnings

Jared pulled off his shoes, letting them drop to the floor, and slumped forward on his bed.

"What is wrong with me?" he spoke into the silence, massaging his forehead. His mood had swung like a pendulum for the past two weeks—euphoria one moment, depression the next—back and forth to extremes, until he thought he'd go completely mad.

Perhaps he was going crazy. There were the voices.

He hadn't heard them that night; they'd been silent, giving his frayed mind a brief reprieve. Perhaps that could be attributed to the upswing of the pendulum into elation. He had been on such a high that he had spent most of the auction suppressing the sporadic laughter building in his throat, like the carbonated contents in a shaken soda can. The part of his mind that hadn't succumbed to the rush had reasoned that he was sitting across the table from the most beautiful girl in the room. *His* girl.

Who wouldn't be walking on air?

But then his psyche would counter this argument, rationalizing that he had no reason to be happy, no matter how much Cassidy meant to him. He had lost his father, a man he'd never really known. He had only known the creatures that were controlling his *real* father's brain.

Maybe his *real* father would have been the dad he had always wished for, a dad like Drake.

Maybe his *real* father would have never left his mom and him.

A tear trickled down Jared's cheek. He swiped it away.

"Up and down, like a freaking rollercoaster," he admonished, pushing himself off the bed and to his feet. "Stop being mental. Get a grip!"

Aggravated, he snatched up the jar of crickets. The swift motion triggered their frantic chirping.

"I know how you feel." Jared examined the startled insects that were hopping around the jar, bumping into the glass and one another. "Trapped, waiting to die, and there isn't a darn thing you can do about it."

He stopped talking and wondered where that sick thought had come from. On the heels of this contemplation, his tormentors returned.

We won't let you die, the voices promised.

Jared squeezed his eyes shut and delivered a punishing blow to his forehead with his palm, as though it could knock the voices loose.

"Shut up!" He gritted his teeth so hard that it felt like they would shatter. Pain shooting through his jaw forced him to relax the muscles. Shaking his head, he drew in a ragged breath and went back to his task. He would ignore the voices. Pretend they weren't there. Maybe then they would go away.

Jared, they summoned.

Jared captured a cricket and dropped it into the terrarium.

Find your father.

"How am I supposed to do that?" he snapped, and then reprimanded himself for answering the voices. They had been telling him for days to find his father and Patrick Grimm.

An image of his dad watching Joe pull him from the water materialized in his mind's eye. His dad had just stood there, looking on. Sure, he had protected him from that psycho Ashlyn, but he hadn't lifted a finger when Constance attacked him, flinging him into that pool swarming with parasites.

Jared rubbed his ear, remembering how the parasites felt squirming around the canal. If Joe hadn't saved him, maybe they would have eaten his brain.

Maybe they did. Maybe that's why I'm schizophrenic now.

"That's it!" He plucked up another cricket. "I need to tell someone what's happening to me—"

You can't, the voices insisted, just as they'd done every time he'd entertained the notion of confessing that he'd gone crazy.

Even without the demands of the voices, Jared could feel himself retreat from the idea. The instinct to protect his secret was too strong. No one could be trusted with it. He couldn't confide in his mom, since she didn't know what had really happened to his dad, and the thought of telling *any* Phillipses caused his insides to recoil. They were dangerous people who had their own agenda. The Joneses might have had the wool pulled over their eyes, but he hadn't.

There was only one person he could confide in, only

one person he could trust. Her loyalties to Emery were strong, but he was the person she loved. He knew every time he looked into her eyes that he was special to her. He also recognized that her feelings for Emery were confused. He'd hung back for months, observing them together, waiting for things to progress. They never did. She only had eyes for him, no one else. Cassidy wouldn't betray him.

She cannot be assimilated, the voices interjected. *Her species is our enemy. They must be destroyed. Tell Patrick Gri—*

"Shut up!" Jared bellowed. He stood still, listening for his mom, and heard running water. She was in the shower—thank goodness.

Stop resisting. Open your eyes.

Laughter built in his throat, exploding.

"Fine! I give in." He tossed his hands up in heedless surrender. "I'm totally wacked." He reached into the terrarium for the water bowl. Killer scurried to the corner. "Eyes are *wide* open."

Then see what you can do—

Jared felt raw energy blast from his head, down his neck and arm, and out his fingertips, which were aimed at the water bowl. The ceramic bowl shook, and the vibrating water rose, swirling higher and higher, thinning into something resembling a fine, rotating spike.

His heart pounded with excitement and fear. He moved his forefinger slightly. The thin column followed the motion.

Killer, the voices prompted.

Without a second thought, Jared responded, swinging his finger toward his pet. The water spike plunged, impaling the tarantula dead center in the abdomen. The spider reared up in pain as the water spike disintegrated, droplets splattering the mortal wound.

You are a new man.

Paralyzed with horror, Jared watched his pet collapse, appearing half its size in death.

You are a god.

Acknowledgements

Many thanks to:

My family for their continual support. Thanks for cheering me on. I love you!

My sister, Stacey, for helping with revisions. I'm eternally grateful, sis. Thanks for making it fun!

William Greenleaf for always polishing my work so beautifully.

David C. Cassidy for the killer cover design and book blurb. Your blurb makes *me* want to read my book!

Amy Eye for the fantastic book formatting.

A.L. Phillips, Dana Griffin, and Scott Bury for beta reading and providing great feedback. I appreciate the time you took to really think through the plot.

Neil Low for theorizing about how local law enforcement might handle the unusual occurrences in this story. Luminous, Seattle is ready for you!

My Facebook friends who responded to my scuba diving questions. I will do it one day, maybe...

Last, but never least, Cassidy's fans. Thank you for joining me on her journey. I look forward to continuing it with you!

Elise Stokes lives in Washington State with her husband and their four children, where she is at work on Cassidy's next exciting adventure.

Visit

www.cassidyjonesadventures.com
www.facebook.com/Cassidy.Jones.Adventures
www.facebook.com/Cassidy.Jones.Adventures.Series
www.twitter.com/CassidyJonesAdv

Books in the Cassidy Jones Adventures series:

Cassidy Jones and the Secret Formula

Cassidy Jones and Vulcan's Gift

Cassidy Jones and the Seventh Attendant

Cassidy Jones and the Luminous

46098502R00214

Made in the USA
Lexington, KY
23 October 2015